To: Dear Joan

With Much Love as always.

From: Alma xxxx

Jane Edward.

1998.

THE GIPSY'S CURSE

Jane Edward

MINERVA PRESS
MONTREUX LONDON WASHINGTON

THE GIPSY'S CURSE

ISBN 1 85863 608 6

First Published 1996 by
MINERVA PRESS
195 Knightsbridge,
London SW7 1RE

Printed and bound in Great Britain by
Antony Rowe Ltd, Chippenham, Wiltshire

THE GIPSY'S CURSE

CONTENTS

Part Three – Rightful Heritage

Chapters

Introduction

Cornwall is Celtic Country, once known as Kernow.

One could stand amongst the gorse and heather on windswept moors, or high upon the cliffs that overlook the vast and perilous Atlantic Ocean, and view the wild sea that, greedy for its prey, swallows endless ships, and countless human lives.

One could dream of past days, of legend and ancient history, and as well conjure up pictures of smuggling activities that happened all over the Cornish coasts, famous for its contraband running to and from France, with such cargoes as silks, muslin and china. Everyone gathered their coppers and pounds to purchase smuggled goods. This was the support - in many cases - of tradesmen, so secrecy was essential, but it was the small Cornish crafts, and the French brigs that carried the more popular cargoes of tobacco; jewels, and all important liquors - brandy, rum, whisky and wine that lent a livelihood to the poorer working class so, through 'free-trading' as it was mostly known, men were able to support their families.

People who were wealthy and held in high esteem, namely lords of aristocrat families, gentlemen squires and in some cases the clergy, as well as certain inmates of the lesser strict convents - these, and many others benefited from illegal import and export goods, that would be conveyed into the shadowy coves, with the utmost secrecy, mainly by daring adventurous sons, chosen to sail from France and Cornwall, in well armed and fast sailing vessels. Many enemies waited in dark corners. But the most dangerous was the sea.

Prologue

Cornwall 1774

Lady Cara hurriedly donned her warmest riding-habit and top boots, in readiness to leave The Grange. She had already packed a lightweight bag, with a few toiletries and some night garments. That was all she could take with her, under the circumstances.

Walking across the room, she opened the door, and turned – momentarily to take a wistful last look around at all her personal things that she had grown up with. Things that would no longer be a part of her everyday living; with the choice she had made...

Sighing, she stepped out into the corridor, closing the door softly behind her, and hurriedly – but quietly – descended the elegant staircase, then crept across the hall, out through the front entrance, and down over the wide steps without a backward glance. She hadn't wanted another confrontation with her parents, that could have been far worse than the one she had suffered a few hours previously.

It was only natural that she should experience certain qualms in the pit of her stomach; with the growing realisation that her life-style would change quite drastically. But, at least, she was sensible enough to accept whatever may lay ahead. At this point in time, her heart ruled her head. And, where it must lead, she would follow...

She had no doubt in her mind, whatsoever, that eventually, love would conquer all. But, first and foremost, she had to gain control of her equilibrium – which had been sadly depleted; and was playing havoc with her emotions, since a few hours previously when she had received a devastating shock.

She was still reeling from the enormity of the ultimatum that had been cast at her by her father – out of anger. He hadn't been prepared to consider her feelings, or her side of the argument at all. In fact, the confrontation turned a might nasty, as she recalled with a certain agitation...

* * * * *

"I am sorry father, I have made up my mind, and nothing that you or mother can say will sway me from my decision."

Lady Cara faced her formidable parent across the other side of the room, from where he stood – stern of face – with his back to a roaring fire.

Although she felt somewhat in awe as to what she was about to disclose, she showed it not.

"In any case father," Cara continued speaking with feeling. "Something of the utmost importance has presented itself; which makes it all the more reason for me to marry the man I love. I am afraid it will come as a shock to you, I know – but I have to tell you: I am carrying his child."

Lord Wendamere – momentarily devoid of speech – looked aghast at his daughter, and paled visibly at the impact of what he had heard. And then, as suddenly as his speech and colour went, each returned in full force; with his features suffused by the rage and anger spreading from within, as he began remonstrating with her, so profusely; that he chose not to consider his words; intent only on venting his spleen on his wayward daughter – as he saw her – for what she intended.

"You have dared to defy me again on this matter, Cara, even after the numerous times of late that I have begged you to discontinue with this… this… unhealthy and impossible liaison. And, now you have the gall to admit to this… this…" he spluttered, "person's passion – who is well below your station. Or, Cara, is this just a plausible excuse to achieve what you desire? All I can say, either way; is you must have taken leave of your senses."

Lord Wendamere's face changed continuously with the inner emotions that he struggled, with great difficulty to control.

Cara couldn't understand her father's ridiculous stance – after all, she would have thought he would be grateful for someone to take her off his hands. He had spent all these long years, completely ignoring the fact that he had a daughter, which had caused her to be terribly lonely, and now that she had a chance of happiness, she intended to take it.

"I have a good mind to lock you in your room until you come to your senses." Lord Wendamere carried on. "But what good would that do? You would leave the house to visit your lover at your earliest opportunity; that is certain. I know you are over age, and I cannot stop you from doing what you wish, but, I am asking you – no, begging you to consider the consequences. We could arrange something with regard to the child you carry, although it is against my better judgement to suggest anything untoward at this stage," he told her. "You must make up your mind Cara, now – right away. This has gone on long enough. I want your answer right away, that you will forget this foolhardiness. What do you say?" he asked:

"It is no good father, I do not intend to change my mind, so there is nothing more to say." Cara looked him straight in the eye as she said it.

"Then be it on your own head Cara. You have made your decision, and now I shall make mine. I have no alternative but to deprive you of your inheritance, and banish you from my home. I consider that I no longer have a daughter, and reject you as my heir." He spoke vindictively.

Cara drew herself up to her full height – she wasn't tall, but she had dignity. "If that is your decision father, then, so be it." She turned on her heel, and walked towards the door, as her father gave his parting shot.

"If you are thinking of doing so, it is pointless trying to wheedle around your mother," he sneered. "She will take my side, as always."

Cara didn't answer. She walked out through the door, closing it quietly behind her, thinking all the while of what her father had said. That he was serious, she had no doubt. She knew her parent only too well. His word was law. And her mother, kind enough in her own way when her husband wasn't around, otherwise showed little affection for her daughter. She was quite a simple soul – small and timid, who lived in a world of her own. She was a very feminine type – with a great liking for the frills and falderals. A woman who would agree emphatically with whatever her lord and master would say; irrespective of whether he was right or wrong in his arrogant assumptions.

Cara's mind was in a whirl, as she hurried towards the stables. On entering she walked straight across to where her horse, Jasper, was stalled, and patted him lovingly as he gave her a welcoming neigh. It wasn't yet dark, so she could see to saddle him. The groom who was present offered her his assistance, but Cara refused in a kindly manner, wanting to work, rather than stand around waiting. Cara had had plenty of practice in her young life of dealing with horses. Her love of the noble animals led her to spend many hours in the stables, and often she would assist the grooms to currycomb and tend them. The men had also taught her – from a very young age – to saddle and ride. The Grange could boast of at least a dozen of the best breeds – and she loved them all – Jasper in particular, who to her was almost human.

Not too long afterwards, Cara eased herself up on to the saddle, patted Jasper, and turned his head in the direction of the drive, and on out through the gates into the country lanes.

* * * * *

The rhythmic thud of the horse's hoofs, as they hit the partially moss-covered country lanes to ricochet through the undergrowth, was quite noticeable in the silence of the late afternoon; darkened earlier than usual by overcast skies. The grey blanket of clouds showed only too clearly that threatened rain was not too far away, and Lady Cara could only hope that it would hold off until after she had reached her destination...

Jasper knew the area very well, and could travel blindfolded, being so used to the roads. Cara allowed him to move at his own speed. She would never push him to exhaustion – in any case, she had to be careful herself, at the start of her pregnancy – for Cara dearly loved Jasper, he was so trusting; and a most lovable animal. Uncle Phillip, her father's younger brother, had purchased him for her when she was just twelve years old. He had been aware how lonely Cara was, and he knew how good she was with horses, by the way she treated them. The gift of Jasper went straight to her heart, where it swelled to bursting point with love for him for his kindness. Ever after, he became more of a father to her than her own parent, who rarely gave her the time of day. Her only crime being that she had been born a girl – and not the son that her father had so desperately wanted. Matters deteriorated to a greater degree for Cara, during her young years, when it was discovered that her mother could have no more children – making her father a most disagreeable man; and rather worse to his daughter than he already was. His attitude drove Cara from the house to spend more time outdoors, as well as in the stables. She had always been a bit of a tomboy – a strong trait in her make-up which had led her to the situation she now found herself embroiled in. She was well aware that she had burnt her bridges; that there was no going back, and committed herself irrevocably to a new life ahead.

What it would hold for her, she could not fathom at this early stage. All she could think of, was to be at last with the man that she loved to distraction – and had done so, in secret, for some little while. Luke loved her, she knew, and their gipsy marriage had been arranged, and would take place in a few days time.

Luke was no ordinary gipsy. He was a leader of one of the many smaller groups of Romany nomadic people who first came to England from Europe and the East as early as the fourteenth century. A decidedly handsome man, with thick black curly hair – worn long – Luke had a swarthy complexion and expressive black eyes, fringed by long lashes. His features were chiselled and clear cut, with a fine aquiline nose – of average height and slim build, he was older than Cara, by some eight years.

* * * * *

The evening sky had darkened alarmingly, with large spots of rain hitting the dry ground as Cara reined in Jasper at the fringe of the wood, just as the figure stepped forward out of the shadows and moved quickly to lift her down from the saddle to the ground, where he held her protectively within his strong arms in an effort to comfort her. Luke sensed that she was very distressed, and held her close. Cara felt safe at last, and as they moved forward toward the clearing where the group of caravans stood, she knew then, that she had made the right decision.

* * * * *

The gipsy camp was in mourning. Everyone moved around in silence – stunned by the death of Lady Cara. She had expired a few hours earlier giving birth to a girl-child – of the chosen name – Esmeralda.

The birth had been troublesome and lengthy, and Cara's strength had, at last, given out. She was beyond human help…

Luke sat by her side where she had been laid out, his head buried in his hands. The only sound – his heartbreaking sobs.

When eventually the sobbing ceased – albeit momentarily – Luke raised his head to glance into the crib, where the babe lay quiet and asleep – exhausted after her long fight to come into the world.

Luke looked long and hard at his daughter, his eyes red-rimmed with weeping, and loss of sleep.

After an interminable time, the gipsy spoke his thoughts aloud to the child.

"I shall always hate you Esmeralda, as long as I live, for robbing me of my beloved wife; and for that, I curse you, and all those who will - in the future - become most dear to you..."

* * * * *

News reached Lord Wendamere that his only daughter, Lady Cara, had expired giving birth to a baby girl - by the name Esmeralda. The child was faring well.

* * * * *

PART ONE

Antony and Esmeralda

Chapter One

Seduction

As Esmeralda set forth on her enforced journey, low black ominous clouds raced rapidly across a very dismal and already partly darkened sky, driven on by the seemingly impending storm that had been gradually brewing for some little while. Even so, although the hour was late afternoon, daylight still persisted. 'But, not for long,' Esmeralda told herself, as she stared anxiously ahead at the narrow and dreary road stretching out before her, as though there would never be an end in sight. She could not help but feel a certain amount of not unexpected trepidation as to what was to become of her, as well as what the future would hold for such as she. She felt distinctly lonely too. But then, hadn't she always suffered from constant loneliness throughout her young life? Her father had seen to that right from the start, by discouraging even their very own 'kith and kin' from proffering any likelihood of friendship, whatsoever. And now, through no fault of her own, she had been turned from the only home that she had ever known – such as it was – to fend completely for herself. She had had no choice in the matter. So, in such devastating circumstances, it was as well she had little to carry as an extra burden. Her belongings were so frugal as to be contained and tied within a large red coloured 'kerchief, that hung from her right shoulder.

The long winding road that appeared to go on for ever, seemed longer by the minute with each step that she took, bringing no living habitation within sight of the weary and most distressed girl. The hedgerows had long since become menacing shadows to her, as every little sound thereabouts – presumably of wildlife – gave the impression that someone or something would pounce out upon her, and show her no mercy. She had no idea how long she had been walking, but to her it seemed hours – literally. At times, Esmeralda nearly succumbed to laying down by the wayside, but fear of the unknown, and sheer determination kept her on the move, although she had the greatest difficulty in putting one leg before the other. And, to make her position worse, darkness was fast falling. The realisation came upon her as well, that she was approaching the open sea, as she could hear quite close by, the roar of the waves as they lashed against the rocks far below her. And it was this that gave her much cause for concern, having as yet, found no shelter. Then suddenly, at the end of a long winding bend, there it was, just come into view – standing high; gaunt and stark against the sky – a large mansion house of forbidding appearance, set well back from the road, and enclosed by massive wrought iron gates that separated the long driveway from any potential intruders – but to the young gipsy girl, a most welcome sight, when she was almost ready to drop to the ground from sheer exhaustion.

This great granite structure stood near to the sprawling cliffs on the rugged coast of Cornwall, overlooking the vast Atlantic Ocean. The name Pendavan – which Esmeralda noticed in the fast waning light – was spread in imposing letters right across the top of the gates, adding mystery to the place.

Suddenly, as the winds whipped up into her face, striking icy cold blasts, Esmeralda shivered, whether from the cold or just apprehension, she wasn't sure, as she approached the side wall where she noticed a large bell which she supposed she would need to ring to gain entrance to the house.

Hesitating momentarily as to whether she should pull the bell to make her presence known, Esmeralda felt a certain amount of uneasy anticipation, and as well, extreme anxiety as to how she would be greeted, and by whom, and if because of who she was, and the condition she found herself in – she may not even be invited inside the house, when it was well known in the surrounding districts, that mostly all unmarried mothers to be, would most certainly be frowned upon, especially by the clergy – many of whom considered such a condition an enormous crime. Had this not been the case, the gipsy girl would have had no hesitation in approaching any church for assistance. It could have saved her considerable distress, not knowing where she would end up. Panic seized her, with the notion that she may have to venture further afield, and in these bitter cold winds which, since she had been standing there, had considerably worsened. She shivered once more as stronger gusts whipped around her urging her to make a move one way or the other. She decided to pull the bell and face whatever should befall her, for good or for ill. This done, the resonant sound as she released the knob, vibrated and echoed all around to startle her somewhat. She listened, and had not long to wait, as a door of a cottage-like building – set back at the side of the driveway – opened, letting out a welcome light to the girl, as well as to reveal the caller to the man who stepped outside, as he walked with heavy footsteps towards the gates.

"Who is it please?" a voice asked. "And can you state your business at such a late hour," the voice added, not unkindly.

Esmeralda, lifting her head, saw the face – she presumed – of the caretaker loom before her. Almost ready to swoon, she lent against the gates in her weariness, and answered, "I am lost, and need help. I beg of you… can I come inside?" she pleaded, dreading the thought that she could be turned away,

The man saw how terribly distressed the young visitor was, and immediately opened the gates to admit her.

Esmeralda didn't know how to struggle up the driveway to reach the front of the house, which to her seemed completely inaccessible from where she stood, only the kind support from the caretaker when he proffered his arm for her to lean on and her own eagerness to enter the house, and be in the warmth, gave her the strength she needed. On reaching the entrance, they stepped inside the hall, and no sooner had they done so than, with a suddenness that quite startled the young gipsy, the largest dog that she had ever seen came bounding towards them in greeting, until another man appeared from the other end of the massive hall, and walking towards the little group, spoke to enquire what the commotion was about, as well as to order the dog to cease its noise. "Good boy!" he said, patting the animal's head affectionately, whilst at the same time with a puzzled look upon his face – looking down at Esmeralda from his great height, and enquiring once again what the trouble was, and how he could be of assistance?

Esmeralda's heart almost stood still, when she realised that the handsome man who stood there before her was none other than her seducer. For a moment she could not answer, she was so shocked, and completely lost for words. She was also astounded, as he showed no recognition of her whatsoever.

Perhaps he didn't want the caretaker to know what had occurred between them, so she decided to say nothing for the present, but how could she stay in this man's house? For she certainly wouldn't feel safe under the same roof with him, but where else could she go at this time of night? She didn't relish the prospect of venturing very much further in her weary state, as she was ready to drop right where she stood. If only she could have a night's rest, she could then journey on the next day, and hopefully find someone who might be willing to help her. 'But, for now,' she told herself, 'there must be other people in the mansion, so surely he won't do anything at this stage,' and on the morrow she would be gone.

"I know not in what direction I am heading," Esmeralda answered, her soft voice hardly discernible, even to herself. "Can you give me shelter for the night?" she asked, almost at the end of her tether.

The Master of Pendavan could not but help notice how terribly pale his visitor was looking when suddenly she fell to the floor in a dead faint, completely startling both men, who were, momentarily, lost for words. Lord Antony was the first to recover his equilibrium to a certain extent by saying: "Quickly, Albert, go and fetch Mrs Rushton, she will know what to do for the poor girl," and taking a coat from the cloakroom, Lord Pendavan covered the limp body of the girl, who lay as one dead, her beautiful hair – revealed by the hood that had dropped back – spread around her face, in its masses. He felt quite helpless as he stood looking down at her, whilst he waited for the caretaker to return with assistance. He was getting anxious by the minute what to do next, when the motherly housekeeper arrived, looking very flustered, and most distressed to see such a wan face.

"Oh! the poor mite," she said, quickly cradling the lovely girl within her arms, whilst Lord Pendavan hurriedly poured a glass of brandy, and holding it to her lips, watched the colour gradually return to her ashen cheeks.

Struggling to rise to her feet, Esmeralda heard her seducer say in a most kindly manner, which surprised her: "Take our young visitor to one of the spare bedrooms Rushie" – using his favourite nickname for his very devoted housekeeper – "and see that she is made comfortable and warm, where a good night's rest should see her much better in the morning. Good-night my dear," he went on to say, speaking directly to the gipsy girl, "and rest well. Come King," he added, turning away to enter a door at the end of the hall, the mastiff following at his heels.

As Mrs Rushton removed Esmeralda's scant clothing, which was barely sufficient to keep a body warm in such atrocious cold weather, the housekeeper became aware at once that the girl was with child. Some six months on she thought. It must have been the pregnancy that hastened the weakness that had caused her to faint. Added to this, the comatose state that she was in made it impossible for the girl to be questioned. However, she was able to glean her name, which was something, at least, to tell the master. But, for now, their young patient needed all the rest she could get, and was relaxed, and sleeping. The housekeeper, having administered all the necessary requirements, quietly left the room.

With Esmeralda having retired for the night, Lord Pendavan sat in the library, deep in thought. 'What is such a beautiful girl doing wandering around at this hour?' he asked himself. Had she fallen into bad company, and was now in trouble; and what was she doing in this vicinity? To his knowledge there were no gipsies anywhere near for miles. He knew immediately on sight that she was a gipsy, for one could never mistake them, although this one was different, he could certainly sense that.

He arose and rang for Mrs Rushton, who immediately appeared.

"You rang, Sir?" she asked, noticing the worried look on her young master's face.

"Yes, Mrs Rushton, has the young lady settled down for the night?"

"She has, Sir, the poor child has fallen fast asleep, and I am sure that nothing will disturb her, but I think you should know that she is with child."

Lord Pendavan looked very thoughtful. "It would appear that our young visitor will need help, which we shall most certainly give. In the meantime let her rest as long as she wants, and I will have a talk with her on the morrow," he told his housekeeper. "Incidentally, did you enquire her name?"

"Yes, Sir, she is called Esmeralda, and what a pretty name, if I may say so. I could find out nothing else, Sir, in her present condition," she added.

"Have no worry Rushie," he told her. "I am certain that she will confide in us as soon as she is ready to do so. Good-night now, and thank you for your help."

After she had left the room, King, the mastiff, rose from the hearth, where he had been lying near the fire, not asleep, for he sensed that his master was concerned and rested his huge head on his master's knee.

"You sense a mystery, don't you boy?" he remarked to the dog. "Come, let us go for a walk."

Both man and dog made a very handsome pair as they left the comfort of the house. Lord Pendavan wore a long cloak, as it was quite fresh outside. As he reached the gates, the caretaker approached, asking him if he would be very long.

"No Albert, King and I are a bit restless tonight, and I need to do some serious thinking, for as you know I always work out any problems whilst out walking," he replied.

"Very good, Sir, I will lock up when you return," he said.

When his master had disappeared from sight, Albert found himself thinking about the young lady, and why she had come to this place. Mind, she was a very nice little thing, and she certainly was in a bad state when he took her to the master. He kept wondering who she was, and where she had come from. Well, it would all come to light soon enough, and Mrs Rushton would be the first to know, so he must wait until then.

Meanwhile, Lord Pendavan was striding across the top of the cliffs. He was an extremely good-looking man, with thick long brown hair, shaped very close to his head, and tied back in a ribbon. He looked very strong, and one sensed that he would be a good friend to anyone in need, provided they were both honest and genuine. In repose, his mouth was stern, and looking at him, anyone could see that he had suffered.

At present, his thoughts were centred around Esmeralda. He kept remembering how beautiful she appeared to him, and couldn't wait to see her again. To him, at first, she seemed very refined, and not the usual type for a gipsy. How had she let herself become pregnant; for he could swear she wasn't a loose girl? Perhaps she was married, and her husband had deserted her; but he had seen no wedding ring on her finger. He thought too, of her family – if she had one – what were they thinking of to allow such a young girl to be wandering the streets, and lonely roads? 'She should not be out on her own' he told himself. Who knows what could have become of her, had she not found Pendavan first?

He could ponder all night, and be no further ahead, so it was best to leave things as they were until he could speak to the gipsy on the morrow.

"Come King, let us return now," he said.

* * * * *

When Esmeralda awakened, the bedroom was bright with sunshine, showing a beautiful day outside. As she lay there feeling warm and comfortable, she looked around the room, noticing how attractive everything was, and by beautiful furniture arranged within the room, she could only surmise that her seducer was a very rich man.

The most prominent colour in the bedroom was rose pink, consisting of beautifully draped curtains, made of the most exquisite velvet, reaching from ceiling to floor. The window took up the whole wall, lending much light to the room, and overlooking the sea. There were two relaxing-chairs, covered in the same material, and a matching bed cover.

The wall decorations were really magnificent, being white and gilt, with panelling, whilst the ceiling was covered mostly by little cherubs, and to complete the picture, a lovely leaf-patterned carpet.

Esmeralda was completely fascinated by everything, particularly the luxurious bed, with sparkling white sheets and pillow-slips. Never before had she been in such a state of physical well-being; and as she stretched herself she felt just like a queen, but reality took over, as she became aware once more of her swollen abdomen.

What was to become of her? Would she end up in the workhouse as others before her had done? Now that she was fully awake, Esmeralda could not but help have butterfly nerves in the pit of her stomach. She felt an extreme state of anxiety, and fear, as she remembered whose house she had been taken into, and that she must come face to face with her seducer once again, and, for certain, be on the move to find another place, which she hoped would be more helpful to her, and a safer haven. When she had at first sighted the mansion, her feelings were that she had been guided to the place in her hour of desperate need, but under the present circumstances, her hopes were dashed, when she considered where she should go from here, and what lay ahead. Of one thing she was certain, her child would more than likely be born by the wayside, with no assistance, and this worried her considerably. The thought of the unborn child recalled to her mind the almost unbelievable nightmarish events which were responsible for her presence here in this magnificent mansion that seemed to her for the most part, a fantasy. There was no question whatsoever, that she had been subjected to an extremely cruel act which had involved both physical and sexual abuse, the result of which had now rendered her homeless, and put her in the condition in which she now found herself.

Firstly, her mind reverted to the trauma of her childhood, and the treatment that her father had bestowed upon her.

Esmeralda understood that her mother – of noble birth – had expired giving birth to her, after having married her gipsy lover against her parents' wishes, and thereafter, having been disowned by them. From the day that she had come into the world, her father's consuming hatred of her increased daily. She had been ignored; shown no affection whatever, and left mainly to her own devices. So it was understandable that she should seek other areas to explore; and find new interests as she blossomed into a young woman of great beauty. One of her favourite haunts had been the forest, also of some considerable beauty, and a goodly distance from the gipsy camp. She made frequent visits to this area, mainly to gather special plants and wild flowers, for the sheer joy of doing so. It was on such an occasion as one of these that she ventured much deeper into the forest. She already held a selection of such specimens within her hands, when, without any warning she was grasped from behind, and held captive within a strong pair of arms. When she faced her captor, it was to find herself looking at the most handsome man she had ever seen, but there was that in his face that frightened her, as he looked her over. She struggled furiously, but it was of no avail, as she was forcibly imprisoned within his arms. She cried out in terror, but knew there would be no one near, as she had wandered far from the camp, so could expect no help. Her head was covered, and she was thrown unceremoniously over her captor's shoulder.

She had no idea where she was being taken, only, that after what seemed an endless time to her, she was sure that they were near the sea, and felt they were going downwards, as she could not only hear the crunch his footsteps made on the stones, but was aware of the force he had to use, carrying his burden to a lower place.

Eventually, she was dropped to the floor, in what appeared to her, a cave, as her head was uncovered, and she was able to look around her. At long last she could breathe freely again, but her terror persisted, as her captor tied her hands and feet. She could hear voices in the distance, but couldn't make out what was being said.

"What do you want with me?" she asked. "Let me go; and I shall say nothing of this," she pleaded.

He just laughed, and walked in the direction of the voices. How long she sat there, she had no way of knowing, when suddenly two hooded figures approached her, lifting her bodily. She screamed, but they only laughed, telling her that no one would hear her. She wondered what they were going to do to her, when suddenly they came into a large clearing of an underground cavern, which she could not help but notice, was most strangely furnished, with low lying seats, covered by misshapen furs, and arranged around the perimeter of the area. It was on to one of these that Esmeralda was, once again, thrown, with much inconsiderate force, it would seem, for a further interval. But, for how long, she had no way of knowing.

Looking around her, the terrified gipsy girl had plenty to observe, which did nothing to abate her fear of the unknown. Her heart, racing at a terrible pace, threatened to burst, or choke her, as she noticed, as well, many other hooded figures occupying some of the old gnarled stools placed around an oblong trestle table of considerable dimensions. On it was a tall lamp that threw its light eerily around the cavern. The drone of voices was unmistakable, but nothing made any sense to her. Eventually, as her eyes became accustomed to her surroundings – in all directions – she could see, quite close by, to where she lay, hollowed out cavernous sections through one of which, had she not been tied at the ankles, there might have been a chance, even with her hands tied – if only a slim one – to escape. These would, for certain, lead to other tunnels, and although the danger of becoming lost in one of them would not be pleasant, anything would be better than what must be in store for her here. However, it was no use conjecturing. There was no escape for her, of that she was certain. But the thought did help her somewhat, for the longer she had to wait, the more anxious she became. Then, all of a sudden, everything happened at once to completely confuse her, and grip her with an emotion of impending danger, as well as of evil. Heavy curtains that she had first observed on entry into the cavern, which she had presumed, covering some form of opening, were dramatically drawn back on either side to reveal an altar, flanked by several candles, and a large platform of stone, also partly covered by fur. Behind this gruesome object stood a tall and menacing figure, covered from head to foot in a multi-coloured cloak and hood – the 'High

Priest' of the proceedings, Esmeralda decided, as the hooded figures she had seen draw back the curtains, hurried towards her, one to untie her hands and ankles and stripping her of her garments until she was naked, and the other to forcibly make her swallow a liquid, which tasted very sickly sweet. As Esmeralda moved her head in a futile attempt to try not to take the substance, a certain amount missed her mouth, and trickled down her neck, but it went unnoticed by her captors, who lifted her bodily between them, and carried her over to the platform of stone, where they placed her length-ways on to the fur in front of their leader.

Esmeralda could see the glistening of his eyes through the narrow slits, before she succumbed to the drug. Her last memory, before falling into unconsciousness was her conclusion that what was taking place now, was some form of ceremony, and she was at their mercy. So, she thought, this was to be her end, and no one at hand to save her. Then she knew no more.

* * * * *

Eventually, on slowly surfacing from her drugged sleep, Esmeralda found herself lying just inside the entrance to the cavern. Still feeling somewhat comatose, she thought, at first, that she must be asleep, and dreaming. For that is what the scene before her eyes must surely have been. 'How could it be otherwise?' she asked herself, on seeing groups of scantily clad men and women in their sensual indulgence of perverted debauchery, whilst others revelled in licentious and lewd wild dancing, and excessive drinking, that left nothing to the imagination, and Esmeralda was old enough to realise that she was witnessing no dream, but a sexual orgy, with everyone present disregarding accepted rules. She was no fool, having always lived within a gipsy camp, and had seen and heard plenty. Lying there, her mind went back to some of the embarrassing episodes that she herself had experienced from time to time, even before she reached her teens, not unexpected amongst the multitude of gipsies in the camp, where she was famed for her fast developing beauty, when so often she had had to ward off amorous attempts on her person. She supposed they must have considered her worth pursuing, but of late they had kept their distance, until this very latest attack on her from outside the camp. This thought brought her out of her reverie, to once more be aware of her present predicament. Seeing what was taking place before her very eyes made Esmeralda suddenly realise that she must have been misused, whilst under the influence of the drug. She felt noticeably different, somehow, and terribly uncomfortable. Her body ached, and she admitted to herself that she was really frightened of what was to become of her. Of one thing she was now sure, the drug should have lasted longer, so that she should not have witnessed what was going on around her. The wasted substance must have been the reason.

Looking around her, Esmeralda could see that no one was taking the least bit of notice of her. As her eyes focused better now in the dim light, she could see a pile of black clothing, just a few yards away on the other side of the entrance, and suddenly came to the conclusion, that the items were the cloak and hoods belonging to the cult members, gathered there.

Without considering the consequences should she be caught, Esmeralda edged forward, inch by inch, until she was out of view. She quickly grabbed the top garment, and pulled it over her as a disguise. 'If anyone saw me,' she told herself, 'they would think I was one of them.' She hoped that no one would speak to her, for she would know not what to say, and dreaded the thought of being returned to the cavern, to face she knew not what.

Esmeralda had to admit to herself a deep seated fear that her destiny could be death, should she be recaptured by the cult. So, the sooner she escaped, the better she would feel. Her heart was pounding uncontrollably. Her eyes peered through the slits of the hood, which allowed her to see where she was going. Thankfully, dimmed lights were positioned here and there along the tunnels, to help her progress. She could see in the soft damp ground different sized footprints before her, and hurriedly followed them, which eventually brought her out on to the shingle. Fortunately, the tide was out, and dawn was breaking. It didn't take her long to find one of the many paths to the headland, although her effort to reach it was a struggle, but soon she found herself walking towards the forest. She dreaded walking through it, to reach the camp, which was still some distance away.

After an endless time, Esmeralda arrived at the outskirts, where a small number of the caravans were situated. In no time at all, she came very near to her father's place of abode, after wending her way carefully between the many other such dwellings, that were dotted all over the piece of land. Dressed as she was, in such a gruesome outfit, Esmeralda surmised that she must have made a most formidable figure, as she moved stealthily amongst the caravans, and could only hope once again, that no one would have risen so early as to be able to see her. In her present state, she was not at all ready to explain her unusual actions. That must come later... much later. But, for the moment, all she could think of was to discard what she was wearing, as quickly as possible. She knew she could not enter the caravan, for fear of disturbing her parent, so she removed the cloak and hood, and reached on the line for one of her dresses that she had washed and hung out to dry; that seemed an age ago. Once she had put it on, she bundled the offending items between two boulders surrounded by bushes. She knew it well, as it was one of her very own hiding places that she had used so many times before, though not for anything so drastic as this. She was lucky that no one was yet astir, it being such an early hour. She crawled under the caravan, behind the huge wheels, and in a few minutes fell fast asleep, quite exhausted after her journey back to the camp. She had used this method many times throughout her young life, mainly to keep out of the way of her father, unless, of course, the weather should be inclement; then she would share the caravan with him. This she hated, much preferring to sleep under the sky.

Some time later, the sounds around the camp awakened Esmeralda, and as she came to, and remembered what had transpired, she could not help but wonder if what she had experienced was true, or had been some terrible nightmare. She was to discover the alarming truth a few weeks hence. She was with child... there was no mistake.

When Esmeralda tried to relate what had happened to her, no one believed her story, until the pregnancy began to reveal itself. Her father - already embittered - turned his daughter out of her home, such as it was, and she was told to leave the camp. She felt desperate, for where could she go and who would help her? As well as this worry, she was also terrified of being accosted again.

Esmeralda came back to the present with a jolt. Here she was in this beautiful house, but with the man whom she believed had seduced her, yet the face that had looked on her last night, was different somehow, it was kinder. Perhaps he had a split personality, for it could happen, and it had been known before, especially in aristocratic families. Well, she would soon find out she supposed, for he would, for certain, summon her to his presence shortly.

Just then, as Esmeralda pondered on what the outcome would be when they came face to face, Mrs Rushton entered the bedroom with a tray, which consisted of a pot of tea, some hot buttered scones, and marmalade.

"Good morning, my dear," she said. "You look refreshed after your night's rest."

Esmeralda decided she liked her, for she seemed a very kindly soul, and felt she had a friend here, at least. This in itself gave her silent support, for what she could have to face.

"Yes, I feel very much better thank you," she answered, looking at the appetising food placed before her, "and I am hungry too."

The housekeeper, delighted to see such a complete change in her patient, could not help thinking what a lovely picture the young gipsy girl made, and how at home she looked, sitting up in the very large bed. As Mrs Rushton was leaving the room, she said that Lord Pendavan would be in the library, awaiting an audience with her, when she was ready. Left on her own again, Esmeralda wondered what she could say to this man, and how he himself would retract from his behaviour towards her.

Meanwhile, in the library, Lord Pendavan's thoughts were swirling around inside his head. He could have sworn that he had seen recognition in Esmeralda's startled glance, when she first looked at him, but he knew he had never set eyes on her before, as he surely would have remembered her unusual beauty. He now recalled her to his mind once again, but then she was already imprinted on it. He could think of nothing else, and was longing to see her again. Her features were elfin like, and she had the most expressive eyes, grey in colour, which looked very sad, but could light up with excitement at the right time, he felt sure. He found himself wanting to bring them alive again.

Suddenly, there was a knock on the door, and certain that it was Esmeralda, he bade her enter. She walked into the room like a lady, even though her dress was quite ordinary. Her bearing was good, and she appeared very mannerly to the man standing before her. He couldn't take his eyes from her, and felt fascinated by her beauty, and her forthright manner. She was very slightly built, and even though he could see her swollen abdomen, he knew that after the birth of her child, she would revert back to an extremely petite young lady.

"Good morning my dear," he said. "Won't you sit down?"

"I wish to thank you for your kindness in allowing me to stay the night in your house, Sir," Esmeralda said. "But surely you know me? You cannot have forgotten already, for I have you to blame for my condition; which you must have noticed, for I am with child, and have been disowned by my kith and kin."

"If I say that I have never set eyes on you before, will you believe me, my dear?" he answered.

She surely couldn't be hearing aright. That he could tell such an untruth to her face, she couldn't comprehend. "How can you say such a thing," she continued, "when you know you set on me in the forest, abducted me, and took me to a large cavern, where everyone present was attired in black grotesque hoods and cloaks, and most formidable looking to anyone not used to such activity, in particular, the ceremony that was being performed, where as their prisoner, I was drugged, and abused! Can you explain that to me?"

Lord Pendavan looked very shocked, losing what little colour he had. 'My God,' he thought, 'so Adrian is up to his old tricks again is he? He has gone too far this time, the scoundrel, and he will pay for what he has done to this lovely girl. I have covered for him many times, but not for this abominable crime.'

He looked at the girl sitting silently opposite him, so young, yet old in years already. She was to suffer through his brother's dastardly act, with her life ruined almost before it had started. What would it mean to her, to have a child born out of wedlock? And what would become of her? He must try and explain about Adrian; to clear himself, for he wanted them to be friends.

"Esmeralda, will you bear with me while I tell you something of my life, so that you will understand? I have a twin brother, identical in fact, but unfortunately he is the black sheep of the family. He has been in numerous scrapes all his life, and I have nearly always taken the blame for him, trying to cover up his many heinous misdeeds to save our parents more distress than was necessary. So, understandably, I was, more times than not, considered the real culprit. Unfortunately, they were both killed in a coaching accident when we were eighteen years of age, so they never discovered the truth of Adrian's behaviour. To them, he was the apple of their eye.

He has always been the weaker of the two, and I have shown only love and kindness to him because of this, especially when he was younger. However, as he has matured, he has become far more difficult, keeping the wrong company, and he has gone from bad to worse.

"The most vile thing he has ever done to me, and I can never forgive him for his action, was to steal my wife, whom I loved very dearly. He couldn't rest until he had won her over, as from a small child, he has always wanted what belonged to me, and he has never changed.

"As I was the first-born, I am heir to this estate, so I have forbidden him entry, other than on urgent business. I haven't seen him for many a month, although I have heard certain stories which have given me food for thought. Now this latest crime of his has completely stunned me beyond belief.

"Naturally, I shall do all in my power to help you, and I think you should stay here, where you can have the best of attention."

Esmeralda looked at Lord Pendavan with a new feeling. How could she have thought badly of him, for he looked so kind and honest? He was completely different from his brother.

"Thank you for explaining everything to me, Sir, for now I can understand, and I am sorry that I wronged you, but it was a genuine mistake on my part; as you can see. Perhaps I should tell you something of my life as well, but there will not be very much to relate, as I have been left to my own devices.

"My mother expired when I was born, and because of this my father has hated me from the day that I came into the world.

"I have always been very grieved at not having the love of a mother and father, so my life has been a most unhappy one. However, I had hoped to find a better existence for myself one day, but never had any idea it would change this way.

"When my father had to be informed of my pregnancy, he turned me away from the camp without any due warning. I cannot begin to tell you how desolate I felt with the uncertainty of my future lying bleakly ahead, but now I feel happier than I have ever done. I would like to remain here as you kindly suggested," Esmeralda went on, feeling a warm glow spread all over her, with the thought of a whole new world before her, "that is, if I may, Sir? I can do some form of work, to repay you for all your help," she added.

All the while Esmeralda was speaking, Lord Pendavan hardly took his eyes from her face. What a lovely creature she was, to be sure.

"I take it you will not wish to keep the child when it is born," he said to her, certain in his mind that this would be her decision. "If this is so," he continued, "I think it best that the necessary arrangements be made for the babe to be taken into a home before you see it, so as to save you any more distress. It will be well cared for, I can assure you," he added, aware that this could cause her some anguish. After all, it would be her own flesh and blood that she would be parting with, and for certain, would not be easy.

"Yes, Sir, I do agree with you that I would not choose to keep the child, as it was not conceived of love," her face colouring somewhat, as she used the expression in front of this man, whose scrutiny of her she was very well aware of.

"When I recall to mind the look on your brother's face as he abducted me, I can only feel extreme anxiety," Esmeralda explained. "He should be punished for what he has done, because," she emphasised," you must realise that I am only one of many, that he could have treated the same."

"You are right of course, Esmeralda, we must investigate my brother's activities, for I suspect far more serious actions on his part with the help of his so-called friends; I shall not rest until I have brought him to justice, for what he has dared to do to you."

Lord Pendavan felt a great sympathy and understanding for the young gipsy, and the thought of the suffering she must be put through because of Adrian's dastardly act, inflamed his anger against him.

Esmeralda, on the other hand, looked around her, feeling safe at last. She felt she had now come home. This had always been her dream, to live in a beautiful house, but she had never thought it possible in her circumstances. There was the saying, "out of evil comes good", and this certainly appertained to her.

She wondered what this handsome man's name was. Should she ask him, or would he think she was trying to be familiar? 'But I am sure he wouldn't think me rude, now that we have met this way,' she told herself. 'Perhaps he will tell me about his wife, and where she is, for I feel I want to know everything about him.'

"May I ask you, Sir, what I am to call you, whilst I am under your roof?" There! she had done it; and it wasn't as bad as she had thought.

"As you already know, Esmeralda, my brother and I are identical twins, his name is Adrian, and mine is Antony, so, as I am only a few years your senior, and consider we are to be very good friends, I would like you to use my Christian name," he answered.

"Thank you... Antony," Esmeralda said, looking slightly embarrassed at her slight hesitation in coming to terms with his request. 'I will have to get used to this,' she thought, feeling so wonderful inside that someone really wanted her for herself. She could have cried with sheer relief.

Lord Pendavan arose from his chair, and went towards the bell pull to ring for the housekeeper, who appeared almost at once.

"Rushie," he said, "would you show Esmeralda over the house, and tell her where everything is, so that she can feel at home? I want her to rest as much as she can, and I will seek medical advice on the morrow. We do not want to take any chances, I feel responsible for her now."

When they had both left the library, Lord Pendavan walked towards the other side of the room to the window which overlooked the beautiful gardens. He was deep in thought looking out on the peaceful scene before him. As always, when he moved, King was at his side.

'I feel very protective towards this girl, so I must see Daniel on the morrow, he will give me any advice on her condition. After all, she may be suffering from the ordeal she has just gone through, and walking for miles cannot have been good for her,' he thought.

"I must do some very serious thinking King," he told the dog, who was as sensible as any human. "There is her good name to be considered, and it is up to me to do all I can, even to go so far as to offer her my hand in marriage."

* * * * *

Chapter Two

Proposal of Marriage

The next morning found Lord Pendavan out riding on his horse Caesar, who was a fine specimen of his breed, accompanied by King. There was much understanding between the three of them, as anyone could see.

The coats of both horse and dog glistened and shone with sheer health, and their strength could be felt by just looking at them. They made a magnificent sight together, with the fine looking man who rode the horse.

This exercise each morning was something that Lord Pendavan really looked forward to, and enjoyed very much, this day in particular, as he felt much happier of late. He couldn't help thinking of Esmeralda, and her beauty. She was certainly different from his wife, who had been blonde and pretty in a way, but hadn't had the looks of the young gipsy.

He remembered how he had first met her, at a ball given by her parents, a few miles from his home. Her family had been rich, and were seeking a suitable husband for their daughter. They did in fact fall in love at first sight, their courtship was hurried, and they were married a few months after their first meeting.

Lord and Lady Rush were both delighted with Rosalind's choice of husband, particularly as he was extremely wealthy, as well as good-looking, so she would enter into her married life with all she had been used to. She had been completely spoilt by her parents of course, being an only child, and giving in to her every whim had been a mistake, but, they would not admit to their error of judgement. Not where their child was concerned. They loved her to distraction, and nothing was too good for her.

Not long after they had been married, she began to show herself in her true colours. She both liked and wanted excitement, and her husband was often at a loss to know how to keep her happy, as she was easily bored, and very moody. Their happiness was soon at an end, and they just existed; to the outside world, their marriage was successful, but they knew better.

Eventually, she began to take an interest in Adrian, flirting with him outrageously.

Antony remembered one evening in particular, when he had arranged a ball for her benefit. How humiliating it had been for him. She had looked very pretty in a beautiful gown he had purchased in London, on one of their visits. It had been a lovely shade of blue to match her eyes, and she had looked really exquisite in it. Adrian couldn't take his eyes from her, and pursued her most of the time, claiming many dances.

From that evening on she seemed to change, and took to going for long walks. Adrian always seemed to be away from the house at these times also, not that he was ever home much in those days. Antony knew that there was something wrong, but couldn't quite put his finger on it. He was to find out very soon, and was stunned beyond belief.

Rosalind came to him one day, saying she wished to talk. He thought she had been looking very pale of late, and certainly not herself. What she had to tell him, was a dreadful shock. She was pregnant, and Adrian was the father. She had also been mixing with many of his so-called friends, whom she had found both exciting and peculiar, at the same time, but wouldn't give any more details. She did tell her husband there had been several meetings where they had all gathered together, in some form of a cult, and she had become so involved, that it was most difficult to break free of it.

She broke down and cried, saying again and again, how sorry she was, and what a scandal it would cause. What on earth could he say to her, for although he had no love for her, he felt very sorry that this had happened? He blamed Adrian for going out of his way to steal his brother's wife. After talking for hours, and getting no further ahead, they decided to retire for the night.

The next morning loomed grey and formidable, as though something was about to happen. Never in his life could he have imagined anything so terrible.

Rosalind was missing from the house for several hours; not that this was unusual in itself, as she had done this often of late, but after what she had related to him the night before, he thought she would have wanted to stay at home. As the day wore on she didn't make an appearance, so it was a shock to him when in the early evening,

Albert came into the house to say there was someone to see him, regarding his wife.

It was a Constable, come to tell him that his wife's body had been found at the bottom of the cliffs, on the rocks where she had presumably fallen, or thrown herself.

He couldn't speak for several minutes, as of course he realised that Rosalind had taken her own life. He was dreadfully shocked, and couldn't take it in, for it was so unexpected. Poor Rosalind, what a terrible state she must have been in. He couldn't feel any anger towards her, only pity. It must have taken considerable courage for her to do such a thing. Surely she must have known that he would stand by her, for no man worth his salt could stand by and let his wife suffer, even though she had betrayed him.

He felt a deep anger towards Adrian, and was determined to break with him, once and for all, for this was the final sin. But this was easier said than done, to cut him right off. By rights, he should never welcome him into the house again, but Adrian had a way with him to get around his brother, as he had always done. If anything ever happened to him, Adrian would become heir to Pendavan, and this worried him constantly, as everyone on the estate would be made to suffer. It would be a disaster.

There had been an inquest of course, which was very upsetting for the family. People talked, naturally, as can be expected in a small community. Rosalind's parents were completely devastated when they heard of their daughter's death, and were still in a state of shock for many a long day.

Lord Pendavan had no intention of telling them what really happened, and they always believed she fell to her death by accident. He could remember it now, as though it only happened yesterday. What a nightmare it had been; how could they ever forget it?

Now here he was again, implicated in the same way, except that a stranger was involved this time, and a beautiful one at that. Well, he must return to the house now, as there was much to see to, and discuss.

* * * * *

Esmeralda saw the master of Pendavan return, and thought how handsome he looked in his riding habit, but then he would look good in anything, she told herself.

As she stood lost in thought, she realised what a wonderful place this was to live in. There was much for her to see, and she was really looking forward to browsing around. The gardens alone would take some time to view, and she was looking forward to exploring every nook and cranny.

Esmeralda very much liked Mrs Rushton, and felt she could – should the need arise – always confide in her. Here she was now, come to fetch her to see Lord Pendavan, or Antony, as she was to call him.

She followed the housekeeper, and found herself standing before him once again. He beckoned her to a chair, placed quite close to where he was reclining, and told her to sit down, which she did in a slightly nervous way, although she felt quite excited at seeing him again.

"Would you like a drink my dear?" he asked. "Perhaps a small sherry would suit you; it is a light alcoholic beverage, after all," he told her, "and will not hurt you. I would not suggest it, if I thought that it would," he insisted, rising from where he sat to pour the drink, and place it on a low table at her side, whence he returned to his previous seat opposite to Esmeralda, who sat with her hands folded demurely in her lap, waiting for him to speak, which he did, almost at once.

"Esmeralda," he said, "I have sent for my friend, who is a doctor, and have explained the position to him, regarding your condition, and he will be calling to see you later, but in the meantime, I wish to talk to you, and put a proposition to you. I have been thinking about what you have related to me, and your position, and I am going to offer you my hand in marriage. I am free to do so, and think it will be the best thing for you. What do you think of the idea of becoming my wife?"

Esmeralda was astounded at what she had heard, and couldn't believe her ears. What a wonderful person he was, to make this very kind offer. She couldn't accept of course, it just wouldn't be right, as he could marry any lady of his choice, with his background. What could she say to him other than that she wasn't good enough for him? Also they didn't love each other, and, in her unaffected manner, she believed that a man and woman should marry for love, and not convenience.

"Well, Esmeralda," Lord Pendavan said, "what do you think? Am I so terrible that you are not able to answer me?"

At last she found her tongue. "No, Sir, I cannot let you make this sacrifice for me. You may find that you don't even like me later on, then what could you do? For it would be too late once we are man and wife!"

"Will you not let me be the best judge of that?" he said. "I suppose you haven't had an offer of marriage before, being so young, so I can understand how you feel. It must have been a shock to you, but I will expect nothing from you unless you approach me first. That I can promise you, my dear. Who knows! We may even learn to love each other, after a while. I feel it is the least I can do to make up for my brother's terrible crime, and his disgraceful behaviour towards you," he continued. "I also feel a responsibility for your future. I think you are far too young to fend for yourself, and after the child is born, you would feel bound to be on your way again, whereas, if you were married to me, I could look after you, and save any embarrassment that could materialise."

Esmeralda told herself that perhaps it would be best for her to have a husband, for she would be safe from Adrian, and others like him; also, she had to admit, that it would be so pleasurable to live in this beautiful house, with so charming a man.

"Antony," she said the name shyly, her face blushing prettily. "I am very tempted to accept your offer, for I know that we shall be good friends at least, and perhaps one day, I could grow to love you, as you say."

"You agree then, my dear?" he asked.

"Yes, I will do as you suggest, and I do want to thank you for being so kind to me, for I know not where I should have gone after the confinement had taken place. Had it not been for you," she went on, "I may have died by the roadside. And alone," she added, reaching for the glass of sherry, and, raising it to her lips, savoured a few sips, mainly to try and hide her increasing shyness, mixed with feelings of sheer excitement, and tender emotions, that developed inside her with every passing hour. "I shall do all in my power to repay you," she continued, "and try to be a good wife to you."

He crossed to where she sat, taking both her hands within his own, and drawing her to her feet, said: "You will never regret your decision, Esmeralda, for I know we shall be happy together. I shall be proud to show you off to my friends, of which there are many, as my wife, and a very beautiful one you will make, my dear."

Lord Pendavan knew that he was a very lucky man to be able to marry such a lovely girl. Although many people would say he was choosing a wife far below his station, he knew otherwise. A gipsy she may be, and nothing could change that, but hadn't he tried someone within his own class, and where had that got him, other than much trouble and sorrow? This time, he knew, somehow, that this girl would be the right one for him, for after all, she was of good blood, from one parent at least, and he was positive of her integrity. Also there was a feeling between them, although he could not explain to himself how far this went with either of them. Looking at her now, he realised how much he wanted her for his wife.

"Perhaps one day we shall have a family of our own, and a son as heir to Pendavan," he told her.

When Esmeralda heard him say this, she blushed again, feeling a pleasurable warmth steal over her body. "May I be excused now, Sir?" she asked.

"Certainly, my dear," he answered. "Have you forgotten already, that my name is Antony," he went on to say, with a smile spreading across his handsome face. You will have to get used to calling me that from now on, will you not?"

She walked from the room, almost on air. Never in her wildest dreams had she expected anything like this to come about. She felt a great peace within her, and her happiness knew no bounds, knowing, that, at last, that she was with someone she could trust. She was more certain than ever now, that her feet had been guided in this direction, and that everything was going to work out well for her. God was by her side.

She reached her bedroom, where she collapsed on to the bed, and tried to regain her composure. She could hardly believe that this had happened to her, and pinched herself, to see if she were really awake, and not dreaming.

Later that day she was visited by the doctor, who was a very charming man. He was short and stocky, with wonderful twinkling eyes, and a most endearing smile. He had a delightful manner, and

Esmeralda took to him right away, feeling as though she had known him all her life.

He knew the full story from Lord Pendavan, so by the time he had introduced himself to the young gipsy girl, he had been put in the picture, and knew just what to say to her.

She didn't feel in the least bit uncomfortable with him, and was able to talk to him quite naturally.

He was accompanied by the housekeeper, who was flushed with excitement. 'I think she knows,' Esmeralda thought.

After the doctor had examined her, he left her for a while, saying that he would return within a short interval, to have a word with her. She wondered if everything was all right, and what she would have, a boy, or a girl, not that she was in the least interested, how could she be, under the circumstances? There must be a few more weeks to go yet, she was sure. Meanwhile, she would have her wedding to look forward to, and plan her trousseau.

As she was sitting there, she had the feeling of another presence, and of someone watching her, but surely not, for she had been left on her own until the doctor returned. She tried to shrug off the feeling, but it persisted. Perhaps someone had died in this room who had been unhappy; she must remember to ask Antony, for he would be sure to know.

She rose, and walked towards the window, looking out on to the scene before her. The sea looked calm, and beautiful, making a magnificent sight to the watching girl. How lucky she was to be able to live in such lovely surroundings, she told herself.

The doctor returned eventually, with Mrs Rushton, who started to fuss around her patient, just like a nurse. She had been told by the doctor, that Esmeralda must have a certain amount of rest each day, until after the birth of the child. He intended to call again the following week, to keep an eye on her. As he left the room, his parting remark was for her to take care, after first asking if she would mind him using her Christian name, as they were to become very good friends, he knew.

"Esmeralda, my dear," he said, "you are marrying a good man, and he will look after you, so you need have no fear."

After he had gone, she closed her eyes, and tried to relax, but she felt too excited with so many things to think about. However, after a short while, she began to feel very sleepy, and soon was lost to the world. When the housekeeper returned later, to summon her to the library, she found her in a deep sleep. She stood looking at the young girl for a moment, thinking how sweet she was, and how restful she looked in repose. She decided not to disturb her for a while, poor child, she looked very worn. The master would understand, and she could come back later.

After Mrs Rushton left the room, nothing could be heard but the deep breathing of Esmeralda. Suddenly, there was a very slight movement at the far end of the room, and had anyone noticed, they would have seen one of the eyes, in the picture, which hung on that particular wall, open, and immediately close again.

Fortunately, Esmeralda wasn't aware of this, for had she seen the face of the man on the other side of the wall, she certainly would have been terrified, so it was as well she knew nothing about it.

Meanwhile, the man's face took on a sinister look as he moved away from the wall, to descend the steps which led down into the caves, far below the house of Pendavan.

What was the beautiful gipsy doing in the house? And how had she come to be staying there with Antony? After all, her camp was several miles away, as he had cause to remember. He noticed she was with child too. His! of course! He recalled with extreme relish his barely controllable emotion as he raped the gipsy, in the presence of his companions, in an intense sexual attack. He thought if the plans that had just come into his scheming brain were successful, he would repeat the performance as many times as he wished, until, of course, he tired of the gipsy.

Adrian hated his brother, Antony, and had every intention of making him suffer, as much as he considered he had suffered himself. He had loved Rosalind as much as he could love anyone, and Antony had – in his eyes – taken her away from him, not intentionally, of course. Antony was always the favourite with everyone, and for that he hated him, anyway. He had won Rosalind away from his brother, only to lose her again for ever. He would never love anyone as much again, and this in itself, fed the consuming hatred that he harboured in his heart for Antony.

He had been away for some months, visiting his old haunts, gambling his easy money away, which Antony generously supplied, and often ending up at the usual brothels, for this was how he lived.

The light ahead brought Adrian into the clearing, leading into the larger cave, which Esmeralda had seen when she had been accosted in the forest, and brought here by her captor.

He was the first to arrive, but then he lodged near, so that he could be on the spot when needed. They were all to assemble here tonight, after their break, and he would have much to relate. Meanwhile, there would be time for a rest, and to continue with his scheming within his devious mind, before the others arrived.

* * * * *

Esmeralda awakened refreshed after her sleep and decided to wear a gown that Antony had given her, one of Rosalind's. He had already mentioned taking her to London, as soon as he could arrange it, to purchase all she would need. The gown was very tight across her swollen body, but it was a pretty style which suited her elfin beauty. It was a lovely shade of green, and with her hair brushed until it shone, she made an attractive picture.

She left the room, making for the staircase, which was circular, splendid in its style, and carpeted throughout. Portraits lined the high panelled walls down to the magnificent hall. Antony's ancestors, she supposed, for they all had similar features.

She felt like a queen descending the stairs, for everything she looked at, or touched, was so luxurious. Just to think, she told herself, this will be my very own home, and I shall be sharing it with my husband very soon. As yet she was extremely shy with Antony, which was only to be expected, although he did his best to make her feel as comfortable as possible.

On reaching the door of the library, Lord Pendavan, hearing her gentle tap, bade her enter, and what a sight met his eyes when Esmeralda stepped over the threshold. How lovely she appeared to him, he who was still in a state of sheer unbelievable incredibility that this very young gipsy girl was soon to become his wife, and, as such, the mistress of his estate, Pendavan. He was impatient already, and growing fonder of her by the minute, had made up his mind to do all he could to make her happy. To start with, he had already made arrangements to travel to London, on the morrow, which would take several days. The miles were many on such a journey, and therefore would necessitate stops at traveller's accommodation inns, where food would be available and a good warm bed – in this case, two separate rooms – would be put at Lord Pendavan, and Esmeralda's disposal. Having made this journey so often, the master of Pendavan and his future wife would be treated with the best of attention by the hostelers, and their good ladies, who would fawn over the gentleman and his companion. The horses, too, would be changed for fresh ones. All in all, it would be a very exciting time for the young gipsy, and a new experience for her to see all the things that went to make up such a vast city. She would have need to get used to London, for as his wife she would have to travel with him from time to time. He would take her to Jacqueline's, and let her decide which garments would suit Esmeralda, at least until her pregnancy would be at an end, after which he would purchase anything that she could wish for, and spoil her.

The delight in Esmeralda's eyes when he told her was good to see. She had never been to this big city that everyone from all walks of life talked about. Even in her gipsy camp, she had heard talk of it. She wondered what it would be like, and couldn't wait to get there.

"We shall leave early on the morrow, my dear", he told her. "Meanwhile, why don't you take a walk around the gardens, for there is plenty to see, and then retire reasonably early, so that you will be fresh for the journey."

Esmeralda wandered out into the sunshine, feeling so happy, and contented, with her spirits high, but suddenly, she came down to earth with a bump. If only she wasn't pregnant, or had it been under different circumstances, being married to Antony, and bearing his child, she could have looked forward to the birth of the baby; instead, her condition now somewhat marred her coming happiness. Still, she felt safe at least, and knew he would be by her side in her hour of need. That was all that mattered.

* * * * *

Chapter Three

A Friend in Need, is a Friend Indeed
Enter 'Jacqueline'

The hooded figures sat around the large rectangular trestle table, and one could, if one appeared on the scene, sense the mounting excitement amongst them.

Adrian was doing the talking, and had Antony heard what his brother was discussing, he would have had good reason to be, not only disturbed, but considerably frightened for Esmeralda.

"I suggest we take the gipsy girl prisoner again," Adrian said, "arrange for the birth of the child, and when it is born, we will use it for our sacrificial rites. The time for this is drawing nigh," he added. The expression on his face showed the sheer cruelty within him.

He had already explained what he had discovered in the mansion way above them, and emphasised his sheer hatred for his brother. The group was well aware of their leader's dangerous intensity. They would never be surprised at him.

"What of the mother? Will you let her go after it is all over?" one of them asked.

"No," Adrian answered. "I have other plans for the gipsy, which will keep for the time being."

With a break in the conversation, it was time for refreshments, and some form of beverage. Needless, to say, intoxicating liquors would be the favourite choice for most present. They would drink themselves into a stupor, but this time it would seem they wished to remain level headed, afraid they would miss something of importance.

Had anyone looked in on this scene, it would have appeared eerie, with the grotto dimly lit, and the figures slumped over the table. The altar behind them, lit by the many burning candles, showed very clearly the platform of stone, which had at the head a long, ugly-looking knife, nestled in the centre of a large red velvet setting.

Adrian continued making his plans to abduct Esmeralda from the mansion. As he did so, his face took on a malignant look, added to a gleeful expression in his eyes, as he savoured what he intended to do. There were two methods in which this could be accomplished. He could either use the secret panel, which led into her bedroom, or he could pretend to be Antony. He would – if he chose the latter – need to wait until he was sure that his brother was out of the house, and then gain entrance, suggesting she should accompany him on some pretext or other. But he would have to content himself for the present, and observe their daily routine, as there must be no blundering whatsoever, on his part.

Unfortunately, Adrian knew nothing of his brother's forthcoming marriage to Esmeralda; had he done so, he would have thought twice about abducting her. Whereas he would want his brother to think she had left the mansion of her own accord, Antony would know otherwise.

After these discussions were completed, the group set about making other plans for their orgies, which took place regularly. Now that all the talking had come to an end for this session, one hooded figure repeatedly filled the many glasses so that all were well on the way to becoming intoxicated, but not Adrian, who preferred to know what was happening. He could think of nothing else but his extreme pleasure in abducting the gipsy and upsetting his brother. Perhaps, after the child had been disposed of, he could make further plans to punish Antony completely by discrediting him; then he could take his place as heir to Pendavan, but this would need careful planning and much scheming for it to be successful.

As we leave Adrian to his plotting, we return to the mansion, where Esmeralda was getting acquainted with the gardens. She was in her element, amongst all the beautiful trees, plants, and the blooms surrounding her. Suddenly she came upon a magnificent fish pond, very beautifully set out, with water lilies peeping through the water. Occasionally, there was a slight splash, showing her the coloured fish jumping in the sunlight. In the centre was a most unusual waterfall setting, which gave one a most restful feeling. There were also many seats placed here and there, some under shady trees, whilst others were situated in the bright sunshine. She would spend many hours here, she knew.

Suddenly a figure appeared, and Esmeralda, who had been lost in thought, jumped to her feet to greet Antony, who was looking particularly handsome in his immaculate clothes, followed by King, who came bounding towards her, to greet his new-found friend.

"How do you like the gardens, Esmeralda?" he asked, noticing her liking for the fishpond, which had always been a favourite with him, even as a small child, for whenever he was missing, his mother knew where to find him.

"I think it is a beautiful area of the gardens, and I really love the whole place," she answered

"Come, let us walk towards the summer-house, which is another old haunt of mine," he said.

They walked in silence, both occupied with their own thoughts, when suddenly Esmeralda halted in her tracks, for before them, in a large clearing, stood the prettiest sight she had ever beheld. A small circular building, with the smallest windows ever, was surrounded by tiny separate beds of most beautiful coloured flowers. What a picture it made, certainly something never to be forgotten. She held her breath in wonderment, and drank in the beauty of the place.

"You like it Esmeralda?" he asked, watching the different expressions flit across her face.

"Oh yes, it is a wonderful spot, and I would love to come here each day, if I may," she answered. "I could spend hours here I know," she added.

"You can come here whenever you so wish, and no one will intrude on your privacy," he told her. "In fact, I think I shall leave you alone now, and perhaps you would like King to stay with you, for he knows his way back to the house, and will see that you are safe while wandering around on your own."

She agreed, and Lord Pendavan left both girl and dog, amongst the beautiful foliage.

King sensed that Esmeralda wished to be quiet, so he stayed by her side, silent, and ever watchful, whilst she relaxed, thinking of all the events that had taken place of late.

Naturally, her first thoughts were of Antony, and his kindness to her since her arrival at Pendavan, and there was her forthcoming marriage to him, which he had suggested, to help her. She felt quite excited at the thought of becoming his wife, her visit to London, and meeting Jacqueline, as well as choosing a selection of clothes that had been planned for her. So much had happened in such a short time, that she could hardly take it in. Her one worry at the moment, was if she should come in contact with Adrian again, and her fear of what he may do. Although Antony would be taking care of her now, and hadn't he already said that he had refused his brother entrance to the mansion? So was it likely that he would force himself upon them?

Perhaps she was concerning herself unnecessarily. She shrugged it away.

"Come boy," she said, "we must return to your master, as darkness is fast falling, and it is a little chilly."

* * * * *

Once again, Esmeralda awakened to a lovely bright morning. The bedroom was flooded with sunlight, making her feel good to be alive.

She could hardly contain herself, in her excitement for the coming journey, and forgetting all about the child within her, jumped out of bed on hearing unusual sounds coming from below the window, in the drive, and looking out, she observed a coach and horses, stationary at the entrance, with Antony standing alongside, talking to the driver.

She had already been given her first meal of the day, sitting up in bed. Mrs Rushton seemed to be determined to spoil her future mistress, and, as was to be expected, Esmeralda thoroughly enjoyed it all.

She was dressed and attired in her coat and hood in less than half of the hour, when the housekeeper came to fetch her, to say that the master was ready to commence the journey.

She accompanied Esmeralda to the coach, where Lord Pendavan was waiting patiently for her. He helped her up, covering her with a thick rug, making her feel warm and cosy, for although it was fine and sunny, it was quite fresh.

At last they were on their way, sitting in close proximity to each other. The horses, turning out of the driveway through the gates which Albert closed directly behind them, gathered a little speed, then settled down to a steady pace. Antony would never have them pushed too hard. This the driver understood, and was ready to do his master's bidding. There was much harmony among all the workers on the estate, and Lord Pendavan was greatly respected and liked for his kindly manner.

* * * * *

Inside the coach the conversation was varied, for there was much to talk about. Esmeralda seemed to lose some of the shyness that had been noticeable in the last few days. There were deeper feelings inside her now, and each time she looked at her future husband, her heart did a quick turn, and she was fascinated by his attentions. She still could not believe her good fortune in meeting such a person, and felt so safe with him. She loved him already, and knew this was so because of the pounding of her heart. Her thoughts went on and on, and she was blissfully happy to be near him.

Esmeralda came out of her reverie to hear Antony speaking again.

"You will be sure to like my good friend Jacqueline, for she is a dear person, always ready to assist anyone, and will certainly be of great help to you my dear," he explained. "I suggest you lie back and rest for a while, as you are sure to be somewhat tired by the time we reach our first halt."

Esmeralda didn't answer, as she was almost asleep, the movement of the coach lulling her senses.

Lord Pendavan, watching the sleeping girl, thought again how lovely she looked in repose. He began to think of the coming birth, and it worried him more, as each day passed, bringing the time that much nearer. He was anxious that everything should go well for her, but realised the suffering ahead for her. He brightened slightly, with the thought that she would be in good hands with Daniel and Mrs Rushton looking after her, but she was so young to have a child. Would that it had been his own, but please God they would have a family eventually, for he knew that he was fast falling in love with this beautiful girl, and if everything worked out as he hoped his dearest wish could be answered, but first he wanted her to enjoy her excursion to the city. He wondered if perhaps she would like to stay with Jacqueline for a few weeks, whilst waiting for the birth, as long as he brought her back before anything might happen. He decided that he would mention it to her when she awakened.

Lord Pendavan looked at his watch, to see that in a matter of an hour they would arrive at their first stop – the King's Head, where the innkeeper, who knew him well, would give good service.

When Esmeralda opened her eyes, the horses were pulling in at the wayside inn. She felt really rested, but would be glad to stretch her legs after the journey so far. Antony helped her from the coach, just as the innkeeper came outside to welcome them.

"We shall stay here for a few hours Esmeralda," Lord Pendavan informed her. "That will give us plenty of time to freshen up; have something to eat, and rest in our respective rooms."

Esmeralda, on entering the inn, noticed how clean and sparkling everything looked, and coming towards them, was the happiest looking woman that she had ever seen, with the rosiest of cheeks, and very homely looking.

"Come in my lord and lady, and sit ye down," she said, "and good-day to you both. Would ye like some fresh ham and eggs, with bread and cheese, and some ale to wash it down with?" she asked. "Perhaps you would like to freshen yourselves," she went on, "whilst I am preparing the food."

Both eagerly accepted what the woman had suggested, and within a half of the hour, were seated near to the welcome huge log fire, that burnt merrily in the spacious grate, to partake of their appetising meal.

After they had eaten, and taken advantage of a few hours' rest, the driver entered to say that the horses had been changed, and the groom would be taking care of them until Lord Pendavan returned to the inn.

After paying the innkeeper and his wife, and thanking them for their kindness and trouble, and saying that he would be with them again within a week or so, Antony led Esmeralda to the coach, where once more they were settled, and on their way again. After other halts of a similar nature they finally came near to London. The journey had been pleasurable, and gave them much to think about. Esmeralda talked excitedly, and as she did so, Lord Pendavan watched the different expressions flit across her face. She looked now so full of life that it did his heart good, with the knowledge that he was the instigator of her happiness.

"How would you like to stay with Jacqueline for a while my dear?" he asked her. "I could return for you later. I must go back to Pendavan soon, as it wouldn't be wise for me to stay away too long."

"Oh! I would love to if you are sure it will be all right with you and your friend, but are you certain she will want me, for after all she doesn't know me?" Esmeralda asked.

"Be assured my dear, she will want you, and is sure to love you; I know Jacqueline," he told her.

Up till then the roads had been very quiet, but they were now becoming really busy, which showed their journey was very nearly at an end.

Esmeralda's first sight of London would for ever stay in her memory. She was fascinated by the many pedlars standing at street corners, shouting, and selling their wares.

Lord Pendavan asked the coach driver to stop, as he had noticed an elderly woman selling bunches of violets. He jumped down from the coach, and bought one to present to Esmeralda, which pleased her very much. Her pleasure was plain to see.

Once more they were on their way, eager now to reach their destination, each lost in their own thoughts, Esmeralda trying to visualise what Jacqueline would be like to her, and how they would spend their time together. Antony was telling himself that he was going to miss Esmeralda when he returned home on his own. The mansion would certainly be quiet, and he knew it wouldn't be the same without her. 'Bless my soul, I am acting like a loving husband already.' he told himself.

"We are almost there," he told her, his voice breaking through her thoughts. In fact the coach was now drawing up to a long avenue of houses, which all looked alike, flanked by beautiful trees. To Esmeralda, who had never seen anything of the like, the houses looked like palaces.

Lord Pendavan assisted Esmeralda from the coach, and they walked to the front porch; the door was opened by a friendly maid, who welcomed them inside. Anyone could see that she had a great affection for the master of Pendavan, and as she looked from one to the other, he said, "Rose, I would like you to meet my future wife, who is as excited as a child at the prospect of staying here with your mistress, whom I hope is in the best of health."

Rose, smiling all over her face, answered, "She is, I am glad to say, Sir, and is awaiting you in the drawing-room, so would you both come this way, please?"

They followed in the wake of Rose, who, after knocking on the double doors before them, was bade to enter. They found themselves in a magnificently furnished room, the woman coming towards them being as splendid as the room itself. She certainly was very beautiful, and walked like a queen, Esmeralda thought.

"My dears, how welcome you both are," were her first words. She spoke in a soft and refined voice.

Lord Pendavan took her hand within his own, and kissed it, saying, "Jacqueline, how lovely to see you again, after such a long time. May I introduce my future wife to you?" he continued, drawing Esmeralda towards him.

"I am delighted to meet you my dear," Jacqueline told her, "and I know we shall be good friends."

Esmeralda had seen the look of pain that crossed her face, when Antony had mentioned his future wife. So this beautiful woman was in love with him, and this she could understand, for she herself loved him, and more by the minute. She did wonder why two people so much alike had not married; he must realise her feelings for him, as they were plain to see, but, he had been married before, and she didn't look the sort of person who would take second place.

Jacqueline observed the lovely girl before her, pursuing her thoughts on a similar line. She could understand Antony wanting to marry such a young and beautiful creature, but it had happened suddenly, and where had he met her? No doubt he would tell her all there was to know when he was ready. Meanwhile, they must be feeling very worn, and in need of refreshments, and a good night's rest. Tomorrow would be time enough for things to be discussed.

* * * * *

Esmeralda's first morning in the new city brought a dark and dismal start to the day. It was raining as though all the heavens had opened. She awakened, refreshed after a good night's sleep. She was so looking forward to her visit to Jacqueline's fashion house, but couldn't imagine what it would be like. She knew it would be no easy matter, being fitted out in her condition, but felt sure Antony's friend would find something suitable for her.

What would she feel like, she mused, being married to a man like Antony? He was kind, and a gentleman through and through, but could she cope as his partner, having had no experience with aristocrats? She knew in her heart of hearts, that he would be a good husband to her, but still this did not allay her inward fears, knowing that she was well below his station, and couldn't bear to let him down. She was worried that seeing her in the company of Jacqueline, may force Antony to make comparisons. But she was being silly, she knew. Antony was the only one that could put her mind to rest, and she couldn't wait to see him.

After knocking, Rose entered the room, and Esmeralda came out of her reverie.

"Good morning, miss, and have you slept well?" she asked. What a young girl this was, to be sure. Too youthful by far to be entering into marriage, but then, she couldn't choose a nicer man to become her husband, and she did look a nice little thing. "The mistress is waiting for you in the drawing-room, so would you go down to her when you are ready?"

"Has Lord Pendavan risen yet?" asked Esmeralda.

"Yes miss, he is in the drawing-room, also," Rose replied.

"Will you kindly inform them, that I shall be down as soon as I can manage it," she said.

Esmeralda hurried over her toilet, and made her way downstairs, where, on entering the drawing-room, she found Antony and Jacqueline deep in conversation and looking very serious.

Jacqueline walked towards her, saying, "So here you are my dear, I hope you have had a comfortable night, and feel more rested."

Lord Pendavan greeted her with a smile also, thinking how fresh and beautiful his future wife was looking. "I suggest we make an early start, my dear," he said, "and I will leave you with Jacqueline so that she can fit you out with everything that you will need. Meanwhile, I shall go to my club, and will call for you later this afternoon, which should give you plenty of time, and choose what you will."

They left almost immediately for the fashion house. The coach and horses wound in and out of many streets before they reached their destination. Eventually they drew up before a large building, which looked nothing from the outside, but on entering Esmeralda could not fail to notice the brightness of the place, and everything appeared neat and clean. There was much activity going on, with many young ladies dashing around everywhere. Jacqueline approached a section which housed bales and bales of material of all kinds and shades. Never before had Esmeralda seen so many beautiful colours, all at once, and it made her feel like burying her face in the soft and shimmering fabrics. It was going to be a very busy day, with fittings and trying on garments, but she was going to enjoy every minute of it, she knew.

Jacqueline came hurrying towards her, accompanied by an older lady, who was armed with scissors, pins and tape measure.

* * * * *

When Lord Pendavan returned for Esmeralda, he noticed how tired and weary she looked. It must have been very wearing for her, he thought, standing for hours in her condition, but it had been necessary, and she certainly seemed happy.

Esmeralda was actually more than delighted with her promised apparel. She had been very lucky with the ready made clothes, that needed only slight alterations to comply with what Jacqueline wished for her, and in her mind would suit the young gipsy girl. Fittings for very special occasions had been necessary, and now Jacqueline was explaining to Antony, how her work force were intending to stay at the fashion house for many extra hours, to get everything completed in as short a time as possible.

It was towards early evening before they all settled in the coach to return to Jacqueline's house, after a satisfying day.

Lord Pendavan thanked his friend for all her valued help. But, then, hadn't she always been kind and thoughtful towards everyone? It was her nature. He was, he knew for certain, in her debt. Especially, as she had welcomed his future wife with open arms, and would spoil her, for sure.

* * * * *

Silence prevailed in the coach, while the three passengers relaxed, and pursued their own thoughts. Antony was the first to speak.

"I shall be returning to Cornwall tomorrow," he told Esmeralda, leaning slightly towards her, on the opposite seat, where Jacqueline sat beside her, taking her hands within his own, showing openly his deep feelings of tenderness towards her, "and shall leave you with Jacqueline, as I said before," he went on. "I hope you will be happy with these arrangements, my dear," he added, giving her soft hands a slight squeeze. He tried not to embarrass her in front of his friend, aware of her shyness still.

Esmeralda returned his affection with a heart-warming smile, thinking all the while how very much she was going to miss him when he was to leave on the morrow, but to be able to stay with Jacqueline would be a wonderful change for them both, as it appeared to her, that her new friend led a lonely existence, apart from her work at the fashion house.

The remainder of the evening passed very quietly, as they all partook of a sumptuous meal; a nice ending to Esmeralda's first day in London.

* * * * *

Lord Pendavan awoke with a slight feeling of depression the following morning. Could it be that he had fallen deeply in love at first sight with the young gipsy? She was so vastly different from anyone else that he had ever known, and Pendavan would be very quiet without her. Even in the short time that she had been there, a gloom had been lifted, that had descended on the mansion for so long. He couldn't remember how long ago it was that he had heard laughter in his home, but things would be different now, he knew. Anyway, there must be no more reminiscing now, for he had to prepare for his journey to Cornwall. It would seem longer, with only himself for company, but at least he had plenty to think on.

After saying his good-byes to both Esmeralda and Jacqueline, and giving his promise to return and collect her within a month, he left on his lengthy journey.

There had been a wistful look on Esmeralda's face, as she had said goodbye, giving him a shy kiss on the cheek. She was going to feel lost without him, and hated to see him go, but whilst she was here with Jacqueline, with his blessing, she intended to enjoy her stay, and gain knowledge of how to become a real lady, like Jacqueline, and the new mistress of Pendavan. She wanted Antony to be proud of her.

Jacqueline broke through her train of thoughts, to suggest a sightseeing spree. "How would you like to visit one of the respectable coffee houses on our travels?" she asked.

"Oh yes! I would love that," answered Esmeralda, "and I would also like to visit the streets, where the people sell their wares. It was so exciting to hear them shouting, and singing, as Antony and I passed through in the coach."

To Jacqueline, the young gipsy girl radiated extreme happiness, and her excitement was captivating, and quite infectious.

* * * * *

Chapter Four

Treachery

The coach drew up before the vast, impressive gates. The horses would deserve their well-earned rest, for they had really shown their paces during the latter part of the journey back to Cornwall, after Lord Pendavan had collected them at the inn. They were fine beasts, and excellent runners. Just then they were steaming with perspiration, but a good rub down, fresh water, and some hay, would refresh them.

Albert opened the gates and let his master in, whilst the groom ran forward to unharness the tired horses.

Lord Pendavan entered the house, to be greeted ecstatically by King, who was beside himself with excitement at seeing his beloved master again. The housekeeper came forward to greet him also, showing her pleasure at his return.

"Are there any messages for me?" he asked her.

"Yes Sir," she answered, "Master Adrian called, and wishes to see you as soon as possible."

Looking very thoughtful, Lord Pendavan thanked her, and said he would be in the library until dinner was served, whereupon, with the huge dog nuzzling against him, he entered the room, closing the door behind him.

Pouring himself a large drink, he asked himself what Adrian wanted with him now? He supposed he was in trouble with someone regarding money, as was often the case. Anyway, it must be something serious to bring him here again, to dare show his face, and after what he had done to Esmeralda, Antony would hardly be able to contain his anger. 'It is as well that she will not be here when he calls,' he told himself, for the last thing he wanted, was for Adrian to get wind of his marriage to Esmeralda, as he didn't trust him at all. He must make sure that no one, other than his closest and most trusted friends should know of his forthcoming wedding. 'Time enough after it happens for Adrian to know, then it will be too late for him to do anything.' There was one thing he couldn't understand, and that was why his brother had discarded such a beautiful girl, and had not made any move to see her again. Still, if he had been in London for a few months, and up to his old tricks again, he would have been too busy visiting his equally dishonest friends, whom he, Antony, had always found most objectionable. There had been many visits from these friends in the past, and not one of them did Antony like the least bit. Adrian would never change now, he was too steeped in his vices to turn back, which was a great pity, as surely there must have been something good in him once. Antony had to admit, however, that he couldn't recall one decent thing at all. After the tragic loss of their parents, he had taken over the very demanding task of trying to keep his twin out of trouble, but it had been of no avail; hopeless, as he knew to his cost.

He was so thankful that his parents weren't alive to witness this latest dastardly act against an innocent young girl, and how many others, he knew not yet, but it had to come to light eventually.

Whilst we leave Lord Pendavan at home, in his mansion, to await his brother's visit, we return to London, to Esmeralda, and Jacqueline, to find out how they are faring.

* * * * *

The days had passed very quickly for Esmeralda, who was enjoying every minute she spent with her new friend. She had seen many sights, and such an abundance of places, that she felt as though she had lived in London all her life, for they were implanted on her memory.

Jacqueline had been wonderful company for the young gipsy girl, and most thoughtful for her welfare. Her concern touched Esmeralda, and in the short time they had spent together, she had endeared herself to the girl.

For the last few days Esmeralda had been feeling very tired, even though she had rested a part of each day, following the doctor's orders. Now that her stay in London was nearly at an end, she found herself wanting to be back at Pendavan with Antony. He was due to collect her on the morrow, and she couldn't wait to see him again. She had missed him dreadfully; more than she had thought possible, even though her days had been very full.

She had some very attractive clothes to take back with her, and she felt the warmth stealing over her, as she thought of how her future husband would react at the sight of her.

She had chosen a beautiful golden coloured gown, topped by a cape edged with fur, and a hat to match, to wear on her return journey to Cornwall. The days were becoming much colder than of late, winter was setting in, so she would need to be warmly clad.

The movements inside her made her realise that the child was eager to come into the world. She couldn't help but wonder what it would be, and how she would feel on parting with her baby, although she was sensible enough to know that this was the only alternative for her, under the circumstances.

She asked herself how Antony must feel, regarding the birth of his brother's child. She would be thankful when it was all over, as in her heart she was very nervous, her mother having died in childbirth, and she couldn't forget this.

Jacqueline had observed Esmeralda for some time now, and wondered what was passing through her mind. She was deep in thought, and she could tell that the young gipsy was concerned about something. The poor child was too young by far to have problems, and it was so unfair that she had to go through having a child at her age, especially when she could not keep it. Still at least she would have a good husband in Antony. Would that things had turned out differently, for she, herself had loved him for a very long time, but it was on her side only. If he hadn't met and married Rosalind, she was sure she could have won him over. Anyway, she must be content to love him as a good friend, that was infinitely better than not seeing him at all, for his friendship meant so much to her. Likewise his future wife, Esmeralda, was dear to her already, and she must never know her secret love for Antony.

She knew she was going to miss her when she returned to Cornwall, but at least she could now spend a holiday at Pendavan, whereas before it was unthinkable.

It looked as though she would have to settle with Stuart, who had been her admirer for as long as she could remember. Dear faithful Stuart, he would do anything for her, and had begged Jacqueline many times to marry him. Well, she couldn't do better, so it was time she thought seriously about it, for Antony was lost to her now. She didn't want to be on her own for ever, as it was a lonely life, especially living in London. Stuart was kindness itself, and would certainly be a good husband to her. He was ten years her senior, and a fine looking man with a wonderful disposition. He was also a comparatively rich man, so she wouldn't want for anything, he would see to that. Only a few weeks ago she had been offered a good price for her now flourishing business, so perhaps she should seriously consider the possibility of a sale. All in all, they would have a good foundation for a happy marriage.

Anyway, there would be plenty of time to make her plans, after Antony's wedding, which was to be fairly quiet, or so she understood, because of Esmeralda's condition. Thinking about this made Jacqueline realise how near the dear girl was to the approaching confinement, and looking at her now she thought an early night was called for, as the journey would be very long and tiring for her, and she knew Antony would expect to see her looking better for the change.

* * * * *

Mrs Rushton was rather flustered, for there was much to do and see to, before her master and future mistress returned from London. All the guest rooms had been turned out and cleaned, and the master's bedroom had been changed completely in readiness for his forthcoming marriage.

She had a great affection for the present Lord Pendavan, as she had had for his parents before him. She had been housekeeper for many years, serving the Pendavan family with the loyalty they rightly deserved, and had watched the growing up of the twin boys with the love of a mother. Widowed whilst still a young woman, and having no children of her own, she had poured out all her love for the twin baby boys born to her beloved mistress. There had been a nanny to give some support, until they were ten years of age, also the very best of tutors, and, as well, they were showered with all the love that was possible from their doting parents.

It had been a dreadful day for the housekeeper when news of the tragic death of the then Lord and Lady Pendavan reached them. It had been so very sudden and so final. Never to see them again. Mrs Rushton had never really recovered from the shook of losing two people who were so dear to her. As expected, Pendavan was never the same again. Happiness was one of the many ingredients missing for a long time to come, but she decided there and then, to devote the rest of her time at Pendavan, to caring for the kind-hearted boy, who was in line as the new heir to the estate. As for the other twin, Adrian, the housekeeper tried her hardest to overlook his devious ways and obvious sadistic streak, which was, more often than not, directed at Antony, causing her young master considerable sorrow.

She was very aware of the anxiety he carried in his heart, constantly, and as the years passed, things worsened, bringing about open hostility. Feelings had deteriorated between them to such an extent that Antony had shown him the door – literally, for him only to return when he needed money.

Now, Mrs Rushton wondered what the reason was for Adrian's visit just over a week ago, whilst Antony was in London. Whatever it was, she felt sure he was up to no good; she had seen the ugly look upon his face when he took his departure... She sensed more trouble for her beloved master and wished he could be left in peace, for he had suffered enough.

She had hoped for his complete happiness with the coming of the young gipsy girl, for she had seen the tender look he had bestowed upon her, and knew how happy he could be, if left alone.

Thinking back to when Master Antony had departed on his journey to collect Esmeralda, just three days ago, he had come upon her suddenly, to enquire if there were any problems, and to wish her good-bye.

He had been so excited at seeing the lovely girl, who was to become his wife in a very short time.

"I shall be leaving in less than half of the hour Rushie," he told her, "and hope to reach London with all possible speed, for I cannot wait to have Esmeralda back here with us once again," and added, "I have missed her so."

He had glanced out of the window, on to the driveway, to see if the coach was coming, showing all too plainly how impatient he was to be on his way.

Antony had decided not to use his own coach and horses on this hasty journey, although the animals would still be entitled to a deserved rest; he would see to that, even though they were owned by another.

She had explained to him that everything was proceeding as planned with the wedding arrangements, and wished him a safe journey.

"Is Master Adrian likely to call again, while you are away?" she asked.

"I sincerely hope not," he had answered, looking very serious, "but should he do so, he is not to enter the mansion under any circumstances. He must await my return."

At that moment, the coach and horses pulled in towards the front entrance, allowing only minutes for Master Antony to say good-bye, and patting King's head affectionately, he hurriedly crossed the hall, out through the entrance, and entered the coach.

* * * * *

The journey was uneventful, if lonely, but Antony had plenty to think on, to help pass the time. He closed his eyes, and let his thoughts dwell on Esmeralda, and his coming marriage, and all that had transpired since she came so suddenly into his life. He also remembered his meeting with Adrian, just a few days before. He experienced again the mounting anger he had felt, knowing what his brother had put the gipsy girl through, and knowing also, that he had to stay silent for the present, at least until she was his wife. What would he have said, had he known, that the gipsy girl he had seduced was soon to be the mistress of Pendavan? He couldn't wait to tell him, and watch his reactions. He had a feeling that Adrian came to see him for something more than money - which he, Antony was committed to provide - but couldn't think what it could be, only aware of an undercurrent always prevalent in his brother's sadistic and jealous nature. He would know about the wedding soon enough, and once Esmeralda was wearing his ring there would be nothing that he could do about it. However, he would be very thankful when it was all over. There would be time enough to deal with these problems later, for his eagerness to see Esmeralda again drove all other thoughts from his mind.

* * * * *

Lord Pendavan would have been very surprised had he known his brother was himself in London at that very time. Had he seen the company his brother was keeping and heard the conversation that was taking place, he would have had good cause to be more than worried for the safety of Esmeralda.

For, right at that moment, Adrian was talking excitedly to the owner of one of the brothels which he visited regularly. She was a huge woman, with her face so heavily painted with make-up that it could be scraped off. She looked repulsive with flesh that bulged everywhere. They were discussing a plan that Adrian had put to her.

"I have a beautiful girl for you, very shortly, if you are at all interested, Mrs Tootle," he was telling her, "and she could be your number one. She is a handsome creature," he went on, "and would, for certain, be an asset to your profession. However, there is just one problem, she is pregnant; and I believe, due to have the child very soon."

As he continued talking to this coarse being, lounging in a huge chair quite near him, he could feel the usual excitement mounting within himself. This always happened when he was planning something that was as unthinkable as this scheme, which he considered by far the best.

Mrs Tootle also felt very elated, thinking of the money that would come her way, through the help of this unscrupulous man, who was one of her most valued customers in her thriving business. He had put many an unsuspecting girl her way; and once in her clutches, they stayed at the brothel, for with their character smirched, where else could they go?

She realised that Lord Pendavan was speaking again, and forced herself to listen to the remainder of his plan.

"How would it be, if I brought the girl to you for the birth, and afterwards, I could come and take the child away? I shall, of course, expect to have first call on her when I return here from time to time. Is that understood?"

"I shall be delighted, I'm sure, my lord," she replied. "You can depend on me, for it sounds as though she will be of great value to my business, and I cannot wait to look her over."

She chuckled to herself, thinking how lucky it was for her that she was a friend of this handsome man. She knew without doubt that his character left much to be desired; that he would stop at nothing to get what he wanted; and felt sure that he would be a dangerous enemy. However, she happened to be on good terms with him at present; and intended keeping it that way.

"When shall I expect this young lady, Sir?" she asked, "for I should like to be ready for the event, which, as you say could happen at any time."

"I hope to have her here in your care, within a few days," he told her. "I shall have to bring her during the night though, for I do not wish her to be aware of her surroundings. Also I shall have to be very careful that no one sees her enter this place, for all our sakes."

After saying his good-byes, Adrian left the house of prostitutes, feeling pleased with himself. The scheme to get back at his brother had really commenced at last, and with luck, everything should go the way he wanted. His first move was to return to Cornwall with all possible speed, for Antony had mentioned to him that he would have a guest shortly, not knowing, of course, that Adrian already knew that Esmeralda was staying at Pendavan. He needed to have access to the mansion as soon as possible. He had to work fast, for his plan to be a success.

He had already decided that he must abduct the gipsy girl and take her through the secret panel in her bedroom, for he sensed that he wouldn't be able to trick her by pretending to be Antony. He also suspected that his brother knew more than he admitted, regarding his twin's seduction of the young gipsy. Adrian couldn't understand why Antony hadn't made any reference to it.

He had already considered that the best way to outwit Antony was to make it look as though Esmeralda would have left the mansion on her own accord, and told himself that his brother would never see her again. Antony would never dream of looking for her in a brothel, especially in London.

Feeling satisfied with his clever – as he saw them – arrangements he lay back, and closing his eyes, hoped he could sleep, for he was impatient to have the girl in his power, again, to see the expression on her face, when she would be aware of who her captor was. Her terrified reaction would fan the flames of his sheer sadism, his enjoyment of inflicting pain and suffering upon others. All Adrian wished for was for the gipsy girl to be a prisoner in the brothel, and to ensure that she stayed such. Once there, it would be too late for anyone to help her, least of all Antony. The subject of his unscrupulous plans was at that moment, travelling back to Pendavan, with her future husband.

How wonderful it had been to see Antony again, after a whole month, which to her had seemed much longer. She had missed him, even though Jacqueline, her new friend, had made her so comfortable, and had made a real effort to see that she enjoyed herself. The whole episode had been a new experience for her.

Now she was eager to reach her new home, and to start a new life. She felt safe with Antony; and although she had been thrilled to see London, she certainly wouldn't wish to live there.

Of one thing she was certain, that during her absence from Pendavan, she had grown to love the handsome man sitting at her side in the coach; and could hardly contain her excitement at the thought of becoming his wife. Perhaps he too, would fall in love with her after the confinement. She often wondered what she would feel like, clasped in his arms; and to be told that he loved her.

She lovingly scanned the face of her future husband in repose, and knew that her happiness would be fulfilled once she belonged to him. The colour crept into her cheeks, as she looked at him.

The horses suddenly gathered speed, and Esmeralda felt that they were as eager to reach Pendavan as she was herself. Could she have seen the passenger in the coach not so far behind them, she would indeed have been far from happy, and very disturbed as well as terribly frightened.

He, unlike his twin, had no thought for the horses. He had failed to take advantage of the halts available for the horses to be changed and fed. The poor beasts could fall by the wayside from sheer exhaustion, as far as he was concerned. In his impatience to reach his destination before nightfall, he drove them at a furious pace. He couldn't wait to relate to his so-called friends what had transpired between him and Mrs Tootle and their plans for the gipsy girl.

They all needed more excitement from time to time, and once the child was within their grasp, they could derive infinite pleasure, from the gruesome action they intended taking. Of course, Adrian was the instigator of the whole thing, being the leader of the group he had formed sometime since. They bent to his every whim, never daring to cross him under any circumstance, for he could be highly unpleasant and dangerous if put out, as they had good cause to remember.

They recalled an episode that took place, when one of the members of the cult, quite a good friend of Adrian's, had taken one of the girls before their leader, and his punishment had been diabolical.

Adrian had had the culprit – as he saw it – tied to the stone slab and tortured for an hour, until he became unconscious. The other members were expected to watch, and they all knew, that their leader would stop at nothing, even murder. Each one knew far too much about the other, so it was impossible for any one of them to cease to be a member.

They were at that very moment gathered together, awaiting their leader.

* * * * *

Esmeralda couldn't describe how happy she felt to be back at Pendavan once again. The welcome she received from Mrs Rushton showed how much the housekeeper had missed her. King was absolutely ecstatic at seeing his new friend and his beloved master once more. He leapt towards them both with his usual unbounded energy.

"Your rooms are ready for you, Sir," the housekeeper informed Lord Pendavan. "I expect you would like to freshen up before you have dinner," she said, turning towards the young girl, who looked very weary. "I will unpack for you later on my dear, for you must be tired after your journey."

Esmeralda felt completely devoid of energy; and she couldn't wait to reach her room, where she could rest a while. Her body felt heavy, and the movements within her made her feel most uncomfortable. Oh to be slim again, and able to put all this behind her! The nearer the time came, the more anxious she became, so the sooner it was over, the better.

The bed looked so inviting to Esmeralda, that after slipping out of her outer garments, she fell back on to it with sheer abandonment, and within a few minutes was fast asleep.

When the housekeeper entered the room after knocking and getting no reply, she could not awaken the young gipsy girl from her deep sleep. For a moment she stood looking down at her, thinking how vulnerable she looked. Poor child, she thought, she had to suffer very shortly, when the birth would be upon her, and so young too. How could Master Adrian have done so dreadful a thing? Still, the master would look after her, as his wife, for no one could be kinder than he was. How different things could have been, had the child been his own. What excitement there would have been, in this old, and silent house. She knew that he had hoped for a family when he had married Miss Rosalind, but it wasn't to be, unfortunately.

'I'll not awaken her, for the rest will do her far more good than a meal,' she told herself.

When Lord Pendavan was told that Esmeralda had fallen asleep, he didn't want her disturbed. "I'll eat alone tonight," he told his housekeeper. "Perhaps you could make your future mistress comfortable, before you retire for the night."

Left alone with his thoughts, he told himself that he would be relieved when it was all over and she would be back to normal. Before many days were to be over, Esmeralda would be his wife, and he intended to be by her side when her labour started, for he sensed that she was very nervous. Thank goodness Daniel would be attending her, for the thought of anything going wrong worried him constantly. She had become very dear to him since he had left her in London, with Jacqueline, and each day had seemed a lifetime until he had seen her once more. He hoped they need never be parted again.

This beautiful girl had found her way to his heart, and helped to heal it from the terrible blows he had received in the past. He now felt an extreme happiness that had seemed impossible for him. The one worry that nagged at the back of his mind was Adrian, for he knew in his heart, that while he existed, there would be no real peace for them. He must meet any trouble, if or when it came, because he did not intend his future to be marred by his twin and any schemes he may have up his sleeve. He could never trust him now, more than ever, and knew he would be expected to help him whenever he appeared.

How long he could keep up this constant drain on his purse, for each time it doubled, more or less, he couldn't foretell. Adrian's gambling debts were by far the worst, he never won anything worth winning, and the amount of money he spent on his many women was unthinkable. Antony felt sure there were other activities he could be involved in and felt his twin would stop at nothing to get what he wanted. He made up his mind, there and then, that he would have him brought to justice, brother or no brother. His future wife must have peace. She deserved that.

He would have some busy days ahead, what with the wedding, and other things as well, but now he must abate his hunger, and get a good night's rest.

* * * * *

Apart from her deep breathing, not a sound could be heard in the room where Esmeralda was sleeping, as the dimly lit area showed the onlooker on the other side of the panelled wall.

Adrian knew he had to make his move now, this minute, while the gipsy girl was still asleep. He could overcome her, before she could put up a fight and raise the household.

At the touch of a lever, which was cleverly hidden, the panel slid open silently, giving no warning to the unsuspecting sleeper. Adrian crept quietly to the bedside and stood, momentarily, looking down at the beautiful girl whom he had seduced. The thought came into his head that he would do what he pleased with her, once she was at the brothel, and in the Madam's grasp.

He decided he must move fast, and put an end to his musing. He worried in case she came to before he reached the other side of the panel. Once there, no one would hear her should she call out. Of that, he was certain.

He bent over the girl and lifted her in his arms, hurrying to the other side of the room, as quickly as he could, for she was a dead weight. By the time he had stepped through the panel, she had awakened, and started to struggle.

Adrian dropped her to the floor, and taking some strong string from his pockets, quickly tied her wrists and ankles, then gagged her with his handkerchief. He could see that she was terrified, by the look in her eyes, but it pleased him to know that she now realised her seducer had her once again, in his evil power. She was aware, he could see, that she was at his mercy.

The journey to the caves wouldn't be easy, carrying his burden, but he was a big man, and in any case he could rest when he needed to, with no fear of being followed. It would be morning before anyone would miss the gipsy girl, and by the time the alarm was raised, they would be well on their way to London, where eventually, behind the closed doors of the brothel, no one would be able to find her. She would have vanished off the face of the earth.

It gave him great satisfaction to imagine his brother, frantic with worry, combing the whole area, searching for his missing guest, for he knew how Antony would feel, being an honourable person.

When Esmeralda saw who her captor was she was sick with worry, and absolutely terrified. She was also feeling dizzy, and uncomfortable with the gag in her mouth, for she couldn't breathe freely, and this made her panic-stricken. Was she to be taken to the caves again? And for what reason this time she asked herself. And what of the child? It wouldn't be too long now, she was sure. What would Antony think? And where would he begin to look for her? Was it possible that he might think she had changed her mind, and not want to marry him after all? Surely he couldn't believe that of her, he must be aware of her feelings for him.

'Please, please Antony, find me quickly!' her heart cried out in despair, 'for I would sooner die, than live without you.'

At that moment, she was thrown to the ground with such force that her head hit the wall, and she passed into blessed oblivion.

* * * * *

Chapter Five

The Mills of God Grind Exceeding Small

When Esmeralda came to again, she saw that her captor had been joined by another. She was propped against a stone structure, whilst her two companions were conversing with each other. She could, of course, have no idea where she was, only that she felt they must be near the caves, for the sounds of the sea were far more prominent here.

What had this dangerous man in store for her now, she wondered, and how could she expect to escape from his clutches in her condition?

She had no idea of what the time could be, and wondered if Mrs Rushton had discovered her absence yet. She may not even have realised that her future mistress was missing, for many mornings before she had left for London, Esmeralda had been given to wandering out of doors, before the first meal of the day would be in evidence. So it could be many hours before discovering she had gone.

Surely with happiness in her grasp, she couldn't lose it like this. She felt in a hopeless position; and was well aware that she could expect no compassion from her captor. 'How could two brothers be so different?' she asked herself.

Her head was splitting, and her breathing was becoming more irregular as time went on. How much longer could she exist like this, feeling constant nausea, caused by her anxiety?

She suddenly felt herself being lifted again, and none too gently. Whereas before, Adrian had carried her on his own, now the other man was helping. She could feel their urgency as they moved as quickly as possible. After what seemed an endless time to her, they suddenly came to the cave where she had been brought before, where once again they threw her unceremoniously to the ground.

Adrian was feeling exalted, although very tired after his arduous journey carrying the girl, who was heavier now.

Well, it wouldn't be too long now before she would be far from Pendavan, and out of Antony's reach. He would give anything to see his twin's face, when he discovered the young gipsy girl's disappearance. By that time it would be too late for him to do anything, because even Antony, with his generous temperament, wouldn't want the girl after she had been used at the brothel, for she would be unclean in his eyes.

When he thought of having his way with the beautiful gipsy eventually, he could hardly contain himself. The fact that she wouldn't want him would make her put up a fight, and his conquest would be more exciting. He didn't like his women too passive. It would be better and more thrilling, because now she would know her seducer, whereas before, she had been oblivious.

Anyway, there was little time to pursue his own private thoughts, as he must be on his way with the gipsy within the hour. He had decided to drive the coach and horses himself. He had hired them, which was usual for him, with his regular trips to and from London, on his many jaunts and escapades. He had already arranged an alibi, so that no one could connect him with the gipsy's disappearance. He was quite confident that nothing could go wrong, but he wouldn't be satisfied until he had reached his destination, and carried out his wicked scheme, by depositing the girl at the brothel.

Esmeralda was shivering with the cold, and still very uncomfortable, although the gag had been removed from her mouth and she could breathe more freely.

'What is to happen to me?' she asked herself. And was she to give birth to the child here, without any comfort? Her mind was so jumbled, and she couldn't think straight any more. If only she knew what was going to happen to her, for the suspense of not knowing was quite devastating! Surely she must find out soon.

Momentarily, she closed her eyes, trying to relieve the pain in her head, when suddenly her captor came towards her with another figure dressed in a cloak and hood. Adrian was cloaked also, so where were they going, she wondered?

She was gagged again, and lifted off the ground. Her muscles felt considerably cramped, and she ached all over. It looked now, as though she was soon to find out what her captor had in mind for her.

They were carrying her across the shore now, and making for a man-made path, winding upwards towards the top of the cliffs. Their ascent was difficult, but with much puffing and panting, they eventually reached the top.

'We must be some way from Pendavan,' Esmeralda told herself, for there was no one around. The sea lashed against the massive rocks, leaving the white foam in its wake, and the terrified girl was reminded of the night that she first arrived here, which to her now, seemed an age ago.

She noticed a coach and horses a few yards further on, and suddenly realised that she was to go on a journey with her two captors.

She was lifted on to the seat and partially covered by a rug, which she was grateful for, as she felt so cold having no outer garments.

Adrian jumped on to the coach, and taking the reins, whipped the horses into a gallop, eager to be on his way. His companion sat opposite Esmeralda, inside the coach, watching her all the while. He had thrown off his cloak and hood, showing a man about Adrian's age, who looked so pale and wan, that she thought he would faint on the spot. Not a word had been spoken between the two men since leaving the caves, and the girl knew that her passenger did not intend speaking to her.

She was utterly exhausted and shocked beyond anything. She wouldn't have believed it possible that she could be abducted for a second time, and by the same man.

Adrian drove the horses at such a speed that the coach lurched continually, and Esmeralda had to cling to the side to keep her balance, as did her companion.

Suddenly, without any warning, the coach tipped sideways, throwing its occupants out. The last thing Esmeralda heard, before she fell into unconsciousness, were the frightened cries of the horses; and a terrible piercing scream which swirled around in the night, and was abruptly cut off. Then darkness enveloped her, and she knew no more.

The prostrate form of the girl, lying stretched out a few feet from the coach, looked lifeless, whilst her passenger lay trapped beneath the vehicle. One of the horses was lying very still, and in a twisted position, whilst the other had broken free when the accident happened.

The man, spread-eagled on the rocks far below, looked at the sky with lifeless eyes.

God works in mysterious ways.

* * * * *

Lord Pendavan was happy. He had awakened early to a bright and sunny morning, well satisfied with his lot. Esmeralda was here, under his roof at last, and in a few days they would be man and wife. Never in his wildest dreams had he expected to feel this way, for he was happier now than he had ever been, and very much in love.

He couldn't wait to see her, but knew she was sure to be still in the land of dreams, so while he waited with as much patience as he could muster, he decided to go riding. So, with Caesar saddled and King for extra company, he set off at a canter.

It was good to be alive on this magnificent morning, and Antony hoped that Esmeralda was as happy as he was. He would see to it that she never wanted for anything, and as soon as the child was born, and she had recovered, he would make arrangements for the ball he had promised her.

He would be so proud to show her off to his many friends, and was sure she would endear herself to all of them in time.

The most important thing he must see to had to be done that day. There were the enquiries he intended to make about his brother, and to try once and for all to flush him out, and to keep him away from Pendavan permanently, for Esmeralda would never be completely at peace with the threat of Adrian's presence.

Lost in his thoughts, he had let Caesar wander on. King was bounding far ahead, enjoying every minute of his outing.

Just then, the master of Pendavan came in sight of the headland path leading towards the open road, and as he looked ahead, he saw what appeared to be a coach overturned, and someone lying very still beside it. He couldn't make out from this distance exactly what was wrong, so urged Caesar into a gallop, just as King set up a furious barking.

He noticed that one of the horses had strayed from the overturned coach, and was grazing lazily a few yards away, but could see no other movement, whatsoever. As he reached the spot, his heart practically stood still when he saw the still figure of the girl who looked so familiar to him, then the man trapped underneath the side of the coach.

What had happened? he asked himself, and what was Esmeralda doing here, dressed only in her undergarments, looking so lifeless?

King was nuzzling the girl, whimpering all the while. He just couldn't understand why his new friend was ignoring him.

Lord Pendavan reached the girl's side, dropping to the ground beside her, calling her name repeatedly. Thank God, she was still alive, he thought, but she must be suffering from shock and exposure, so the sooner she was moved, the better.

He could hear the trapped man moaning, and called to him, saying he would get help to him as soon as possible. Meanwhile, lifting the girl very carefully on to the horse, and supporting her, he jumped up behind her, and urged Caesar into a light trot, for he must get Esmeralda home as quickly as he possibly could, and fetch the doctor. Daniel was going to have a very busy time, for he would have to treat the trapped man as well as his beloved Esmeralda. Was he to lose her, just as he had found complete happiness?

The horse, feeling the urgency of his master, broke into a gallop, eager to reach the house, likewise King, who had already arrived at the gates, which were open to receive them.

Lord Pendavan lifted Esmeralda from Caesar, and Albert, seeing that something was radically wrong, had hurried as quickly as he could to warn the housekeeper, who was now waiting to help. She was a very tactful person, so asked no questions, and was only ready to assist all she could.

"Rushie, get her into bed as quickly as possible, and keep her warm, while I fetch Daniel, for I am beside myself with worry," he told her. "I pray to God we are not too late. I must also send help to the scene of the accident, for there is a man trapped under the coach. He may be dying, or he could even be dead already."

Mrs Rushton, with Albert's assistance, got Esmeralda to her room, and sending the caretaker for hot water bottles, wrapped the unconscious girl in as many blankets as she could. She placed the hot water bottles around her, and as the warmth started to seep into the lifeless body, colour gradually returned to her cheeks.

The housekeeper drew up a chair and sat by the bed, to await the return of Lord Pendavan and the doctor, watching the gipsy girl very closely. What could have happened for her to be in this state? And why had she gone out of doors without her outer garments? There was a mystery here all right, and not of the girl's making, she was sure.

Meanwhile, Lord Pendavan rode with all possible speed, his one thought to reach his friend's house as soon as he could. He had already wasted valuable time, having to report the accident to the local watch house; but the man, whatever he had done, was a human being after all and needed help.

He kept asking himself who the man was, and what connection had he with Esmeralda? Nothing made sense any more, only that he felt his twin was mixed up with it somehow.

"Please God, don't let it be too late to save her!" he cried aloud in his anguish.

Daniel was just turning into his gateway, when Antony rode up, and seeing the look on his friend's face halted him in his tracks. What had happened to put that horrified expression on his face? he wondered.

"Daniel, can you come to Pendavan at once?" he asked. "It is Esmeralda, she has met with an accident, and I fear she may already be dead."

"I'll come at once Antony," his friend answered. "My horse is already saddled, I have just returned from visiting a patient. Try not to worry, for things may not be as bad as they seem," he said. "Perhaps you can tell me what happened as we go along?"

The two men set off, riding together, as they had done many times before. They had been childhood friends, and had drawn closer as the years had passed. Daniel had married his childhood sweetheart, Mary, who had adored him always. The marriage was an extremely happy one, bringing up their young family; and the doctor, who was a very hard-working man, became most popular over the years. He could be seen most days, riding his horse over the many rough paths, in all weathers, to visit someone who was sick.

He was most concerned at that moment as he accompanied his friend to Pendavan. What would he find when they arrived? And what would it do to Antony if Esmeralda died? He dreaded to think.

The horses galloped up to the entrance, and the men leapt from their saddles, disappearing into the house.

On entering the bedroom, Antony held his breath, almost afraid to look at the figure lying so still in the bed. Whereas, before, she looked like death, she was now terribly flushed with fever.

Daniel would help her, he knew, but anxiety nagged at his heart, making him feel very hopeless. How could she survive, after being exposed to the cold night air, and for how long they had no way of knowing.

The housekeeper left the room, after telling the doctor that Esmeralda hadn't yet spoken, although she had been very restless. She had taken it upon herself to hold a cool cloth to the young girl's forehead hoping it would help.

The look on the doctor's face became very serious, as he examined the young gipsy girl. "I am afraid she has a slight concussion, and a severe chill," he told his friend, "and she will go into labour at any time now, so we must prepare everything at once. Can Mrs Rushton help me, for I shall need plenty of hot water?" So saying, he removed his jacket, and rolled up his shirt sleeves in readiness for the worrying time ahead.

"If there is anything I can do Daniel, don't hesitate to ask," Antony told him. "But, I beg of you, please bring Esmeralda safely through, for I know not what I shall do if I should lose her."

* * * * *

Chapter Six

A Life Held in the Balance

As the man was extricated from beneath the over-turned coach, he moaned, and tried to speak, but his jumbled words made no sense to the men who were carrying his broken body. They knew he would be dead within a few hours. Suddenly his extra effort got through to one of the men, who heard him say that he must see Lord Pendavan at once, or it would be too late.

"There now, Sir, do not distress yourself," he told him, trying his hardest to keep the poor devil calm. "We shall take you to the gentleman right away."

The dying man closed his eyes, and tried to ease his aching body. Why had he let himself be a pawn in Adrian's diabolical plan? Where had it got him? And was he to die before making his peace with God? He wasn't a bad man, just easily led. He had been used continually by Adrian, and as things went from bad to worse, he had become more involved, and found himself unable to break free from him. He had tried numerous times, God knows, but to no avail. Now it was too late, for his life was almost ended, he well knew. At least he could try to do something good, by warning Lord Pendavan of his brother's plan regarding the gipsy girl, and, as well, of his other wicked deeds. Perhaps then the cult could be disbanded before anything else happened.

Adrian had formed the cult for his own ends, and if he was allowed to continue, many others would suffer because of him. He must be stopped before it got out of hand. The girl looked a nice little thing, and was certainly terrified, not knowing what her captor had in store for her. If he could live long enough to relate all he knew of Adrian's plans to Lord Pendavan, he would at least go to the next world feeling less guilty.

* * * * *

Lord Pendavan couldn't rest, for he was beside himself with worry. He knew that Esmeralda was desperately ill, her life now hanging in the balance, and only a miracle could save her. Could

Daniel help her, or was she too far gone? If only the birth could have been held off for a while, but of course, one could never halt nature.

He stood at the window looking out on to the scene before him, as he pursued his thoughts. He imagined himself married to Esmeralda, having a young family, and watching them play in the sunshine, amongst the haunts of his own childhood.

A knock at the door awakened him from his reverie. Thinking it might be news of Esmeralda, he hurried across the room, to find the caretaker at the door.

"There is a Constable asking for you, Sir," Albert informed his master.

"I expect it is about the accident, Albert. Would you show him in please?"

As the man entered the room, Lord Pendavan beckoned him to a chair. "How can I help you?" he asked, thinking only of the life and death struggle which was taking place above, in the room upstairs.

The man told him he had bad news. "I am afraid your brother, Lord Adrian, has been killed in the accident which you reported earlier. We think he was driving the coach which overturned during the night - and was thrown from his seat to the rocks below, where we found his body."

Lord Pendavan could hardly believe his ears; but that his twin was dead, he now had no doubt. He couldn't feel sorry, how could he, after all that had transpired? He just felt a wonderful relief.

His one thought now was for the miraculous news of Esmeralda's recovery. He could tell her then, that she need have no more worries, as her seducer was dead.

"I expect you know that one of the passengers in the coach was badly injured; is in fact dying, and wishes to speak to you, Sir." Antony realised that the man was speaking again. "We have brought him here, as we understand it is urgent that he speaks with you," he continued.

"I will see him immediately," said Lord Pendavan, walking across the room. What did this dying man want with him, and who was he? He must be one of Adrian's friends of course, and had most likely been a visitor here at sometime.

When he reached the man's side, he could see that he wasn't long for this world. He did recognise him as one of Adrian's circle, remembering that he hadn't taken to him at all. He had appeared an easily led youth, and must have been a puppet in Adrian's hands.

Antony found it very difficult to catch everything that the man said, but what he managed to hear was enough to make him realise what a dangerous man his brother had been, far more than he had ever thought possible. His face became grim, and somewhat mystified, with the knowledge of what had been going on around him. He could hardly take it in. Why had Adrian been so wanton? He, Antony, felt somehow, that he had failed his twin in a way. But in his heart, he knew Adrian had been bad all the way through. No individual could have swayed him one way or the other. Antony had no illusions; had Adrian lived, Esmeralda would have been in constant fear all her days.

"I didn't want to get involved, but you must be aware how persuasive your brother can be," the dying man continued.

This unfortunate being doesn't know that Adrian is dead, Lord Pendavan told himself, so to put the man's mind at rest he must be told. He deserved that, anyway.

The shock Antony received, with the knowledge of what could have become of Esmeralda, had Adrian succeeded with his fiendish scheme, he couldn't describe. She would have been lost to him for ever, degraded, and wretched, with no hope for the future.

Dear God, how could he live the rest of his life without her? It certainly didn't bear thinking about, for to lose her now was inconceivable to him. What she must have gone through those last hours! Would he ever know what really happened? There were so many questions he needed answers to, and would, more than likely, never get.

Meanwhile, upstairs, the struggle for Esmeralda's life was being fought. Never had a birth been so difficult, for the child had to do all the work to come into the world. The mother could give little or no help at all. Daniel was completely exhausted. Never before could he remember such a terrible ordeal. The child died, as he feared it might from the commencement of the birth. It was best that it happened this way, under the circumstances. Now the life of the girl was in the balance. It would be touch and go he knew, and if she died what could he say to his dearest friend, to console him in his hour of grief? Surely such a lovely girl couldn't die so young. Married to Antony she could have had so much wealth and happiness, and the main thing of all, love, for he was well aware that his friend loved the young gipsy girl.

She must have constant attention if they were to save her. If only the fever would abate, there might be a chance, however small. Mrs Rushton had been such a help already. How he would have managed without her, he knew not. He could sense that the girl had endeared herself to the housekeeper, as she had done to Antony, and she had so much to live for. His biggest concern was if pneumonia set in. Should this happen, there would definitely be no hope for her whatever. The crisis would come in a few hours, and with God's help, she might pull through, and live to marry Antony.

* * * * *

Chapter Seven

Loss of Memory

The silent onlookers had kept vigil for many anxious hours, hoping for any sign of change in the condition of the unconscious girl. The strain could be felt in the atmosphere of the sick room, as the doctor moved closer to the patient.

"Praise be to God!" he remarked to the housekeeper, "I do believe Esmeralda's breathing is a little easier."

Daniel felt there was some hope at last, but she wasn't out of the woods yet, by any means. At least she was now in a very deep sleep, which would be good for the sick girl.

"You must be very tired, Mrs Rushton," he said, "but if you could just manage another hour or so, I would appreciate it. I must go down and talk to your master and let him know how Esmeralda is, for he must be very anxious. Meanwhile, would you watch her closely until I return?"

Feeling exhausted, Daniel descended the staircase and made for the library, where he found his friend deep in thought. Antony brightened visibly when he saw Daniel, hoping for good news.

"The child is dead, Antony," he told him, "and Esmeralda has had a very rough time, although there is some slight improvement. She will need very careful nursing if we are to pull her through, but try not to worry, my friend." He could tell by the look of anguish on Antony's face how much his friend was suffering, and it pulled at his heart strings to see him like this, but Antony couldn't be given any false hopes at this stage.

"Would you like a drink, Daniel?" Lord Pendavan asked, pouring himself a stiff whisky. "I have some disturbing news to impart, and I cannot really believe it has happened myself, as yet." He looked into space, not seeing Daniel, at all. He couldn't grasp everything that had happened, and wondered how his friend would react when he knew.

"Adrian is dead," he told him. "He was involved in the coach accident, and thrown on to the rocks below, where his body has just been recovered. I must admit that I am stunned by the news of his death, but the worst shock of all is what he had planned to do to Esmeralda."

Lord Pendavan quickly related what the man had told him, watching his friend's expression change to one of consternation and horror.

Daniel was aghast at what he had just heard. That this kind and honest man standing before him could have had a brother so criminal, who had violated the law in so many ways, he couldn't comprehend. Adrian had met a violent death, no one could deny, and no more than he so rightly deserved, but it could cause his friend more mental pain. He dreaded to think what would happen should the girl die.

"There will have to be an inquest, of course," he told Antony, "but we must do everything we can to cover up Adrian's activities, for the good name of your family. Leave it to me Antony, for I will do all in my power to save any scandal which could fall on this household.

"The people in the village know of various happenings," he continued, "as I have often heard, whilst on my rounds, but it is my belief that they could not connect it with your brother. Now that he is dead, I think it will fade out, as he, always being the leader, must have had a great hold on many of his circle, consequently, they will, I believe, be very relieved at his death and disband quietly."

Lord Pendavan brightened momentarily, knowing Daniel would help him all he could. Now he could give all his mind to Esmeralda, and hopefully, her recovery.

"Daniel," he said, "I am thinking of asking Jacqueline to come to Pendavan for a while, to help with the nursing, for, if as you say it is going to be a long process, Mrs Rushton will be glad of some assistance. It would also be a change for her to get away from London. What do you think of the idea?"

"I am all for it," he answered, "especially Jacqueline, for they took to each other, and I think she will do Esmeralda a power of good. She is going to need constant supervision."

"Can I see Esmeralda for a few minutes?" he asked the doctor. He couldn't wait to feast his eyes on his beloved, even if only a short visit was permissible. It seemed to him an endless time since he had discovered her at the cliff edge that morning. Much had happened; and an explanation was needed, but there would be plenty of time for that, if she recovered, and once she was over the worst of her illness.

The doctor followed him from the library, and both men climbed the stairs to the bedroom that housed the sick girl.

On entering the room, they saw Mrs Rushton leave the side of the bed where she had been sitting, keeping vigil. Her eyes were red with tiredness, but she appeared satisfied with the patient.

"You must retire now," Lord Pendavan told her. "I will stay here for the remainder of the night, bless you, Rushie," his voice demonstrating his heartfelt thanks.

"She is certainly sleeping easier now," Daniel said, taking his young patient's pulse. "I think she is over the crisis, Antony. She is a strong girl; and with the will to live, I am sure she will come through all right. Her colour is improving already, but do keep a close watch still; and if there should be any specific change, either way, let me know. Meanwhile, I will snatch some sleep."

After Daniel had left, Antony settled down beside the sleeping girl.

If only she would open her eyes, and recognise him, then he would be really happy.

The room was so still that even a pin could be heard to drop. He began to think over the day's happenings, which had been nightmarish. That Esmeralda had gone through a most harrowing time, he knew, and would expect it to be some time before she could erase the experience from her mind, if at all.

If she recovered fully, he would tell her of Adrian's death, and could almost picture the immense relief in her eyes. As soon as she was, hopefully, on her feet again, he would take a trip to London, and choose for her the most beautiful gown that money could buy. Nothing would be too good for her.

That this beautiful girl would be his wife very soon, God willing, he could hardly believe. He moved his position within the chair, and rested his head on its back, but kept his eyes on the lovely girl, who was sleeping peacefully now, by far the best medicine that she could possibly have.

Fortunately, they could keep her name out of the inquiries, as no one had been aware of her presence in the coach apart from the other passenger, who must be dead by now.

He would arrange on the morrow for Jacqueline to come to Pendavan, and felt secure in the knowledge, that no one could help Esmeralda as much as his greatest friend.

* * * * *

Dawn showed the man tired and weary after his all night vigil at the bedside of the girl. He had been listening constantly for any alteration in her laboured breathing, which had improved hourly, bringing a complete change as morning broke.

"Thanks be to God!" Lord Pendavan explained, as he looked at her, his devotion mixed with relief, she suddenly opened her eyes, looking first around the room then at the man who sat beside her, hollow-eyed.

Esmeralda felt hazy, and couldn't regain her equanimity. What was she doing here, lying in this beautiful bed, in such lovely surroundings? Who was this man sitting at her side, with so serious a look on his handsome face? It hurt her to think, so she closed her eyes to help relieve the feeling of nausea which had come over her. She couldn't remember how she came to be there. Perhaps her companion could put her mind at rest. She wanted to ask him, but couldn't form the words; and suddenly felt herself sinking into oblivion again.

A knock on the door, which opened to reveal the housekeeper, brought Lord Pendavan to his feet. He had the greatest difficulty in keeping his eyes open and they ached continually.

"I have come to take over from you, Sir," she told him, thinking how exhausted he looked.

"Thank you, Rushie; I could do with some rest," he answered. "She regained consciousness just now, but showed no recognition, and immediately fell asleep again," he told his housekeeper.

"Were you able to sleep?" he asked her.

"Yes," she answered, "and I feel much refreshed, thank you, Sir! Perhaps you would like your breakfast, for it is ready?"

He realised how hungry he was feeling, as he detected the odour of the cooked meal awaiting him. He felt somewhat impatient for Esmeralda's rapid recovery, and wondered if he could rest away from her side, but accepted he must be sensible, as Daniel had implied it could be a long time before she became herself again. He would be calling later on in the day, and then perhaps he would have better news and more hope, so until he arrived he must take the opportunity and get some rest.

Mrs Rushton could see that a vast improvement had taken place in their patient, in less than twenty-four hours. She couldn't wait to see her sitting up, and taking notice, but realised that would be some way ahead yet.

She settled down beside the bed, to watch over Esmeralda, when suddenly she stirred, bringing the housekeeper to her feet again, anxious to see if there was something that she could do for her. As her eyes opened, and fastened on Mrs Rushton, the older woman could see no recognition whatsoever, and was aware that the girl had lost her memory. Would to God that it was only temporary, for it would be such a tragedy for these young people.

"Where am I?" she asked the housekeeper, "and who are you?"

"You are with friends, dear," Mrs Rushton answered, thinking it best not to mention her forthcoming marriage, for fear of worrying the girl. "You met with an accident, and have been ill," she continued. "We are nursing you back to health, but you mustn't worry, dear, as that would be bad for you."

"Who am I?" she asked, "and what is my name?"

"You came to visit us, and your name is Esmeralda," the housekeeper answered, watching the girl very closely. How could she possibly begin to explain to this vulnerable young girl that she arrived here a homeless gipsy, forsaken by her own kith and kin? The poor child would need to be better in herself to accept what she would eventually be told, and of the trauma she had been put through. No one at the mansion could have foreseen her loss of memory, except the doctor, who may have had his suspicions of something like this happening. Esmeralda must have taken quite a knock, to be thrown from the coach. It was a wonder she hadn't been killed in the process. The whole household was anxious to know how she had come to be involved in the coach accident, but if her memory loss persisted, it would be her secret, alone, with her abductor and the other passenger both gone from this world.

"The doctor will be calling to see you again shortly," Mrs Rushton told her, "so perhaps I should tidy you a little, in readiness for him."

"How long have I been ill?" she asked. "And where is this place?"

The housekeeper was worried now, as she felt the doctor wouldn't want their patient to tire herself asking questions, but she had to answer the girl, to satisfy her curiosity.

"You were taken ill yesterday, and are staying here with my master, who owns this mansion house," she told her, hoping this would suffice for the time.

Esmeralda closed her eyes again, and Mrs Rushton could see that she was exhausted. She must try and keep her quiet until the doctor arrived, for Master Antony would still be asleep and she had no intention of disturbing him until it was absolutely necessary.

She settled down again, after first straightening the bed covers. She could tell by the regular breathing that her young patient had again fallen into a deep sleep.

She must have dozed off herself, for the next thing she knew, the doctor was in the room.

* * * * *

Chapter Eight

A Sense of Foreboding

Daniel was looking very thoughtful when Lord Pendavan came upon him, walking in the gardens.

He felt better now, and able to cope after his rest. He was surprised that he had slept at all, worried as he was. King was at his side as always, happy to be near his master. Every now and then he nuzzled against him.

"What news have you regarding Esmeralda?" he asked the doctor. "Is she going to be all right?"

"Thanks be to God, she has much improved, Antony, but I am afraid she has completely lost her memory," Daniel informed his friend. "I didn't say so to you," he continued, "but I was afraid this would happen."

"Do you mean to say she remembers nothing?" asked Lord Pendavan, aghast at what this could mean to him.

"Her mind is a complete blank, and I have no way of knowing if there is any permanent damage." Daniel told him.

"Then she will have no knowledge of me, or that she is to become my wife," remarked Lord Pendavan. He was stunned by this news, as it hadn't occurred to him that should Esmeralda recover, there could be other complications. She must have suffered a more serious knock on the head than they had first imagined, and if, as Daniel thought, there might be permanent damage, then where did that leave him? For certainly there would be no future for them as man and wife.

Why, oh why, did this have to happen? he asked himself, that such a young and beautiful girl could become inactive, and lack interest in the rest of her life, for that is what could happen. He couldn't imagine anything so terrible, seeing her suffer, and not being able to do anything to help. There was one thing he was certain of, she would never have to leave Pendavan, for he would look after her always. Even had he not fallen in love with her, he felt a responsibility towards her, because of what Adrian had done to her, and he would never see her want. She must have every comfort and all the love and attention he could give her, if not as a husband, then at least a father figure.

"We must go carefully with her, Antony, and not force her in any way," Daniel was saying, "as this could do her more harm than good. It will take much patience on all our parts, and the sooner Jacqueline can take over, the better, for with a good friend to watch over her, I feel it may help her to recover her memory, if anything will. She is certain to feel more comfortable with another young woman around her, rather than yourself, as she is sure to feel shy with you."

Lord Pendavan had to admit that Daniel was right, that if anyone could help Esmeralda it was Jacqueline. She would be here soon, if all went well.

Meanwhile, the subject of their conversation was awake, and taking stock of her surroundings. The room somehow seemed familiar, but how could that be, for surely she had never been here before? She wished so very much that she could remember who she was. Who did she belong to? And where did she come from? For someone, somewhere, must be very worried about her. Who were these people who were so kind to her? And what accident had she been involved in? She liked the motherly looking soul sitting by her bedside, who was so attentive to her.

Perhaps the gentleman who had sat with her earlier, would come again soon. She liked the look of him too, for he seemed so kind, and was most handsome. She wondered if she had a family, and if so, when she would see them again? The answers would come sometime she supposed but for the present it hurt her to think, so she must refrain from trying. Her head ached constantly with the thoughts jumping around inside. She must sleep, for then she could forget her present problems.

* * * * *

Jacqueline was travelling post haste towards Pendavan. What could have happened? she kept asking herself. Surely things could not have gone wrong for Antony again, just as he had found his new happiness? She would know soon enough, for another hour or so, should see her at the end of the journey.

She had made her plans for the future, starting with the selling of her fashion house. As she had expected, Stuart had again proposed to her, and this time she had accepted. Theirs should be a happy marriage, for he was a good man, and very much in love with her. He had told her that her happiness was the most important thing to him, and he intended devoting his life to her. He knew of her fondness for Lord Pendavan, and understood the feelings for the man she had grown up with.

They were to be married in the spring, which to Jacqueline was the most beautiful time of the year. Antony and Esmeralda would have been married some few months by the time she herself went to the altar.

She felt very happy now that she had made her decision at last. She told herself that she should have done this long ago.

Now her thoughts reverted to her friends again. In the message Antony had seemed very distressed and had begged her immediate help. There had been no time for any explanations, other than that there was trouble at Pendavan.

She couldn't wait to get there, and find out what was wrong. It must be serious for her to have to drop everything, and leave London immediately.

* * * * *

Meanwhile, back at Pendavan, Lord Antony entered the bedroom, and crossing to the bed, stood looking down at the beautiful girl, who in repose looked so vulnerable, and even more lovely.

He couldn't help wondering what the future held for them. Would she fully recover, or would she get steadily worse? Daniel had given him to understand, within the last hour or so, that her condition could deteriorate rapidly should there be any damage to her brain, and there was nothing that could be done under these circumstances. He had prayed to God for help, and although he fully understood the seriousness of her condition, he still held out hope that they could become man and wife.

He felt so helpless, and incapable of thinking any more. The time dragged incessantly, making him impatient, and unsettled. Perhaps he would feel better when Jacqueline arrived, for he knew he could rely on her. She should be here soon, providing she got away on time for her journey, which would have taken five days, at least, so she would be exhausted on her arrival.

“This must be her now,’ he thought, for he could hear the sounds in the drive of the coach and horses, as they were pulled to a stop. He descended the staircase just as Jacqueline made her entrance. He crossed the hall to where she was standing, taking her hands within his own, showing his relief as well as pleasure at seeing her.

“Will you come into the library, my dear?” he asked his guest. “Albert will take your luggage to your room, where you can rest later. But first I must tell you what has happened.

“Would you like a drink?” he asked, pouring one for himself. “We shall have a meal in just a short while, when you have freshened yourself.”

Jacqueline sat back, relaxing her aching body while listening to Antony relate all the events that had taken place within the past few days.

The news of Adrian’s death shocked her, but aware of his character, she accepted this was the best thing that could have happened. When she heard what had befallen Esmeralda, she was horrified and distressed beyond anything. That this should have come about, just as everything had been working out well for Antony, was a tragedy. No wonder he looked worn with anxiety, she told herself. It must have been a nightmare for him, and still would be until Esmeralda was fully recovered, if at all.

What twist of fate had brought this about? Hadn’t he suffered enough? She made up her mind there and then, that she would devote every waking hour to nursing this unfortunate girl who had become so dear to her, and to the man sitting opposite. To be able to bring back a smile to the tragic face of her dearest friend, would be reward enough, for it grieved her to see him looking like he did, and what of Esmeralda? What had it done to her? Would she ever be the same person again? And would they ever be able to find out the true facts? She couldn’t wait to see her, and wondered how she would look after what she had endured.

The days and weeks that followed were very trying indeed for the whole household, particularly Jacqueline, who spent every minute of her time with the young gipsy, who at times had taken to wandering off towards the cliff paths, leading down to the beaches and caves far below Pendavan. This in itself was most worrying for everyone, as she seemed to have no fear, although one slip and she would be gone for ever. It was almost like looking after and talking to a child, as no one could get her to see the danger which surrounded her. She seemed lost in her thoughts, staring for hours out to sea, as though looking for someone or something. Other days she was quite content to stay in the gardens, where she would sit beside the fish pond, gazing into its depths.

It was here one day that Lord Pendavan came upon her. He was expecting Daniel, who only called once a week now, having done all he could.

The sun shone high in the sky, showing the gardens and beautiful plants to advantage. It certainly was a magnificent sight to any onlooker, but particularly to Antony, who had always loved the place, and now more than ever, seeing the girl that he loved amongst all his favourite haunts. He looked on his home with fierce pride, as that of an Indian for his ancestors. The mansion had so much character, and every part of it held many memories for him. If only Adrian had been different they could have done so much together; as it was, everything had fallen on to his shoulders. He had always been disappointed knowing he couldn't rely on his twin, and now with his death, he, Antony, was last in line.

The girls were each lost in their own thoughts, and Antony momentarily pursued his, thinking, perhaps, that a change would help Esmeralda recover her memory. Different surroundings might do her the world of good. He decided he would suggest it later, for he must try all that he could. Nothing must be spared. She was happy in his company, he knew, even though she was not aware of who he was. Looking at her now, he couldn't accept that she would never recover.

After enquiring how she was on this wonderful day, and being told the same thing that he heard each time, he decided to go and meet Daniel.

Esmeralda watched him go, thinking how charming he was. If only she could remember some little thing, it might start her off on a train of thought which could help to restore her memory, for it was a constant worry, not knowing her identity. How could she continue like this, being an anxiety to others? For instance, this sweet woman sitting beside her, who was her constant companion each day and night, never tiring in her undaunted duty. Who was she? And what was her relationship to the kind man whose house she was sharing? For they certainly were not man and wife, of this she was sure.

Questions buzzed around inside her head, but she still could find no answers to them, and it hurt her to think.

Suddenly she heard Jacqueline saying they should return to the house, so she rose rather reluctantly from her favourite seat, to walk slowly and silently towards the home she had grown to love.

* * * * *

Chapter Nine

Miraculous Recovery

Esmeralda felt restless and her head ached continually. She was on her own at that moment, Jacqueline having decided to have a bath.

The house was very silent. Lord Pendavan had retired earlier to the library, followed by King, who hated to be away from his master. He had plenty to think about, for Daniel had implied that Esmeralda would not improve in her present state. He had told his friend that he intended marrying the lovely gipsy girl, even should she stay as she was, for he would never be completely happy unless he made her his wife, as he loved her so very much. At first, he had thought marriage was unthinkable, in her condition. It was the desperate shock of her not knowing him, and the love he had for her which she could not return, that absolutely threw him, and caused him untold distress. As the days progressed, with no outward improvement, he tried to visualise what life would be like at Pendavan without her. He had no illusions as to how quickly her health could deteriorate, and he decided that he wanted to be by her side whatever happened. As her husband, he could do this without any questions asked. So, his decision was made, and the issue conclusive. The wedding would take place on the morrow.

His thoughts darted from Esmeralda, to Adrian, and the inquest. The verdict had been death by misadventure, so no one was any the wiser as to his twin's misdeeds. He had made some discreet enquiries around, and not a thing was known of any groups being seen or anything untoward happening since the news of Adrian's tragic death, so it looked as though his friends had gone to ground. Nothing more was heard about them from that fateful day.

The relief from the extreme tension that Lord Pendavan had suffered over his brother's death had momentarily distracted his thoughts from Esmeralda, so he immediately turned his mind back to her. Had he but known or guessed what drastic events were to befall them, he would have been truly heartbroken. As it was, he was oblivious to what was about to happen around him.

* * * * *

Esmeralda had thrown her cloak around her, and closing the bedroom door quietly behind her, silently descended the stairs. The large heavily studded door before her was unlocked, it being far too early in the evening for everyone to retire for the night.

As she let herself out into the darkness, her one thought was to get away. She must, for how otherwise would she be able to find out who she was, or where she came from? These people were kindness itself, but she could not depend on them indefinitely. Perhaps if she mixed with others it might help to restore her memory, as this was no life for her in her present condition. She felt sure her new friends would be distressed when they discovered her missing, but they would soon forget, because wasn't she a nuisance to everyone?

She found herself walking towards the headland and cliff paths, with the treacherous rocks far below. The sound of the sea dashing against them, was the only noise to be heard in the otherwise still night.

Esmeralda felt herself drawn towards the spot where she would always sit looking out to sea. In her eagerness to reach it, she had gone too far to the edge, and suddenly, she felt herself falling into space.

The sudden jolt as her body hit the hard surface winded her completely, and as her head came into contact with the cliff edge she fell into a bottomless pit.

The gulls screeched as they circled the still form of the girl.

* * * * *

Jacqueline felt very relaxed and refreshed after bathing in the warm water. Her thoughts went to Stuart, wondering how he was faring. She missed him already, and this pleased her, for it proved that he meant more to her than she had realised. She could now look forward to her forthcoming marriage with hope. With her new found happiness, she compared it to Antony's continual plight, with his perpetual worries over the young gipsy girl, who had endeared herself to everyone with whom she had come into contact. She knew already of Antony's steadfast decision to marry Esmeralda, irrespective of her condition. In his love for her, he was completely devoid of logic as to the consequences that could arise, should she become pregnant. There would be disastrous results, should this happen, but she could not blame him for wanting to snatch what happiness he could. She was quite aware that he loved the girl to distraction, and dreaded to think what it would do to him should she die. And this was a definite possibility, as had already been explained to him by Daniel.

Slipping into something comfortable, Jacqueline made for Esmeralda's bedroom, whereupon, entering, she was more than surprised to find it empty. Where could she be? she asked herself. Perhaps she was downstairs with Antony, the hour not too late? As she approached the library she could not understand why everything was so quiet. If Esmeralda was with him, surely she would hear voices!

At her tap on the door, Lord Pendavan bade her enter, pleased to see his friend, likewise King, who rose to greet her.

"Antony," she said in a worried voice," have you seen Esmeralda for she is not in her bedroom?"

He jumped to his feet, consternation in his face. "Surely she cannot have wandered off at this time of night," he said, hurrying over to the bell rope to summon the housekeeper.

Mrs Rushton came into the room, wondering what could have happened, as it was unusual for her master to send for her at that time. These hours were allotted to her for herself.

"Is anything wrong, Sir?" she asked, looking from one to the other, noticing the anxious look on their faces, and her master - wild of eye, his countenance almost devoid of any colour.

"Is Miss Esmeralda with you, Rushie?" Lord Pendavan asked, afraid of what her answer would be.

"No, Sir, I haven't seen her since she retired early to her bedroom," she replied, feeling a foreboding steal over her.

Antony felt sick in the pit of his stomach. He had been afraid that this would happen, for had she not taken to wandering off at all times? It was unusual for her to do this after dark, and this gave him great cause for concern.

"Quickly, we must search the house thoroughly, and if we cannot find her within the house, we must look around outside in all the most likely places. There is no time to be lost," he told them. "Jacqueline, you go upstairs and see if she has entered any of the other rooms, while Rushie and I check everywhere down here."

Within five minutes they were all back after their unsuccessful search.

Donning coats, they dashed out into the night, each one sensing the other's anxiety. King, aware that something was wrong, bounded ahead of them, stopping to look back every few minutes. They must be looking for his new found-friend, for she wasn't with them as she should be.

A swift look around her favourite haunts in the gardens brought no luck, so they immediately hurried towards the cliff paths, dreading what they might find.

King found her, and raised the alarm by barking furiously at the spot where not long before Esmeralda had slipped down into the darkness.

Hardly able to breathe after their exertions, the searchers reached the frantic dog who was trying to make his way down over the sheer drop in an effort to get to the girl, who was lying some way below on a large ledge.

Lord Pendavan – although it was quite a clear night – held out the lantern, to get a better view, whilst their eyes, now accustomed somewhat to the dark, picked out quite clearly the figure of Esmeralda.

Their first thought was that the girl was dead, for how could she survive this fall? Antony asked himself the agonising question: had he lost her after all?

"I must fetch help," he told the other two, "for the longer she lies there, the less chance we have of finding her alive."

He must hurry to his nearest neighbour, who had two sturdy sons, and with the help of ropes and several strong arms, they should be able to pull Esmeralda to safety. Would that they were not too late! His most worrying thought was that if she should move on recovering consciousness, she could so easily fall down to the treacherous rocks below, with no hope of survival. Thank God the ledge had saved her from this.

He felt so desperate as he rushed up to the large door facing him. The loud clanging of the bell, and the approaching footsteps told him he had been heard.

He quickly related what had happened, and armed with ropes and lanterns, the four men rushed back to the waiting women and dog, who hadn't taken their eyes from the still figure lying far below them.

In minutes the two young men had fastened the ropes and quickly lowered themselves to the ledge, whereupon they tied more ropes around the unconscious girl, moving her as little as possible, in case of internal injuries. One of them had taken her pulse, shouting to the onlookers above that she was still alive.

"Thank God!" Lord Pendavan said, terrified that she might be injured more while hoisting her dead weight to the top, with the help of the older man, but between them they managed to bring her up over the cliff face without undue knocks. To their inexperienced eyes, she appeared to be none the worse for her fall, except for her comatose state. Only the doctor could be sure that nothing was broken.

Carrying their burden back to Pendavan was easier said than done, but they accomplished it as quickly as they could, and eventually, the patient was warmly wrapped up in bed, still unconscious, which did nothing to alleviate their fears for her health. Daniel would come right away, he knew. Whatever would he think, when he was told of the accident, he asked himself.

Once again Antony rode Caesar at a furious pace, hoping to find the doctor at home. As luck would have it Daniel was with his family, and about to retire for the night, with the hope of few interruptions, but he readily agreed to accompany his friend and examine Esmeralda.

Antony tried to explain what he knew to Daniel, but could not give any insight into why Esmeralda went out of doors, or how she came to be where she was found.

As the two friends rode along, the horses gathered speed, aware of their riders' urgency. Neither spoke, for there was too much concern within their thoughts; Daniel's, for this dear man who had had far more than his fair share of troubles. As he glanced at him, he noticed the persistent worried look flitting across his face, silent in his thoughts. Antony couldn't get it out of his head, that his beloved was gone from this world. If this was the case, then his life would be finished.

As Pendavan appeared before them, the two riders rode through the large gates up the driveway, and reined in their horses at the entrance, where the groom waited to lead the tired animals to the stables. Both men dreaded to enter the mansion house for fear of what they might hear. As they half-heartedly, but hurriedly ascended the huge staircase, Jacqueline came dashing out of the bedroom, halting them in their tracks.

"Antony! Esmeralda is all right, her memory has returned and she knows us all!" she exclaimed excitedly. "We haven't let her move as yet in case she has any injuries, but she seems fine."

The three friends looked at one another, each aware of the others' feelings. For Antony himself, he could not contain his sheer excitement. Dear God! was his happiness to be fulfilled after all?

They entered the bedroom, and looked towards the bed where Esmeralda was lying, a look of recognition on her face.

The doctor's examination resulted in good news. "There is not much wrong with the patient that a few days' rest won't put right," Daniel told them. "She will have bruises of course," he went on to say, "which should clear very quickly, as will the stiffness which she can not help but suffer after such a fall, but apart from this I can detect no other problems."

Lord Pendavan dropped to his knees beside the girl, taking both her hands within his own. "My darling, how happy I am that you remember me at last," he told his blushing wife to be.

Esmeralda looked at the man kneeling beside her with a rapt expression. To think that had she not been involved in the accident, which Jacqueline had told her about, she might never have known of her deep love for him. She tried to erase from her mind all the things that had happened, knowing that in their own time they would talk about it, but for the present, all she could think of was Antony.

They had no need of words; their eyes spoke for them, and at long last their lips met in sheer abandonment, yielding completely to a passionate kiss.

The onlookers, not wishing to intrude, walked silently from the room, leaving the two happy lovers alone.

* * * * *

PART TWO

Dark Shadows are Cast

Chapter One

Mistress of Pendavan

The tiny church was filled to capacity. It was Gothic in its architecture, with the pointed arch common from the twelfth to sixteenth centuries. It stood surrounded by old gnarled trees with beautiful foliage shading the gravestones, chipped and broken with age. One could still decipher the remnants of writing on most, enabling the onlooker to notice that many of the buried had died young.

The flagstones, just inside the church leading up to the altar and flanked by long pews of shiny carved wood, were also graves, but on these the words were hardly discernible, worn away over the years by successive footsteps.

Whilst mostly peaceful, on this occasion there was much activity and excitement, for everyone in this small community was gathered together to witness the wedding of the year.

The bridegroom, Lord Pendavan, was liked and respected by all, and, although few had seen his bride-to-be, it was said she was a pretty young thing.

He stood at the head of the pews anxiously awaiting the arrival of Esmeralda, his best man by his side.

"Have you the ring Daniel?" he enquired once again, satisfied only when his friend opened his hand to show it nestling safely within his palm.

Daniel had never seen Antony so nervous in all the years that they had known each other, but when he looked back on his own marriage, hadn't he himself felt much the same?

This was a perfect love match between Antony and the lovely gipsy girl, Daniel told himself, satisfied deep within that his friend had at last found complete happiness. It had eluded him so far with troubles attacking him from all sides. Perhaps now, he would be happier than ever before. Esmeralda would see to that, Daniel knew, for she had shown her innermost feelings of love for Antony every day since her memory returned.

"Here she comes," someone whispered, and all heads turned to where Esmeralda had just entered the church on the arm of a very handsome man, whilst her friend Jacqueline followed behind holding the heavy train.

Esmeralda had never thought a church aisle could appear so long. When she looked back afterwards, all she could remember was the sea of faces all around her, and her eagerness to reach the side of her beloved Antony, who waited patiently at the head of the church.

Her wedding dress, beautiful in its hanging folds from the tiny waist, had a high neckline which, trimmed with layers of dainty lace, gave added height to Esmeralda's petite figure; while the full sleeves, caught into tiny cuffs, were also trimmed with matching lace. Her jet black hair dressed high carried a magnificent multi-coloured tiara, which held the heavy veil back from her face.

Esmeralda felt her hand grasped tightly, and looking up, realised that she was at last standing beside Antony. The contact with him gave her added strength, which had long since diminished during her waking hours.

Having Jacqueline with her had helped considerably. She was a tower of strength, and when she had suggested Stuart giving her away, Esmeralda had been delighted, especially as she had no wish to approach her estranged father.

She thought back on all that had occurred these past months, months which to her seemed a lifetime yet much of which she had little or no recollection, until her memory had returned fully, and with it the full horror of all the trauma she had been put through. She had felt sick to the pit of her stomach, as the devastating events came flooding back to her. She had no wish to discuss any of the details because of the terrible shocks she had received, so she deliberately stored away memories that had developed into recurring nightmares of the worse kind, preferring to pursue her sober reflections of Antony, her deep love for him, and her forthcoming marriage to him.

Antony had suggested the wedding could wait. He thought they should tarry a while, so that she could convalesce after her accident, for a few weeks at least until she recovered completely. "Then" he had told her, "we can be married."

Her argument that she felt absolutely fine and wished not to change any of the arrangements fell on deaf ears. Antony had resisted any persuasion on her part, for her own sake, so Jacqueline had continued to stay at Pendavan until such time as Daniel had considered his patient had returned to health, enabling Jacqueline to return to

London, to make the necessary arrangements for the wedding dress with the new management of the fashion house.

After a week in the city, Jacqueline was informed that the wedding gown was ready for collection, as well as the complete trousseau. So, after first calling at the place of business, she made the necessary arrangements to return to Pendavan, accompanied by Stuart, who readily agreed to give Esmeralda away, delighted to be approached for such an important occasion.

The sight of the dress had almost taken the young gipsy girl's breath away, it was so beautiful. After first stepping into her new gossamer undergarments, she then, with Jacqueline's assistance, donned the magnificent gown, which fitted her to perfection.

As Esmeralda had surveyed her reflection in the full-length cheval-glass mirror, that she could swing into various positions to see herself from top to toe, she could hardly recognise her image, and pinched herself to see that she wasn't dreaming. This was her friend's wedding gift, so she couldn't be more pleased.

Jacqueline helped her out of all the clothes, and hung them away in readiness for the great day, not very far off. That everything fitted well, gave her the satisfaction that there would be no problems on the day.

While Jacqueline had been away, Esmeralda had improved, visiting the various haunts in the huge grounds, but not on her own. Antony was still very reluctant for her to venture far without company. He was terrified that something could happen to his wife to be. His love for her had increased tenfold, and he couldn't bear her out of his sight for any length of time.

With a start, Esmeralda came out of her reverie to realise that Antony was speaking in a whisper, and squeezing her hand tight. "Do not be anxious my darling, it will be all over very shortly."

Only minutes had passed whilst she pursued her thoughts, but it seemed hours since she had first reached Antony's side. And now the clergyman was in the throes of the ceremony establishing the marriage union, with its repeated recital of words between him and the handsome couple standing before the altar. The sentences bandied to and fro, until, eventually, "Wilt thou have this woman to thy wedded wife?" he asked, and Antony, looking first at Esmeralda, replied, "I will."

The clergyman continued: "Wilt thou have this man to thy wedded husband?" "I will," she replied, looking at the ring as it was placed on her finger.

"I now pronounce you man and wife," the voice went on. "You may now kiss the bride," the clergyman finished, with the semblance of a smile spreading across his somewhat doleful face.

Esmeralda held her face up to her husband, who cupped it within his hands, gently kissing her tremulous mouth.

With the wedding over at last, everyone began to relax and enjoy the social occasion. Antony performed the introductions with pride, feeling honoured to be able to present such a beautiful young wife to his friends. He was overwhelmingly happy. So too, was Esmeralda now that everything had been resolved.

A few days before the wedding, the housekeeper had served breakfast to her future mistress in her private boudoir. She was taken quite by surprise when Esmeralda explained how she wished to reveal what had happened to her, which, up to then she had been unable to even think about, let alone open her heart to anyone else. In a matter of hours, both Antony, and Jacqueline knew the full story, and they in turn, informed Mrs Rushton of the devastating events. All had waited patiently for this to take place without questioning the girl, on Daniel's instructions, as he considered that more harm than good could result from such action. Now that everything was out in the open, Antony felt that he could divulge to Esmeralda the information regarding Adrian's death. To say she was startled was an understatement, but the relief she experienced was wonderful, and the days leading up to the wedding, were at last free of anxiety.

The reception over, and the last of the guests seen off the premises, Esmeralda, now the Mistress of Pendavan, and her beloved husband – Lord Antony, consummated their marriage, and their joy knew no bounds.

* * * * *

Chapter Two

First-Born: Jason

"Try not to bear down again until I tell you, Esme," the doctor advised anxiously.

How much longer would it be? Esmeralda wondered, hardly able to contain herself from crying out with the anguish, and each new pain that gripped her aching body appeared far more severe than the last. She clenched her teeth to try and stifle any sound that she may make. Her one thought was that Antony should be proud of her effort, not ashamed.

As a very young girl she had witnessed many births in the gipsy camp, and it was usual for the women in labour to vent their feelings by emitting loud high-pitched cries. This was said to help the birth and the mother, but was most upsetting for the onlookers.

"Push Esme, push!" cried the doctor. "It shouldn't be too long now," he explained to his patient, while helping her all he could.

A few more contractions and it should be over, he thought. Brave Esmeralda had suffered a long and difficult labour, and had made hardly a sound. How different from the last birth, when he had struggled for hours without Esmeralda's help – only to find the child dead on arrival. It had been for the best, he knew.

More anxious by the minute, Rushie stood by the side of her mistress, and dabbed her face and forehead with a damp cloth. The poor dear, she thought, in so much pain and discomfort, and perspiring from the strenuous exertion she had to put into the birth. The whole thing was taking so long, but at least Daniel would see her through to the end, and she couldn't wait to see her lovely face so full of joy, when she would hold the babe within her arms. Both the master and the mistress were overjoyed at the thought of their first child, to be born any minute, by the look of things, with the mother thrashing around on the bed, in the last stages of the birth.

"Good girl Esme," the doctor encouraged excitedly, "here it is, the last one!" With a loud gasp from Esmeralda, the baby slid out into his hands.

The next minutes were busy ones, for while Esmeralda lay exhausted from her physical effort, Daniel, with the housekeeper's assistance, performed the necessary and usual precautions.

On hearing the sudden cries of the baby, Esmeralda asked, "what is it Daniel, a boy or a girl?"

"You have a beautiful healthy son Esme," he answered, proudly placing the child in its mother's eager arms.

He was well satisfied with the birth, especially since the baby was perfect, and Esmeralda too had come through safely. This was always a concern to him, but more so now, when his greatest friends were involved. Antony would be so proud to have a son, and Daniel couldn't wait to see his friend's face.

He must impart the news right away, so after making sure that both mother and son were comfortable he left the room, leaving faithful Mrs Rushton to watch over his patients, knowing they would be in good hands.

As Daniel had expected, he found Antony wandering around outside in the gardens, where every kind of flower stood majestically in abundance. Never before had he noticed so many beautiful colours gathered together at one time. He could quite understand how Esmeralda would stay out here for hours lost in thought and so happy, always looking so much at home among the profusion of colour.

Antony hurried towards his friend, eager for news.

"Well, am I a father Daniel?" he asked.

"You are, and you have a fine healthy son," he answered, taking his friend's hand within his own, and offering his sincere congratulations.

"Both mother and child are doing well," he told him, anticipating his next question.

"Can I see them now?" Antony asked excitedly, eager to be with his beloved Esmeralda and their newly born son. Daniel agreed, provided his patient didn't get too excited, he told him.

The sight of his son nestling within his wife's arms was something that Antony would never forget.

"What a clever girl you are, my darling, to give us a son," he said, kissing his wife gently on the forehead. "He will be a playmate for our Thorley," he continued.

He recalled the shock they had received just after Esmeralda discovered that she was with child.

* * * * *

There was a lady visitor in the drawing-room awaiting an audience with the master, the housekeeper had informed him. "And she is not alone," she added, "she has a young child with her, Sir."

As Lord Pendavan entered the room he wondered who his visitor was, and what she could want with him. She was quite young, he could see that.

"I am very sorry to intrude Lord Pendavan," she commenced, speaking in moderate educated tones, which surprised Antony, as her clothes were very shabby, although quite clean. The young boy with her – he guessed his age around four years old – was neatly dressed and a handsome child, who bore a distinct resemblance to his late twin, Adrian.

Startled beyond belief at this discovery, he realised the woman was speaking to him again.

"As you must already have surmised, I am your late brother's wife – he married me just over four years ago," she continued, "but deserted me a few months later. He didn't know that I was with child when he left, and I was too proud to have him informed of this."

Antony wasn't in the least surprised by this news, this had been Adrian all right, and most typical of him. Here was another dastardly act he had committed, he told himself. He recalled momentarily to his mind, something that his father had related to him a short while before his death, which could perhaps, give an insight into Adrian's behaviour.

It had happened during his father's great-grandfather's time. Lord Hugo – who had then been heir to Pendavan – had married a beautiful Spanish girl, much younger than himself, named Angelita, whom he had met on his many travels abroad.

The eldest son of three, Hugo was the head of the family when his father died, so naturally took his place as the new heir to the estate. Always restless, and on the lookout for new excitement, he could never settle. Often he would make sudden departures, leaving his two brothers to manage as best they could. He was a frequent visitor to London, where he would meet with the so-called 'High Society' who were, more often than not, steeped in vice.

It was nothing for him to return to Pendavan with twenty or more guests at a moment's notice. Their raucous laughter rang through the old mansion long after the Pendavan family had retired for the night – as did the noise caused by their many drunken orgies that sometimes lasted right through until dawn, led on mostly by Hugo, who was the initiator of the perpetual lewdness.

Devious as well as lecherous, he was a man to keep on the right side of, for he made a very dangerous enemy. He literally threw the Pendavan money away on his regular gambling exploits and women. He was given to violent outbursts of temper, and if anyone stood out against him, he had been known to get back at them by discrediting the person or persons involved.

Devilishly handsome, with a strong personality, women continually sought him, wanting to be by loved him or, at least, to be seen in his company. He often played one off against the other, and when they would fight for what they considered theirs by right, he would walk out, leaving them – at times – in a suicidal state. More than one anguished woman had plunged to her death because of him, although nothing could actually be proved – and even if it could, people were afraid to speak out against him for fear of reprisals on his part. No society woman or servant alike was ever safe with him, so there were more bastards born of his seed, than he cared to acknowledge.

The tragedy occurred just two years after his marriage to Angelita, whom he had met, fallen in love with, courted and married in just two visits to Spain. Her parents were rich and when his offer of marriage was put before them they agreed wholeheartedly, showing their delight and pleasure by endowing their youngest daughter with a handsome dowry as a wedding gift.

Hugo brought her to Pendavan as his bride and for the first few months both were ideally happy, but the novelty soon wore off and he returned to his old habits. He dominated his young wife while he remained at home, but was far more interested in spending most of his time away from her, blatantly showing his absolute unconcern for her, as well as his complete and utter disloyalty.

She was a spirited girl, used to being spoilt and having plenty of attention paid her, and she became more and more distressed as the days and weeks went by. She became insanely jealous of her handsome husband and his methods, and was given to severe bouts of rage. It was during one of these rages that she flew at him with a sharp paper knife taken from his desk, and repeatedly stabbed him, until he fell to the floor in a great pool of blood, and while he gasped out his last breath, Angelita struck herself fatally with the weapon, falling across his dead body.

The whole scene had been a most gruesome sight for the Pendavan family, as well as a terrible shock, but eventually they realised she had only done what so many others had wanted to do for a very long time.

Perhaps some of Hugo's traits had been passed down through the generations to Adrian, especially the misuse of young women, Antony explained to himself, as he came back to the present with a start. Looking again at Adrian's widow, he couldn't help but wonder if his brother had used any others in the same way as her, through the marriage vows. He was sure that his twin would have had no compunction in satisfying his ardent desires this way, if it had suited his purpose.

"I wish, Lord Antony, that I could have met you under better circumstances," the young widow went on, speaking with conviction. "I would never have entertained asking for your help, had it not been both necessary, as well as urgent. I have no family of my own to approach, so when I heard the news of Adrian's death, I thought of you." Her voice suddenly broke, and she ceased talking, appearing quite agitated, as though worried about something she had to say.

Antony had a strong feeling that this gentle creature carried a heavy load within her heart, and whatever it was, he knew before she would be ready to tell him, that it was of a most serious nature. A secret so closely guarded, and of such severity that in her desperation she could hardly find the words, or the strength to divulge it to anyone, but she had come to him for his help – in her own words, and in her own time he felt sure that she must confide in him.

"Please do not distress yourself my dear," Lord Pendavan told her. "Make yourselves comfortable while I send for some refreshments." This would give her the opportunity to collect her thoughts, he told himself. "Incidentally," he asked, "what are your names?"

"Mine is Petra, and my son is called Thorley," she answered shyly, overcome by the kindness shown to them.

In no time at all a tray of tea, butter scones and sweet cakes, were put before them. When they were replenished, and only then, would

Antony hear the rest of her story, he told her. He then had every opportunity to study his visitors.

The young woman - he would put her age at no more than the early twenties - had dark hair and eyes, with good classical features, and was of average height. He noticed the colour had returned to her cheeks, whereas before she had looked extremely pale and weary.

He decided that he liked her, and felt she came from a good class of family. He also liked the boy who, when he looked at his mother, showed his devotion and deep love for her. She had been a good mother to him, he knew without being told. He thought the likeness to Adrian remarkable.

"Have you had sufficient?" Antony asked, seeing that she was ready to speak again.

"Thank you, yes," she answered, "it was most kind of you, Lord Pendavan."

Please call me Antony," he told her. "After all, you are my sister-in-law." He had no doubt of this whatsoever, knowing somehow that she was telling the truth.

He listened intently to what she was saying, first having asked if the housekeeper would take the boy with her, when she entered the drawing-room to collect the tray. Petra had requested this, as she had no wish for Thorley to hear what was being said.

"I will come straight to the point Antony," using his name with some restraint. "I am ill," she continued, "with an incurable disease, and have only a few months to live at the most."

Antony could see that to speak of it distressed her, and felt completely at a loss to know what to say. After considering silence was by far the wisest in these circumstances, he motioned her to carry on speaking.

"Now I shall come to the main reason for my visit here," she went on. "I have no family of my own to take care of Thorley when the inevitable does happen, in which case he would, more than likely, be sent to an orphanage, or worse still, the workhouse, for he will be penniless, and this worries me greatly. So I am asking," here she ceased speaking, seemingly unable to form the words again because of the enormity of her request. After a few moments hesitation, she continued, "would you please consider taking my son into your family, and raising him as your own. If not for my sake, or Adrian's, then for his own," she concluded, relieved that she had said what she had braved herself to come and say.

Lord Pendavan had decided almost at once that he would do what had been asked of him, but first he must speak to Esmeralda, as she would certainly be the one most concerned with looking after and bringing up the boy. He knew without saying what her answer would be.

He rang for the housekeeper, asking her to bring his wife to the drawing-room.

As Esmeralda entered she wondered who the now silent visitor could be. She became aware immediately of an overwhelming sadness surrounding the young woman, little older than herself.

After the introductions were over Antony explained everything to his wife, then waited for her reply, which was as expected. Then she asked to see this young boy who was to become an important part of their household. Esmeralda took to him on sight, and told her husband so.

She looked sympathetically at his mother. What a tragedy, she thought. Suddenly she had a wonderful idea. Why couldn't Petra stay at Pendavan with her son to finish out her last days in comfort and nice surroundings? After all, there was nothing in London for her. It would also save her the terrible anguish of parting with Thorley before she need. She explained her idea to them both, noticing the expression of incredulity on Petra's face who then, suddenly burst into tears.

Antony, taking the boy by the hand, left the room silently, leaving the two young women alone.

* * * * *

Lord Pendavan came out of his reverie with somewhat of a start on hearing the persistent cries of his baby son. He certainly had a healthy pair of lungs, he thought to himself.

As Mrs Rushton lifted the lusty child from his mother's arms, Antony could see that Esmeralda wanted to sleep. So, after kissing her gently he turned and quietly left the room, his heart brimming over with so much love.

* * * * *

Chapter Three

Tragedy Strikes Twice

The weeks and months sped by at Pendavan. Each new day would see Esmeralda and Jason, accompanied by Thorley – who was absolutely devoted to his younger cousin – in the garden.

It had been the hottest and longest summer for years, with clear blue skies throughout each day. The sun shone relentlessly down on to the garden's occupants who were, by this time, well and truly sun-tanned a golden brown, as though they had spent weeks in a hot climate.

Jason – Antony and Esmeralda had both agreed on this name for their first-born – followed Thorley everywhere.

At first they had thought Thorley would be jealous of the new arrival, having been at Pendavan for many months before Jason was born, but no, it was quite the opposite in fact. Thorley had also taken to Esmeralda, watching her every movement, and when Antony had explained that he would soon have a playmate for company, it seemed to help him over the death of his mother.

As Esmeralda had anticipated, the last few months of Petra's life were happy ones, in a sense. She had become very attached to her new brother-in-law and his wife, who had shown her nothing but kindness since she first arrived at Pendavan. During the final weeks of her illness she was confined to bed, which had been placed by the window in the room they had given her as her very own. She could at least look out on to the beauty of the gardens. This in itself helped her considerably. She was never left alone to brood over her circumstances. Even the housekeeper spoilt her, and tempted her often with little dainty dishes, prepared always with devotion for the patient, who had endeared herself to them all. Never a grumble was heard during this unhappy time, when her young body would be racked with pain, and she could no longer take notice of those around her.

Esmeralda stayed by her bedside until the end. Petra died peacefully in her sleep, leaving a terrible void in Pendavan. It was fortunate that Thorley was asleep himself when it happened, and as Esmeralda explained his mother's death to the sorrowful boy during his waking hours, he threw himself into her welcoming arms, and from that day onwards she took the place of his beloved parent.

It was a sad day for all, and after Petra had been laid to rest, it took some little while for everyone to pull themselves out of the doldrums they had fallen into. But life had to go on for Thorley's sake, at least.

* * * * *

Jason was three years of age when Esmeralda became pregnant again. It was at this time that Jacqueline gave birth to twins, a boy and a girl, Clive and Elizabeth. She had been married to Stuart for nigh on a year, and they were ideally happy together. Theirs had been a quiet wedding, with only two witnesses present – a choice both had preferred unlike the marriage ceremony for Antony and Esmeralda, which was full of pomp and circumstance – in this case, his decision, for the sheer joy of indulging his beloved wife, who after all, had had very few pleasures, as such, throughout her young life. It was Antony's aim to give her everything within his power that had been denied her.

Antony loved to reminisce, and his favourite time for doing this was during his early morning rides on Caesar, when the horse would wander at a leisurely pace along the country paths, where at that very moment they were heading. With peace all around him, Antony pursued his thoughts. It was a routine with which he was well acquainted.

Dearest Esmeralda, his wife – he was thinking with deep gratitude. How he loved her. She was such a wonderful person, and so appreciative of everything. He remembered her excitement at the ball he had promised her. He remembered how the mansion became a hive of activity when everyone was employed with the arrangements for the ball. Jacqueline – as he recalled – had organised the guest list, as she knew all the people in the surrounding area who would consider it an honour to be invited to a ball, especially one to be held at Pendavan. The awesome task of arranging all the plants and flowers had been allotted to Esmeralda, who had a flair for this, while many other meaningful duties – that were needed to ensure the success of the great social gathering – had been assigned to, and shared amongst the staff, under the keen eye of the housekeeper.

As to be expected, the ball was a 'grand affair', as Antony remembered, still pursuing his thoughts. He could picture again the whole scene.

The gentry were well turned out – the men attired in cut-away jackets, with their fancy waistcoats, lacy shirts and snug fitting breeches, and the ladies in fine array, bedecked with jewellery that could not fail to enhance their elegant bustled and tiered gowns, that rustled gently as they moved – as of dry leaves blowing in the breeze.

He could still savour the fragrance from the many exotic blooms, arranged so deftly by Esmeralda in corners and alcoves, where seating had been available, with indoor palm plants standing majestically near them. Even now, the different scents still lingered in his senses. But the most important thing of all, that meant so much to him, was how his darling wife had dealt so effectively with everything.

Esmeralda had been an impeccable and charming hostess. She had mingled among the many guests with just the right faculty of perception. If she saw anyone standing alone, she quickly approached them, and immediately engaged the person – whomever – in conversation, to put them at their ease. It had done Antony's heart good to observe how she handled the situation, as well as her obvious sheer enjoyment in what she was doing. It had been always the same throughout their five years of marriage, Antony recollected, when everything Esmeralda undertook to be responsible for, had been of the greatest pleasure to her. Nothing was a trouble to the dear girl, Antony decided, coming out of his reverie with a jolt, as he realised how quickly the time had passed. He must make for home now or his lengthy absence would cause unnecessary anxiety for his loved ones, and that he could not endure. 'Besides,' he told himself, 'in the condition that Esmeralda is in, she can ill afford to suffer any shock, with her tendency to miscarry.' She was so looking forward to having another child, as he himself was. In fact, his happiness was full to brimming with the knowledge. Perhaps it would be a girl this time, which would be nice for his wife, he thought, while patting Caesar's head to encourage the horse to move at a faster pace. Wives almost always wished for a daughter or two, and he was well aware of Esmeralda's hopes in this direction. She had chosen the name already. It was to be Francesca, she informed her husband. "That is if you agree," she added. Antony smiled his answer, knowing full well that nothing would alter her decision. He had no wish to change it anyway. Unfortunately, the early weeks of Esmeralda's pregnancy would be fraught with bouts of terrible nausea. As before, when right from the beginning she suffered violent sickness, and would lie prostrate for hours. At this time, mostly because of her condition he decided to engage a nanny for the boys. So, when the subject was broached to Daniel after he had called to see his patient, he was able to suggest just the right person. "Her name is Kathy," he told Antony, "and she comes from a good family. She is wonderful with children, I know," he went on, "and the boys will be certain to like her."

So it was, that while Esmeralda remained indisposed, Kathy took over her duties as nanny to Jason and Thorley which, as it happened, turned out for the best, because a few weeks later, Esmeralda had been taken really ill, and lost the child. The miscarriage left her weak, depressed and very disappointed.

"The only answer," Daniel said, "is to try for another child, and I wouldn't advise you to wait too long," he added.

There had been one or two false alarms, and at one time, both Antony and Esmeralda had given up hope of having any more family. However, eventually the inevitable happened, and once again his Esme was looking forward with new hope to the happy event, erasing from her memory what had transpired before. This was the reason that he couldn't get back to the mansion quickly enough, to see how she was faring, although Mrs Rushton would be looking after her welfare, he knew, but these attacks happened so unexpectedly, to quite frighten her, that he would need to be close at hand.

Caesar was trotting quickly towards the gates, having just rounded the bend, with only a few more yards to go. Albert, having heard the clumping of the horses' hooves in the quiet of the early morning, was already swinging the heavy gates open for his master to enter the driveway. Thanking the caretaker, Antony reined in at the entrance where the groom waited in readiness to take Caesar to the stables, where he would be tended with much loving care. The master entered the mansion, and took the stairs, two at a time in his eagerness to be with his beloved wife. As it happened, this was one of her better mornings, and looking at her, Antony compared his life to what it had been before Esmeralda had so miraculously entered into it.

"I cannot imagine what I would do without you, my darling," he told her, holding her close within his arms, as though he would never let her go. In their happiness, how could they know that fate was about to deal them a devastating blow?

* * * * *

Grief descended upon Pendavan again; without warning this time. The tragedy occurred just as Francesca had reached her fifth birthday, and while the new addition to their family, Corrina, was still a baby.

Esmeralda had suffered two more miscarriages since her last confinement. These left her dangerously low in health to such an extent that Daniel did deem to point out to his friend the dangers of her becoming pregnant again. He couldn't be held responsible if it happened and they were to lose her, he warned. Couldn't they be satisfied with the family they had been blessed with? he asked.

Antony explained that Esme's health was far more important to him than increasing the size of their family. "After all," he told Daniel, "we have two lovely daughters and our son Jason, and also there is Thorley, who won a place in our hearts right from the beginning, and is as much a son to us now, as Jason is."

The two boys were the best of friends and spent many hours on the rocks below Pendavan.

Thorley, who was now almost fourteen and quite a little man, would hesitate often to go as far out on the rocks as Jason, who was the more adventurous of the two and saw little danger in anything he did. Often they would climb the rocky shore and make for the small coves that could be cut off by the tides, edged on by Jason's abundance of energy, which was never lacking. Occasionally the sea would be calm, and one could hear the sound of the water lapping as it crept through the coves, covering them almost at once, but mostly the sea would be ferociously rough, lashing the barnacled rocks repeatedly.

It was on such a day as this that the boys decided to explore a cave, a cave set well back in a sheltered bay which Jason – whilst climbing out towards the furthermost rocks – had spotted. Calling excitedly to Thorley who could never quite keep up with his younger cousin – Jason leapt from rock to rock in his eagerness to get a better view of the cave. Suddenly, without warning, a huge wave swept relentlessly over Jason, carrying the unsuspecting boy away into the depths of the water. Any cry he may have uttered was silenced.

Thorley – intent on watching where he stepped to reach his cousin – became aware that the excited shouts had stopped, and looking up, could see no sign of Jason anywhere. At first Thorley thought he had climbed down behind one of the larger rocks, but on reaching the spot there was nothing, only the angry white foam, relic of the waves.

"Jason, Jason," he cried frantically. "Where are you?" But his only answer was the sound of the sea and cries of the soaring seagulls.

After a thorough search, and still finding no trace of him, Thorley stumbled and slipped back over the remaining rocks to the base of the cliffs and scrambling up the face, ran all the way back to Pendavan to break the news, he knew not how. Arriving home, breathless, sick with worry and hardly able to talk, he tried to relate what had happened.

Through the intervening years, Thorley was never able to erase from his memory the stunned expression on Esmeralda's face.

A further search was made, which proved futile. Jason had drowned, there was no doubt about it. The verdict at the private inquest was 'death by misadventure'.

* * * * *

Chapter Four

Sole Beneficiary

The day of the funeral service loomed grey and formidable – well suited to the sombreness of everyone's mood.

The tragedy had shaken the very close community most rigidly. Jason, a likeable little boy, and so handsome, had endeared himself to all who had known him, so it was only to be expected that a great number would present themselves at the moving service, to show their deepest respect.

It had become a familiar sight for the tenants to see Jason riding with his father around the vast estates, accompanied by Thorley, who had never strayed far from his young cousin's side. In fact, the very first steps that Jason had taken would always have found Thorley there beside him to pick up the young toddler, if he fell. A great bond had developed rapidly between them, to such an extent, that on Jason's death, Thorley was so completely devastated, and torn by grief, that he was unable to venture into the cove again. The nearest he ever came to it was from the cliff-top, on the headland, where he would sometimes sit, staring across the vast expanse of sea.

* * * * *

The nightmare of that fateful day remained with Thorley as he grew into a man, and now, many years had passed since the death of Jason.

As for Lord and Lady Pendavan, they had never recovered from the anguish of losing their first born. So, it was only to be expected; and quite natural that they should shower their adopted son with all the love and affection they could muster. Neither one had ever regretted taking Thorley, and bringing him up as their son, and they were so proud of him. He was now in his late twenties, and had grown into a very handsome man. His resemblance to Antony was startling, who often felt he was looking at his late twin, Adrian – but, fortunately, without his wicked brother's traits.

As the future heir to Pendavan, Thorley had, over the years, religiously supported his adoptive father in the management of the property, and had gained experience in managing them, should the need arise. His love for his adopted parents went very deep, and their friendship for each other was steadfast. Esmeralda, he adored. He always said if ever he married, his wife must be like her in every way. Not that he was at all interested in wooing any particular young maiden at this period in his life. He was quite content to wallow in the adoration of his adopted mother, and his cousins – Francesca and Corrie – not forgetting Elizabeth, daughter to Jacqueline. They had all grown up together, and were inseparable chums, but they were all different in their attitudes. Francesca reacted, at times, with a certain jealous streak at the love her parents bestowed upon her cousin. Corrie on the other hand – that much younger – idolised Thorley, who was to her the true brother she had so tragically lost. Elizabeth – the shy one of the group – stayed mostly in the background and kept her thoughts and deep feelings to herself. As for Thorley, his time and thoughts were taken up – mostly – with the work that had been entrusted to him as steward of the vast estates. He had quite a flair for the land and agriculture. However, he had now come to a cross-roads in his life. He felt he must try and make something of it and fend for himself. And as well, Thorley had suffered pangs of guilt for sometime now, knowing there were men who could do the work that he was doing for his father – for a sorely needed regular wage.

It was about a month before that he had travelled to London with his father, and being left to his own devices whilst Antony met some business associates, he decided to go along to his club in Mayfair. Both he and his father were members. It was because of his visit to the club that day that he met some businessmen, one of whom was an American, and Thorley became interested in their topic of conversation.

It came about that the American, Mr Grant, owned a sugar plantation in New Orleans, and was on a visit to London with the sole prospect of finding a suitable partner or, failing that, selling it outright if he could get a buyer. He had owned the plantation for many years and, although it had been really hard work, he had certainly been recompensed, as he was now a very rich man in his own right. Of late his health hadn't been too good, so talking things over with his wife Alice, he had decided to make a change. "If I were to have a good man – not too old – that I could rely on," he told Alice, "then I could take things easier."

Mr and Mrs Grant had been blessed with one child, a daughter, and had named her Crystal. They had been most disappointed in not having a son, particularly Mr Grant, for he had visualised help from that quarter. However, Crystal had now grown into a very beautiful young woman, with dark hair and eyes. She was tall, with a graceful figure. She was devoted to her parents, who in turn lavished all their love on her. She had been given the best of everything, including a good education, completing it at a finishing school in Paris. They had decided to take a trip to London, for a holiday, combining business with pleasure. Crystal was to accompany them.

So it was that the American, who had been a member of the Mayfair club for some years since he last visited London, came to be there on this day, and met Thorley.

He had been taking stock of the young man for some little while now, and liked what he saw. Here was a gentleman if ever there was one and a most handsome fellow at that. He decided right away that he must have a word with him.

Thorley couldn't help noticing the American's scrutiny of him, and as he glanced once more in his direction the man walked towards him.

"I am Theodore Grant," he explained, gripping the young man's hand strongly within his own.

"How do you do, Sir," Thorley replied, "I am very pleased to make your acquaintance. I am Lord Pendavan's son Thorley," he informed the American. "My father is up here from Cornwall on a business trip and I was invited to accompany him. We are staying here," he continued, "so my father will be returning later."

"What is your trade young fella?" Grant asked, liking the young man all the more on closer inspection. Just the right kind of person to be my partner, he decided right there and then, but made no mention of what was foremost in his mind at this point.

"My father and myself, with the help of others, manage the estates of our ancestral home Pendavan," he answered.

"I am staying at Claridges with my wife and daughter," Grant informed Thorley. "We would like you and your father to be our guests this evening," he suggested. "The hotel is in Brook Street," he added.

After a few more trivialities, Mr Grant left, with the promise of a very entertaining evening to come. He was looking forward to meeting his father with growing interest, he told Thorley.

Thorley would always remember his first encounter with Crystal, whom he thought was the most beautiful girl that he had ever seen, apart from his mother. As he looked into her eyes, he immediately fell in love.

When Antony had returned to the club, Thorley informed his father of their invitation to spend the evening with the American family. Antony was quite surprised to say the least, and enquired who they were.

Upon hearing about the plantation Antony glanced at his son, detecting a certain amount of excitement in his voice and manner. He pondered on this news, realising that Thorley wished to go his own way. Who could blame him after all? for he must want to see something of the world. He was a grown man and could please himself. He thought of Esmeralda and how she would take the news. She would be heartbroken, there was no doubt about that but, like himself, would only want Thorley's happiness.

When father and son stepped through the hotel doors, many heads turned in their direction, for they made a very handsome pair and, being smartly dressed, represented the perfect English gentlemen.

Mr and Mrs Grant moved forward to welcome their guests, their daughter walking sedately behind them. After the introductions were over, they all settled in the lounge with drinks, to await the meal that was laid on for them.

The Americans were perfect hosts, entertaining their guests with the usual courtesy of their kind.

Lord Pendavan liked them from the very first, listening to and enjoying Mr Grant's many interesting stories, which he related with gusto. There had been no mention of his plans regarding the plantation during the meal so, when all were replete and well satisfied by the first class food partaken, the men relaxing with their cigars, the ladies sitting back ready to listen, only then did the American broach the subject.

It was a foregone conclusion to Antony that Thorley had already made up his mind to accept Mr Grant's offer, with his father's blessing of course, for he knew his son would do nothing without his consent, even though he was now a grown man.

If Thorley had been doubtful at first, now that he had met the beautiful American girl, he was really sold on the idea. That he had taken to her, anyone could see, for he had barely looked away from her all through the evening,

They discussed the proposition, and a sum of money was decided upon, but here the American was very generous, not in the least wishing to rob his new-found friends.

Lord Pendavan was wealthy, so he wouldn't miss the amount needed for this venture. It was what Thorley wanted and this was good enough for him, but he did point out to the Grants, that his wife should know all about it before settlement took place. So with this in mind, Antony made the suggestion that they all return to Pendavan as soon as possible, to discuss matters with Esmeralda. The Grants were absolutely delighted with this arrangement, eager to see these charming English gentlemen in their own surroundings.

The whole evening was most successful, and it ended with plans being made for the journey to Pendavan. So Antony decided to send a courier ahead warning Esmeralda of their visit. They would be travelling several days, so he knew that she would have plenty of time to be ready for her unexpected guests.

* * * * *

By the time Esmeralda received the news, Antony and his guests were part way through their journey. There was much activity and excitement throughout Pendavan, Mrs Rushton taking charge of the preparations. So with help from Esmeralda, who insisted on being useful, with her two daughters, now grown into beautiful young ladies; the eldest, Francesca, married with a child, who was visiting her mother for a few days; and able to assist, the rooms were ready for their guests.

It wasn't often that Antony sprang a surprise like this on to her, but she would be the perfect hostess. All the years that she had been mistress of Pendavan she had never – to her knowledge – let her husband down. Her one thought, at all times, was to please.

She was still an exceptionally beautiful woman, and because of her small girlish figure – even though she had gone through childbearing many times – looked far younger than her years.

Her love for Antony had grown deeper and even more lasting through the passing years, and his devotion to her carried Esmeralda through many sorrows. Never would she forget the desolate grief she suffered when darling Jason was lost to them for ever. That Antony grieved also, she was very well aware, particularly when she came upon him unexpectedly, filled with emotion. They would cry silently together. Always close, the tragedy brought them even closer.

The letter that Antony had sent, suddenly recalled to her the unexpected visitor who had appeared a year ago.

* * * * *

Rushie – as she always called the housekeeper; they were devoted to each other – entered the drawing-room with an air of excitement about her. She carried a silver platter, displaying a printed card, which, after excusing the interruption to her mistress, promptly told Esmeralda that a gentleman, whose employer's name was on the card, begged an audience with Lady Pendavan immediately, as the matter was of the utmost importance.

"He looks rather solemn my Lady," the housekeeper remarked, "and he is a stranger around these parts, anyone can see that," she concluded.

Esmeralda, glancing first at the small and neatly printed card, raised her delicate eyebrows, noting that her visitor was a messenger from a reputed firm of solicitors, Smythe and Tibbs. She asked Mrs Rushton to show the gentleman in. 'Now what could a firm like this want with me?' she asked herself, as to her knowledge she had never heard of them before.

The drawing-room door opened to admit the housekeeper once again who stepped to one side, allowing their visitor to enter, saying as he did so, "Mr Weedon my Lady," whereupon she reluctantly left the room, closing the door quietly behind her. She was curious to say the least.

'What could he want with the mistress?' she asked herself. 'Was there more trouble for the master?' She hoped not, hadn't they had enough already! Anyway, she would be told soon enough, for there were very few secrets between the mistress and herself.

Meanwhile, in the drawing-room, Esmeralda beckoned Mr Weedon towards a chair, and seating herself once more, asked him how she could help.

"You are Lady Pendavan I presume," he stated in a quiet and precise manner, "and," he continued, "was your mother the only daughter of Lord and Lady Wendamere?"

"Yes, I am Lady Pendavan," Esmeralda replied, "and yes to your second question." 'What is this conversation leading up to?' she asked herself, quite mystified at this stage.

"I have been requested by Messrs Smythe and Tibbs, a firm of solicitors, to inform you that you now own the late Lord Wendamere's estates and residue, being his only grandchild and sole beneficiary." He spoke as though he had memorised each word.

To say that Esmeralda was surprised was an understatement. 'There must be some mistake,' she thought. She couldn't comprehend why her grandfather had left her the bulk of his fortune for he had never seen her, and as her mother had died giving birth to her first child, surely that would be reason enough for him to erase them from his memory.

She tried to explain all this to Mr Weedon, who listened intently.

When Esmeralda had finished speaking, her visitor fumbled in a brief-case, which was filled to capacity with papers.

"I can assure you, Lady Pendavan, that you are, most definitely, your late grandfather's only beneficiary," Mr Weedon stressed. "I have all the proof you need right here," he told her, extracting certain documents from the case, which he passed to his client.

There was complete silence in the room whilst Esmeralda carefully scanned the papers. 'So it is true,' she told herself, 'I am an heiress, and a very rich one at that.'

The news was staggering, to say the least, for she could hardly believe it. Her grandfather had requested in his will that a share of his legacy be distributed amongst her children – if any – whilst the remainder was hers to do with as she wished. There was also a large country mansion, called The Grange and farms and estates surrounding it, with many acres of land with good rich soil and plenty of livestock. There were cottages that housed all the farm hands and their families. These provided moderate rents for the estate.

Esmeralda – completely astounded by this time, and having read the information thoroughly – returned the documents, with her signature, to Mr Weedon.

When they were once more safely deposited in his briefcase, he rose to take his leave.

After he had gone, the housekeeper re-entered the drawing-room to find her mistress sitting as one in a dream.

As Esmeralda became aware of Mrs Rushton's presence, she had been busy thinking of the many alterations that could now be realised at Pendavan with the coming of her fortune.

"Are you pressed for time Rushie?" she asked, anticipating the surprise and pleasure her housekeeper would receive on hearing the wonderful news.

* * * * *

To the American family Pendavan was a most refreshing sight. They were intrigued by the grandeur of the old mansion, set high on the cliffs, overlooking a wide expanse of water that reflected the clear sky above. The aquamarine sea glistened, whilst far below the rugged rocks were partly covered by the waves that left behind the white foam in their wake.

The house stood tall and majestic, surrounded by growths of bright yellow gorse bushes and purple heather, whilst the land stretched back as far as the eye could see.

Esmeralda took to the Grant family on sight. She was also greatly impressed with Crystal, whose rare beauty surpassed anything she had ever seen.

She had no idea as to the reason for their visit, but sensed it had something to do with Thorley who, when he came forward to greet his mother with his usual affection, could hardly contain his excitement. Being as close to him as she was, Esmeralda knew she was about to hear something out of the ordinary.

"I could take Miss Grant on a tour of the house and gardens, Mother," Thorley suggested, anxious to have Crystal to himself for a while. There was much he wished to impart, also he had to find out more about this shy and charming girl to satisfy his own curiosity. He had surveyed her quietly in the coach whilst sitting opposite on the journey home to Pendavan. Her unusual beauty fascinated him, and he was already infatuated with her.

Esmeralda watched the two young people disappear into the house with a feeling of apprehension. She couldn't explain this to herself, and trying to hide her anxiety from her other guests, turned back towards them ready to be the perfect hostess.

Mr and Mrs Grant found the whole place quite awe inspiring. Their first day was spent mostly exploring the estates with Lord Pendavan, who explained fully all they required to know. Nothing as yet had been mentioned regarding the business deal between the two men, so Esmeralda was left completely ignorant of the impending shock that was to suddenly descend on her without warning.

The gardens were at their best just at this time. The weather, warm, fine and dry, with bright sunshine, added extra lustre to the beautiful array of delightful flowers and plants. The wide drive – flanked on either side by spreading trees, splendid in their foliage – led to the magnificent door, that gave entrance to the hall. This in itself was enormous in size and full of character. Many large paintings – exquisite in their extreme beauty – looked down from the high walls. The thickly carpeted staircase rose magnificently, losing itself into long secluded corridors stretching out on either side, flanked here and there by beautifully carved wooden doors, massive in their size, whilst beyond each door was housed the most splendid furniture, most delicately worked.

To Crystal, who had never seen so grand a place, it was a wondrous sight. Her parents' homestead was a far cry from this. Pendavan was truly an Englishman's castle.

The tour was a long drawn-out affair, caused mainly by Thorley, who had no intention of hurrying over it. As far as he was concerned the day should never end. His opinion of Crystal was very high indeed and he thought her beauty a sight to behold. The many expressions that flitted across her face, warmed his heart. That he loved her was certain, and it was now a foregone conclusion that he would accept her father's offer. He made up his mind there and then, that he would marry this girl. He wouldn't dare broach the subject yet, for he was almost afraid of what her answer would be. She must have many admirers and have received offers of marriage, with her sparkling beauty, he thought worriedly. She may already be spoken for, and should this be so, he would be devastated.

When eventually the tour of the house was completed, they joined their parents on the headland, where they stood surveying the unforgettable sight before their eyes.

Just as they arrived on the scene, Thorley heard his father relating the many tragedies that had taken place on that particular spot.

"My first wife fell to her death from here," Lord Pendavan was saying, "and my twin, Lord Adrian, also died on the rocks below, whilst our son Jason was drowned out on the furthermost rocks," he concluded, a shadow crossing his face as the memory returned once more.

"How tragic for you both," Mrs Grant remarked, glancing first at her husband, aware of how this news would affect him. He was a tender-hearted man and wouldn't forget what he had been told. She knew that.

This was a tragic place, one could feel it, but a most impressive one, and the owners, well, they were the perfect host and hostess and a pleasure to be with.

Their first day at Pendavan was a memorable one, and something to cherish for evermore.

* * * * *

Chapter Five

Family Changes

The sun shone down on the early morning dew, with the promise of another beautiful day.

Esmeralda stared with unseeing eyes at the fish pond, covered mostly by budding pink tipped oyster water-lilies, that peeped out at the clear skies.

As always, when troubled, she found some solace for herself in her favourite hideaway, which secluded her from everyone.

Thorley had informed his mother of his plans and, although excited now that the decision was made to leave for America, realised how the news would affect her. Always thoughtful and devoted to Esmeralda, this blighted his new-found happiness somewhat; but not even for her, whom he loved so dearly, would he change his mind. His heart was completely lost to Crystal, and nothing, or no one could sway him otherwise.

He was to journey to America with the Grants, an extended, slow journey by sea. Their plans were made accordingly, and they would be ready to leave Pendavan in a day or two, first to return to London, where eventually they would travel to Liverpool to join their ship, the *Eagle Star*.

Thus it was that Esmeralda, lost in thought, tried to visualise what life would be at Pendavan without Thorley. It was hard to believe that he would be gone from them for ever, or at least for many years to come, across the other side of the world, with so many thousands of miles between them.

Mr and Mrs Grant had mentioned earlier that there would always be a warm welcome for their new friends at their homestead, should they ever wish to visit New Orleans.

"Ah, there you are Esme darling," Antony said, coming up suddenly behind his wife and drawing her close.

Startled out of her reverie, Esmeralda turned towards him, burying her face against his chest, her tears flowing unceasingly. Nothing that Antony could say would help, so holding her closer, he let her give vent to her emotions. It was at times like these that he felt quite inadequate. There was little need for words between them, for he knew what it was that troubled her. He too, would miss Thorley, that went without saying.

He glanced over her head, sighting the brightly coloured fish that periodically leapt into the air, returning to the pond with a splash, the sun reflecting them beneath the water, darting between the sturdy plant life, that moved continually.

Devoted, and a good mother to her children, Esmeralda's life was absorbed by them, and their hurts and problems became hers. It had been the same when Francesca had left Pendavan. He recalled to his mind her suffering at the parting, also the continued anxieties she experienced because of the circumstances.

* * * * *

Francesca, having been sent as a young debutante to London, mixing in society and meeting numerous admirers, as was usual in the big city, became involved with a country squire's son, a certain Captain Frisby, Charlie to his friends, who spent most of his time at sea and visited many foreign ports. He was both handsome and debonair, and had a way with the ladies. He was several years her senior and Francesca, who was easily impressed, became obsessed with him. She was a very outstanding girl, startlingly beautiful, a replica of her mother, and tall like her father, with classical features. Her disposition was kind, very soft and most trusting.

She was in love with Captain Frisby, she informed Aunt Jacqueline who, when she met him, could see right away that he was most irresponsible, but nothing she could say would dissuade Francesca.

He rented rooms in a rather dowdy building that housed many people, when he wasn't away at sea. It was a seedy house, grim on the outside, and even worse on the inside.

When Esmeralda had travelled to London to meet him, accompanied by Antony, she had a premonition that all wasn't well with her eldest daughter. From all that she had heard about this man from Francesca, she knew what to expect when she first saw him. Oh yes, he was very handsome she had to admit, but when he bent over her and kissed her hand lingeringly she received a shock, realising that he was far too much a man of the world for her darling daughter, who was much too naive for him.

Antony had disliked him on sight, piercing right through his armour. He decided to say nothing then, for had he done so, it most certainly would have driven his daughter straight into his arms. That Charlie admired and felt some affection for the girl, anyone could see, but how long would he want her, when the novelty had worn off? Antony asked himself. It would seem that both he and her mother could try and discourage her gradually.

Shaking hands with Lord Pendavan, Charlie Frisby looked him over, noticing his good dress sense, and expensive clothing. 'It is a good thing I am on to here,' he told himself, 'if I play my cards right.' He had always managed to get what he wanted in the past, and he wanted this girl, who was a daughter of a lord, and a very rich one at that.

As yet Francesca had no idea of Charlie Frisby's plans, had she done so the romance could have been nipped in the bud. As it was, she was besotted with the fellow who was brimming over with personality, and had used it many times to get what he desired. She should have returned to Cornwall with her parents, but instead was most adamant that she stay with her future husband. She was over age, and had her own private income – which he already knew about – so Lord and Lady Pendavan returned without her, anxious from the onset. There was nothing they could say or do, but they still held out a faint hope that Francesca would see through him before it was too late. It had possibly gone too far between them anyway.

When next they heard anything, it was news of their daughter's sudden marriage. It had been a very quiet wedding, Francesca informed them, and both she and her new husband were, supposedly, ideally happy. She had been promised a new home, which was to materialise very soon, as Charlie wasn't very happy for his wife to live in squalor, he said, but their happiness was short lived. Francesca found her husband out in his true colours when it was too late. She was carrying his child, when he suddenly went to sea. She had heard nothing from him since he sailed. Her dream of a wonderful home shared with a loving husband, and raising a family, was suddenly dashed to the ground. She was heartbroken, to say the least.

So it was that after travelling several days by coach, breaking the journey when it necessitated, she arrived at Pendavan without any warning, tired, desperate and most unhappy. It was to her loving parents that she turned, feeling safe at last. She had gradually related what had happened over the last months leading up to her desperate flight to Cornwall. Heavy with child, and having parted with most of her money to her husband who had frittered it away – she knew not how – she became frightened, doing the only thing that was left open to her.

Lord and Lady Pendavan showed their usual concern for all that had taken place, welcoming their daughter with open arms, anxious only for her welfare, and for the arrival of their first grandchild.

Once again Daniel attended the birth, which wasn't an easy one. It was a little girl this time, and being born prematurely, looked sickly and small in size. Francesca was as well as could be expected, but the birth, having been difficult, had drained her strength. During the next few weeks she suffered from severe bouts of depression from which nothing or no one could lift her. She couldn't cope with the child, and Esmeralda, with help, performed all that the helpless baby needed.

It was during this time that Esmeralda decided upon something that might help Francesca, and perhaps bring her out of the doldrums.

"I believe she would be happier and improve in health if she had her own home in pleasant surroundings," she told Antony. "I would like her to go and live at The Grange. It is fully staffed, waiting for someone to take up residence," she continued. "Don't you think this could be the answer darling?" she asked of her husband.

Lord Pendavan was definitely in agreement with his wife regarding her suggestion, being aware also of his daughter's continual indisposition. In a place of her own, perhaps, and tended by trustworthy servants, her confidence would return; so, too, might maternal feelings for her child, which had been sadly lacking since the birth. Hardly ever did she show any love for the tiny mite, only holding it within her arms when the need arose for its feeding. Francesca had an abundance of healthy milk, and the child rapidly improved, although still very much under weight.

Francesca brightened visibly when she knew of her mother's plans for her, and each new day saw her considerably better – such a marked difference, everyone said. She still had a faint hope that she may hear news of her estranged husband, for although she was well aware of his many faults, her love for him didn't diminish.

She had been at The Grange for just over a month when Thorley broke the news of his impending visit to America.

Francesca had settled in well, and was beloved by all the staff, who were most considerate of both her and her baby daughter. They talked of little else below stairs, for it was many a year since that any young children had been resident at The Grange.

* * * * *

Lord Pendavan, who had suddenly become aware that his wife had ceased her crying, came back to the present with a start. He hated to see any woman in tears, especially his beloved Esme, who only gave way to her emotions when something happened to warrant it.

The idea suddenly came to him. Why shouldn't they both travel to America with Thorley and the Grants? It would be a wonderful chance for a holiday, and there were plenty of willing hands at Pendavan to see to everything, with Mrs Rushton in charge during their absence.

The more he thought of it, the more certain he was that it was the best thing for them both. It would take away the sudden hurt of Thorley's departure. Corrina could go with them also. It would be a wonderful experience for them all.

Lord Pendavan couldn't wait to break the news to Esmeralda, but first he must talk it over with the American family. He could not stay his fast growing excitement at the thought of bringing pleasure to his beloved wife, whom he loved with all his heart.

* * * * *

The ship dipped and rose repeatedly with the swell, waves lashed the decks, running swiftly down the sides and returning to the turbulent sea in readiness for its next attack. The wind howled ferociously, whipping up cold icy blasts into the already frozen faces of the deck-hands, who worked with unceasing dedication, almost until they dropped.

The storm had been raging for some hours now, keeping the passengers confined to their cabins, with little hope of venturing forth until it had abated. These freak storms could end as suddenly as they began, with the sea beautiful in its tranquillity once more.

The *Eagle Star*, heavy with cargo, had slipped silently out into the ocean, the few onlookers at the quayside waving the ship out of sight.

For the last hour before it had left the docks, Esmeralda had observed with much interest the cargo being packed into the hold below deck. She was beside herself with excitement and not wanting to miss anything, remained at the rail. She should be unpacking, she knew, but it could wait. After all, the journey would take from anything between forty and sixty days, so there would be all the time in the world.

The decision to travel with the American family and Thorley was very sudden. Arrangements had hurriedly been made with the shipping company, so with their clothes practically thrown into the trunks, they were at last on the start of the long journey to America.

Corrina and Thorley had remained on deck with their mother, feeling the same inner excitement in the knowledge that a new life lay ahead for them all.

When eventually they went below to their cabins, Thorley hugged Esmeralda to him affectionately, "Good-night Mother," he said. "I am so happy that both you and Father are accompanying me on this venture, for I should have hated saying good-bye." He glanced at his cousin, drawing her into the circle of his arm also, and kissing her lightly on the cheek, remarked, "I have my Corrie as well, to complete my happiness."

They had always been the very best of friends, and there was much understanding between them. Not so with Francesca; he loved her, there was no doubt of that, but there was this barrier between them. He felt extremely sorry that things hadn't turned out very well for her, but felt now – as did the other members of the family – that she had done the right thing by taking up residence at The Grange. At least they knew where she was, and that both she and her baby daughter were in good hands.

Thorley walked away from the cabins, returning once more to the deck above. He couldn't settle yet, for he had much to think about. He felt elated and light-hearted, now that he was in love. Oh yes, he was certainly in love, he admitted this to himself. If he couldn't have Crystal, then he wanted no other. He leaned against the rail staring out to sea, yet seeing nothing.

She was never very far from his thoughts. It was not very long since he had said goodnight to her, yet here he was again, longing to see her and feast his eyes on her beauty. He wondered if she was thinking of him in the same way. If only she would give him some clue to her feelings for him, then he would be satisfied. Instead, he waited with longing to touch her hand, or brush her cheek with his lips. He wanted so much to pour into her ears his love for her. The next few weeks could be courtship time between them during the long journey, if only he could be sure that she felt the same way as him.

* * * * *

The calm that followed the storm was a definite improvement, although now that the wind had ceased completely, the ship was practically at a standstill. The heat was unbearable, leaving little air.

The *Eagle Star* was somewhere in the Atlantic, drifting aimlessly. Five weeks of the journey had been completed already, with very little mishap. Some members of the crew had been taken sick, with the usual maladies that could strike them down at any time. However, according to the ship's doctor, they were well on the mend, and almost ready to resume their duties once more.

Lord Pendavan and his family were in fine fettle, enjoying every minute.

On the other hand, the American wasn't a particularly good sailor, so had been indisposed for most of the time.

Thorley had pursued Crystal ceaselessly and, having reached the decision to declare his love for her, was at that very moment waiting for her to appear on the poop-deck. They had arranged to meet after dinner.

The Captain had invited his passengers to dine with his officers each evening. The conversation was always varied, and the meals pleasant and appetising. Captain Bower, as he was called, was a kindly but gruff man, respected by his crew. He made his passengers welcome, making the journey enjoyable through the long and dreary days.

Thorley waited with as much patience as he could muster. 'Will she ever get here?' he asked himself. He kept repeating what he would say to Crystal over and over again, until he was word perfect. He must know her answer tonight, at all costs. Ah, this was her coming up on deck now, thank goodness. He hurried towards her, taking her arm.

"I am sorry I am late Thorley," she started, explaining that she had returned to her cabin for a warm outer garment, in case of a sudden chill in the air.

Thorley gazed at her, showing his feelings for anyone to see. With a suddenness that took her by surprise he pulled her into his arms, kissing her fully on the mouth, gently at first, and then more persistently.

Her body consumed by a passion she had never experienced before, Crystal returned his kisses, moved by strong emotions that were foreign to her. 'This must be love,' she thought, as Thorley released her.

"Of course, you must realise that I am desperately in love with you Crystal," he told her, "and I want to marry you," he finished.

She was silenced momentarily, not expecting this sudden proposal of marriage although she had been aware for some time now of Thorley's attraction for her. She had had plenty of opportunity to study this handsome man, and always felt happy in his company. Her liking had increased day by day, and she was always impatient to see him. Crystal felt an inner excitement at the thought of sharing her life with Thorley. His next request surprised her further.

"Can we be married right away now?" he asked her. "I do not think we need to wait until we reach our destination, Crystal, for I am sure the Captain would officiate for us. You see my darling," he continued, "I cannot wait until then for you to become my wife, as I love you to distraction." He held her close, as though he would never let her go. "My happiness will never be complete until you are mine for all eternity," he told her. "You will marry me Crystal, won't you?" he questioned anxiously.

She traced his sensitive mouth lightly with the tips of her fingers, more sure than ever now that she was deeply in love with this handsome man, and knew she wanted to spend the rest of her life with him.

"Of course I will marry you darling," she answered, "and I cannot think of anything nicer than being married on this ship," she told him. "But we must speak with our parents first, to have their blessing."

Thorley agreed with her, and suggested doing so right away without any preamble.

As he finished speaking his lips were on hers again, kissing her more passionately than before. His hold on her tightened, until she could hardly breathe.

At last she was able to break away from him, if only to take air, and hid her face against his shoulder, speaking in so low a voice that he could hardly hear what she was saying.

"We belong to each other in our hearts dearest Thorley," she told him. "It will not be long before we are as one when we take our marriage vows, and I have never felt so happy as I am at this moment," she finished shyly.

They walked silently towards the companionway, each lost in thought.

Lord and Lady Pendavan were delighted with the news, as were Mr and Mrs Grant, who considered their daughter a very fortunate young lady indeed to find such an ideal husband.

"And so handsome too," Alice Grant remarked to her husband. "We couldn't have chosen better for her had we searched the whole world over, Theodore," she went on.

"Yes Alice, you are right," he told her. "I am highly delighted myself to have found the ideal partner and a son-in-law in one go." He puffed out his cheeks, anticipating the pleasure he would have in introducing Thorley to his friends and close acquaintances. There would be a few eyebrows raised he knew, smiling quietly to himself, thinking of what he would have to impart, and of the reaction that would take place. He could hardly wait to see their faces, and chuckled softly.

Like most parents, Mr Grant wanted only the best for his daughter. There had been a time, a few months back, when he feared a romance springing up between her and his overseer, Ross. He had nothing against the man, who did his work well and kept good order amongst the blacks who laboured unceasingly on the plantation, but to him he was a hot blooded devil, and not at all suitable for Crystal. Well, that was nipped in the bud now, the better for everyone concerned. He had already decided to speak to the Captain the next day, so that the necessary arrangements could be made. He felt excited at the thought; not so his wife, for he had been aware for some little while of the furrow across her brow as though something troubled her. He stretched his arm across her shoulder and pulled her close.

"What is the matter Alice?" he asked. "Is something troubling you my dear?" sensing her anxiousness.

Alice sighed momentarily, glancing at her husband lovingly, wanting to speak but hesitating to do so, not wanting to take away the happiness that he felt and displayed so openly. To say she was disappointed she couldn't deny, for although she was ready to accept Thorley as her son-in-law, she would rather the marriage took place within their own surroundings. She had always dreamt of a special wedding for their only daughter, who was so very beautiful, and would make a lovely bride, all in white. Only now it wasn't possible, so she would have to be satisfied with a quiet one, with no social gathering, and none of the organising which she, Alice, would have liked.

"Why can't Crystal wait?" she asked her husband. "Surely there isn't that much rush? And she certainly wouldn't want to disappoint us, Theodore," she sighed again.

"Now, now my dear, don't upset our girl's plans," he asked of his wife. "Let the young people go ahead, after all," he explained, "there is no reason why they cannot have a church wedding after we arrive home Alice," he told her.

Mrs Grant cheered up considerably at her husband's suggestion, and made up her mind to speak to Crystal on the following day.

* * * * *

Captain Bower was concerned. The *Eagle Star* was well off course through no fault of the crew, and could soon be in the path of the dreaded Sargasso Sea with its deadly seaweed, that had caused many ships to flounder amongst it, and sink.

The Sargasso Sea, situated in the south-west of the North Atlantic, is relatively still within the swirl of warm ocean currents. This part of the Atlantic has an abundance of Sargassum, or gulf-weed, on its surface. It is known as a graveyard for ships, of every type and size, but even so cruel and desolate a place is the centre of one of nature's marvels. It is a well known fact that baby eels, as small as worms, swim from the Sargasso Sea through the warm Gulf Stream eventually to reach rivers in England and the Continent where they grow and reach adulthood. They then return to where their life commenced, to breed and die.

What other creatures lurk beneath the mighty oceans? Captain Bower often wondered, as did many others who, like him, spent years at sea. He looked around him with a feeling of frustration. He must get the ship back on course at all costs for the safety of the crew and all concerned. 'This could lengthen the journey by some considerable time', he told himself, but at least his wealthy passengers would reach their destination – he hoped -without mishap. With danger averted he could then settle his mind to other matters, for instance there was a wedding he must officiate at, for the handsome young couple who were both impatient to become man and wife.

The wind had risen again, although very faintly, but it was a start. If it could blow in the right direction, that was all Captain Bower asked. It was now in the lap of the gods.

* * * * *

Theodore Grant was feeling ill. He hadn't had a day yet on this return journey to America that he had felt well. At the moment he was lying on the bunk, and feeling most sorry for himself. Captain Bower had recently brought the news that the danger had been averted, with the change of direction of the winds, that had slowly brought the *Eagle Star* back on course!

"Now that things are well with us once more, the wedding of your daughter and her fiancée can take place tomorrow," he had informed the American.

Mr Grant hardly answered him, not in the least able to concentrate even on Crystal's happiness. He wished that he could feel better for this important occasion, but had reached the conclusion, now, that there was something far more seriously wrong with him than he had at first thought. He decided he would see the ship's doctors at once. Having made this decision he struggled to his feet, hardly able to stand because of the terrible nausea and dizziness that threatened to bring him to his knees every time he stood upright.

It was as well that Alice was with Crystal just now, otherwise she would have started fussing as she always did when he was indisposed.

Just as he reached the cabin door, after much effort, someone knocked, and on opening it he saw young Pendavan there.

Thorley was dreadfully shocked when he saw how ill his future father-in-law looked, and taking him by the arm, guided him back to the bunk bed, where Mr Grant fell back on to it, hardly able to breathe.

"Look, Sir," Thorley said, "I must get help, for you are ill."

The sick man nodded his head, too weak now to answer.

* * * * *

The doctor looked grim as he stood surveying his patient. He knew he had a sick man on his hands, and from the look of him, he wouldn't last the night.

Death saddened him and, as always when losing a patient, left him with a feeling of defeat. Doctor Fenton disliked being the bearer of bad news, and knowing that the relations were here on the ship, knew he must witness their sorrow.

The Captain would have to be notified at once, and there would be no wedding on the morrow, this he was certain of. The American's torturous breathing worsened by the minute, causing the doctor great concern.

There was nothing he could do, except watch the man die.

* * * * *

The death of Theodore Grant caused a gloom to settle over the *Eagle Star*. The ship's officers missed his jollity, for although his continual indisposition kept him mostly away from the Captain's table, the few occasions when he did appear with his family and friends had left an impression on everyone,

Alice Grant confined herself to her cabin, stunned into immobility. To her callers she repeatedly explained that her husband wasn't dead, "he can't be," she said, "for haven't I been talking to him a short while ago?" She could shed no tears, for none would fall. Crystal was broken-hearted, for she had been devoted to her father. Her tears came easily. As yet she hadn't considered the cancellation of her wedding plans, her one thought at present being the death and terrible loss of one she had loved so dearly.

Lord Pendavan and his family were utterly shocked, as were the crew of the *Eagle Star*.

It was far too soon yet for anyone to consider the consequences now that Theodore was dead, or what it would mean to the Pendavans and more particularly Thorley.

The American would have to be buried at sea which was a great pity, but it couldn't be helped, especially with the extreme heat, which was upon them most of the time.

The journey would be at an end in just over two weeks, when the *Eagle Star* would dock in New Orleans.

* * * * *

Thorley and Crystal had by now accepted the delay of their marriage. How could they mix pleasure with sorrow?

For the remainder of the journey everyone waited with what little patience they could muster. Thorley himself wondered what would happen, and what his position would be, now that his new partner had passed over. He had to admit that he couldn't visualise working the plantation without Mr Grant, to whom he had taken an instant liking on their first meeting. It wouldn't be the same now, he was sure of that, but he still had Crystal, and that was what really mattered to him, although he knew it was a bad start to his new venture.

As the days slowly passed the heat became unbearable, and most oppressive. There was no change in Crystal's grief. She seemed unable to snap herself out of it, however much she tried.

Alice Grant still hadn't grasped the significance of her husband's death, and spoke as though he was still with her. Lord and Lady Pendavan helped all they could, and Corrina spent many hours closeted with Crystal. They had become firm friends, and nothing could part them from each other. The American girl leaned on her English friend and seemed to gather some strength from her.

The crew, forever busy, were making preparations for the latter part of their journey. The ship, having reached Breton Sound, had dropped anchor to await the pilot, who would be taking the *Eagle Star* into the port of New Orleans.

The Sound was used as it was a natural harbour and eventually the *Eagle Star* would move slowly through the waters, led by the pilot.

Maurice Dupont knew the waters like the back of his hand. Even when under the influence of drink, which was more often than not, he could still be relied upon to take any ship safely into port. An uncouth

Frenchman of ill-repute, he was licentious, lecherous, and would lay any girl or woman he fancied, or so desired. Handsome, in a barbaric way, he appealed to most females, although some kept out of his way. More frequently than not, he would be late arriving at the rendezvous, which was exactly what had happened while Captain Bower waited on the bridge.

* * * * *

The distant beating of native drums travelled across the silent waters, lending an eerie sound to the still night. Captain Bower had heard tales of primitive tribes who practised voodoo, which in itself was a possession of spirits – invocation of the dead – and rites which built up to a crescendo of music and sorcery. Voodoo is the most exotic variety of black magic – a tropical phantasmagoria of zombies, wizards, spells and enchantments – but he, like many others, had no wish to investigate.

'I shall be thankful when we end this journey,' he told himself. It had been a sad trip with the death of his rich passenger, and he couldn't help but feel sorry for the young couple whose marriage plans had been wrecked. What a disappointment for them, and such an ending to the trip, which had started out so well and full of promise. At least they were young, that was all that could be said about it. He looked about him, thinking the pilot had arrived, but no, he hadn't. 'Would Dupont ever be on time?' he asked himself, picturing the Frenchman staggering along on some doxy's arm, blaspheming profanely.

* * * * *

Chapter Six

Obsession

The *Eagle Star* docked at New Orleans where the passengers alighted. Alice Grant clung to the arm of her daughter, bent of shoulders. The death of her loving husband had at last hit home to her. Life would never be the same now, she had to admit this.

They were, with the Pendavan family, met at the docks, so, with plenty of room for their luggage and themselves, proceeded on the last part of the journey to the plantation.

* * * * *

The land around the plantation was vast. There was plenty to see and Thorley, since leaving the dock-side, couldn't quell the mounting excitement which threatened to overwhelm him, although he had certain qualms, which was only natural, now that his new responsibilities were almost at hand. He tried, time and time again, to visualise being married to Crystal, who had with each passing hour endeared herself to him.

The phaeton, driven with expertise and precision, sped over the many miles. The roads, dusty and well worn, spread out before the onlookers, but the route leading to the plantation was most interesting.

Crystal informed them from time to time, of what lay ahead. So it was that suddenly, on either side of the path, they saw groups of black workers with their heads covered, bending over and tending the sugar canes, with the hot sun beating down on them. This scene stretched as far as the eye could see, and Thorley noticed that many of them raised their hats in recognition. He was absolutely astounded when he viewed the vast expanse of land throughout the plantation that was worked by literally hundreds of blacks of all ages. Eventually, the workers and the trees thinned out, and they were once more upon open ground.

The phaeton eased its speed, as slowly the horses turned a long bend, pulling up before a large house, strongly built, with steps leading up to a wide porch. On either side stood powerful iron railings, and surrounding the house was a very spacious veranda. The windows had storm shutters, which Crystal explained was usual with this style of house. It was a most welcome sight to the weary travellers.

Their first impression on entering the homestead, was the space, it being very sparsely furnished. This was an important factor in the extreme heat, Crystal went on to explain further. Her mother had little to say, apart from the introduction between her guests and their maid Rosalie, who was as black as the ace of spades, in contrast with her very white teeth which she displayed in plenty with her ready smile. Her attitude changed immediately when – on missing her master, and being told that he was dead – her face crumpled, and the tears flowed freely as she stumbled blindly from the room.

"She is just like one of the family," Crystal told them, "and she loved Daddy." Her lips trembled with the memory, but not wishing to give way again to her grief, she readily attended to the wants of her mother's guests.

It was a large house, with the necessary requirements and comfort. The bedrooms allocated to everyone were situated on the same floor, Thorley's almost opposite Crystal's. The windows in each room were wide open, letting in small amounts of air, but the humidity was stifling after the bracing Cornish breezes. This was something that he would have to adjust to, Thorley thought to himself, but as long as he had Crystal he could put up with anything. He was here now, for good or ill, and he intended to do all that Theodore Grant would have expected of him, had he lived. But it was little use deluding himself, for he was well aware of the difficulties that lay ahead and must be overcome. His first attempt at taking over the plantation would be to seek out the overseer Ross. This must be his first task on the morrow, but for now he wished only to relax his body and think of Crystal.

* * * * *

The next morning Thorley, always an early riser, was up at dawn. He had decided to visit the stables to choose his horse, as there was a lot of ground to cover, and he couldn't possibly go everywhere on foot. Crystal had already explained that her father's horse, Shandy, was used to the plantation, so knew his way blindfolded. She would ride him and could lead the way.

The groom showed Thorley three magnificent beasts – out of the vast selection of horses – one of which was highly excitable but very strong, so was aptly named Hercules. He was a beautiful chestnut, with a superb shiny coat. The remaining two were called Rufus and, of course, Shandy.

"I favour the chestnut," Thorley told the groom, slapping Hercules on the hind quarters. "He will be my choice William. Miss Crystal will be riding Shandy and accompany me around the plantation, so I shall be glad if you will saddle them for us within the next hour." So saying, Thorley turned on his heel and walked back to the house.

William, husband to the maid Rosalie, watched him out of sight. 'This Englishman will be a good boss man,' he told himself, making ready to do his bidding.

* * * * *

"Can I visit the plantation with you and Crystal?" Corrina asked her cousin. She had also awakened early, much too excited to sleep.

"I don't see why not, Corrie," he answered. "In fact Crystal will be glad of your company, I'm sure of that, but you will have to be ready within the hour," he told her.

Corrina quickly attired herself in a very becoming bottle-green velvet riding habit, with full skirt, complete with hat to match, topped by a thick curling feather that nestled in her golden hair which hung in abundance, cascading over her shoulders.

"You make an uncommonly pretty sight Corrie," Thorley remarked when she joined him at the stables. William had saddled Rufus as most suitable for the young lady. So with both girls sitting side saddle – Crystal suitably dressed in a black riding habit and equally as attractive as her companion, and both excellent horsewomen, having ridden most of their young lives – the three riders urged their horses into a trot.

It was a beautiful clear morning, with the promise of another good day, although the sun was very hot even at this early hour.

* * * * *

Ross Anderson enjoyed his work. He was a brute to his men, and would admit to it, but under his supervision the plantation ran very smoothly. He had been overseer for the Grants for nigh on eight years, in which time he had become known as the man of iron, for he ruled with the rod. The black workers were afraid of him, although they had a certain amount of respect for their overseer, and should there be any trouble brewing they kept away from it, if they possibly could.

He wasn't handsome by any means, but knew he was attractive to certain types of women. He had never married, not being the marrying kind. His strongest feeling, akin to love, was his obsession with Crystal Grant who - apart from the odd conversation with him whilst journeying around the plantation with her father, when she would come into contact with him - was unaware of his existence.

His face darkened with the thought that she always tried to avoid him. He was, at that moment, stretched out on a bunk in his office - which was nothing but a shack - going over in his mind what the runner had just told him, that Mr Grant was dead, and a young white boss had arrived at Manston House.

"He is from England boss," the man had continued, "and a real gentleman." He rolled his eyes up to the sky, feeling the importance of being the bearer of such news. "He is riding out to see you Masta' Ross."

Ross wondered if Crystal would accompany him. The thought of seeing her again set his pulses racing. He wanted to possess her, and waited with anticipation to feast his eyes upon her once more, even though he knew she would treat him with disdain, making him want to pull her into his arms, and kiss her until she cried for mercy.

* * * * *

Thorley rode amongst the black workers. The sweat poured off their faces in the intense heat as they bent over their tasks, but they worked with determination.

"Mornin' Miss Crystal, Mam," greeted some of the older hands, showing their respect for their late master's daughter, although they eyed Thorley with apprehension. This was somewhat different to riding around Cornwall, where the smell of the sea was for ever in his nostrils. Already, he was missing his beloved Pendavan and the sound of the screeching seagulls soaring high around the cliff face...

He wiped his brow and face, the sweat pouring in driblets on to his shirt collar. The girls – even if they were feeling the heat, which they must be he thought – appeared cool enough. Crystal was well used to the climate, but Corrie surprised him, for she looked as beautiful now as she did when she first set out for the plantation.

"Here we are Thorley," Crystal explained, "Ross should be here to meet you, for I sent a runner on ahead to prepare him."

They reined in their horses at a small clearing which showed a shack-like building, of squat appearance, and, standing in the doorway was a man who Thorley presumed must be the overseer. As soon as the introductions were over with, he became aware of the persistent, lustful, covetous looks that were cast at Crystal. She, having noticed as well, remarked, "Oh Ross, I think you should know that this English gentleman – as well as being your boss – is to become my husband as soon as the six months' mourning has passed. Had my father not died on the *Eagle Star*," she continued, "we should have been married by the Captain."

Ross's face darkened perceptibly as he looked at Thorley with suspicion and hatred.

So this was how the wind blew, was it? Well he would see about that. He intended to have her by hook or by crook, by fair means or foul. He would show her, stuck up Miss Madam. He would bring her to her knees and make her want him. He felt that beneath her calm exterior there lurked hidden passions, which he knew he could awaken. His obsession for her was like a fire that threatened to consume him. He stole a glance at the English girl who was definitely a beauty, he couldn't deny that, but she was not his type. She was one of the untouchable kind. No, it was Miss Grant he wanted, and would get little or no rest until he had his way with her. The more he thought about it, the more determined he became.

* * * * *

The weeks and months sped by with the new life for Thorley, who had now begun to settle down to the many responsibilities on the plantation. He enjoyed the varied interests that cropped up daily. He seldom saw Ross Anderson, unless there were any problems. He was reliable, so Thorley left him alone.

He was at that moment riding Hercules away from Manston House on his way to meet Corrie, who during the last few weeks had been helping out at the local hospital. She had – from a small child – shown an aptitude for nursing sick children and animals, often resulting in tears if anything untoward happened to them.

It came about, just after they had settled in at 'Manston' when Alice Grant had felt very much under the weather, that her doctor, Andre Perrie was sent for. Corrie was with her when he called, and liked him on sight. She found out that he was dedicated to his work, particularly at the hospital, which he mostly controlled with little or no help. He was mostly always on duty, and at the end of the day, returned home to an invalid wife. It was understood that she had been this way for many years, confined to a wheelchair after a serious accident.

A month after his visit to see his patient at 'Manston' Corrie suddenly decided to ride out to the hospital, so with Rufus saddled in readiness, she set off. Had she only known, it was an opening to a new start in life, with very little happiness, and much heartbreak. After seeing how Doctor Perrie worked under difficult conditions, coping with black people who were the bulk of the patients, Corrie offered her services. Most days she returned home before the evening pulled in, but on this particular day she was much later, and as it had been dark for some time now, Thorley became anxious, so decided to go and meet his cousin. As he reined in at the front of the hospital, she came slowly towards him, and being as close to Corrie as he was, knew immediately that something was wrong and troubled her.

The cousins turned their horses towards home, allowing them the lead. As always Thorley waited, for he knew Corrie would confide in him when she was ready, which she did almost at once.

"Thorley," she started, hesitating momentarily, "I have fallen in love with Andre Perrie, what can I do?" she asked, looking at him in desperation.

"Corrie, I am so sorry my dear," he answered, his voice full of emotion, unable – at that moment – to think of anything else to say to help console her.

They rode in silence, each lost in thought, until at last they reached Manston House.

* * * * *

Esmeralda had retired to her room with a severe headache. The persistent heat had its effect on her. She hated to say it, but although she had been happy to make the journey here to New Orleans she couldn't wait to return to her beloved Pendavan. She mustn't tell Thorley, for he would be most distressed. At least they would be together for his wedding to Crystal, and this was important to her. Within a few more weeks the mourning time would be complete, then the marriage could take place. Her thoughts were often with Francesca, wondering how she fared at the 'Grange' and if there was any news of her husband.

A knock at the door brought her back to the present with a start. "Can I speak with you Mother?" Thorley asked, as he stepped into the room, closing the door quietly behind him, and walking towards her, bent and kissed her on the cheek.

Esmeralda looked lovingly at him, thinking how very handsome he looked tonight. She felt so proud and overwhelmed with the feeling of love she carried in her breast for her beloved Thorley, and thanked God that he had been brought to Pendavan. At least she had something to be thankful to Adrian for. Despite all his wicked deeds, this was Adrian's own son, born of his seed, so some good had originated from him.

As she observed him, she could tell almost immediately that he was concerned about something, and wished to discuss it with her. This is how it had been between them, from the time he had just thrown himself into the comfort of her arms, and wept silent tears over the death of his mother. Never would she erase from her memory his sorrow when Jason had drowned, that he suffered deeply was evident at the time. Now her only hope was that the coming marriage would be right for him. She couldn't bear to think of him being hurt in any way, although she was sure Crystal loved him very much; but something persistently nagged at the back of her mind, which she could not explain to anyone, not even herself. It was as though she had a premonition of danger.

* * * * *

Crystal Grant was bored and restless. She had decided against riding Shandy, preferring to walk just where the mood took her. It was early evening and quiet everywhere. She kept telling herself that she couldn't wait to be married to Thorley, and felt sure, that once they were man and wife she would be able to settle down to her new role. It was what she wanted, or was it?

Was there some doubt in her mind? Oh! she loved the Englishman all right, and when she was alone with him she could think of nothing else. But it was at times like these, when she was on her own, that she felt uncertain of the future, asking herself if she really wanted marriage, and then perhaps ending up in a rut. Thorley had told her that he wished them to have a family right away, after they were married, but was she ready for this, she asked herself numerous times. She had never told anyone, not even her mother, that she was terrified of having children. The thought of giving birth to a child scared her completely. Whenever Thorley broached the subject she went hot and cold, becoming withdrawn, which he naturally put down to shyness on her part. He had no idea that she felt this way.

She recalled to her mind the evening before, when she had retired for the night. Thorley entered her room, not having seen her all day. There was much he wished to discuss with her, but as always, when they were together, other things were forgotten. He pulled her into his embrace, his kisses becoming more insistent, which she returned eagerly, and found her treacherous body wanting to surrender to his passion. It had become increasingly difficult of late to hold their ardent desires in check, because they were strained to the limit. Although she had had a few amorous male friends, she was still a virgin, and perhaps this fact held her back, but she didn't know how long she could hold out in these conditions.

Completely lost in thought, Crystal suddenly realised that she had wandered a good way from the house. As she turned about she heard a sound that startled her out of her reverie, and being alone she felt scared. She tried telling herself that there was nothing to worry about, as no one would dream of hurting her, particularly the blacks, for they had nothing but respect for her. There it was again, stealthy footsteps, she was sure. She was really frightened now, and hastened her steps in the direction of the house.

With a suddenness that brought her heart up into her mouth, she was pulled to the ground with such force, that it winded her momentarily.

"Let me go you beast," she cried, recognising her attacker as Ross. "I shall scream if you dare touch me," she told him.

The overseer bent across Crystal, pinioning her arms at her sides, and imprisoning her legs with his body. She was at his mercy now, and knew it. The desire in his eyes was plain to see. Although she intended screaming, she found she couldn't, or was it that she didn't want to? She couldn't understand her feelings at all for, although she held this man in disdain, she knew now that she wanted his kisses. Thorley and everything else was forgotten in this wild moment of passion that enveloped them both, as his mouth covered hers with fierce and demanding kisses, and as their love making increased, they were lifted into dizzy heights, her virginity forgotten also.

* * * * *

The evening was very still, with little or no air to breathe. Esmeralda, relaxing out on the veranda, listened to the usual night noises. She had much to think about since Thorley had told her about Corrie. 'Poor darling,' she thought, 'she will suffer much heartbreak, that is certain.' Now both her daughters had problems, and their troubles were hers also.

Esmeralda had made up her mind already, that as soon as the marriage took place between Thorley and Crystal, she would return to England and Pendavan with her beloved Antony. It was where they belonged, she knew that now. She was aware that Corrie would want to stay in New Orleans by the side of her lover and she could quite understand this, but it meant they would have to be parted. It would mean both daughters being at opposite ends of the world but, whereas Francesca was at this moment safely ensconced in a beautiful home with her child, even though she lived there without her husband, Corrie on the other hand had little hope of any immediate future, loving a married man who was dedicated to his work – and if she knew anything about it, loyal to his wife, who could live for many years yet with careful nursing, which she was certainly having.

Engrossed in her thoughts, she hadn't realised how late it must be, so rising from her seat, made to re-enter the house but suddenly stopped in her tracks as she became aware of a figure hurrying towards 'Manston' in a very furtive manner. The shock she received when she realised it was Crystal, who was in such a state of disarray, absolutely stunned her. What was she doing out alone at this time of night she asked herself. And who had she been with? Not Thorley, she well knew.

Her hand flew to her breast to help stay the sudden flutter in her heart. She knew now that without doubt trouble lay ahead for him.

As the American girl disappeared from view, Esmeralda tried to regain her control before entering the house. She must try and act normally and say nothing of what she had seen, so that she could observe closely and piece together the puzzle.

* * * * *

Chapter Seven

Killer Hurricane

There was a feeling of apprehension in the air. Thorley was as busy as ever, with the help of the overseer, and Corrie was hardly ever at home. Her days at the hospital were full. She worked non-stop at the side of Andre Perrie, giving him all the help he so badly needed. He told her more than once, that he didn't know how he ever managed before she had come into his life.

Crystal spent much of her time out of doors, sometimes meandering around, but mostly riding Shandy and going further afield. Today, she was to meet Thorley. On this particular day Lord Pendavan decided to go riding on Hercules, although the weather didn't look at all promising; in fact the sky was very overcast, with heavy low lying clouds, dark and menacing. The lull before the storm.

Thorley was out somewhere on the plantation, leaving Esmeralda alone in the house, with only Alice Grant for company. The maid Rosalie was away nursing a sick sister. A sudden and drastic change in the weather had come about within the last hour, and Esmeralda had been aware for some little while of the high wind, which in its intensity, shook the window shutters noisily. She wished the others were here, for she felt somewhat tensed up and worried. On deciding to close all the shutters in readiness for – she knew not what, hurriedly she fastened them, and settled down to wait.

Lord Pendavan had ventured further than he had first intended. He knew there was a fierce storm brewing for he had noticed the dark clouds rushing across the sky. He had long since reined in Hercules, for in his awareness the horse seemed to sense some form of danger and refused to go any further. There was little or no shelter in these parts, so he would have to take his chances. He wished with all his heart that he was at 'Manston' with Esme, for he knew she must be very frightened. She hated storms at the best of times, and this one would be ferocious in its intensity, he was sure of this, for it appeared to worsen by the minute. This was the first of its kind that they had experienced since coming to New Orleans.

* * * * *

With a suddenness that was startling, both man and horse were carried along in the wake of the hurricane. Without any warning both were felled to the ground by an uprooted tree, and knew no more.

* * * * *

The hurricane was uncontrollable, attacking everything in its path, and devastating the whole area. The river, swollen in its extremity, was littered with dead bodies and debris that were rushed along at a terrible speed.

Many who struggled to survive by clinging to any floating objects in the churned up foam, were dragged beneath the waters by the waiting alligators, who carried their drowning victims to their lair.

* * * * *

The massive tree bent and swayed with the ferociousness of the wind. Thorley, getting weaker by the minute, gripped the tree with all the strength he could muster. He had long since lost sight of Crystal and Ross who had disappeared from view when, after clinging to the lower trunk, both had been whipped away before his very eyes by an extra strong gust. He couldn't even alter his position, and felt himself break out in a cold sweat, when he realised what could happen to Crystal. Even now she could be dead. He was beside himself with worry, fearing the worst. He could only send up a silent prayer for her safety.

Without any warning, something came from above and hit him on the side of the head, which caused him to loosen his hold, and with a jolt he fell to the ground, senseless.

* * * * *

The whole area was completely flattened and unrecognisable, with litter strewn all around and widespread damage. Death stalked everywhere. Those that had survived the cyclonic storm moved around in a daze.

The hospital was full of the injured and dying. Corrie, by the side of Andre Perrie, worked non-stop tending the very sick patients. The doctor, ashen faced with fatigue, did the best he could in the emergency.

If Corrie hadn't already fallen in love with him, she would have done so now, for he showed another side to his nature in his devotion to his patients that endeared him to her for evermore. He sympathised when it was needed, and still fought vigorously for the lives of many, although he knew it was hopeless from the beginning. When Thorley was brought in she had watched Andre at work while she stood there, mesmerised by the shock that her cousin was in a bad way, if not already dead. The wound at the side of his head was nasty, and before it was cleaned appeared far worse than it really was. Andre explained to her that it wasn't serious, but he was suffering from severe shock. With the caked blood and grime removed he looked like death, and so vulnerable, now that he had fallen asleep. Corrie felt a lump in her throat as the ready tears sprang to her eyes.

"Don't upset yourself my darling," he whispered, afraid lest anyone should hear the endearment that had slipped out unavoidably, moved by her grief. His face took on a look of anguish as he realised once more how hopeless their love for one another had become. He had fallen desperately in love with this beautiful girl, and yet he was tied to a wife in name only. His loyalty to Donna would let him do nothing, and he had long since been quite satisfied just to see Corrie and have her by his side during their working hours, at least that was something.

"Doctor, can you come here?" Corrie cried anxiously, as he pushed his thoughts away.

* * * * *

Crystal Grant lay dying. Help had been administered, but it was of no avail. Her broken body was beyond repair. The figure keeping vigil at her bedside, sat with bowed head. Ross Anderson couldn't believe that she was doomed to die. It would all come to light now that they were lovers, and he the father of her child that would have been born seven months from now. As yet, no one knew their secret, for they had covered their tracks very thoroughly. Although he was utterly devastated by what had happened, he did spare a thought for the Englishman, who naturally enough would be in a terrible state when he knew. He would suffer a dreadful shock at the knowledge of her death, but her infidelity must surely affect him most. For the present he was unaware of the impending doom. Perhaps it would be all over before he returned to reality.

* * * * *

The group of rescuers, struggling under the dead weight of their burden, approached 'Manston' with some hesitation. Their find was grim, and worse still, they had to be the bearers of the bad news. How could they tell Lady Pendavan that her husband was dead? What could they say to soften the blow? Their footsteps lagged as the dreaded moment was almost upon them. Death is never pleasant, particularly when one is confronted with the bereaved person, as in this case.

* * * * *

Never had Esmeralda been so terrified in her life. The hurricane while it lasted had been most frightening. The continual roar of the wind that battered and rattled the window shutters, shook the house in its ferocity. Esmeralda's nerves were very nearly at breaking point, as each new gust threatened to rip the house from its very foundations. If only Antony and Thorley were with her, it wouldn't have seemed half so bad; as it was her terror persisted, worsening by the minute.

With only Alice Grant for company there was no one to keep her spirits up. As well as contending with the storm, there was the added worry of not knowing where her loved ones were. She had already accepted that Corrie was at the hospital, where she was sure to be needed with the number of casualties caused by the severe hurricane, but it was because of Antony and Thorley, who were terribly late coming back, that she conjured up pictures of them battling against the tearing winds, that shrieked like demons let loose on the Delta.

"Why oh why can't it stop?" she cried in anguish, her heart thumping uncontrollably, as it threatened to burst.

Completely lost in her sobering thoughts she had no idea that the storm had subsided quite suddenly. She breathed a sigh of relief as this was brought home to her. The deathly silence was suddenly broken as a different kind of sound reached her ears. It startled her momentarily until she realised that it could be either Antony or Thorley, perhaps, even both of them. It came from the veranda, and sounded as though someone was hesitant to make himself known. It must be Antony she thought excitedly as she hurriedly crossed to the entrance ready to greet him, but her look of expectation and pleasure turned to horror as she opened the door and fastened her eyes on the significant object held by the group of silent men.

As in a dream she heard one of them say, "Are you Lady Pendavan?" Esmeralda, her hand clutching her throat, nodded, unable to find her voice.

"I am afraid we have some bad news for you," the man went on, hesitating momentarily. How could he tell this beautiful woman, who looked so tragic, that her husband was dead? He glanced away from her, unable to bring himself to impart such news.

"Are you trying to tell me that my husband is...?" she began, afraid to say the terrible word. Bells rang in her ears as the terrible truth began to dawn on her. Suddenly, and without warning, she staggered and fell senseless to the floor.

* * * * *

Thorley, as one in a trance, returned to 'Manston'. He could never quite remember how he got there.

When he had eventually awakened to reality and had to face the terrible truth, it was as though the end of the world had come.

'Crystal dead?' he asked himself. 'It just can't be true. Surely it is a nightmare, and I shall awaken presently to find that I have been dreaming.' He tried to console himself with this.

Corrie, her face filled with compassion, stood looking down at her cousin, who sat with his face buried in his hands, choking with emotion. What could she say to him in his hour of sorrow? That he was suffering the most terrible grief, she was well aware, but in a few months, perhaps even weeks, he might see things in a different light, for there was Crystal's infidelity to consider, and she knew he would never be able to accept that once he had overcome his grief. There were other more serious things he would have to face yet, that he still had no inkling of. First there was Papa, and his tragic death. Her eyes filled with tears at the memory. Then there was darling Mama, lying so desperately ill, and still not speaking.

Andre had explained: "It's the shock my darling. She will recover, although it may take some time, especially if she doesn't want to help herself," he told her.

Being desperately in love herself, her heart went out to her mother, who she knew had loved her husband to distraction. If, and when, Mama recovered, how was she going to face the future without her loved one? Corrie asked herself. Her thoughts reverted once more to Thorley. What would he feel like, or do, when he knew of the devastation to the plantation? It had been – as well as many others – flattened to the ground, with all the crops destroyed. There was nothing left, but worst of all, was the terrible loss of life. Many had perished, and the whole area was in mourning.

* * * * *

Esmeralda's indisposition was the making of Alice Grant, who had been somewhat strange in her manner since returning to 'Manston', never really recovering from the death of Theodore. She seemed unable to take in the news that her daughter had died in the hurricane, and the fact that her new friend needed help seemed to blind herself to her own grief. She could, at least, share her sorrow with Lady Pendavan.

For the first time in many months, she came out of her shell – her behaviour astounded everyone, including the doctor, but he agreed that this could be the beginning of her recovery.

The days and weeks passed by uneventfully, and as yet there was no significant change in the patient's condition. The owner of 'Manston' nursed Esmeralda with dedication, mixed with devotion. Although everyone hoped for her complete recovery, in their hearts they really dreaded her return to reality, to face the desperate truth, and to witness her pain and sorrow.

* * * * *

Ross Anderson was desolate. The girl he loved was dead. Oh yes, he had loved Crystal Grant to distraction. At first he had thought it was simply just a question of possessing her, and being the victor, but after her surrender to him his feelings had altered and he became a changed man. Now as well as losing her, his work in this area had finished. He could get employment elsewhere he knew, but it would mean starting all over again. He thought of the Englishman and what this would mean to him! For he had travelled to America with the sole prospect of running the plantation, as well as marrying Crystal, and now he had nothing, for hadn't he also lost his father in the hurricane? He felt very sorry for him. For himself, he thought it best to be moving on as there was nothing more here to hold him now, and if the Englishman was sensible, he would do the same.

* * * * *

Thorley took the death of his father and his mother's illness – caused by the initial shock of losing him – very badly indeed. Only once before in his life could he remember feeling so desolate, and that was when Jason had presumably died from drowning. He was utterly shocked at the devastation caused by the killer hurricane, in particular, the loss of life.

He had decided almost at once that he would return to Pendavan as soon as his mother was well enough to undertake the arduous journey to England. There was nothing left to keep them in New Orleans. The plantation was beyond repair, and the fact that Crystal was gone from him for ever, made it so much more final.

* * * * *

Esmeralda's health improved daily, after weeks of struggling to become herself once more. She had been unable to use her legs for some time, and her speech had been very much impaired, but gradually these returned to her.

There had been much concern for her sanity. At times, even Andre had held out little hope for her full recovery.

The doctor, with the help of Corrie, had, with others also, almost run themselves into the ground with the work at the hospital following the awful tragedy, but gradually things returned to some form of order, although it would be a very long time before people could pick up the threads of life again.

Corrie had definitely decided on remaining at 'Manston' and had Alice Grant's blessing. She couldn't leave Andre anyway, for he needed her more each day. Although Corrie was torn between her love for the doctor, and her devotion and duty to her mother, she knew in her heart that she should travel back to England with her, but couldn't bring herself to say good-bye to Andre.

It was Thorley himself who finally made the decision. He informed them that he intended to return to England on his own. He had given it much thought, and nothing would change his mind now. He was very thankful that Mama had recovered at last, he told Corrie, but he didn't consider her fit enough to make the return journey. In any case, he thought they would be needed at 'Manston'. There was plenty of room at the homestead to house some of the unfortunate victims who had lost their homes in the hurricane, and handing out help to others was indeed the right treatment for both Alice Grant and dear Mama.

Oh, he would miss her, that went without saying, but he would just have to get used to being without her. In any case, he wanted to be on his own. He had become a different person of late, he knew it. The change had come about very sudden. He felt a terrible bitterness in losing Crystal, and as Corrie had predicted, his love for her had turned to a hatred that tore at his heart. Never again would he reveal his feelings to anyone he decided. As far as he was concerned no woman was worth the trouble. His continual aggressive manner made him not the best of company, so he decided he was better on his own. 'I shall lose myself in my work at Pendavan for that is where I belong,' he told himself, feeling satisfied that he had made the right decision. He would make the necessary arrangements for his journey home to England.

* * * * *

Chapter Eight

The New Master Of Pendavan

Thorley rode his late father's horse with reverence. He breathed the clear air that mingled with the smell of the sea and plant life. How could he have ever left his beloved Pendavan? he repeatedly asked himself. It looked much the same, with little change, but there was a difference, he was here without dear Mama and Papa. Thorley felt a lump in his throat as he conjured up a picture of his adored parents, and his heart cried out in anguish.

He looked back over the past few months and his homeward journey. It had been most wearisome travelling on his own. There had been six other passengers, as well as himself, but he hadn't wanted to take the trouble to mix with them, or make friends. It was better that he kept to his own company in the state that he was in, for he just wasn't in the mood for talking. Most days would find him closeted in his cabin, other than when he took his exercise. He could then be seen walking to and fro on the top deck, and would retire below as soon as he could. Occasionally he would sit with the others but even then he only answered when he was spoken to. Far from putting everything behind him after leaving New Orleans, Thorley constantly grieved for Crystal. Her death was still a desperate shock, but her infidelity had affected him far worse, he just couldn't put it from his mind, embittering him more with each passing hour.

By the time the ship had docked at Liverpool, Thorley had had enough. The first thing he did after once more setting foot on dry land, was to send a letter to Pendavan warning Mrs Rushton of his impending arrival. He knew she would be both curious and anxious at the same time, when the realisation hit home that it would only be him returning. He then decided to travel to London, and stay the night at his Mayfair club. He would arrange to commence his long journey to Cornwall on the following day, knowing that within about a week he should be at home once again.

* * * * *

As the coach drew up before the imposing gates, the new Master of Pendavan feasted his eyes on all the loveable things that he had so missed. It was good to be back, he told himself. If only he had refrained from moving to America – he had to admit to Crystal being the biggest attraction for doing so – dear Mama and Papa would still be here, and he would have been his fun-loving self, instead of the unsociable man that he had become. He knew he was no good to himself, or anyone else, for that matter. He tried reasoning with his own conscience, also battling with his problems at the same time, but try as he would, he could not pull himself out of the doldrums. He could only try and reassure himself that time would be the governing factor.

* * * * *

Albert eagerly approached the coach which, driven by the now tired horses – although they had only done the latter few miles of the journey home – was ready to turn into the driveway.

"Welcome home Master Thorley," he began, hesitating as to what to say next. The caretaker, always tactful, used his tact now as he sensed something unspoken between them.

The housekeeper was there at the entrance, ready to greet her new Master, but as Thorley stepped from the coach, helped by the livery man, she saw the tragic look on his face and with a sense of foreboding realised immediately that there was something wrong. She had never expected to see Master Thorley for many years, knowing how much his heart had been set on his new venture. So it was with great concern that she waited to hear, she knew not what.

"Dear Rushie," he greeted her, showing his pleasure at seeing her, but his smile of welcome never reached his eyes. "There is much I have to say, and need to relate to you," he told her, "but first I wish to refresh myself after the journey. So shall we meet in the drawing-room, say, in about an hour?" he suggested.

As Thorley ascended the staircase he looked around him, seeing the old familiar objects.

He was certainly glad to be back at Pendavan once more, even though his homecoming brought on a terrible nostalgia.

* * * * *

The housekeeper and housemaid entered the drawing-room at the same time, one to await the young Master, the other to set out a pot of tea and sweet cakes, in readiness.

Mrs Rushton, first thanking Trudie, waved her away, anxious to have her own company until Master Thorley should appear. Her heart was in her mouth, for she knew she was about to hear terrible news. 'It has to be something serious,' she told herself, 'to have changed the Master from a young man full of life, and laughter, to an older and sorrowful man, who, as well as being withdrawn within himself, seems to be an embittered person.'

Thorley entered the drawing-room, completely startling the housekeeper, who continually twisted an already well screwed up handkerchief between her nervous fingers.

He strode across the room, not looking in her direction and poured himself a drink from a crystal glass decanter, that clinked against the other glasses as he replaced it with a shaky hand. The sound echoed in the silent room, putting them both on edge more than ever.

Thorley, after taking a long gulp from the glass, came right out with, "My father is dead Rushie, and Mama has been seriously ill with the shock." He was brutally frank, knowing no other way in his bitterness, to tender the blow lightly.

Mrs Rushton collapsed back on to the settle behind her, feeling as though all the air had left her body. She shook as with a chill, she couldn't speak, and just sat staring into space.

"I have also lost Crystal," Thorley continued. "She died through fatal injuries caused by the hurricane that hit us without warning." He paused, hating to think about it again. "It was terrible Rushie," he went on, recalling the terror he had experienced. "Father was killed instantaneously whilst out riding, and the rescuers brought him home to Mother," he explained. "She lost her speech, and the use of her legs you know, and has only recently recovered."

He finished his drink and rose to replenish his glass. "Would you like one Rushie?" he asked. "I think you need something after the shock you have received." Sorry now that he hadn't been more gentle in handling the bad news.

The housekeeper nodded in acceptance, still unable to put into words what she felt for the new Master of Pendavan. She had already experienced this before, when her first Master and Mistress had left the house very much in love and in good spirits, to return no more because of a terrible tragedy. This was history repeating itself all over again. 'And now what of Master Thorley?' she asked herself. As well as losing his much loved father, and his betrothed, he had returned to Pendavan to live alone. What would this mean to him in the future? Would he become a lonely man, aged by sorrow? It distressed her to think of it.

"I left Mama at 'Manston' with Mrs Grant and Corrie," he continued. "Incidentally Rushie, we didn't send the news to you, as I knew I would be in England before it could reach you.

"What am I going to do, Rushie?" he asked. "My dreams are completely shattered, I'm heartbroken, unsociable, and a changed man." His voice broke with emotion, as he turned towards the window, looking out unseeingly on to the scene before him.

Much of Thorley's anguish transferred itself to the housekeeper. What could she say to comfort him in his hour of need? That he would need some sort of solace, she was well aware, but would he find it here at Pendavan without his loved ones by his side?

His hurt, sorrow and bitterness was written all over his face, and there for all to see.

* * * * *

Lord Pendavan threw all his energies into the work on the estate. Everyone, tenants, farm-hands and the lower workers alike, knew their new Master as both agreeable and steadfast. He had won their hearts and trust when he had accompanied his father around the estates. They found difficulty in hiding their grief for the late Master of Pendavan. Many openly cried, while others bowed their heads in memory of a lost friend.

The whole place had been ran on smooth lines since the family had first departed to America, with everyone pulling their weight. Mostly all would have laid down their lives for their beloved Master. So it was that the community went around silent and sorrowful, doing their work, with the joy of reunion forgotten momentarily.

Before leaving New Orleans, Esmeralda had asked Thorley to call on Francesca, to relate what had happened and give her news of the tragedy. She also wanted Jacqueline and her family to know. So, after his first week spent at Pendavan Thorley decided to visit The

Grange. He knew Francesca would be shocked to see him, and to hear of her father's tragic death, but at least he would be on the spot to comfort her. He intended to stay two or three days, and then journey on to Jacqueline's home.

This was something he wasn't looking forward to, hating to be the bearer of such news.

During the past week he hadn't had much free time to think about what had happened, but now that he was preparing for the journey, his thoughts centred around Francesca, wondering how he would find her, and if she had heard fresh news of her estranged husband.

* * * * *

Lord Pendavan glanced out of the open window of the coach, and breathed into his nostrils the fresh country air that wafted inside. He noticed the picturesque views, magnificent spreading trees, giant in their size, and landscapes that brought home to him how much he had missed it all. There were lonely farmhouses dotted here and there, with gentle cattle grazing in and around the surrounding fields.

He knew now that he should never have gone to America, and blamed himself for what had happened. He wished with all his heart that he could revert back to what it was before, with dear Mama and Papa safe at Pendavan. He was stricken with remorse and sighed, remembering what had gone before.

The nearer he was to the end of his journey, the more anxious he became. How could he break the news to Francesca that she had lost her father for ever? He wondered how she would take it.

The horses gathered speed as they neared the little village where The Grange was situated. The stately mansion nestled amongst a group of spreading trees displaying tender green foliage, that shaded the group of people who sat beneath them.

Lord Pendavan alighted from the coach, and turned in the direction of the voices.

Francesca, when she realised who her visitor was, jumped to her feet and ran towards him.

"How good to see you Thorley," she said, greeting him with a kiss on his cheek. "What are you doing here? And why have you come?" she asked. "I thought you were still in America." Francesca turned towards her companions, surprise written all over her face. "Look who it is," she cried.

Thorley approached the group thinking all the while what a restful sight they made. He noticed Jacqueline, her husband, and the twins, Elizabeth and Clive, while a few feet away, playing silently, was a pretty child who had the good looks of Francesca. She must be nearly twelve months old now, he thought.

Francesca surprised him by her attitude. She had changed from when he had last seen her. She appeared more serene in her manner, and much happier, which lent an inner beauty to her classic features.

"Can we walk for a few minutes?" he asked. "I have some news to impart, and I think you will want to be on your own when you hear it," he told her.

She agreed, and walked away from the circle, already aware that something was terribly wrong, having noticed the drastic change in her cousin.

"Francesca my dear," Thorley began, hesitating as to how he could soften the blow, but there was no other way. "Papa is dead," he continued, "he was killed in a hurricane that hit us suddenly, and Mama has been terribly ill. She nearly died too."

Francesca looked up at Thorley, who suddenly seemed to tower above her. Her vision became blurred and difficult, and clutching her throat, she fell to the ground quite senseless.

Thorley dropped to his knees beside the limp body of his cousin, chaffing her hands all the while. He was completely startled at the feeling of gentleness that stirred within him as he looked anxiously at Francesca lying so still, her face void of any colour.

After an interminable time, her eyelids fluttered and she opened her eyes to rest them on the stern handsome features looking down at her.

Thorley immediately jumped to his feet whilst holding out a hand to help her to rise. Francesca looked like death, and as realisation took over, instead of giving way to her grief, she remained dry eyed, but completely stunned.

They returned to the others, she resting her hand lightly on her cousin's arm that offered assistance.

Jacqueline hurried towards them, seeing right away that something was very wrong. She looked at Thorley for an explanation, but what she read in his eyes stayed her question so, tactful as she was, she focused her attention on Francesca, who she could see needed help.

* * * * *

While Jacqueline supported Francesca to the house, Thorley explained to the others what had happened and why. He was more than surprised to see that Elizabeth had grown into an attractive young woman, unrecognisable as the lean and lanky girl that she had once been. He hadn't seen her for some years as she had spent much of her schooldays abroad, and now materialising before his very eyes was a budding beauty. He couldn't believe it. He realised at that moment that he wasn't completely immune to other women, although he was still very bitter about what had happened. He was very deeply affected by Crystal's betrayal of him, but even so, he tried to make allowances for her behaviour, thinking perhaps that the shock she received at the death of her beloved father may have had something to do with her change of heart.

He would like to think this was so; then perhaps, he could, in his heart, forgive her infidelity. He glanced towards Roberta who toddled around, and tried to visualise what he would feel like had she been his child. He was still a romantic at heart.

* * * * *

Chapter Nine

Deeper Feelings for a Cousin

Winter had set in with full force. The clouds, low, dark and menacing, raced across the sky, shadowing Pendavan standing tall and majestic. The gales blew themselves into a frenzy on the outside, whilst inside everywhere was warm and cosy.

Autumn had shed its leaves late, encroaching on winter, bringing Yuletide ever nearer. There was much activity going on in preparation for the festive season. The housekeeper supervised the decoration, so under the busy hands of housemaids the whole place glistened and sparkled with swinging multi-coloured lanterns and bright shining stars, with sprigs of holly and mistletoe tucked in and around all the likely places. It was certainly a sight to behold, as Lord Pendavan remarked to his housekeeper, while they stood surveying it all.

He had decided quite suddenly to have a Christmas party, which a year before he wouldn't have considered under any circumstances, but the new Master of Pendavan had changed of late, due mostly to the fact that he now felt he had something to live for. After his return from America his first few months were very grim indeed. He worked himself almost to a standstill, trying to erase from his memory all that had befallen him. However much he loved his home, there were times when he felt stifled by the very place he held such affection for, so he would most times visit The Grange to see Francesca and Roberta, who had taken to following him everywhere. The child had become very dear to him of late, as she was a tiny replica of her mother, in her serenity.

Thorley had been aware for sometime, that the barrier between himself and Francesca had disappeared completely, and a feeling of understanding had taken its place, bringing a closer relationship.

During some of his visits to The Grange Thorley saw Elizabeth – she frequently stayed with Francesca – who had helped his cousin over a bad patch, and had become very firm friends. Francesca had for some time now noticed the adoring looks her friend cast in his direction, and realised that Elizabeth was fast falling in love with Thorley.

As for Elizabeth herself, she had no illusions as to how things were between the two cousins. She had seen their friendship blossom into a deeper feeling that grew daily. He had eyes for no other.

* * * * *

Christmas had come and gone, with Pendavan back to normal once more. The festivities were something to remember by all who had participated. Naturally Thorley missed his parents, and longed with all his heart for the old days. He had at last put Crystal from his thoughts.

Quite a gathering had congregated at Pendavan for as well as Francesca, Roberta, Jacqueline, her husband, Elizabeth and Clive, Thorley had invited some of his parents' friends, including the doctor and his family. When Daniel had first heard the tragic news of Antony's death, he could hardly take it in. Always the best of friends with Antony, the news had come as a great shock to him. Antony was a great loss to the community as well as to himself. At first he had wished to reject the kind invitation to spend Yuletide at Pendavan but on an afterthought decided to accept, if only for young Thorley's sake, although he knew it wouldn't be the same without his dearest friends, for Esmeralda's presence would be missed also. Daniel when he had first seen Thorley and heard about the tragedy, was terribly shocked at the change in him. He couldn't believe that he was the same young man who had eagerly ventured forth into a new life, for he had aged considerably, and was more severe in his manner to everyone. He realised, too, that there was nothing anyone could do, least of all himself, as Thorley was suffering greatly from severe delayed shock, and one could only hope that something or someone, at some time, would help bring him out of it.

Daniel had seen something during the Yuletide celebrations that had given him much food for thought. The incident had occurred during the afternoon of the second day. It happened as Francesca descended the stairs after settling Roberta down for her afternoon rest. As she had reached the last few stairs she tripped, and losing her balance, fell to the bottom and lay there stunned and immobilised.

Thorley had been the first to reach her side, with Daniel following close behind. He had surprised the expression on the young man's face as he bent over Francesca. There had been a mixture of sympathy, concern, affection and, he was certain, love. Daniel was completely baffled, particularly so because he knew Thorley and Francesca were first cousins, and she a married woman, even though estranged. The doctor was distressed for if, as he thought, there was a deeper feeling between these two young people, then this could only present more problems for the new Master of Pendavan.

* * * * *

A badly sprained ankle and bruised leg was the result of the fall, and Francesca was indisposed for several days. Elizabeth took on the role of nurse and nursemaid at the same time, which surprised everyone, especially her own mother. She had always been somewhat shy and timid, holding back in most things, but in this Elizabeth availed herself in every way. She took charge of the invalid, ready to do her bidding at all times, and pampered her continually.

Roberta, already devoted to her new nursemaid, clung to Elizabeth and followed her around the place, showing her contentment in her baby gurgles.

So, whilst the other guests returned to their own homes, Francesca, Roberta and Elizabeth remained at Pendavan for a few more days.

* * * * *

Jacqueline, saying good-bye, hugged her daughter to her. She had already sensed that Elizabeth had fallen in love with Thorley, and knew that only distress and sorrow could lie ahead for her, as anyone could see that he had eyes only for Francesca. Jacqueline was choked with emotion, not only at the thought of Elizabeth being hurt, but the grief she was experiencing because of Antony's demise. It had come as a desperate shock to her, and her heart went out to Esmeralda, who was so many miles away across the world, and must be suffering in her anguish for the loss of her beloved husband.

Death was so final.

* * * * *

Caesar set off at a canter, moving at a steady pace. Lord Pendavan gave the horse his head, leaving him to gallop where he wanted.

The early morning air was quite fresh and exhilarating, with the sea breezes filling his nostrils. He had no intention of returning to Pendavan for some little while, as he needed to be alone, with time to think.

Much had happened within the last few days, and when he thought back on what had transpired, Thorley wondered if he had imagined it all.

Francesca's indisposition had improved but, because Roberta seemed so contented, and she herself had felt happier than she had done for some time, she decided, after the invitation had come forth from Thorley, to stay a few more days, providing Elizabeth could remain also.

The Master of Pendavan knew he was fast falling in love with Francesca, and closed his eyes to the most important facts. He was aware in his heart that the feeling of love was on his side only – although she seemed very much fonder of him – and realised the impossibilities of such a love. He was also sure that his cousin still held a deep feeling for her husband, and because of this resisted him. Had Francesca been informed of his treachery to her, or his death, then it was quite possible that she might have returned Thorley's love. He thought deeply about this, telling himself, that should they be able to marry they were cousins, so there could be no children of his seed, for fear of imbecility. But even he – who would have dearly loved a family would be willing to sacrifice that so that they could be together indefinitely.

So it was, that while it had appeared more hopeful, something happened that completely dashed his new hopes to the ground. It was the day before Francesca was to return home to The Grange – she had decided this herself that Thorley had a visitor.

* * * * *

The housekeeper closed the door quietly behind her. She stood momentarily, her face set in earnest. She could hardly believe that the man waiting to see her Master, was Captain Frisby, Francesca's husband, for he had changed completely. Mrs Rushton couldn't help but wonder how the young wife would take this news. She had also changed somewhat of late, and seemed more resigned to her husband's neglect, so what would this mean to her now?

* * * * *

Lord Pendavan reined in his horse at the gates and leapt from the saddle. As the groom ran forward to take Caesar, Thorley hurried into the house, eager to set his eyes on Francesca again. This was the last day that he would have her to himself before she left Pendavan, and he wasn't looking forward to it at all. He had used himself to having her around, and he would miss the sound of laughter, also the patter of little feet.

Mrs Rushton moved forward halting Lord Pendavan in his tracks.

"There is a visitor in the drawing-room, Sir," she started, twisting her fingers nervously, and looking away from him.

"What is the matter Rushie? Are you worried about something?" he asked, showing his impatience.

"It is Captain Frisby, Sir, and he is asking for his wife."

Thorley paled visibly, the shock hitting him in the pit of the stomach. So this was the end of his dreams, with the future grim once more.

Thanking the housekeeper, he moved towards the drawing-room, momentarily hesitating outside the door. This was a reunion he couldn't look forward to.

Thorley threw the door open at a touch, startled at the drastic change that had taken place in Francesca's husband. He would never have recognised the debonair and irresponsible man, who had married his cousin – how long was it, two years ago? It seemed more like twenty-two to him.

They greeted each other with restraint, neither feeling at ease.

"I understand, Thorley, that Francesca is staying here at Pendavan. Can I see her?" he asked, appearing very agitated.

"This will be somewhat of a shock to her," Thorley told him, "so I had best break the news gently before she sees you." He crossed to the bell pull and rang for the housekeeper, to arrange for refreshments to be brought to Captain Frisby, whilst he made haste to speak to his cousin.

The sight that met his eyes was pleasant indeed, and one to store in his memory with many others.

Francesca was reclining on the settle, whilst Roberta played at her feet. The whole scene displayed one of contentment to Thorley who looked lovingly, and at the same time, dejectedly at them.

"Francesca my dear," Thorley began, as he approached her, "I have a surprise for you." And as she looked enquiringly at him, he finished, "Your husband has returned and wishes to see you. He awaits your appearance in the drawing-room."

When Francesca heard this she was completely startled, and as she rose from the settle her hand pressed her breast to stay its heaving. She looked disbelievingly at Thorley, questioning him with her eyes.

"It is true Francee," he told her, using his nickname for her. 'If only it wasn't,' he thought to himself. 'Would that things could have stayed as they were,' his heart cried out in anguish.

Hiding his feelings as well as he could he said, "You must be prepared when you see your husband, for he is a changed man."

Francesca bent low to gather Roberta into her arms, and as she left the room, Thorley accompanied her across the hall to the drawing-room, where closing the door behind her, he discreetly left them alone. He had seen the look of incredulity on the face of Captain Frisby, as Francesca entered with their daughter. Thorley wished with all his heart that he could have changed places with him.

* * * * *

Chapter Ten

Sudden Clarification

Two years had passed since Francesca had been reunited with her husband.

Lord Pendavan had suffered intermittent bouts of emotional jealousy, that tugged at his heart. He became more and more depressed as the weeks and months sped by. Winter turned into spring, with buds bursting into flower, and the summer following closely on its heels, then autumn crept in, but he wasn't even aware of the changing seasons.

Thorley would never forget the day that Captain Frisby arrived at Pendavan and Francesca's joy and excitement at his return. When she had sought him out after their meeting, and explained her husband's reaction at the sight of their daughter, her eyes spoke volumes, and her face was filled with an expression of love.

Thorley couldn't bear to watch her feelings of devotion for Captain Frisby. "Why did he have to come back and spoil everything?" How many times had he spoken these words out loud, to the trees, the sea and the sky? The feeling of hopelessness had crept over him stealthily, and the future looked very black indeed. There was one consolation however, and that was the change in her husband's character, which had improved considerably, giving Francesca the happiness she so badly needed.

Captain Frisby had explained how, when he first returned to sea, he had little thought for his wife, and how she would feel at their first parting. He had regretted their marriage, only wanting to be free, but it had taken a dangerous event at sea to bring home to him how lucky he was to have such a beautiful and loving wife. His life had been in danger through injuries received when his ship had been lost at sea, with most of his hands drowned in tropical waters. He lay for months, almost dead and in a stupor, delirious most of the time, and oblivious of where he was, or who he was. He recalled that the heat had been unbearable as he had thrashed around in his delirium. Eventually, after what seemed an interminable time, he came back to life and reality, slowly recovering to take stock once more.

The journey to England had taken many more months at sea, with the usual trials and tribulations, but his main objective was to see Francesca, so this drove all other worries from his mind. He had eventually reached London to find she had returned home to her parents. So it was then, that he had travelled post-haste to Pendavan to be reunited with her, and to find he had a daughter. Their life began all over again.

* * * * *

Jacqueline and her husband had been most concerned for their daughter Elizabeth for some time. She had, if anything, become more withdrawn within herself since her last visit to Pendavan.

The love she felt for Thorley had never diminished. It had grown in her breast. They had tried to interest her in other suitors, who were many, but she only treated these young men with extreme politeness - being the well-mannered young woman that she was. She had no inclination to begin a friendship with any man, and explained this most vehemently to her parents.

Jacqueline had news occasionally of Thorley and Esmeralda, who were never far from her thoughts. The last time she had heard, it was news of Esmeralda returning to England, so she was anxiously waiting to hear of her safe return.

So it was, that around this time, that Thorley, after being somewhat of a recluse for the past two years, invited them all to visit Pendavan for a reunion.

* * * * *

Esmeralda drank in the sweet smelling air and sea breezes that had always been part of her life. It was this she had missed these past three years. She couldn't help recall the excitement she had felt when they, as a family, had commenced their long journey away, many hundreds of miles across the other side of the world. It had certainly been a happy start to a new venture and they all had welcomed it with open arms. They couldn't see into the future, the tragedies and sorrows that were to befall them. When fate had struck, and robbed her of her dearest love, she hadn't wanted to live without Antony, for nothing seemed worthwhile any more.

It was when Thorley returned to England to take up his rightful place as heir to Pendavan that she came out of her lethargic reverie, to realise how many other people, apart from herself, needed help. So with this in mind, Esmeralda offered her services, and joined Doctor Andre at the hospital. She worked, almost until she dropped from sheer exhaustion, with dear Corrina by her side. Everything that could be done was done. It gave her little time to think, which was good medicine in itself. Days ran into weeks, and weeks into months.

Another death followed closely on the heels of all the others but, whereas those left sorrowful mourners, this one released two people, giving them the happiness they so rightly deserved. Doctor Andre's wife had died in her sleep, allowing the two lovers to look forward hopefully to the future.

Esmeralda wanted nothing better than her favourite daughter's happiness and now that she had a secure future ahead of her, it was time to withdraw gracefully. So Esmeralda made the necessary arrangements to return to England and her beloved Pendavan. News was sent on ahead to warn them of her impending arrival.

She couldn't wait to see Thorley, and dear Rushie as well as Francesca, of course, again, for she had missed them constantly.

* * * * *

The nearer the coach came to Pendavan the more apprehensive Elizabeth became. That she looked forward to seeing Thorley she couldn't deny, but she couldn't stay the feeling of nausea that gripped her stomach.

"You are pale Elizabeth," Jacqueline told her daughter. "Are you feeling unwell dear?" she asked, realising as she spoke that Elizabeth was troubled, not with sickness, but with love. She, and none better, knew only too well what her daughter had suffered these past two years, loving someone who could not return the same feeling. Had she not experienced the same anguish, loving dear departed Antony? Although she was now dearly fond of her husband, and extremely happy, her thoughts often reverted to her first love.

Jacqueline glanced at her daughter again with affection. She was good to look at, and would make some man a perfect wife. Would that Thorley could have loved her, she mused, things then could have been simplified. She would have fitted in at Pendavan, Jacqueline had no doubt of that.

Elizabeth sat forward in her seat as the tired horses were reined in before the same imposing gates that led to the drive, and would bring them once more before the majestic house.

Jacqueline was reminded of the time many years before, when she had travelled post-haste from London, to help nurse Esmeralda during her illness. She would never forget the day that Esme fully recovered her memory and knew she was to marry Antony. The joy that appeared on both their faces was something to remember, but today, after a long parting, she was to see her greatest friend in the role of a widow, instead of a blushing bride-to-be. Jacqueline sighed, very much aware that their reunion would be a sad one indeed, for all concerned.

* * * * *

"Good-night Elizabeth," Thorley called to her as she ascended the stairs. "Sleep well. Oh! and welcome again to Pendavan."

He watched her disappear into the corridor at the head of the staircase, his thoughts centring around her. He had forgotten that Elizabeth was such a beautiful girl, for he had never really noticed her with Francesca around. He had been much happier of late, since dear Mama had returned to Pendavan. It was a memorable time for him the day she arrived. He had hugged her to him, loath to let her go. They were both choked with emotion at their reunion, and vowed never to be parted again. They spent their days riding around the estates and countryside with a feeling of peace. Jacqueline's visit with Elizabeth completed Esmeralda's happiness. The two friends had much to discuss after their tearful meeting, so wandered away to their once favourite haunts, leaving Elizabeth with Thorley for company.

Her hair could be likened to a lion's mane in colour, dressed high on the crown, with masses of thick ringlets hanging down her back. Her classic features were enhanced by the deepest of blue eyes that lifted at the corners, whilst her mouth, generous in size, had a sad look. Of average height, she dressed exquisitely, making an effective picture.

To Thorley, she appeared very restrained in her manner – caused without his knowing by embarrassment.

* * * * *

Elizabeth couldn't sleep, for she was far too excited. She had tossed and turned for hours, seeing the dawn appear on the horizon. The reason for her sleepless night was the expression she had caught on Thorley's face, when he had looked at her. It was as though he had seen her for the first time, and liked what he saw. She had lost her heart to him completely, and loved him so desperately, and now, as she lay there, she tried to imagine how she would feel grasped in his arms, and to be told that he loved her too. She longed for his kisses which she knew could awaken a consuming fire within her. Surely he must know how she felt about him, she couldn't hide it from him any longer, and asked herself if she should make the first move.

Whilst her thoughts were full of him, sleep came to her at last, and she knew no more.

Just a short distance away from where Elizabeth lay asleep, Thorley in his bedroom stood by the window looking out on to the peaceful scene below him. He too was unable to sleep, with jumbled thoughts flitting through his head. He had suddenly realised what a lonely existence he had led since Francesca had been reinstated with her husband. He knew within himself that it wasn't normal to be like this, but he couldn't help it, for he deliberately set out to deter anyone who made any advances towards him. It was time now to change his attitude and make something of his life, he told himself. It was seeing Elizabeth again after such a long time that brought home to him what he was missing. He decided, there and then, that on the morrow he would take her riding, and the thought of this set his pulses racing. He would sleep now, he knew, and as he relaxed upon his bed and closed his eyes, his last thoughts were of Elizabeth, and their future.

* * * * *

Elizabeth rode the horse at a terrific pace. She had left Thorley far behind on Caesar, who was quite content to canter, although he would only need the slightest flick on his flanks for him to catch Tristan.

A week had passed since Elizabeth came to Pendavan accompanied by her mother. With the weather fine and bracing, most days would find them riding together, or climbing the rocks below the mansion. Thorley hadn't been so happy for a very long time so, because of this, the days passed far too quickly.

Elizabeth entered into everything with much zest, enjoying every minute, bringing about a considerable change in the young Master, which was good to see. He could laugh now, and did so quite openly.

Jacqueline had decided to return home, but was quite happy to leave Elizabeth at Pendavan with Esmeralda as her chaperon. The colour had returned to her cheeks, and with the continual outdoor enjoyment, Elizabeth looked a picture of health. It would be a wrench for her to leave Pendavan now, and she dreaded to think of her departure. Thorley had been a wonderful companion and her love had increased even more.

Thorley himself looked forward to each new day. He couldn't imagine what it would be like without Elizabeth, who had grown on him to such an extent that he dreaded the time when she would have to leave. He recalled the night before, when she had descended the stairs dressed for dinner and looking like a queen. As he had moved forward to escort her to the dining-room, he suddenly realised how much she had come to mean to him, and how much she fitted into his way of life. She certainly seemed very much at home in his surroundings.

He was at that moment thinking about it and, wanting to be near her, urged Caesar on. He could hardly contain his excitement as he breathed the rushing air. It was good to be alive. Caesar, feeling the urgency of his master, galloped at such a speed that Thorley was almost unseated. He could see Elizabeth ahead, tawny hair flying in the breeze, sitting Tristan as though she had been born in the saddle.

He came abreast with Elizabeth just as Tristan pulled to a halt with a suddenness that threw her to the ground, where she lay still.

Thorley leapt from his horse and dropped to his knees beside her, and seeing her lying there so pale and still, he realised that he loved her. He hadn't expected to feel this way ever again, but he knew now that what he felt for Elizabeth was a deep lasting love, and not the hot passion he had experienced for Crystal, or the infatuation he had felt for Francesca.

"Elizabeth," he called her name frantically. "Elizabeth darling, speak to me," he cried.

Her eyelids fluttered, and she opened her eyes. She must have fainted when she fell, for her sight was hazy, but the mistiness suddenly cleared as she beheld the handsome face looking anxiously down at her. She struggled to sit up, feeling at a disadvantage lying there.

"Elizabeth my darling, I was so frightened, for I feared you were hurt," Thorley said, as he helped her to her feet.

Elizabeth tried to brush herself down, and pat her hair into some order. She could have sworn she heard Thorley use an endearment that could only mean one thing, that he returned her love. As she glanced at him, Thorley pulled her against his chest and, encircling her within his arms, rained kisses upon her responsive mouth. Elizabeth, starved for his love, returned his kisses with a passion that had been awakened within her. Time stood still, as she realised her dream had come true.

* * * * *

Lord Pendavan stood at the window looking out on to the scene before him, as his father Lord Antony had done many years before.

Elizabeth sat with their young son amongst the profusion of colour, her body heavy with child.

They had been married three years, and their happiness was at last complete.

* * * * *

PART THREE

Rightful Heritage

Chapter One

The French Smuggler

'When times could be difficult in Cornwall.
By 'smuggling' they tried to get by.
Free traders versus the revenue, was the cause for which many died.
In sandy coves by moonlight, shadowy figures toiled.
Fear in their hearts that their dealings would be unexpectedly foiled.
When the winds blew fierce on the hillsides, the tub-men were walking the moors, making haste for the miner's burrows, where the "blessings" could be safely stored.
And, so we'll end the story, of these times in many a town.
When men said "God Bless the Runner", and "Beware the 'Men' of the Crown".'

Rudyard Kipling.

By a strange quirk of fate, the destiny of the Pendavan family is to be reshaped.

With ceaseless rapidity, lightning flashed across the sky, followed in quick succession by thunder that rolled and crashed about the hillside, causing the low menacing clouds to burst their sides, and send torrential rain streaming down in a deluge. Swirling white foam rushed in over the treacherous rocks, and the foundations shook beneath the cliffs, as once again the thunder crashed even more violently than before.

Not a night to be caught out of doors unaware, that was certain, when the lure of a room full of warmth from a blazing log fire would be more acceptable to the average person.

The intermittent flashes made visible the group of men huddled together at the cliff face, battling against ferocious winds and blinding rain.

"There it is," one of them shouted, "coming straight towards us."

"She'll never make it," stated another emphatically. "She is too near the rocks."

News travelled fast amongst the smuggling fraternity, passed from one to the other. The French brig *Navire de Long Cours* was expected this night in the year 1811, filled with a cargo that would delight many a smuggler, as well as any wrecker.

The brigantine tossed and heaved about on the storm-ridden waters, almost heeling over on to her side as the heavy waves lashed the deck with a terrible force. With the expertise of the small crew, she could have reached safety through the perilous rocks, had the sea been tranquil, instead of which, unable to ride the storm, she was lifted out of the water by hurricane gusts of gale force winds, tossed on to huge jagged rocks, and disintegrated, with her back quite broken. The crew were thrown unceremoniously into freezing churned up seas, whilst the cove and innermost rocks became littered with remnants of the brig, and her cargo.

The watchers, immobilised momentarily, came to life suddenly one and all to dash to the aid of the drowning men, the booty forgotten in the urgency to save lives. Although the darkness as well as the storm hampered the rescue considerably, after a seemingly endless time it became obvious to the would be rescuers that all the crew had perished, apart from one man who was already unconscious, and was thought, badly injured. After another unsuccessful attempt to find the rest of the crew, the search was abandoned for the more pressing state of affairs confronting the Cornishmen, that of hiding the French smuggler, and whatever cargo could be retrieved. Most urgent, of course, was to procure some form of medical attention for the sick man, which was easier said than done, for a word uttered in the wrong ear could bring the 'Preventive' men on their trail. Already, it was imperative they hide any evidence of the brig's wreckage which could be sighted from the headland. Fortunately, the pounding seas would destroy most of it by morning, and any fragments remaining would have to be buried by the smugglers to remove any signs of what had occurred.

The men worked with feverish urgency to collect whatever contraband they could find intact. They had decided to carry it to safety in a cave, where collection would cautiously take place on another night.

The cave, situated on the rocky shore, opened upon the sea. It was twelve feet high and wide, of irregular shape, and extended back into the rock formation some thirty feet. It had evidently been excavated by the ceaseless action of the waves upon portions of rocks somewhat softer than their surroundings. At high tide, part of the cave would be under water, but at low tide it could be entered dry shod. The back of the cavern emerged into a deep tunnel, hollowed out to lead under the cliffs. At the far end, in a high position, a cleverly hidden lever opened an entrance in the wall, to reveal a shorter tunnel that rose to a sharp incline, which in turn led to a long and very steep flight of rough hewn well worn steps, at the head of which, on the facing wall, another lever, hardly discernible to the naked eye, opened a secret panel into a bedroom at Pendavan. An ideal hiding place for the Frenchman.

This exit from the shore to the huge old mansion had, no doubt, been the ingenious work of earlier generations.

The journey through the tunnel and the ascent of the steps, which seemed endless as they carried their burden, was arduous for both Ruan and Michael Pendavan, but eventually the unconscious man was lifted through the panel and laid gently on to the broad bed that, with its faded drapes, dominated the room. It had at one time been a beautiful room, but as the years passed, its beauty disappeared gradually, from neglect. Little used, and hardly spoken of, it remained unused until the boys discovered the hidden compartment, and that which lay behind it. As they grew with the years, this became their very own secret room, where they could plan exciting adventures, just as in times gone by, their forefathers plotted and schemed on a much larger scale.

* * * * *

Lady Pendavan had retired for the night, and it would appear that it was to be a sleepless one. She had always hated storms, and this one was quite ferocious in its intensity.

She let her thoughts wander back into the past, to all that had occurred.

Her seduction, and eventual abduction from Pendavan, by Adrian; her illness and memory loss before her marriage to Antony; her love for him; the arrival of Adrian's son Thorley, and the tragic loss of her first born child, Jason; the journey to America, and the devastating hurricane that caused Antony's death, and her near fatal illness caused by the shock of losing him. There was her inevitable return to

Pendavan, Thorley as heir to the estate, and his marriage to Elizabeth. The birth of their two sons, Ruan and Michael. There was, too Elizabeth's death during the stillborn birth of a baby daughter, leaving him a broken man who lost interest in everything, including his sons who, when he moved away to London, were left to their own devices. As the years passed Thorley's health deteriorated quite rapidly, and his visits to Pendavan became less frequent. At their young age, the boys had rebounded with great resilience after the death of their mother. Having someone to shower them with love and affection was all they needed. But when their father left Pendavan, although only temporarily, the gravity of the situation had quite the opposite effect. Their ready tears burst forth on that day, and gradually their whole personalities changed completely. They became both difficult, and very secretive. So it had been necessary to humour them during the past ten years, and accord them plenty of understanding as they approached manhood.

She had known for quite some while now of their close involvement with the smuggling fraternity, so showed little surprise when Ruan appeared before her at so late an hour, and in such a shocking and dishevelled state. Having seen both boys in the same situation so many times, she was used to it.

"I am sorry to disturb you grandmother," he began, hesitating momentarily, not knowing how to begin explaining the presence of the injured man in the secret room, but the urgency of the situation drove him on. "There has been a terrible disaster down at the cove. The French brig *Navire de Long Cours* which we were waiting for has been wrecked, and all but one of the crew have drowned. We tried to save them," he added, "but our effort was of no avail."

Lady Pendavan looked long and searchingly at her favourite grandson, dreading to ask that which was foremost in her mind. God forbid that it were true, but she had to know.

"Was the wreck planned Ruan?" she asked. "Were you waiting with those terrible people, the 'Wreckers'?"

The young man's face already pale with weariness, went ashen as he replied.

"Oh! no! grandmother, Michael and I could never do anything so dreadful, I can promise you that. We would not have saved the Frenchman had we been one of them," he went on to explain. "He is here in the secret room, and will need your help. Can you come right away?" There, he had told her.

Lady Pendavan reached for a warm shawl to cover her elegant night coat, her relief unmistakable. She thought quickly. Rushie, who was the soul of discretion, would have to help. Housekeeper at Pendavan for many years, Mrs Rushton had never failed the family in any crisis, and there had been many.

Having sent Ruan post-haste to awaken her, and assist with plenty of hot water, towels and white sheets to tear into strips for bandages, reluctantly she made her way to the room that had nothing but distressing memories for her.

That she dreaded her mission, was plain to see. She had no idea what she was to find, but on entering the pressing need for secrecy drove all other thoughts from her mind. She spared a quick glance around her, but it was the man laid out on the bed who drew her full attention, and compassion. That he was in a bad way was obvious. The little of his face that could be seen behind the full beard and matted blood was deathly pale, and he lay as one dead. There was little or nothing she could do single handed, so while she waited she took stock of him. Ruan had already loosened the clothing at his neck and chest, and removed his thigh length black leather boots now lying discarded on the floor. His clothing, at first glance, looked the usual type worn by most smugglers as she had imagined, but on closer inspection Lady Pendavan noticed the material was of finer quality, worn mainly by the rich. This surprised her, and she sensed a mystery, but her train of thought was broken with the arrival of Rushie, armed with masses of towels and rough pieces of sheeting, with Ruan following in her wake carrying two very large pots of steaming water, and looking as though he would fall asleep at any moment.

As always, the housekeeper took command. Her charge now retired for whatever was left of the night, along with Michael, who must already be asleep, she set about removing the wet and torn bloodstained clothing. This was no easy task with the dead weight of the patient, but even so his outer jacket and loose fitting breeches came off fairly easy, and as Rushie dropped these to the floor, she was aware, albeit subconsciously, of something heavy amongst them.

Suddenly, as the last of his garments were removed, the silence was broken with a sharp anguished cry from Esmeralda, as she leapt back from the bed, her hands pressed to her breast to stay its fluttering, her eyes staring, and face ashen.

"Rushie," she whispered. "The mark – it can't be – surely it can't be – Jason, he is dead!" She stared fixedly at the unusual, and irregular star-shaped birthmark, lying at the base of the Frenchman's left rib cage. Her eyes were bright with unshed tears.

"It is your son, my lady, back from the grave!" The housekeeper spoke with conviction. She should know. Hadn't she seen the birthmark almost daily during the boy's very short existence? It was Jason all right. She would bet her own life that no two men could possibly have the same distinguishing mark. It was a miracle, that was certain, and she was as shocked as her mistress, but more pressing at the moment, was treatment for him.

With all the love she could muster, Rushie washed the patient. She cleansed and dressed his wounds which, with the blood removed, convinced both women that they were not quite so serious as first envisaged. He had a nasty gash at the right side of his forehead, reaching below the eyebrow to the cheekbone. It still bled freely, but Rushie made a good job of padding, and bandaging the whole head. This way, the flow of blood could be stemmed. Nasty bruises were most prevalent on his arms, back and legs, but these contusions would heal without treatment, and gave less cause for concern. His unconscious state was the greater worry, especially as they both knew it would be unwise to bring anyone in from the outside to treat him; but a good night's rest, in a warm bed, with night clothes taken from Thorley's wardrobe and nourishment as soon as he could take it, should, hopefully put him on the road to recovery. That it would take time, they both knew.

Esmeralda stood at the bedside, looking down at her son. It was Jason, she now had no doubt. Her motherly instincts were uppermost. In repose, he looked so vulnerable, and her heart went out to him. With his beard, there was no visible likeness to Antony, or to herself. This she felt was a godsend, for his identity must be kept secret at all costs. She had decided on this as soon as she realised the truth. She recalled the terrible anguish she had suffered, along with Antony, who had continually grieved for his first born. He couldn't accept Jason's death, and never really recovered from the loss. It had been easier for herself, with the other children to mother, and Thorley, of course. He had filled a terrible void, taking the place of their dead son, and for this she could in no way cause him any more hurt, especially after what he had already been through. She just couldn't denounce his title, not at the moment anyway. So, secrecy was imperative.

She stooped to retrieve the pile of clothing, and as she did so, another shock presented itself. A beautifully marked leather draw-string bag, its perimeter about a foot in size, was full of magnificent jewels of tremendous value, she knew. There were necklaces, some of clear diamonds, whilst others had varied coloured stones, and bracelets of all styles and shapes, superb in their beauty, with glamorous ear-rings to match, and sparkling clustered rings, many priceless antique gems amongst them, that the aristocracy or even Royalty might wear.

This discovery startled Esmeralda, and panic seized her. She felt very afraid for Jason, and shivered with apprehension. She was aware that smuggling was his livelihood, and suspected the jewels were stolen property, for certain, from a very rich, and most probably well known aristocratic family.

A gasp from behind her brought Esmeralda around to face the housekeeper, who had just returned to the room with an extra cover for the patient, and noticing the leather bag, and its contents, remembered the heaviness of Jason's outer garments. A knowing look passed between the two women as they realised what the outcome of this could mean to them all. Although by now Esmeralda knew what must be done.

"Rushie," she said, "we have much to discuss dear, but not in here. Our patient is still comatose, and I am sure he will not regain consciousness yet for a while, so, we shall go to the library. Take everything of Jason's out of this room," she went on, "and bring it with you."

As Esmeralda entered the largest and most beautiful room in the mansion, she shivered. The temperature had dropped considerably, now that the night was part over, even though a log fire had burnt in the grate all day. The library had always been Antony's favourite room, and since his death a cheerful fire was always in evidence, whatever the weather. This is where she felt closest to him, closeted with his books, and although he was no longer with her, his presence still dominated the room.

Dear faithful Rushie was already busy trying to re-kindle the residue of faintly glowing embers in the hearth. She was successful, and soon the fire burned merrily.

Taking up the whole wall the main attraction in the room was a splendid bookcase. It reached from floor to ceiling, and was filled with beautifully bound volumes, many of which were relics of former times, and could never be replaced. Antony had always been proud of the collection, and spent hours browsing through them.

It was on a day just after their marriage, Lady Pendavan recalled, that she came upon her late husband's hiding place. It came as a surprise to her, to know of the hollow cavity positioned ingeniously behind a set of well worn books that, out of reach at the top, would never receive a second glance. She had decided there and then that she would not intrude on Antony's privacy, and felt he was entitled to keep his family secret without her curiosity causing him distress. It was only after his death that she became aware of the contents of the cavity which intrigued her, and had done so to this very moment as she stood before the object of her thoughts, and made her decision. Here she would hide the jewels, safe from prying eyes. They would take their place beside Antony's secret hoard, which included a diary written with great precision. It recorded daily events in his great grandfather's early life, and the contents explained fully that his ancestor had been a very successful highwayman until he reached the age of thirty and nine years when, to save himself from the gallows, he sought shelter in France, for a few years, until the hue and cry had died down, after which he eventually returned to his family at Pendavan, his former hair-raising escapades put behind him, once and for all.

Other objects comprised of a three-cornered cocked hat, along with an eye mask, and a musket, with a supply of gunpowder. There was a noticeable absence of valuables which, according to the diary, had once been plentiful. No doubt these had been exchanged gradually, for money.

Apart from herself, and Rushie, no one else knew of the cavity. Even Thorley had no knowledge of it, and it must remain thus. She had her family secret to preserve now. She had no intention of allowing Jason to go to prison, or worse still, be put to death by the French authorities. Either way, his life would be ended, as he would never survive the French dungeons. She had heard tell of these God forsaken places where poor wretches, both male and female were spirited away from their loved ones, their only crime – in most cases – not to be wanted. The apertures, where they would spend the rest of their days, were so cramped, damp and dismal, with only rats and mice for company, that many of them pined away after only months of captivity, their backs bent permanently with no room to stand. The vile 'Bastille' had been an horrific prison, where victims never saw the light of day again. Their hair and beards would grow and become matted. The sordid squalor and grief would bring about their early death, if the plague hadn't attacked them first.

Lady Pendavan shivered, worse than before. Her thoughts made her more determined than ever to do what she had to. She slid the portable steps, inserted in two uprights of wood to ascend the high bookcase, in position and commenced climbing, calling to Rushie as she did so to bring the leather bag. In a matter of minutes the jewels were safely concealed, and the steps replaced to the opposite end of the case.

A sigh of relief escaped her lips as she moved towards the fire. She sat down on a low settle, inviting the housekeeper to do the same. The room was warmer now, and a little colour had returned to her cheeks. That she had suffered a severe shock was obvious, but she refused the offer of some refreshments, concerned only for the urgency to speak of her fear for Jason.

"Rushie," she began, toying with the ribbon at her throat. "It is imperative that we keep silent about the jewels. No one must know of their existence, not even Thorley, or the boys, and definitely not Jason. If he should ask, and he will," she went on, "he must believe they were lost in the storm. It is after all for his own good, and silence could save his life." She looked into the fire as she continued. "You realise, of course, that they must be stolen heirlooms, and you do not need me to tell you what this could mean if they come to light. It is our secret, Rushie. Yours and mine, at least, until Jason may possibly become heir to Pendavan, but Rushie, he must not know his true identity, not while Thorley is still alive."

"You can rely on me my lady, you have my word." The housekeeper spoke with feeling. She would rather die than break a confidence, especially where her beloved mistress was concerned. Her lips were sealed. She gathered together the discarded clothing which would have to be destroyed, and left the room, Esmeralda following in her wake, to make her way once more back to the secret room to watch over their patient.

* * * * *

Chapter Two

The Blackmailing Count

The silence in the room was broken only by the flick of the cards. No one spoke. In the distance a clock struck on the hour which, in the quiet of the night, sounded like a death knell.

The faces of the men sitting around the table in the dimly lit room were set in grim lines, for the game, involving very high stakes, had reached its climax, and the youngest member of the group, Dario de Laffiette, paled as the distinguished looking Frenchman, sitting opposite him, placed his last card face upwards on the table.

Count Jean-Philippe Maille, a very rich man, was the winner and, as he spoke, his face took on a sinister look.

"Well, de Laffiette, you have increased your already very large debt to me by another twenty thousand francs." He glanced at the small black leather book now held in his hand, and slowly, with great deliberation, flicked over the pages, his long white tapering fingers hesitating momentarily as he found what he was looking for. Waving the book in the young man's face he said, "You are now my debtor to the tune of fifty thousand francs, and you certainly don't need me to tell you what will happen if you fail to return it," he added.

Dario hesitated before he answered then, after a long pause he asked, "How much time will you allow me Monsieur?"

"No time at all!" the Count replied, as he left the table.

The other players had already retired from the gambling room when the men commenced their conversation. They were fully aware of the Count's blackmailing tactics, and sensing hostility between the two, preferred not to get involved.

"Why did you play for such high stakes tonight, De Laffiette? I told you I would win," the Count remarked boastfully, his eyes narrowing to slits, as his mouth took on a sardonic leer. "I have already allowed you one month to repay your first debt, and that was longer than I had intended." He took out a diamond snuff box, and inhaling fastidiously, savoured his victim's discomfort.

Immaculate in appearance, with almost the look of a dandy, the Count, extremely tall – head and shoulders above his victim in fact – sauntered across the room with the air of a victor. Slim of stature, he was lean, almost to emaciation. His eyes, dominating his features, were deepest black, and piercing, the left one emphasised by a monocle. A hooked nose and tight-lipped mouth, completed the face of an evil looking man.

"I shall need more time, especially now," Dario told the Count. "I have tried really hard to raise the money, and failed, so there is nothing left for me. I played the way I did tonight, as I felt lucky, and was sure I could win," he explained. "My family are disgraced and, because of this, I should put a gun to my head." His despair was plain to see.

Again, the Count's eyes narrowed to slits. This wouldn't do at all. He could see his victim slipping through his fingers. The poor weak fool meant what he said. 'He will be no use to me dead' he told himself.

"I have a plan," the Count began. "It could save your life, and I shall get what I have wanted for a very long time. This way, we shall both be satisfied but, should you be the cause of my losing that which means more to me than anything else, then be it on your head," he finished.

Dario listened to the Count, brightening visibly. He couldn't begin to visualise what the man had planned for him, but whatever it was, couldn't be worse than his probable premature death. He was desperate now. Jean-Paul had been his last hope, and he was dead. He had lost a good friend, and the last chance to raise such a large sum of money, in so little time. Had it not been for his crazy gambling, Jean-Paul would still be alive, and he wouldn't be in this evil man's clutches. It was what he had done to Semire that grieved him so much. She had lost the man she loved, and had very little interest in anything. And, as well, there was the matter of the jewels. The family heirlooms. Even those were lost for ever, and their mother could not be informed of the loss. He came to with a start, to hear the Count speaking of his scheme.

"I intend to marry your sister," he stipulated in clipped tones. "I shall need an introduction, of course, this is where you come in De Laffiette. She will need persuasion, and must not refuse. I shall not take no for an answer, you understand? For your own sake," he added.

Dario was completely startled at the Count's audacious and daring proposition. He knew without asking Semire what her reaction and answer would be. Even for his benefit he couldn't, under any circumstances, allow her to make this sacrifice. It was unthinkable that she should marry such a wicked and evil man. They could stall him, and play for time, of course. Or perhaps there could be some other way, but for the life of him he was unable to think how, or what. It was unforgivable to have placed her in such a difficult position, and he was filled with remorse. He must speak to Semire this very night, however late the hour. At least, she would listen to him, and perhaps between them they could reach a solution. He must leave at once. The Count had already donned a long vermilion lined black cloak which almost reached the floor, and as he pulled a large brimmed hat jauntily on to his head, and sauntered towards the door, he called back over his shoulder: "I can offer you a seat in my coach to your place of abode should you so wish young sir, but we must depart at once. After all," he added, sneeringly, "we must appear to be friendly, if I am to be your future brother-in-law."

Dario accepted the Count's unexpected offer of conveyance with a certain indecision. How could he ever be on good terms with such a man; but time was essential, so following in his wake he made his way to the coach standing in the shadows. Impatient to start, four fine black horses of the thoroughbred breed pulled the coach along the narrow cobbled street.

Once settled in the luxurious carriage, Dario thought seriously of what he could say to this most devious of men, to pacify him for the immediate future. He had no elusions as to the seriousness of the problem now facing both him and his sister, and realised that the Count would be adamant in his demands, and desirous of gaining his own ends with little delay.

"Have you nothing to say regarding my proposition?" asked the Count. His drawling voice breaking through Dario's thoughts. "I always get what I want you know!"

"I shall speak with my sister tonight. Does that satisfy you, Sir?" Dario spoke with feeling. "I think you are mad though! She doesn't even know you," he went on, "and for certain, will hate you," he added.

"I shall rectify that by calling on her on the morrow, and it worries me not what her feelings are," stated the Count, letting his young victim's outburst go over his head. "I have had your sister under constant surveillance for some time now, and shall not be satisfied until I possess her, as I do with all beautiful objects. I must say though," his voice droned on, "I did wonder how I could accomplish this, but the fact that you have played right into my hands, has made it much easier for me." He thought for the moment, looking intently at the young man sitting opposite him with a dour look on his face. "I shall, of course, give her everything that she can want. Surely, that should be reward enough for cancelling your debt!" he remarked sarcastically.

"You can put me down at this point if you will Monsieur," Dario said, ignoring completely the man's jibe. The coach had neared his destination.

The Count hit the roof of the coach with his silver knobbed cane. He gave two sharp taps, and as the driver drew the carriage to a halt, Dario stepped quickly out on to the Boulevard. His "Goodnight, and *rendre grâces* Monsieur," was lost in the sudden noise, as the horses pulled away at breakneck speed.

Houses in this residential area, outside Paris, were much of the same style. Thick white pillars surrounded the porches, and black wrought iron railings guarded the dwellings. The entrance doors were heavy, but attractive, with intricate wood patterns.

Dario entered his mother's house, discarding his outer jacket as he hurriedly mounted the splendid curved staircase, encased by an unusual, but richly designed banister.

He wasn't a tall man, so to others he appeared quite stocky, although very light on his feet. His special skill in fencing gave him much agility. He was quick, and very active, so his build was deceiving. Dark hair, and fair skin, with twinkling eyes, gave a striking and vivid representation of a very likeable young man.

* * * * *

The intermittent taps soft, but insistent at the door of Semire de Laffiette's bed chamber, eventually wakened her from sleep, to realise the urgency of the sounds disturbing the silence in the house. It must be the early hours she thought as, reaching for her negligee, she moved quickly towards the door, showing great surprise on opening it to admit her brother.

"What is wrong *mon frère*?" she asked. "Has something untoward happened? You look so terrible!"

"Forgive my disturbing you at so late an hour *ma soeur*," he said. "I have depressing news which can only afflict more mental pain upon you." He threw himself down on to a low canapé, its back just high enough to rest his head, and momentarily closed his eyes. He felt exhausted, and sad now that he had to relate something even worse, which she could never have envisaged. He hesitated even to think about it, but it had to be done.

Looking at Semire, he was of one mind with the Count, on this, at least. She certainly was a very beautiful woman. There was no doubt about that. Her dark hair, usually worn high, hung low, almost to the waist, its shining glory due to painstaking brush strokes. She was slim of build, and half a head taller than her brother. Chiselled features, with high cheekbones, and a very straight nose, gave her the outstanding beauty for which she was famed. Winged eyebrows, and long curling eyelashes shadowed eyes of deepest blue which, at times of distress, could change almost to violet. Her mouth, full, soft and sensitive, was at the moment showing signs of stress and strain which, in itself, wasn't surprising, after hearing the devastating news of Jean-Paul's death. When Dario had relayed the sad news to her, she collapsed with grief, and had since suffered severely. The sorrow had gone deep and now, because of him, it would go even deeper.

"Semire" he began. "I know not how to tell you this, but I must. Believe me, it grieves me greatly to bring more sorrow upon you, and through my selfishness, this I have done." He hung his head, too ashamed to look at his sister. If in any way he could have spared her, he would have done so, but, as it was, he couldn't even take his own life, as he had at first planned, because she would still be in the Count's power, and have to face him alone.

He couldn't do that to her. He must remain by her side, whatever the outcome.

"Forgive me ma soeur. I have this night increased my debt to Count Jean-Philippe Maille, by an additional twenty thousand francs. I asked to take part in the game, hoping I could successfully obtain the money through a winning hand. It was hopeless, of course," he continued. "How could I expect to overcome such an accomplished player as the Count, with his known expertise at cards? Now I have disgraced you further, and embroiled you in hostility, even danger. And that isn't all," he went on. "He will release me from the debt, if you consent to be his wife."

Dario paced to and fro, sliding his fingers through his hair in an agitated manner. "I cannot let you agree to this preposterous suggestion Semire, even for me," he told her. "We must think of something, and quickly. He is calling on you in a few hours, for your answer and, according to the way he spoke to me earlier, he will expect it to be yes!" He groaned with dismay at the thought.

Semire de Laffiette, up to that moment, had uttered not a word. She was unable to do so. She was startled, to say the least, but absurd as the proposition might be, and surely was, it was Dario's future that was at stake, and however much she would loathe being married to a complete stranger, she could, at least, be a Countess in her own right, and obtain security for her family. Things had been far from easy since the death of her father, Louis de Laffiette, who was snatched with his friends, and taken to the guillotine. From that time on, their wealth had gradually diminished, and although their reputation was based on trust, with regard to creditors, there would come a time when the need would arise for the family to realise the money on their ancestral jewels. Now, with their loss, this was impossible. Her greatest concern had been to keep what had happened from their mother, Anne-Marie de Laffiette. The unseemly behaviour of her adored son would certainly cause distress, and the shock could kill her, should she know the real truth. Semire loved her brother too, they were very close, and even though he had brought probable disgrace into their home, she could not forsake him in his hour of need. No sacrifice, however great or small, would be too much for the love of her family. She knew where her loyalties lay.

Relating all this to Dario, who was completely astounded at her acceptance of the bizarre situation, she realised how impossible everything seemed, and with Jean-Paul gone from her forever, knew that her marriage to the devious Count would be the answer. As Dario had played into his hands, so now the position could be reversed. All that remained for the immediate present, was the meeting with her future husband.

* * * * *

Chapter Three

Missing Heirlooms

Jean-Paul came back from his unconscious state with some difficulty. He was still slightly comatose, although aware of his surroundings and identity.

At first, as he had struggled to open his eyes, he could not comprehend what he was doing here in this faded room, of an era long past. He could see winged creatures, with human faces. It was as though he had reached another world, with divine spirits of angelic qualities surrounding him. Certainly, the woman standing by the bed, and looking down at him could not be real. After minutes of indecision, as to her ethereal and heavenly beauty, it suddenly dawned on him that she was, without a doubt, very real, and the cherubs looking down from above, were the decoration on the ceiling. He hadn't drowned after all, he was very much alive.

His mind reverted to the trauma of the storm. He remembered the terrible fear that he had experienced as the crew fought to control the vessel. It had been quite obvious to them all that they would never reach safety, and his last recall was of the frantic struggle in the angry seas, with the force of the winds and the waves throwing him toward the massive rocks.

The Frenchman, easing himself with difficulty into a sitting position, became aware of his bandaged head, and making bewildering and worried gestures with his hands he asked, "*Qu'est que s'est passé*?"

"Do you understand English?" Lady Pendavan enquired of her patient. She found it hard to behave as though she had no idea whom he was. Her innermost self wanted to hug this vulnerable man to her breast, and greet him as her long-lost son, but being sensible, she knew she had to pretend he was a stranger.

"Yes I do, Madame," he answered, eager only to ascertain what had taken place, where he was, and in whose care he was. His body ached, and his limbs felt stiff and sore, bringing home to him with sudden clarity his sense of helplessness. This fact gave him cause for concern, as having glanced furtively around the room, he could not see any of his clothing. Lady Pendavan, noticing his obvious distress, felt the time had come to explain everything. She was well aware of what this would do to him, as what she had to impart to him he wouldn't want to hear.

"I know not what you remember," she began, "but during a terrible storm, the brigantine in which you were travelling was wrecked right here in the cove directly below this house. You have had a narrow escape from death. Your companions, however, were not so lucky. They all perished. My grandsons can tell you far more than I can," she continued, "as they helped to save your life. They brought you here in a somewhat irregular manner, which no doubt they will explain when they see you. But at least you are safe here, and we shall nurse you back to health."

Jean-Paul hesitated before he answered, his thoughts in great disorder. "I am, as you English say, very much in your debt Madame." He pointed at his head in a perplexed manner. "Unfortunately, I remember very little, so *naturellement* I shall be anxious to hear all, but for now I need to know how to address you, and your family. I can then tell you who I am."

"I am Lady Pendavan," she told him. "My grandsons are Ruan and Michael, and our housekeeper, who shares your nursing, is Mrs Rushton, although we call her Rushie, as I am sure you will be doing before you are well enough to leave us." She smiled as she said it, thinking how Rushie would wallow in it.

"Lady Pendavan, you may call me Jean-Paul," he stated. "I am known as Jean-Paul de Leon, and I live near to the outskirts of Paris." He looked away from her as he added, "I think it only right, and fair that you should know I am a *contrabandist* and have been such for some time. This is my mode of living, *vous comprenez*? I wasn't born to it. My lifestyle materialised because of very unusual circumstances, and through my adoptive father, who snatched me from the sea, just as your grandsons have at this time." He crossed himself as he raised his eyes upwards. "I was at the tender age of six years," he continued, "and it was no time at all, before I discovered accidentally, I may add – my *père's Claire-de-Lune*. His lands grew with the years, as did his involvement with smuggled spirits, as an illicit distiller. These operations brought to him considerable wealth, and with it a complete change of character. He became the meanest of men; stingy, malicious, and ill-tempered." His face shadowed with sadness as he spoke. "My *mère adoptée* died from his harsh treatment of her, and her inevitable death, my forced entanglement with the 'moonshining', and the continued worry for concealment, has made me secretly ashamed. So much so, I intend to break away eventually, and make a new life for myself," he went on. "You see! I cannot offer the woman I love my hand in marriage, unless I can prove myself worthy of her. But I talk too much! Here I am, as you call it, babbling on when you must have many other duties to perform. Forgive me Madame," he said. "I meant not to command all your attention."

"Not at all," Esmeralda said, wanting only to hear all about the way he lived, without him becoming too suspicious of her interest.

"It will do you good to talk of your experiences, and whatever you have related to me, will be in the strictest confidence, I can assure you."

She thought deeply of what he had divulged. She couldn't say why, but she had the feeling he hadn't unburdened himself to anyone before. He seemed so intense. It disturbed her greatly to have to lie about the jewels, but she had to do it and, she decided, right now.

"I know you are wondering where your belongings are," she began, quite dreading his reaction, "but they were in such a terrible state of disrepair, I had no alternative but to destroy them. Certainly, they would have been little use to you, sodden, badly bloodstained, and torn almost to shreds," she added. She thought for a moment, watching him closely, aware of his sudden emotions.

"Have no worry Jean-Paul," she said, playing for time. "There is an abundance of clothing apparel right here in the mansion, from which you may take your choice, as little or as much as you wish. They belong to my son," she told him, "who is much of the same build as yourself."

Her heart lurched as she spoke of Thorley. She did love him as her son. He had always been so from the very first day she had taken him into her fold. Would that she could have told him Jason was miraculously alive. He had loved him too. But Pendavan could not have two heirs. There would come a day, she knew, and in the foreseeable future, that she would be put into the impossible position of having to make a choice, but how could she possibly choose between those she loved equally? Circumstances could change without her having to do this, she thought, but she wasn't able to think how unless, of course, Thorley, who now had little to do with

Pendavan, were to relinquish the title of his own free will. Then the problem would be resolved.

"I comprehend you did what you had to do," Jean-Paul's voice broke through her thoughts. "But did you find a leather bag containing a few... baubles, and such like?" he asked, making an airy gesture, as though the contents of the bag had little interest for him. "It is no matter," he added, after a slight pause, and a shrug of the shoulders.

Her son's feigned flippancy, as to the priceless jewels being trifles of little worth, put Lady Pendavan into a complete state of perplexity. She wanted to inform him of their safety, but desisted as his making light of so serious a problem, only proved to her that what she had done was essential for his safety. Of one thing she was certain, he wanted no one to know of their existence. Now she had to answer the question she had dreaded.

"We salvaged nothing but your boots I am afraid, and even they are very badly battered, and somewhat sodden. We are drying them out for you, of course, and they should be wearable. I am sorry I cannot be more helpful," she told him, unable to meet his searching look with a lie on her lips. She moved closer to the bed, making a pretence of straightening the covers.

With a loud groan Jean-Paul subsided slowly down amongst the bedclothes, his eyes closing like shutters, but not before Lady Pendavan had seen the sheer look of despair mirrored in them.

It saddened her to witness his discomfort, and her heart went out to him. There was nothing she could do, or say that would help just then, also she realised he had closed her out, wanting to be alone, no doubt, to try and come to terms with the shocking discovery, for knowing about the loss of the jewels, and accepting it, were two different things.

Lady Pendavan walked quietly from the room, closing the door behind her, and as she turned in the direction of the library, her thoughts were racing. She had a plan, which was slowly beginning to take shape. She had pondered over it for a few days now, but as yet it wasn't the moment to suggest what she had in mind. It could be the answer, and the more she thought about it, the more excited she became.

* * * * *

Chapter Four

Return to France

The fog rolled up from the sea, laying a mist over the valley that sloped to the coast.

It was very early in the day, but once the mist swirled away into thin air the sun would shine high in the sky, so brilliant, that one would need to shade one's eyes to view the Atlantic. In the distance one would then see the ridge of low hills, fresh and green, and the sky, blue in its entirety, would be mirrored in the waters, with the promise of a lovely day. Light breezes would occasionally ruffle the waters at the fringe of the cove, causing them to lap gently over the carpet of pebbles dressed with shining seaweed. And, if one happened to be on the headland looking down over the bay, one would be sure to notice the solitary figure in the cove moving around in different directions, first bending here, and then crouching there; looking for something of importance, it would seem.

It was on this first day of Spring, in the year 1811, that a neap tide brought the water level to its lowest, lending to the cove – always of considerable spread – an even larger area, and to the screeching gulls that circled and glided over the surface of the water, a chance to rummage among the dull-hued rock crystal stones for tiny creatures, other than fish. It also gave Jean-Paul the opportunity to search once more for the leather bag that housed the jewels. He still had the absurd notion that it could be lodged between one of the many small fissures, chinks or crevices scattered over the cove. He had to be sure in his mind there was no trace of them before he returned to France, to break the disturbing news – he knew not how – to both Semire and Dario, for to convey such tidings would indeed be far from easy; but thinking on it, how could he be held responsible for an 'act of God'? What had happened was not of his making. Of that he could be sure.

He stood for a moment, resting his acting back. He glanced behind him at the cliff rising high and stark above the bay, while high on the hills at either side, he noticed the winding paths curving upwards. Pendavan was up there above him, somewhere, he thought. He could not see it beyond the cliff, from where he stood, but on the water, from a boat, it must come into view. This beautiful and stately mansion on the inside, with its forbidding external appearance. How one could be deceived! The place fascinated him. He had explored it at great lengths, and now felt he knew it well, as he did the people within its walls. How kind they had been to him, making him feel as though, somehow, he belonged there.

He had fully recovered by now, although his progress had been slow due mostly to the dreadful shocks he had received.

His near loss of life in the sea still remained a formidable experience, and had caused him numerous nightmares, even though two months or more had passed since the tragedy had occurred. His surface wounds and contusions had healed reasonably quickly, but the head injury was another matter. The wound had gone deep, so the healing process was slow, but eventually the gash knitted together and it made rapid progress. A livid red scar was the result. It would stay with him for all time, he knew, even to his grave.

When Lady Pendavan had given him the news that she had found nothing of any value on his person, Jean-Paul refused to believe that the jewels were lost. He had to admit though to the possibility that if they were lying on the ocean bed, they would for certain, be beyond recovery but this he found difficult to accept, however true.

He could not begin to describe the terrible sinking feeling in the pit of the stomach, as he realised that his effort to raise the money for Dario, could be in vain. He had been entrusted with the mission, and had felt very confident, but through no fault of his own, he may have placed both Dario, and Semire, in a far worse predicament than they already were.

The whole series of events had taken its toll, leaving him at a low ebb, and it was some while before he could lift himself out of the doldrums.

Days had run into weeks, and weeks into months, during which time both Esmeralda and Rushie had taken it in turns to nurse their patient back to health. His open admiration for Esmeralda was plain to see. This lady of the 'great' mansion was an exceptional person. He had to admit it. Her bearing was grand. Dark hair, streaked with grey, she had in abundance. It was magnificently styled, which must take some little while to arrange each day. She never approached his part of the house unless her toilet was complete, so Jean-Paul never saw her any other way. She must have been a very beautiful woman when she was younger, he told himself. But now, even in her maturity, she was something to behold, with her arresting features. He hoped that she would not feel embarrassed at his obvious enjoyment in continually gazing at her.

He began to wait eagerly for her visits. There was nothing she would not do for him. It was as though he were one of the family, as was the *femme de ménage* or as the English say, 'housekeeper', Rushie, as she was known; the older one, with the ample bosom. His affection for her grew daily. She completely spoilt him and mothered him at the same time. This he enjoyed and wallowed in it.

Both Ruan and Michael – when they were not fulfilling their obligatory duties on the estate – spent lengthy periods with him. Tales of their many escapades interested the Frenchman and eventually his good nature prevailed, and he accepted them as friends. There was a mutual understanding between them, for after all, were they not involved in the same occupation 'Moonlighting' or 'Smuggling' as it was more commonly called?

Jean-Paul had also heard from them the rest of the story. How they had actually witnessed the destruction – in the storm – of the wrecked French brig: the tragic loss of the crew, and how they rescued him from a watery grave. He also heard how he was brought to Pendavan, and by what means.

As an avid adventurer and a *contrabandist*, the secret panel and what lay behind it intrigued him very much, as did the surprising appearance of both brothers. He could see no similarity whatsoever between the two.

Ruan was tall, and slim of build, with dark hair and eyes, 'Like my father,' he said. Michael, on the other hand, was as fair as his brother was dark. He was the shorter of the two, and not so slim. His looks favoured his mother who, Jean-Paul understood, had been quite exquisite in her beauty. The mention of her early death saddened him. What a tragedy, he thought. She must have had everything to live for with a handsome and kindly husband, as Lady Pendavan had explained – plenty of friends, a splendid home, and in particular, her two sons. He liked these young men of gentle birth, and their spirit of adventure.

As he improved, and gradually became stronger, he accompanied them to the cove by way of the secret panel, the underground tunnels and caves. Without their knowledge, he was able to – under the pretext of gathering unusual specimens, and such like – search in the most unlikely places for the leather bag. It had become an obsession to find the jewels, even though in his heart he knew the whole procedure was useless.

So it was. That on this wonderful Spring morning he had decided to have another last look, however futile it now seemed.

He could not delay returning to France another day. As it was even now, it would be a most terrible shock for both Semire and Dario to suddenly see him, for they must surely believe him dead after all this time, he told himself. News would have reached them of the tragedy, and when he did not return within a certain time, they would have accepted the inevitable, that he had perished with the crew.

Although he would like to have sent word through a courier, he decided against it. His message would only have had to fall into the wrong hands – like the 'Preventative men' – and all would be lost. In any case, he was far too ill for a while to do anything.

As well as the loss of the jewels, which occupied much of his thoughts, he now had something else to mull over in his mind. It was a plan presented to him by Lady Pendavan, and an excellent one, he thought. It could be the answer to his prayers. His precarious lifestyle had, for some time, jarred on him. He had to change it, and as soon as possible. He recalled the conversation that had taken place just a few days before.

The hour was fairly late in the evening when Lady Pendavan had called on him in his room. It had been a bitterly cold day, so he sat huddled over the fire, that still burned merrily in the large grate. He had, for some little while, been contemplating retiring to bed, but was loathe to leave such welcoming warmth. The wind howled down the chimney, causing him to shiver, and move even closer.

It surprised him to hear the light indecisive tapping at the door at such a late hour. It surprised him even further when he opened it to reveal Lady Pendavan.

He waved away her apology for the late visit. "It is no matter," he assured her. "I am always delighted to see your charming self, whatever the hour." He stooped over her hand in the customary manner of a Frenchman and, with dignity, brushed her fingers with his lips. He then led her to the chair by the fire where, drawing a low backless seat towards her, he sat at her feet.

"I hesitated to disturb you Jean-Paul," she began, looking directly at him, mystified still, that she could speak so normally when her heart was racing with excitement. "But I saw your light, and I need to speak with you whilst the boys are asleep," she still looked on them as such. ""It would appear," she said, "they are never far from your side. Even, I believe, neglecting some of their duties to do so," she added. A slow smile played around the corners of her mouth. "You are their hero, you know!"

"I must, how you say, make an apology, Lady Pendavan. I had no intention of taking too much of their time, but I very much like Ruan and Michael. It is as though they are my very own kith and kin," he told her. A shadow crossed his face as he stared into the fire. "I always wished for a brother or sister, or even both," he said. "Instead of which, my growing years have been lonely ones."

"I know what you mean, Jean-Paul," she said. "I suffered the same kind of loneliness as a child. But my life changed for the better when I came here to Pendavan. And although I have lost the one I love, I still have wonderful memories. Something good could happen to you," she suggested, "if you accept a proposition of mine. I have noticed your gradual restlessness, and feel the time has arrived for me to say what is on my mind. I have had plenty of opportunity to think on it," she told him.

She waited momentarily to let this penetrate before she continued.

"You did give me to understand, did you not, that you would like to change your mode of living?" she went on. "After all, it is precarious."

Esmeralda could see he was interested. His eager look was genuine enough, and told her that she wasn't wasting her time, or his, for that matter.

"I am part owner, with my daughter Corrie, of a very profitable cotton plantation, in America," she told him. "It is known as Mon-de-Vue, and covers a considerable area. There is room for expansion," she went on, "because the land is good and fertile, but my daughter will need someone whom she can trust to undertake the financial side of the estate," she explained, hoping he would accept what she had to offer, but she must not try to force him; he must be allowed to make up his own mind. That was important.

"Do you think you would be interested in this advantageous position?" she asked. "I should tell you though, that the work will be rather exacting, and must be of absolute precision. But you will be paid well for your effort. Of course, you do not have to decide immediately," she went on, "but the sooner I know if you wish to accept, the sooner I can send word to my daughter, so that she can hold the position for you. She does need help rather desperately, I can tell you." She paused, a shadow crossing her face, as she spoke of Corrie. "Recently widowed," she continued, "her husband, Doctor Andre Perrie, was a dedicated man in his medical profession at the hospital. But, although his concentrated work occupied much of his time, he did manage to help towards the plantation, and this she will miss. So do not delay too long," she warned.

Esmeralda could not, at this stage, inform Jean-Paul of her intention to make him a gift of her share in *Mon-de-Vue*. With his present mode of living, she must first be certain of his complete integrity. And what better way of ascertaining this than working for the family of Pendavan?

She rose from the chair, and wishing him goodnight, walked with him to the door.

"You will think seriously on what I have said to you. Will you not?" she asked, "for I am sure a fresh environment will be tolerably good for you."

Jean-Paul, bending from the waist, treated her, once more, with the same courtesy as he bade her goodnight.

"I promise you Lady Pendavan, I shall have an answer for you, and," he added, "soon."

As the door closed behind Esmeralda, he stood momentarily, unable to move, his senses reeling. Emotions coming uppermost, he felt shocked surprise. That he, a complete stranger to this family, should be given the opportunity to do honest work, for an honest wage, with promise of security, and certain happiness was to him, unbelievable.

* * * * *

Jean-Paul came out of his reverie with a jolt. He glanced around the cove as though he was seeing it for the last time. There were no jewels here, and the sooner he accepted this, the better. Things had happened fast during the past few days. He was to return to France on the morrow. Arrangements had been made for him to travel across the channel in a yawl – a small two-masted fore-and-aft sailing boat, with four or six oars – which would be moored further along the coast. Two reliable seafarers, one a good friend of Ruan, and Michael, would handle the boat. The two young men had already explained to him - weather permitting, and a fair wind - that they would sail on the tide. "It is fortunate," they said, "that Spring is here, for the sea will be mostly calm. But October to February would have been a different matter, when flurries of light winds can change - without warning - into violent gales, making such a journey impossible." They were unaware who he was, so his secret was still safe.

Jean-Paul had given his answer to Lady Pendavan. He had accepted her most generous and desirable offer without undue hesitation. There was just one stipulation he had to make. It was, that Semire, the woman he loved should, if she so agreed, accompany him to America. Providing there could be some form of accommodation available.

"You see, Lady Pendavan," he told her "it would be good to begin my new life with a wife beside me. I shall be able to support her now, because of your extreme kindness, whereas before there was no guarantee of happiness for her. You comprehend?"

Esmeralda understood, and agreed wholeheartedly. She remembered how well she had been received in her hour of need. When Antony had offered her his hand in marriage, she recalled the feeling his kindness had invoked in her. Therefore, was it not her duty to make the same effort for someone she loved even as much as she had loved Antony?

* * * * *

Chapter Five

Chateau Abbaye

Dario de Laffiette stood as one turned to stone. He was seeing a ghost. That was certain. For standing at the far end of the large drawing room, was his dear friend Jean-Paul. He pinched himself to see if he was dreaming. He was not, for the ghost was fast approaching the *cheminée*, before which he was standing. 'But how can this be?' he asked himself. 'Was he not dead? Had he not perished in the wreck of the *Navire de Long Cours*?'

Dario moved forward in greeting, holding both his friend's hands tightly within his own. "I cannot believe my own eyes Jean-Paul," he said. Sheer amazement spread over his face. "To see you, my friend, is quite miraculous, but what has happened to you?" he asked. "And where have you been all this while?"

Questions followed questions. They poured out, one after the other, from Dario's lips, while his mind recoiled at that which he must relate concerning Semire. He was also shocked at the way his friend looked. The scar, seared deep at the side of his head, stood out, red and livid. The lines about the eyes were deep. And his face, pale and wan, and still showing signs of extreme stress, made him appear vulnerable to Dario, whose heart went out to him. He could see that Jean-Paul had suffered a terrible experience. But at least he was alive, and that was all that mattered, although Dario was fully aware that only a short interlude could pass before sorrow would also etch itself on to his features, already fraught with emotion.

"Do come over here and sit down by the fire," Dario suggested. "It is very cold outside, and you look as though you could do with a good warm through. A brandy would help. Would you care for one?" he asked. "I was about to pour one for myself, anyway. And a strong one at that," he added softly, almost to himself.

"*Rendre grâces*, Dario. That would indeed be most acceptable. But where is Semire?" Jean-Paul asked, glancing inquiringly around the room as though she would suddenly appear from behind one of the many recesses.

Passing him his brandy, Dario immediately took a long drink from his own glass, almost emptying the contents, supposedly to give him Dutch courage. 'Dear God! How am I to tell him,' he thought. 'Is there no way to lighten the blow?'

Jean-Paul, seeing Dario's face cloud over, and noticing also his obvious hesitation, began to feel concern.

"Has something untoward happened?" he asked. "Please tell me! I must know! Has Semire been injured or something... or even worse?" He could see his plans for her slipping through his fingers, as a feeling of apprehension stole over him. He shivered, as with the ague.

"No! Nothing like that," Dario said, speaking with haste. "Semire has taken to herself a husband!" He saw the look of incredulity spread across Jean-Paul's face, but he couldn't stop now. He must conclude his tale, whatever the outcome. "She is married to Count Jean-Philippe Maille," he continued, "and is now living at the Chateau Abbaye."

Dario waited. The silence was unbearable. He gulped back the remainder of the brandy in his glass and, in a subdued manner, moved towards the buffet to refill it. He would have given anything to keep from his friend, the knowledge that he had lost the woman he loved to another. But there was nothing he could say to lessen the blow, or relieve the terrible grief that Jean-Paul must now be suffering.

"What in heaven's name possessed Semire to do such a thing?" Jean-Paul asked with feeling. "Surely she could not have had any great liking to embark on such a madcap scheme," he remarked, with a distinct edge to his voice, "but then I suppose, Dario, she has done this for you."

He buried his face in his hands, his dejection plain to see. If only he could have foreseen this happening! But then, what could he have done under the circumstances? He felt sick to his stomach with the shock.

"Yes, Jean-Paul, Semire did do this for me, but I begged her not to, indeed I did," Dario told him. "God help me, for I know I am to blame, and I am contrite in spirit because of my sins." He stared into space, hesitating momentarily.

"That she had made up her own mind was certain," he went on "and there was nothing I could do to change it." He threw his hands in the air, in a gesture of despair.

"Please do not think too badly of us, I beg of you. We did what we did for the best. After all, we believed you had perished, and Semire was quite devastated at your supposed death," he added.

"I do understand, my friend, more than you think," Jean-Paul replied, his voice now devoid of any emotion, as reality set in. "But it is deuced hard for me to accept."

"I know," Dario said. "I feel the same way." He paused for thought, remembering the day the Count had called on Semire. She had handled the situation with extreme finesse.

Firstly, she had dressed with the utmost care. She had wanted to look the part of a future Countess. And this she accomplished most gracefully, to such an extent, that even the Count – a hardened man – appeared quite taken aback. He had also been astounded by her ready acceptance of his unusual proposal.

She wore a gown of pink velvet, soft to the touch, styled high at the throat, and fastened with numerous tiny buttons – of the same fabric – reaching to her waist, so small, to accentuate the bodice drawn cleverly across her jutting breasts. The front skirt, straight, and reaching the ground, hugged sensuously her shapely hips, and long legs. The back, hanging in pleats, was topped by a tiered and prettily fluked bustle. The sleeves, full to the elbows, fitted tightly to the wrists, also fastened with matching buttons. Her rich dark hair, puffed out at the top, was held in place by diamenté combs, to correspond with the fancy buckles on her dainty footwear.

The picture she presented to the Count must have been to him completely startling. Dario had seen his reaction to Semire's beauty, and was mystified that she had, without knowing it, evoked some kind of feeling, unusual in a man so strangely cold.

Dario had introduced them, and after, had thought to leave them alone. But, at Semire's insistence, he remained in the room – as an avid listener and was more than surprised at what he heard. He could not believe aright his sister's audacious suggestions, which really she had no right to put forward, in the position they found themselves. But Semire held the floor, and, in a clear voice, and steady forthright manner, had come straight to the point.

"I am in agreement with your proposition, Monseigneur Count," she began. "But I must insist it can only be possible if you accept certain conditions of mine, which are of the utmost importance to my family...” Semire paused before continuing, and as the Count had seemed about to speak, asked if she could be allowed to finish.

“The conditions are these: firstly, that on the day our marriage is arranged you cancel my brother’s debt to you with a signed and sealed document, to be held in my safe keeping. Secondly, that a reasonable sum of money be paid to him at quarterly intervals, and lastly, that you allow me access to a part of your vast income, so that I shall be able to maintain the upkeep of our mother’s house and, as well, pay for her constant nursing, which could span over a lengthy period, as she is suffering considerably...”

Slightly aghast at what she had suggested, Semire paused, waiting for the Count to speak, but he remained silent, and tight-lipped. She suddenly realised, by the look on his face, that she may have thrown away the opportunity to clear Dario’s debt. Even so, she began to speak again in a very clear, clipped tone, to hide her embarrassment.

“If this is rather too much to expect for taking me as your wife, then I cannot go through with your scheme, and shall refuse to marry you... It would mean, of course, that my brother and I shall need to find another way of repaying your debt,” she added, as an afterthought.

The Count mused to himself. So, she was clever as well as beautiful, and it impressed him. But he must not give in too easily, at least, not without a little fight.

“Zounds! woman,” he blurted out. “You certainly drive a hard bargain. But you should remember you are in no position to barter. I do, do I not, hold the ace?” He clasped his hands behind his back, and paced the floor.

‘Why should she not have that which she asks?’ he asked himself. After all, she would earn that and more with the tasks he had planned for her. And quite considerable they were too, but as yet there was no good reason for her to be aware of them. Time enough when she was safely housed in the Chateau, he thought, for he intended to use her, and use her well. That was for sure.

The Count halted suddenly in front of Semire and, looking down from his great height, raked her with his eyes.

“I could almost laugh at your sheer audacity Mademoiselle,” he told her. “But I admire your spirit. Therefore, in consequence, I shall accept your... somewhat extreme conditions.” He let this sink in before he said, “Ah! but only in return for one of my own.”

He smiled knowingly, watching her all the while. He liked this feeling of having a hold over her at this early stage. He had accomplished this so often with many of his victims. That is what she would become, as his wife. A victim, and as such, her spirit would be broken. He would see to that, and enjoy every minute.

"My condition," the Count told her, "is that you contact no one outside the Chateau, for at least three quarters of the year. This way, you will accommodate yourself to your new way of life. After the time has passed you may, if you so wish, see whom you like, within reason. Do you understand?" he asked.

"We shall take our marriage vows very quietly, in the Chapel at the Chateau," he explained, hardly able to contain his excitement. Witnesses will be selected from my very large, and most competent staff, one of whom, Michelle, will be your very own *femme de chambre*. She is, at all times, to be at your beck and call. You will have few decisions to make," he went on, "as Gorte, the *chatelaine* is in charge. She holds the keys, and will take orders, only from myself. And, I should add, she is devoted to me."

Taking a generous pinch of snuff from its brilliant precious stone container, and savouring it in his usual manner, the Count turned away from Semire, a derisive smile playing about his mouth. He felt very pleased with himself, for everything had gone just the way he had planned; even more so. A meticulous man in his habits, and over-scrupulous about minute details, he wished only for the matter to be finalised now, today.

"I hope Mademoiselle you will also be in agreement with that which I am about to suggest," the Count began. "I would wish to take you in wedlock, one week from this day. Everything has been provisionally arranged with the *Aumonier*, my dear. He will perform the ceremony at three of the clock. What say you to this?" he asked.

"It would be quite pointless to impede your plans Monseigneur Count," Semire replied. "But should I not be granted a little more time to prepare my trousseau?"

"You need not concern yourself with any wedding attire," he told her, "for it is my command or, if you so prefer, my wish that you wear a very special heirloom, once possessed by my great, great, great grandmother. It is her wedding gown that has been handed down to all brides of the many sons of the Maille family," the Count explained. "This became something of a fetish with my ancestors, so much so, that it has continued irrationally, with reverence, down through the years. You must now realise, of course, that the gown has been used many times," he went on. "But it still holds its extreme beauty. It is an exquisite garment, delicately laced, and covered with hundreds of miniature seed pearls, and so well preserved, that it is certain to suit you," he told her.

"I have little, or no choice in the matter as, of course, you are aware, so naturally I shall accept what you ask of me, and surrender myself into your hands." Semire answered resignedly. After all, she thought, what would be the use of prolonging the agony. Whichever way she looked at it, everything came down to one fact. She was doing this for her family, and that was all that mattered. Her feelings must not come into it. She was committed to this absurd marriage for good or bad, and must make the best of it by accepting the inevitable without repining.

She realised suddenly, that the Count was, once again, speaking, his voice intruding on her thoughts.

"Two days before the ceremony I shall send Michelle in the coach for you, and to collect whatever baggage you have, such as portmanteaux, hat boxes and the like. The driver can make a return journey for any cumbersome trunks, or surplus garments," he told her.

"I am aware, certainly, from the way you appear in your personal aspect, that you must be the most elegantly dressed woman in Paris and, as such, should surely be able to boast a considerable selection of exceptional attire which, of course, you will need as hostess to the acquaintances that call on me from time to time," he explained.

The Count smirked at his description of his victims. Naturally, he could not acclaim them as friends. How would it be possible, he asked himself, to have friends in his kind of business? In any case, he could never imagine showing any good-will towards his numerous clientele. The only feeling he allowed himself was to gloat over their misfortunes. And here he was now, through his own wit and cunning, drawing another victim – and a beautiful one at that – into his already closely woven web. But he must desist this musing and, without more ado, bring his visit to a close. There would be ample time to contrive over this one, he thought.

"Well Mademoiselle, there is little else to discuss at this stage. So I will, if I may, take my leave of you." So saying, he bent lingeringly over her hand, and clicking his heels in salute, walked from the room accompanied by Chebec, the principal manservant, who had been summoned by Dario, to show their guest out.

* * * * *

Relating all this to Jean-Paul, had been far from easy for Dario. It had been one of the most difficult tasks he had ever had to perform. And he hoped with all his heart never to have to do anything like it again. Of the wedding ceremony he could say nothing, for no one outside the Chateau had been present, due to the ridiculous stipulation of the Count. This for Dario, disturbed him somewhat, not knowing how things were faring for his sister. He missed her more than he cared to admit, even to Jean-Paul, for he certainly could not rub salt into his friend's already deep wounds,

As Dario concluded the disturbed tidings concerning Semire, he could not help but observe the look of complete resignation on his friend's face, and felt that this was just as well, for nothing could change what had happened, however much he would wish it to.

Dario also sensed Jean-Paul's slightly impatient manner in wanting to impart his own startling news. So, replenishing both their drinks, he settled near the fire, anxious to hear all that had transpired since they had last seen each other before the fateful storm.

* * * * *

Dario listened intently to what his friend had to say. Jean-Paul's voice was intense as he explained how he had struggled for his life in the freezing cold and treacherous seas as the brig was smashed to pieces on the rocks. He told of his miraculous rescue by the two sons of Lord Pendavan and his feeling of despair on discovering the precious jewels had gone to the bottom of the ocean. He spoke also of the struggle to regain his health, that was at a low ebb for many weeks. He went on and on, leaving nothing out. He made known in detail the kindness shown to him by the Pendavan family, their devoted nursing, and described fully the magnificent mansion. His voice changed suddenly from its intensity, to extreme excitement as he gave an open account of the extraordinary offer he had received from Lady Pendavan, to begin a new life in America, and what it entailed.

When Jean-Paul reached this part of the tale he paused, and taking a long drink from his glass, studied Dario over the rim.

"I had a plan my friend, involving Semire. Oh! and yourself, of course." Jean-Paul told him. "But then, because of the present circumstances, I am afraid it is now of little use."

Again, he paused for thought. This farcical marriage to the Count could have been prevented if only he had returned to France earlier. In which case, he could now be a happy man, instead of one emotionally distressed.

"I knew with the loss of the jewels, that you could in no way repay your debt to the Count," he went on. "So, I decided to take both you and Semire to America, to the port of New Orleans, where on my arrival, I shall take up my position on the cotton plantation *Mon-de-Vue*. Word has already gone ahead with news of my journey from Marseilles. And through the extreme kindness of Lady Pendavan – who has connections with certain shipping lines – I have arranged a berth on the *Marie-Louise*, a cargo ship. And I leave at dawn on the morrow," he explained.

"It was my sole intention to ask Semire for her hand in marriage and, if she had accepted, we could have taken our vows on board the ship, where the Captain would have, I am sure, conducted the ceremony," he added.

"It is a sobering thought Dario, to know that all this has changed," he said. His voice saddened at the realisation that he had lost the woman he loved. But, even with this knowledge, Jean-Paul could not quell the excitement within himself. To go to America, and make new friends, would be a challenge.

"This is something I have always dreamed of Dario," he went on, "and even now I can hardly believe it has happened. But now that it has, and because Semire has taken to herself a husband I can, at long last, sever my connections with France. After all," he added, "there is nothing to keep me here now that I have lost her. And in any case, as far as everyone is concerned, I perished in the storm on the Cornish coast so let it remain thus, for Semire especially. It would be pointless now for her to discover the truth, and could only distress her further. I shall miss her, certainly. How can it be otherwise. And you... my friend. It saddens me deeply to leave you. That goes without saying. But I am sure you understand that I must grasp, with both hands, this heaven-sent opportunity. I would indeed be mad not to. What say you, my friend?"

"I wholeheartedly agree with all you have imparted to me Jean-Paul, and if this new venture is what you desire, then I wish you all the luck in the world. I shall miss you, naturally," Dario told him, "and so will the young blades. How will they cope without their master swordsman, I ask you? Of course," he said, with a sheepish grin on his face, "they will still have me, but I am second best, and not so fast with the sword as you. We have had some good times at the fencing instruction class, have we not my friend? And it will be deuced difficult imagining Paris without you," he hesitated momentarily, staring into the fire. He felt decidedly wretched about everything.

"Would that I could go with you to America, my friend. God knows I have had my fill of Paris, and of living the only way I know how. So, I too could do with a change of scenery, but for the time I must remain here with my mother, whose health, as well as her mind, has somewhat deteriorated of late," Dario explained.

"It is a fact Jean-Paul," he went on, "she knows nothing of recent events, such as the loss of the jewels, or Semire's marriage to the Count, or even that she has left the house to live at the Chateau. She is completely immune to everything, and everyone around her. It means, of course, that I now have no need to tell her the untruths I had first planned," he added.

Dario refrained from telling Jean-Paul that Semire was also another reason for his remaining in Paris. In no way could he bring himself to desert her, even though it would be some weeks still before he would be allowed to see her. He could not explain why, but he had the feeling that all was not well with his sister. He could not get it out of his head that the Count, with other ulterior motives in mind, had let her walk into a well planned trap. So, until his visit to her should come about, he would not rest easy.

"I do sincerely hope Jean-Paul, that your departure from Paris will not mean severing all connections between us," Dario said, his brows knitting together over eyes that were troubled. "I should be sorely grieved to lose touch with you, and not be aware of how you fare."

"Naturally, I have no thought of ending our friendship, Dario. I intend to send word to you as soon as I am established in my new venture," Jean-Paul told him. "I pledge my devout promise on it.

But then, you can always journey to America, and visit me when you no longer have a commitment to hold you here. Can you not? You would be more than welcome, I am sure. Who knows!" he added. "You may wish to stay, and make for yourself a new life. For, from what Lady Pendavan told me, the Americas welcome newcomers to their country."

Glancing at his friend, Jean-Paul could not help but feel sympathy for the plight Dario was in. But, even so, he was sure they would see each other before too long.

With sudden forethought Jean-Paul rose from his seat by the fire, and reaching inside a deep pocket of his waistcoat, brought forth a velvet pouch. On loosening the drawstring, he emptied the contents, consisting of several solid gold coins, into the palm of his hand, which he held out for Dario to see.

"These are of great value my friend," he told him. "And there are twenty and five in all. They were given to me as a gift by Lady Pendavan. Yes! given to me," he repeated, as he noticed the look of disbelief on Dario's face.

Jean-Paul gazed into space as he recalled the day he had left Pendavan. The gift had been presented to him quietly, without any fuss. To refuse would have offended, he knew. So he graciously accepted, but also decided, there and then, that he would, at his earliest opportunity, return the value of the gold pieces to Lady Pendavan. To him, this way, it could be just a loan. That made him feel better. And he felt even better now that he had decided to provide some form of help for the future, for Dario, who he then realised was sitting as one mesmerised, his eyes glued to the gold coins now displayed in their brilliance on the round, and highly polished table where they were placed.

"I want you to have these my friend," he said, counting out five of the coins, and placing them in a neat pile in front of Dario. "And, I should suggest you keep them safely on your person, in a money belt perhaps, as I shall do, particularly on the ship, during my journey to America. Then, if the need arises for your swift departure from Paris, you will have no concern for raising such a sum. They can be your mainstay," Jean-Paul told him. "It is little enough to do for two I hold so dear. After all," he added, a teasing grin on his face. "With your great love of gambling you may have a far more urgent need to flee the country. And, perhaps, sooner than you might imagine."

Dario smiled at Jean-Paul's quip. He was right, of course. His craving for gambling could put him in the position his friend had suggested. He had no qualms about his failings. Gambling was in his blood and, no doubt, there to stay. But now, all he could think of was how he could make up for his misdemeanour to Semire, and try somehow to stay away from the gaming tables, for her sake if not his own. It was up to him to make her sacrifice worthwhile.

"I do hope you are not going to try and dissuade me from this," Jean-Paul said, breaking through Dario's thoughts. "It is what I wish, and I shall have peace of mind knowing you have something of your own to fall back on. You understand?"

"Of course I do, my friend," Dario answered. "But you are too good. I do not deserve this kindness you show me. And I am concerned only that if I accept your most generous offer, and things do not work out for you the way you plan, will you not find yourself somewhat short?"

"In no way Dario, I can assure you. Two gold pieces will be ample for my journey by ship, with more than enough to spare. So please! I beg of you! Do what I ask my friend, and whatever you do, don't part with any of the coins other than for your journey to America. Any Captain of his vessel will accept what you offer him, for the distance you will expect to travel," he added.

Dario, his face openly displaying his emotions, grasped Jean-Paul by the hand. Eventually, he replied:

"Whatever can I say, other than I am eternally grateful for your kindness. And I shall certainly do as you advise me," he added.

"Think nothing of it," Jean-Paul said. "Are we not staunch friends? And would you not do the same for me were our circumstances reversed?"

He rose from his seat by the fire, and glanced at his ornate fob watch, which told him the hour was fast approaching for the commencement of his journey.

"I must away soon my friend, for time is becoming extremely short to hail a carriage to take me direct to Marseilles. But first, may I quickly use your writing *secretaire*?" he asked.

"Certainly," Dario answered, gesturing with his hand in the direction of the splendid piece of furniture positioned near a large window, where the light reflected on a pair of magnificent silver inkwells, with an elaborately coloured quill.

Jean-Paul walked over to the *secretaire* and, selecting a sheet of paper, he set down in a clear hand, details of his destination which he then gave to Dario, after first sprinkling the damp ink with powder, and blowing the surplus away.

Both men, lost in their own thoughts, walked silently from the house on to the Boulevard, where in a matter of minutes a carriage came into view, the horses trotting at a steady pace.

Jean-Paul waved the carriage down and, asking the driver to wait, turned and clasped Dario's hands tightly within his own.

"My friend. The time has come for us to say adieu! But I know we shall meet again. Never fear! Until then, God go with you." His voice choked, and to hide his emotions, he climbed into the carriage. Dario heard him say to the driver, "You shall have ten extra francs if you get me safely to Marseilles, and in good time to board the *Marie Louise*."

Dario was still standing there long after the carriage pulled away, and was out of sight. He felt at a very low ebb.

* * * * *

Chapter Six

Passage to New Orleans

Never would Jean-Paul forget his first sight of Mon-de-Vue. It stood in the centre of a wide semi-circle of massive oak trees, their branches long and thick with rich shining foliage spreading shadows across the neat clearing.

The house, majestic in its grand surroundings, and a typical specimen of the period, favoured the popular ante-bellum style of the average plantation home with its two storey galleried frontal appearance, and as well, the Greek Revival architecture – adopted, and often imitated – by the up and coming wealthy cotton planters of the lower Mississippi valley.

Steps leading to the ornate front entrance, flanked on either side by stucco plaster walls, began wide at the foot, narrowing gradually towards the top, whilst iron grillework, embellished with decorative patterns adorned the galleries, giving the delightful building a secluded look. And with windows, of which there were many, prettily curtained in white flimsy lace, and framed with storm shutters, the whole scene was one of complete charm.

Travelling in a carriage drawn by two fine greys, and controlled by Ned, the driver – who had waited at the wharf for the *Marie-Louise* to dock so he could collect his passenger – Jean-Paul's approach to the plantation had been somewhat of a surprise, for the land around Mississippi was vast, and far beyond his expectations.

The carriage had passed other plantations on the River Road, but as Ned explained, they were on a much smaller scale than that of Mon-de-Vue. Even so, it still came as something of a shock to observe the wide area of each landed property, completely covered with ripe cotton crops – ready for the picking – that spread white, like sheets, as far as the eye could see. And, when the house came into view, Jean-Paul could scarcely believe what he saw.

And if he was astounded at the grandeur of the place, he was more than unprepared for the startling beauty of its owner... the widowed Madame Corrina Perrie.

After first pulling on the elaborate crystal bell at the front entrance to summon Betsy, the second in command at Mon-de-Vue, Ned deposited his passenger's only portmanteau at the top of the steps. This was all that Jean-Paul had brought with him. It contained just a few choice garments selected from Thorley's clothing apparel, which Lady Pendavan had kindly given him to suffice for his needs until he was in a position to order a complete wardrobe, appropriate to his own style.

Because of the presumption of his death, Jean-Paul had been unable to visit his adopted father, to regain possession of his considerable wardrobe of elegant clothing. He had dressed always with good taste befitting any occasion, and it grieved him somewhat to leave behind so many of them, for perhaps, someone else. But at least, he could start afresh, now that his mode of living had changed for the better, and he knew just where there was an excellent tailor who, he understood, followed his prolific trade in the French Quarter of New Orleans. Lady Pendavan had said that Monsieur Edouard Duvalle was famed for his good cut, and well fitted garments, and treated his customers with the utmost courteous manner.

Jean-Paul carried a sword that nestled in its scabbard, attached to his sword belt. It was part of his dress, and he wouldn't dream of going anywhere without it. He also carried a hollowed out walking stick, that held a sword blade, with a very fine edge. This was an essential weapon for use in any conflict, especially when he could perhaps, be waylaid by would-be robbers, and despoiled of his property. It made him feel safe.

* * * * *

When Jean-Paul stepped through the double doors, following in the wake of Betsy, who had greeted him as the new 'maitre', he became aware of the wide centre hall, attractively furnished, and vast enough to lend a certain coolness to it. He noticed also, the tall spiral staircase. A most becoming asset to the house, he thought. And, as well, walking behind Betsy, he was able to take stock of her.

Being short and round, of ample proportions, she moved slowly, although her gait was sure-footed. A typical 'Mammy' of the Deep South, she wore the adopted style of clothing – black dress, full from the waist to the floor, topped by starched white collar and bibbed apron. And to complete the picture, a pleated cap, edged with lace, fitted snugly over her mop of black curly hair.

"The maitresse, she an gon to de fields fo Zeb. Hem vere sick. Hem big boss over nigras, to see dat dey sho work. But de maitresse, she sho tired, andt I scairt dat she don too much," Betsy told him.

She talked, her voice high-pitched, and clear, as they walked across the huge hall, and through open double doors leading into the boudoir, a small sitting-room-cum-library, housing a great number of books.

"She, the maitresse hab tol me I hafta look after yo," she added, as Jean-Paul glanced around the room, taking everything in. To him, it was almost like a den, where supposedly the business side of the plantation was administered. For ledgers, reams of papers, notes and such like were piled high, but tidily on a broad desk, set near to a window where the light could reach it. The room housed two doors at either end, one which led into a spaciously furnished bedroom, and the other, a lounge of good proportions, quite comfortable, with pretty chintz curtains, and covered chairs to match.

"Yo sho be comfy al de time now massa wit Betsy lookin hafta yo," she said, aware by now that the new maitre – as she thought of him – was a real gentleman, and handsome at that.

"The maitresse, she back vere soon. So, whilt yo git yesself ol spruced hup, I go now to de kitchin an fitch a leetle food fer yo." So saying, Betsy ambled from the room mumbling quietly to herself.

Left to his own thoughts Jean-Paul realised that this part of the house must have been used solely by the late doctor, for the whole area was typically male. Now, according to Betsy, it was to be his place of abode. And, as he saw it, more than enough for his needs. He would be happy and contented here, he knew.

On entering the bedroom he noticed there was plenty of clean towels, fresh water and soap put ready for his use. Seeing the toiletries reminded Jean-Paul how dusty and dirty he felt, and must look after his journey from the port which, with all the excitement, had left him drained of vitality. But he knew he would bounce back once he had washed and changed into fresh clothes, suitable for that part of the day when they would partake of the main meal. A real 'Southern dish' was how Betsy had described it. "Yo'll sho lak hit massa. Yessuh massa. Betsy gittin hit fo yo, and the maitresse. She lak hit too," she had explained. Her large eyes rolling from side to side, bright and friendly, whilst her ready smile had shown teeth white and pearly.

Jean-Paul walked towards the mantelpiece, and looking into the mirror above, fingered his beard. He moved closer to his reflection, musing quietly to himself, whether to remove the offending hair completely. He had been toying with the idea for some little while now. It had grown very thick since the storm, when it had been shaved away because of the facial injuries he had received. He liked the beard, and would feel lost without it, he knew, but he was still undecided, and had been ever since the journey from Marseilles, in fact.

For the closer the ship sailed into warmer waters, the worse the heat had become. He recalled how unbearable it had been.

He very nearly didn't make the journey, arriving at the wharf with only minutes to spare. The Captain, who had given up on his only passenger, had been about to give the order to cast off, when he heard the sudden commotion of horses racing along the cobbled wharf. As they ground to a halt, steaming with sweat Jean-Paul leapt from the coach, and paying the driver the money he had promised, hurried up the gang plank to board the ship, apologising profusely for the delay. He presented to the man at the top the introductory note from Lady Pendavan, along with two of the gold pieces, explaining as he did so how one of the leaders had thrown a shoe a mile or so from Marseilles, forcing the driver to retrace his route and call at the nearest inn, where the ostler gladly substituted a fresh horse.

The man glanced first at the paper, then surveyed the two gold pieces laying in the palm of his hand, whilst with the other stroked his chin as he pursed his full lips. He looked directly at the Frenchman as he said proudly.

"I am Captain Renaulde, Master of the *Marie-Louise*, so let me welcome you aboard my ship Monsieur de Leon. But I must inform you now that the gold you have given me for your passage to New Orleans, is far and above what I would ask."

Jean-Paul grasped the naval man firmly by the hand and clicked his heels in salute as he replied.

"If I reach my destination safely I shall regard the extra gold well spent, Capitain. So please keep it with my blessing."

"Your generosity is much appreciated Monsieur, and you may rest assured that your safety will be my concern. However, I should mention that the ship could come under attack from the African pirates, or even slave traders," the Captain warned. He paused momentarily, and looking thoughtful, added, "I trust Monsieur, that as a Frenchman you can wield a sword, for should we encounter these marauders, it will be every man for himself. It is no good my making light of this potential situation, for there is every chance it could happen. There is a certain risk, each and every time we sail across the Gulf of Lions, to the Spanish coast, between the islands of Mallorca and Ibiza, where the waters swarm with them. It is here unfortunately, on the way that I must delay to collect a cargo of slaves, a commitment I have very little liking for Monsieur, I can assure you, but my livelihood, and the support of my family depend on my carrying out the instructions of the ship's owners. It is fortunate, however," he went on to explain, "that I have only to make such a distasteful detour one trip in four, and take only the number of slaves I can cope with for feeding. In any case, I refuse to pack them in the hold of my ship like animals, as so many Captains do, only to lose many of the poor wretches through death and disease. Myself, I choose to treat any slave with respect," he continued. "After all, they are human beings, and should be treated as such."

Jean-Paul nodded his head in agreement. There was little he could say at this stage, only listen to the Captain who was speaking again.

"Perhaps foisting the problems of my ship upon you Monsieur may seem unfair, especially as my fears may be unwarranted. But I am sure you will understand, and accept why I have imparted such news, not to spoil the journey for you, but merely to put you on your guard. After all, as a paying passenger, it is only right you should be made aware of the dangers that could befall the *Marie-Louise*. I should mention," he went on, "that we hug the coastline in the hope we shall not be seen for, apart from the slaves, we carry other cargo which would interest any sea-robbers, who will stop at nothing to get what they want when making their plundering raids. This is the reason why I have engaged a larger crew and, regrettably, press-ganged more men on to my ship. It was necessary to take this step, for the first few weeks will be anxious ones for us all."

The Captain turned, and beckoned to a black boy standing just a few feet away.

"This is Josh, Monsieur, our cabin boy who, I am sure, is eager to do your bidding. He will look after you until I see you at a later hour."

Captain Renaulde knew his passenger would be well cared for by the youngest crewman on his ship. Now he could concentrate on his immediate duties he thought, as he moved towards the helm, where the helmsman was already at the wheel. He could ill afford any more delay.

Even the Captain's warning could not quell the excitement Jean-Paul felt, with the commencement of the journey. It grew inside him as he watched the crew go about their tasks, after hearing their Captain issue orders to the boswain to cast off. He saw some of the crew lift the heavy rope hawsers whilst more crew winched up the anchor, and hoisted the sails to catch the wind which was fair, and ideal for the start of the long voyage.

Dawn was just breaking as Jean-Paul followed Josh towards his cabin. He could feel the steady movement of the ship beneath his feet as she slipped quietly and unobtrusively out into the harbour. The cabin was a small cramped compartment, but, he noticed, very clean. And the bunk looked inviting, bringing home to him how terribly weary he felt. He would sleep now, he told himself, as loosening his elaborate neck cloth, and shirt collar, he flung himself down on to the rough covers.

* * * * *

Surfacing from his sleeping quarters at five of the clock, Jean-Paul made his way along the 'tween to the top deck. He was more than interested in the running of the ship, and knew he could observe the crew without becoming a hindrance. An invitation from the Captain to share the meal at his table came via Josh. But, as yet there was still an hour to wait.

The ship, moving rhythmically, was carried along by the fair winds, which filled the large sails. Different sounds that excited him fell upon Jean-Paul's ears, with the creaking of the timbers and yard – arms as the *Marie–Louise* rose and fell between the waves. Glancing aloft to the rigging he could see the lookouts already in the crows' nests, and the remainder of the crew at their respective posts. He couldn't explain why, but he felt reasonably safe, somehow, although he had no illusions as to the possible risks involved. The journey would be fraught with dangers. Of this he was convinced, even at this early stage; if not from the pirates, there could be storms, hurricane gales and, as well, the usual maladies amongst the crew which could bring death to the ship. But for the present, at least, there was nothing untoward happening, in fact, everything appeared quite restful. Even the helmsman turned the wheel gently, with a look of contentment on his face.

Glancing at his fob watch, Jean-Paul realised that only minutes were left to him for joining the Captain in his cabin.

* * * * *

Eventually, sitting at the rough table Jean-Paul compared the meagre meal with that to which he was accustomed, and hungry though he was, he didn't relish the meats arrayed before him - brined beef and brined pork, with hunks of bread and cheese, water biscuits and French haricot beans, with a bottle of rum to wash it all down - not favourites of his by any means, although no doubt after days at sea the food would be more edible, and possibly taken with less objection. But Jean-Paul's thoughts of food were put to one side as the Captain commenced speaking.

"May I enquire Monsieur. Do you intend settling in New Orleans? Or are you just paying a visit?"

"I am taking up a position at the plantation, Mon-de-Vue, and hope to remain, certainly," Jean-Paul told the Captain. "Do you know the place?"

"Yes! I know the estate, and the owner, well. It is very large and most profitable, holding nigh on five hundred slaves," the Captain explained. "There, the slaves are treated well. When they become sick or reach the end of their working life they are not discarded, and left to die by the wayside. There is provision on the plantation for them to finish their days in comfort. And, as well, with Christianity being forced upon the slaves down by the riverside, places of worship are a necessity, so plantations that are now becoming more in evidence around the Mississippi area are having chapels built on their lands. Mon-de-Vue already has a fine chapel, and a cemetery as well. Naturally, white people on any plantation would be buried in separate plots from the slaves," he added.

"You will be happy, I know, working for Madame Perrie," he went on. "She is a real lady, much respected, and the slaves are devoted to her. I suppose you know already that she is a widow and," he added, "a most beautiful one at that. And wealthy to boot."

"Yes! I am fully aware of her husband's unfortunate demise," Jean-Paul said, ignoring the Captain's jocular innuendo and, as well, hoping he wasn't thinking of him as a fortune hunter, seeking a rich wife.

"It is a very sad day for Madame Perrie," the Captain began again. "Her husband was such a valuable asset to her, that she must miss him terribly. They were extremely close too. I understand there is a daughter from his first marriage who returned recently from Europe, where for several years she has been a pupil at a finishing school for young ladies. Unfortunately," he went on, "she has no interest whatsoever in the plantation, or in her stepmother, for that matter. In fact, there is little love lost between them, and I believe she has recently gone to stay with her late father's family. So Monsieur, it looks very much as though Madame Perrie will lean heavily upon you for support, especially as she can expect no quarter from her only near neighbour, Earl Revington, a planter on Chartenelle, who is a cruel and callous man. He is well known in the area for his savage brutality towards his slaves. He is far too mean to maintain the actual number of slaves needed to work the cotton crop on his land, so those who work in the fields are forced to toil long hours, under the pitiless sun. When the weakest collapse with exhaustion, they are beaten almost senseless. After such bestial treatment the slaves become too ill to work, and mostly die where they fall. I have heard some terrible tales," the Captain went on to explain, "mostly from my brother Shaun who, before deciding on the sea for his future livelihood, worked as overseer for the Perries' estate. Macabre happenings at Chartenelle almost certainly point to its owner who, it is known, dabbles in Voodoo. Cemeteries are robbed of bodies for use in witchcraft. Bones, fingernails and hair are essential to the system for performing rites by the Voodoo queen. And for ritual sacrifices, it is thought that female slaves, acting as nurses or crude midwives will, for certain favours, falsely pronounce the deaths of new-born babies. The addiction to the ritual I may tell you, has consisting impact on all followers, who are mostly Creoles and Negroes. But there are whites who find the 'Act' quite realistic, and startling at the same time. They become completely bewitched. Because of insufficient grounds nothing can actually be proven against

Earl Revington, so one can only conjecture that he is deeply involved in these grim deeds. It is even possible he is steeped in other depravities," he added. "After all, the man is a sadist, and most immoral. It is common knowledge that he will violate young male bucks of his choosing, and lock slaves up in confined buildings for breeding purposes, should he feel so inclined. He will also rape any female slave on his land, even though he has a wife, and a mistress as well. She, as a slave of extreme beauty, is given special privileges, and wields an awful lot of power. It is through her that punishment amongst the slaves is meted out by such atrocities as castration, and, in some cases, if it taken his fancy, he will have them hung, drawn and quartered. For runaway slaves, of which there are always a few who will take their chances of freedom, the Master of Chartenelle will inflict another kind of penalty on the offenders. Permanent injuries to their legs and feet are deliberately induced to render them incapable of repeating their effort to be free. They would, of course, prefer death to this frustration. Poor devils!"

The Captain paused to partake of some food, gesturing to Jean-Paul to follow suit. The naval man seemed to eat with relish, being used to it by now, for certain. He broke off some hunks of bread to go with the large slice of cheese already placed before him, and drank from his full tankard.

With a lull in the conversation, and eating on the agenda, Jean-Paul gingerly sampled a piece of cheese which he thought quite stale, but being hungry the flavour did pass muster, and he found himself enjoying it, especially with some bread, which surprisingly enough, was really fresh tasting.

Eventually, with the meal over, the Captain, once again, reverted to the subject of the slaves.

"It is no wonder that the eyes of the slaves on Chartenelle never laugh," he continued. "And they rarely sing, which is such a pity, for it is the custom for slaves to gather in groups, in front of their cabins where they relax and talk amongst themselves, and sing and chant Negro Spirituals. There is nothing, and I mean nothing," the Captain emphasised, "to compare with the sound of slaves in the Deep South singing their favourite religious song *Swing Low, Sweet Chariot*, accompanied by their instruments, mainly the Jew's-harp, a small lyre-shaped musical contrivance played by holding the frame between the teeth. A plantation that has no vocal music bursting forth is, to my mind, a dead place," he added.

"All in all, Monsieur, Earl Revington is rotten, through and through, and one to steer clear of. Mind! he is not alone in his bestiality. Cruelty is taking quite a hold throughout the Mississippi area. Would that it wasn't," he added. His face took on a serious look. "With plantations coming into their own, masses of slaves have already been traded and bartered for by the planters who, in the main have little time for their would-be workers. Families are, in many cases deliberately split up to cause distress. Coarse blacks, both male and female, work in the fields, whilst good-looking females are sent to plantation houses, some as nannies to white children, others as cooks, and a few so highly thought of as to become second in command to their mistress. Conditions on earlier plantations are extremely poor," the Captain went on, "especially the sleeping facilities, where slaves are herded together in cramped rough shacks that reek with damp, and give little comfort. And, as well, eatables and drinkables are, more often than not, quite frugal. So it is not at all surprising that with continual brutish treatment from their masters, and the overseers who crack their whips at the least excuse, feelings must run deep, and fester amongst them. Things will, I am sure, go from bad to worse, and could eventually lead to horrific consequences throughout the Deep South. God help us all," he added, grave of face.

"The more recent plantations are improving though," the Captain began again. "Larger tracts of land are now being purchased by new people who, like yourself, Monsieur, have arrived from the European countries to begin a new life in the Mississippi cities, many of them drawn by the lure of expected prosperity from cotton, which, I may add, is fast becoming a major crop. We are well into 1812, and I believe, before many more decades have come to pass, that the Mississippi will become a wealthy cotton empire, and planters will amass many riches, and great possessions from their fertile lands. At least, it looks that way to me," he stated further.

"There is such a great degree of information about the area where you are to establish yourself Monsieur, that it would be impossible for you to absorb everything at once," the Captain told Jean-Paul. "But, with the lengthy time we shall spend at sea there is much that I can relate to you. It would certainly help you feel less of a stranger when you step ashore at New Orleans," he added, reaching inside his breast pocket for the hunter's watch lodged there and, glancing at it, realised how quickly the time had passed since first he entered the cabin.

"I suggest Monsieur, that we adjourn for the night," the Captain said, rising from the table. "I had no idea it was so late, and I feel regret, for you must be exhausted, your first day at sea. I realise," he went on, "that my conversation has been somewhat time consuming, but I discussed the subject at greater lengths only for your interest, and I became carried away."

"You are right," Jean-Paul replied. "I am interested, and very much so. I too put the time from my mind, but I am deeply grateful for what I have learnt tonight Capitain. It has, as you say, opened my eyes." So saying, he too rose from the table and, after wishing the naval man goodnight, went his way.

* * * * *

The days and weeks went by, and the weeks reached into the second month of the journey when the *Marie-Louise* creaked and groaned her way out into the warm Spanish waters after collection of the arranged freight of slave labour. The ship's hold now housed an extra cargo of one hundred bemused male and female slaves. The Captain had secured them with little trouble, although there had been a few upsetting skirmishes when some families were parted. Jean-Paul had been invited to join the Captain when he stepped ashore to carry out the necessary transaction on the Island of Ibiza, but witnessing such distressing scenes troubled him greatly, especially to see the look of grief and helplessness on the faces of the slaves involved. There were those amongst them who seemed to accept the inevitable with a certain dignity and calm, whilst others broke down, sobbing uncontrollably as their loved ones were taken from them. He was troubled even more to see so many young blacks, some still only children climb aboard the ship in a state of stupor and lethargy, and even though the Captain explained this attitude was quite characteristic of them, Jean-Paul's heart went right out to the poor wretches as, with faces now completely devoid of any feelings, shoulders bent, and legs faltering under the restraining fetters locked around their ankles, they shuffled across the deck, and stepped down into the hold as best they could.

* * * * *

Silence at last prevailed as evening drew nigh. It was the time of day that Jean-Paul enjoyed, when the searing sun had subsided, and the breezes blew cool. He lent against the gunwale, looking down on to the shadowed waters reflecting the early night clouds, his thoughts in a tumult, one moment excited, the next confused and, like everyone else on the ship, on edge, unable to relax with the *Marie-Louise* still exposed to the risk of attack. Danger lurked on all sides, even more so now that the ship had reached the open seas. For the umpteenth time Jean-Paul glanced along the bulwark, taking stock of the rows of mounted guns pointing menacingly out to sea, and ready for action against the enemy.

The cutter-rigged ship, built on a larger scale than the seventeenth century sloop, had sixty of them, fifteen on either side of both the top and lower decks. He only hoped the crew would have time to use them if the ship was taken by surprise. He looked about him, his imagination running riot, for any minute he fully expected to see a pirate ship, with skull and cross-bones ensign displayed high on the mast, appear from nowhere, and bear down upon them. He came back suddenly with a jolt to the more mundane things that were really happening.

The crew had taken over their regular watch, whilst those relieved from their duties retired to sleep, albeit in a somewhat lighter vein.

The crew walking near to where Jean-Paul was standing, touched their caps in respect as they wished him goodnight. They had become used to the French passenger, who regularly witnessed the watch rota, where the crew were divided to take alternate duty. The whole ship relied implicitly on the watchfulness of the men who vigilantly carried out constant observation for what may come.

Jean-Paul moved away from the gunwale, shuddering as he did so, either from fear of the unknown, or the fact that the temperature had dropped quite considerably within the last hour. Whichever it was, he began to feel cold, and positively weary as he made his way back to his cabin. 'But will I sleep?' he asked himself.

* * * * *

As dawn broke over the horizon, a warning shout, eager in its intensity, rent the early morning air.

"Ship ahoy!" hailed the lookout from the crows-nest facing aft.

Alerted by the not unexpected sounds, the whole ship came alive, with the crew hurrying to their posts to prepare for action stations.

When Jean-Paul tottered sleepily from his bunk, he heard the news that a ship had been sighted dead astern, and the feeling of impending danger hit him more forcibly, now that the Captain's warning was, it seemed, about to come true, not that he could see anything himself. It was, he understood, just a tiny speck on the line at which earth and sky appear to meet, not visible to the naked eye, but there all the same, although as yet no one could justifiably ascertain her identity.

The next few hours were anxious ones, especially for Captain Renaulde, who spent them walking around the top deck, peering through his telescope. He was at a loss to understand why the tiny speck became no larger. If he didn't know any better, he would think the *Marie-Louise* was in the throes of being shadowed, which made little sense in these waters where attacks would be mostly swift and deadly. As adventurous marauders, it was known they never held back.

Perhaps the unknown vessel would abstain from any action until nightfall to enact her dirty deeds, although by then it was wholly possible the *Marie-Louise* could lose her adversary, which would be the ideal situation. But as things stood, with all the odds against them the Captain held out very little hope of the problem being resolved so easily.

He had experienced fear before, many times, but never could he recall such unbearable suspense affecting a whole ship. It was strange, now he came to think on it, for prior to his departure from Marseilles, he had had a premonition of certain peril. And the feeling was still with him.

He had to admit that the Master of the ship most likely following in the wake of the *Marie-Louise* was, whatever his reasons, persistent in his pursuit, albeit in a somewhat stealthy manner. His game of cat and mouse was, to say the least, off-putting for the crew, who could withstand any danger when it came upon them if forewarned. But to be kept completely in the dark as they were, frayed their already taut nerves…

Everything was now at a standstill and all they could do was to wait.

The time dragged until at last the daylight was lost in the shadows of the night. It was then that the atmosphere could be felt, as it very quickly enveloped the ship.

Captain Renaulde was, at that very moment, staring fixedly at the dark waters stretching wide as far as the eye could see. With the absence of light, now that nightfall was upon them, the sea, rippling with gentle breezes that ruffled the surface, its colour very nearly black, appeared sombre and gloomy, whilst the deadly silence brought forth continuous sounds of wavelets lapping as they enfolded caressingly against the lower sides of the ship.

He wasn't sure how long he had been standing there. For certain many hours had passed, but he had completely lost count of time. He couldn't sleep, not now. His mind was too alert for that. Right now he was more concerned for the very worst that could happen, than retiring to his cabin.

The crew were ready and standing by, every man Jack of them. Stalwart and true they would, he knew, if the situation arose, lay down their very lives for the *Marie-Louise*, as well as their Captain.

He glanced up at the sky overcast by flurrying clouds that intermittently extended over a full moon. From time to time she would cautiously emerge and then, would again be obscured from view.

The air, sultry and oppressive, made him realise how uncomfortably hot it must be down in the hold.

The slaves occupied his thoughts more often than not, particularly now, when danger was imminent. They had missed their daily airing as there was no way he could risk bringing them up on deck to face he knew not what, for if sighted in groups the poor wretches, were they not cut down where they stood, would most certainly be tossed unceremoniously overboard to surely drown. The fetters would determine the outcome of such barbarity.

It was at that precise moment, as the Captain came out of his reverie that, once again another shout was heard from the crow's-nest, where the lookout had made another sighting. Whereas before it was practically a shadow, and ghostlike in appearance, now the mystery vessel began to take shape, growing larger in stature. There was still a fair distance between them but, as the *Marie-Louise* carried a heavy cargo, she progressed slowly, whilst the other ship advanced at a far greater speed, establishing the fact that her cargo, if any, was lighter.

The suspense was over at last, and calm prevailed amongst the crew now that the enemy was almost upon them.

When it seemed as though the mystery vessel was about to ram the *Marie-Louise* she suddenly and very quickly turned about avoiding close contact as both Masters observed each other's ensign. The suspected enemy carried the English flag and, according to the rapid conversation between them, was on her way to Gibraltar. She had stalked the *Marie-Louise* believing she was a pirate ship.

The relief was unmistakable as cheer upon cheer rent the air.

With danger averted, and in safer waters, the *Marie-Louise* could now resume her journey.

* * * * *

Daring the remainder of the journey Captain Renaulde – true to his word – spent much of his spare time relating information to his French passenger. He talked in such fine detail, that Jean-Paul had a very clear visual impression of the Deep South.

The Captain discussed fully the system of the Mississippi River, that derived its name from the Choctaw Indian phrase "mish sha suppukrie" which translated means "father of waters."

He told first of how the French landed on the gulf coast in 1699, to find the Old Southwest inhabited by the Choctaw, Chickasaw and Natchez Indians. It was thought these tribes were the original inhabitants of the Mississippi until evidence indicated human habitation as long ago perhaps as eight thousand years. So from this, it could only be assumed that the Indian tribes were not, after all, the first comers to the tracts of land surrounding the river.

"The Mississippi, all two thousand three hundred miles of it, is known for its enormous proportions Monsieur," the Captain went on. "A giant among rivers, used regularly by colourful paddlewheelers, their wheels turning and pressing backwards against the churned up murky waters, make a most welcome sight with their two-way transportation. And now to add to this conveyance, earlier this year the steamer *New Orleans* put in an appearance at Natchez for the first time, bringing about the beginning of a new era for steamboats.

Perhaps, in a decade or so there will be a good many more plying the river," he added.

The Captain ceased talking to puff deeply on the pipe he was smoking. The bowl fascinated Jean-Paul; it was such an elaborate style, one he had never seen before. It was quite large too, and would hold a considerable amount of tobacco. He couldn't stomach the offensive weed himself, but the Master of the ship appeared to be enjoying it. No doubt it relaxed him.

"If only the river could talk," the Captain began again. "To be sure it must have seen some tremendous activity through the ages."

Once again he fell silent, engrossed only in using his thumb to press the burning tobacco further into the bowl then, flourishing it so near as to pass the odour beneath Jean-Paul's sensitive nostrils, causing that gentleman considerable queasiness, he continued once more.

"Why, even now in our day and age it has become quite a common sight to perceive men from Kentucky, and parts of the Western frontier, floating products such as flour, pork, tobacco, hemp, iron, sassafras and, most important of all, pelts brought by backwoods trappers from mid-America. This method of trading began around 1785," the Captain explained, "when goods would be systematically poled down the Mississippi on flatboats by these rivermen, whose expertise came about with the regularity of such distance travelled in a specific time, as well as being zealously loyal to the river's normal function which at times could be most unaccommodating. With the goods redeemed for money at the markets, first at Natchez, and finishing at New Orleans, the men would then trade their flatboats, making the return journey the only way available to them, through the 'Natchez Trace' But what a journey!" he added.

"Although you may never frequent the place Monsieur, the story of the 'Trace' is a wholly interesting narrative, and well worth a mention," enthused the Captain, smiling broadly at his passenger as he paused momentarily to partake – with noticeable relish – of a long and satisfying swig from his already replenished tankard.

"Talking is dry work," he remarked, wiping his mouth, and chin – where the liquid had spilt – with the back of his hand and, easing his body into a more comfortable position, resumed where he had left off.

"In bygone days the 'Trace', known as 'Path to the Choctaw Nation', was just a wilderness, trampled into some semblance of an exit by scores of Indians who used it to and from Natchez, the tract of land of their own choice. It became, gradually, a recognised footway, although narrow and devious, not constructed into anything like a road for walking or riding, but merely beaten and ground under foot in recent years, to a greater degree, by pioneers, missionaries, boatmen, Indian traders and such like. Travellers have always faced enormous discomforts through each and every one of the four hundred and fifty miles the trace consists of, where danger could lurk in every shadow, and although around four years ago in 1808, great improvements were carried out to make the growing thoroughfare more presentable, those that use it still have to contend with vaporous swamps, alive with detestable insects and poisonous snakes. Travellers could fall foul of sickness, accidents, and most dangerous of all, unfriendly Indians and would-be robbers who would lie in wait to pounce upon their victims. All in all Monsieur, not a very pleasant place to venture into by any means," the Captain added.

"It remains only for me to describe New Orleans," he went on, "by which time, and by the grace of God, we should reach the end of our journey."

He made to rise from his seat when an interruption at the cabin door revealed Mr Ketch, the first mate, accompanied by the ship's bos'un, who was in charge of sails and rigging.

"Will ye come aloft now Cap'n surr?" the first mate asked. "A storm be a brewing, an' it looks a might nasty."

With a thoughtful look upon his face the Captain turned once again to his passenger.

"You have little need to concern yourself, Monsieur" he told him. "You are in good hands with my crew, but all the same I should confine myself to my bunk if I were you. We are in an area of known disturbances," he explained, "and unless one is accustomed to such storms it can he most distressing."

He had hardly finished speaking when the ship suddenly lurched to one side causing several articles to fall to the ground with a loud clatter, quite startling the occupants, who to regain their balance, had to cling tightly to items of sturdy furniture.

"You can sit here if you so prefer," the Captain suggested to Jean-Paul, as he vacated his seat. "It holds wholly fast to the floor, and is quite safe. It will only move if the floor gives way." He smiled at his own quip as he moved towards the cabin door, trying to make light of the situation.

"You are right as always Mr Ketch," the Captain said, agreeing with the first mate wholeheartedly. "This disturbance certainly has all the signs of a bad 'un." There was no mistaking the significant rate of increase in the velocity of the storm, as the ominous sounds now reached their ears.

"Make haste, bos'un. Lower the sails, and ride the storm," the Captain told the seaman, his face expressing concern. "We're in for a very rough time, but let us hope the good Lord will bring us safely through," he added, as the three of them hurriedly left the cabin.

Alone with his thoughts Jean-Paul had to admit he was scared. There was no use denying it. The winds whistling and howling through the ship had, by now, reached a crescendo, and the sounds were terrifying. It did nothing to abate his fears, but served only to bring back terrible memories of the Cornish storm.

He had decided he would stay here where he was, in the Captain's cabin. He didn't feel so hemmed in, and felt too nervous anyway to lie on his bunk, so the stalwart seat would do very nicely.

The winds grew stronger by the minute, and became even more violent. He heard, unmistakably the muffled crack and rumble of thunder breaking overhead. Naturally he couldn't see, but could visualise the persistent sheet lightning, that would be shooting across the skies: a frightening experience for the crew, as well as an added peril. Also the rise and fall of the ship in the raging seas, as well as the continuous lurching from side to side must be horrifying for them. He could hear the dull clumping of their feet overhead as the crew struggled to keep their balance. He knew without seeing them that they would be grim-faced, and desperate in their attempt to keep control of the *Marie-Louise*.

He could picture also their faces cold and wet from the heavy spray, and sense the despair they must feel as the deck would be awash with the mountainous waves, that rising high against the mast, would hit the ship with terrible ferocity, to scare even the bravest of men.

'Am I after all to lose my life at sea?' he asked himself. He, who had twice been miraculously snatched from the jaws of death!

Again, the ship pitched and shuddered. She dipped and rose with the swell, and the timbers strained against the pegs that held them together. She then plunged perilously deep down into the swirling waters that slammed the ship to such a degree that she heeled over very close to capsizing.

Added to this, and the expected discomfort that anyone would experience in such circumstances, Jean-Paul fought to ward off the mounting nausea which threatened to overwhelm him... and as well, his thoughts began to run amok, playing havoc with his emotions, which were brimming over with anxiety for the slaves down in the hold. They would, for certain, be huddled together, as far as the fetters would allow. The poor wretches must believe that each lurch of the *Marie-Louise* was a step nearer death. They would be aware, even in their state of stupor, that the belly of the ship could burst its sides, spewing them unceremoniously into the raging seas, where they would drown without dignity.

Now and then, above the sounds of the storm, Jean-Paul was sure that he could hear frightened cries from the hold. This distressed him to such an extent, that he could not help but conjure up a picture of ships that housed cruel Captains, and their crews who would, on hearing the torturous cries of the slaves in the holds, climb down amongst them flaying their whips across the many bodies shining with sweat from close proximity of too many humans in too small a place. This barbaric treatment did exist, he knew only too well, and was a reality more often than not. He thanked God that the Captain of the *Marie-Louise* was a kindly soul, and not given to bouts of temper and savagery.

A lull in the storm must have sent him off to sleep, for suddenly Jean-Paul was awakened by a noise outside the cabin door, which opened to reveal the Captain, who looked completely exhausted and strained of face, his oil-skins dripping with water to such an extent that from where he stood a pool spread rapidly across the wooden floor.

"This is the first chance I have had Monsieur, to come down and find out how you fared in that atrocious weather," the Captain began, looking around the cabin to see if anything was amiss. "Only, with the severity of the storm the ship has sustained some damage, even though she rode it well. At times, up there, I thought our end would come, for we could so easily have been devoured by the sea, but luck was on our side, and by the grace of God we were brought safely through. But not all of us," he went on to explain. "I am sorely troubled by the loss of two of my crew. They were swept overboard as the ship suddenly listed to one side, when heavy waves struck her amidships with full force. There was nothing we could do to save them," he added. His weary face clouded over with emotion.

"Please accept my commiserations Capitain," Jean-Paul said, feeling a great sympathy for the Master of the ship. "For it is a terrible tragedy," he added. What else could he say?

"You are a most courteous passenger Monsieur. I speak for everyone on the *Marie-Louise* when I say this," the Captain told Jean-Paul. "Your kind condolence is much appreciated, I can assure you." He suddenly ceased speaking, and listened intently.

"It is just as I thought," he began again. "The rain is still falling in a deluge, but at least the storm has, at last, blown itself out. When the rain clears, and it will, it is my intention to conduct a short service to show respect for the men who perished," he went on. "If, Monsieur, you would like to attend, you are most welcome, for I am aware that you have, at times, spoken with those that died."

"I shall be honoured to be present," Jean-Paul told him. "Meanwhile, I shall return to my cabin and freshen up in readiness."

"It won't be for a while yet," the Captain said. "I have to supervise the repairs that are being carried out, and I must see to the wants of the slaves, and bring them up on deck for an airing. They have been confined too long as it is. When everything is in order, and it is time, I'll send Josh down for you anyway," he added, as he moved to open the cabin door, and stepping outside in the passageway, quietly closed it behind him.

* * * * *

At twelve of the clock, as arranged, Josh escorted Jean-Paul from his cabin to the top deck, where the whole crew were assembled before the Captain. Heads bowed, and caps in hand, sadly subdued by the death of two of their own kind.

The entire ship refrained from speech or noise until Jean-Paul and the cabin boy walked quickly across the freshly scrubbed platform of planks, their footsteps echoing all the way.

As the Captain predicted, the rain had cleared, and the sun shone high in the sky, so blue as to mirror its deep colour in the waters below.

With everyone present, the Captain commenced the service. His voice carried loud and clear across the deck. He wasted no time, coming straight to the point. He spoke with conviction, ending by praising both seamen who, he said, "had given their lives for the safety of the *Marie-Louise*, and her Captain." There were no bodies to slide dramatically into the deep waters, so after a full minute spent in silence, Captain Renaulde dismissed the crew, and they quickly dispersed to take up their respective duties. They had paid their last respects.

Jean-Paul decided to stay up on deck in the hope that the fresh air would help to ward off the queasy feeling that still persisted in the pit of his stomach. He walked across to join the Captain who was leaning against the bulwark still looking somewhat exhausted, which was not surprising with the trauma he had been through of late. He felt bad enough himself, and that was without having taken any active part in the storm. The whole episode had been a most frightening experience, and one that Jean-Paul wished to put far behind him. He couldn't wait for the *Marie-Louise* to dock at New Orleans, and felt sure that the Captain and his crew would feel much the same. In any case, it wouldn't be too long now as he understood the end of the journey was only days away; a week at the most, allowing for any technical hitches.

* * * * *

Since the cyclonic disturbance the weather had remained unbearably hot and, at times, very oppressive, too uncomfortable by far for Jean-Paul to stay in his cabin, except during the nights, when it would be cooler. He spent hours on deck, standing by the bulwark, looking out to sea which, calm and unruffled, stretched as far as the eye could see on to a scene of extreme tranquillity.

The Captain would join him when his duties permitted and, as well, Jean-Paul was a guest every evening at the Captain's table, where he was able to partake of the food with a little more relish, now that he was used to the meagre menu. In any case, it was either eat, or go hungry, and he had made his choice.

Even the slaves enjoyed extra airings which were considerably lengthened during the hottest part of each day, when the hold would be swilled, cleansed and aired in readiness for their return, more relaxed, and seemingly happier in themselves.

* * * * *

The few remaining days passed quickly enough as Jean-Paul listened intently to Captain Renaulde's narration of New Orleans. The extreme pleasure he had derived from the detailed rendering of the Mississippi was, if anything, slightly dimmed in comparison to the French Quarter, which the Captain was now in the throes of describing.

"Known as Vieux Carré, meaning 'Old Square', it is the actual birthplace of New Orleans," the Captain told Jean-Paul. "It's a dry expanse of high land surrounded by swamps on a sharp bend in the Mississippi River."

He paused momentarily to ease his position from where he leant against the bulwark. He felt stickily hot, and pulled at the top fastener of his reefer jacket to clear the perspiration that had gathered in droplets inside the neck collar. How he prayed for a cool breeze. It was so damnably hot!

"Vieux Carré," the Captain began again, "is romantic, elegant, vibrant and even bawdy, but very real to the mixed races that grace her streets – such as the French, Spanish, Italians, Irish and Germans – to name but a few. And, as well, she has gathered much wealth by being so advantageously placed with the two-way transportation source of the river for all kinds of produce. Talking of produce Monsieur, one of your many duties will be that of supervising the loading of cotton for transit at the Square. It is brought there in 100-pound packs from the plantation – in the main – strapped to the backs of strong slaves although, depending on the amount of picking, and the time factor, carts are used as well to bring the bulk of the crop. Also," the Captain went on to explain, "it is where you will trade and barter for slaves on behalf of your employer, and your decision and final choice will stand firm with her. But a useful tip, Monsieur! One my brother Shaun mentioned when I last saw him. Be sure to examine each slave by looking for any defects in the throat, ears, underarms and groin. You understand?" he asked. "But then, you will soon be used to the routine, and when you do you'll know just what to look for, and the rest will come easily."

To satisfy himself that all was well with his crew, the Captain paused once again to glance aloft, and then around that part of the deck that he could see from where he was standing. He glanced too, out over the still waters, his thoughts in some turmoil. A picture of his wife and children, vivid in his memory, sprang forth before his eyes. He waited with growing anticipation to see them again after so long at sea, so the break at New Orleans couldn't come quickly enough. And when it did, whatever time would be allotted to him would be spent with his family. His wife – part Creole – would fuss over him, and spoil him with many tasty dishes 'to make up' she would say 'for all the food that had been denied him at sea.' Between them they had a good understanding, so gratifying when he had to spend so many months away from home. He was not sure how much longer he could cope with this way of life, although he loved the sea with its excitement and challenge. And he was proud too that he was Master of the *Marie-Louise*. But, she had become part of him, and had encroached on his marriage making him feel somewhat guilty. Therefore, he was now of the opinion that his wife must need him more than he needed the sea. So, when he would eventually return to France, he should have decided whether to relinquish his position, and give up the sea. It was a big decision to make, and he pondered on the outcome.

He came out of his reverie to once again face his passenger who, aware that the Captain needed a break from talking, remained silent at his side, taking in the scene before him.

"Shall we stroll around the ship awhile Monsieur, and afterwards partake of some refreshments in my cabin?" the Captain asked Jean-Paul, who nodded in agreement as he became aware of how famished he was.

An hour or so later found both men back at the bulwark well replenished, and eager to return to the absorbing subject of the French Quarter. It was still much too hot to remain in the cabin for any length of time. Because of the constant heat, the grille of the hold had been pulled right back to give the slaves a little more air – if at all possible – and, as well, the crew with their exacting duties were, one and all, stripped to the waist. Even Jean-Paul had removed his outer cut-away coat, leaving him arrayed in an elaborately coloured waistcoat over a white silk shirt, loosened at the neck. Of one thing he was sure; he would never become accustomed to this persistent heat. Even so, such a thought couldn't deter the excitement that stirred continually in his breast, as each hour brought him that much closer to his longed-for destination. If he had suffered any qualms with regard to his future, these had now been quelled, which he credited to Captain Renaulde who, he suddenly realised, was speaking again.

"When you have good reason to frequent the French Quarter Monsieur, you are certain to notice that a goodly number of houses are incredibly grandiose, like mansions, with their striking Spanish architecture, their elegant courtyards and semi-tropical gardens," the Captain told Jean-Paul. "Naturally, it is only the very wealthy that can boast of such a home, and your employer is one of them. Madame Perrie," he went on to explain, "procured the mansion La Demeure through the unfortunate failure of a once prosperous planter whose crops broke down over three successive years, to make the poor fellow insolvent. The circumstances were most tragic as I remember them," he added.

The Captain fell silent, his expression saddening as the memory came flooding back. It was five years since he had heard the grim tale from his brother, but even so, the event was still as fresh in his mind as though it had just happened.

"After the delayed shock of his insolvency," the Captain continued, "not many days had passed before news of his untimely death became known. He had borne his losses badly, and unable to face ruin, or his family, he walked into the swamp, and shot himself. With creditors waiting to recover vast amounts of money, the widow had no alternative but to sell her much loved home, and this is where your employer showed her good character – as a caring person – for not only did she recompense her with a relatively higher price, she gave the grieving widow the opportunity to stay at the mansion as the *chatelaine*. This, she accepted, and has since become invaluable to Madame Perrie, especially when organising the annual ball, held each year in the Fall. A very grand affair it is too," he added as an after thought.

Reaching inside his jacket pocket for his watch, the Captain had to peer to see that it showed the time as almost ten of the clock. The day had long been over without either of the men noticing the darkness coming down, and the night drawing nigh. Shadows had already spread rapidly across the sky, only permitting a star, here and there, to peep through.

Suddenly, a distinct change came about in the atmosphere as the warmth went out of the air, and a thick haze came down over the inky black waters that rippled and rolled into the base of the ship, as gentle winds developed, and heaven sent breezes blew a fine salt spray into their nostrils.

Both men gulped in the fresher air with relief and much relish, as they moved away from the bulwark, to make their respective ways back to their cabins.

* * * * *

The remaining part of the journey was quite uneventful, although very tedious, and this, coupled with impatience, made the time drag persistently for everyone, as the ship crawled along through the smooth and tranquil waters, but the end was in sight as the last day arrived and the *Marie-Louise* slipped quietly and slowly into harbour, and after a short delay was piloted to the port of New Orleans.

For himself, Jean-Paul was more than eager to step off the ship on to terra firma.

* * * * *

Reminiscing about the journey had somewhat slowed down Jean-Paul's dressing...

It was some time since, he now remembered, that Betsy had called from the lounge to say she had placed some refreshments on the table so, with his body cleansed, and his long dark hair groomed and arranged back off his face with a ribbon, he slipped into a stylish dressing gown to partake of the daintily cut sandwiches, with a choice of sweet-cakes to follow and, as well, a welcoming fruit drink to finish with.

Eventually completing his toilet, he was ready to meet his new employer. His apparel consisted of a three-quarter length rich burgundy velvet cut-away coat, deeply flared into pleats from the waist, with matching waistcoat set over a silk cream shirt with lacy cuffs extending well below the coat sleeves, and a jabot to match, caught at the throat with an elaborate pin. To complete the outfit, he wore cream suede breeches tucked into thigh length black leather boots.

He looked the perfect gentleman, and as he glanced once more at his reflection in the full-length mirror, he felt more than pleased with what he saw, particularly his beard which he had decided to keep after shaping it so meticulously.

Little did he know that his appearance would cause a passionate heart to beat faster.

* * * * *

Chapter Seven

A New Beginning

Madame Perrie was at that moment reclining in the drawing room. She had returned from the plantation on horseback, and ached in every limb. It had been a very long day, and the oppressive heat hadn't helped very much. It would happen like this today of all days, she thought, when she needed to be on top form to meet her new employee. She had no qualms that he would pass muster, coming as he did highly recommended by dear mama. She couldn't deny the eagerness she felt, and perhaps, not unexpectedly some anticipation as to the outcome of her decision. She hadn't been forced to employ the Frenchman, and had she objected to the arrangement, mama would have fully understood, and accepted her judgement without question, although she couldn't help but suspect that dear mama had an ulterior motive in what she had suggested. Well, it would all come to light eventually, that was certain, for Lady Pendavan was one who would explain her reasons fully when the time was ripe. There was a great bond between mother and daughter. It had always been so. She knew already that the Frenchman had endeared himself to her mother and she had nursed him back to health, following the terrible storm at sea, when he had so nearly lost his life. She understood also from mama's letter that Ruan and Michael, as well as Rushie, had taken to him also. It would be wonderful to have someone trustworthy to take over the exacting duties, and such a relief for her. For since her husband Andre had passed away, she had thrown herself completely into an expenditure of energy by taking on extra work. But to what purpose? she often asked herself. What did it mean to her now? She was a wealthy woman and still young. There was nothing she wanted for, and up to the devastating time that Andre had been taken so suddenly from her, she had been deliriously happy, when every day had meant something to her. He had felt the same way. So understandably, her life had turned completely upside down. She suffered days of terrible depression so, to try and overcome these feelings, work seemed to be the only answer. It was an achievement that was beginning to take away the terrible hurt, but by the end of each day she was completely exhausted, especially now that Zeb – her overseer – was ill. Things were piling up on her, and she definitely needed help. Happily, it was available now through dear mama, with her choice of the Frenchman.

Madame Perrie tipped her head against the high chair back, and closed her eyes. She soon began to relax fully, and within a few minutes was fast asleep. The next thing she knew was Betsy awakening her with her usual refreshments, and to inform her mistress that the last meal of the day would be ready in one hour. Time for her to change into her evening wear, and ready herself to meet her new employee.

* * * * *

When a short while later Betsy escorted the Frenchman to the drawing room, she stood at the side of the open door, and called in very clear tones.

"Maitresse! the new Maitre, ee is ere." She spoke with feeling and pride, and by the look on her face, Madame Perrie realised that her second in command was already smitten with the handsome man.

Jean-Paul walked towards the centre of the room and, as his new employer rose from her chair to greet him he had reached her side, and taking her hand within his own, gently placed it to his lips, lightly brushing the fingertips.

He took in everything about her at a glance. She was tall and slender, with beautiful features. Her hair – tawny blonde in colour – was really magnificent. This hung in ringlets down to her shoulders, and was accentuated by the splendid low necked black velvet gown she was wearing. And, as well, it set off to perfection her flawless milk-white complexion. Her beauty surpassed anything Jean-Paul had ever seen. His glance became searching, and although he realised he was actually staring, he could do nothing about it, in any case, he was reluctant to look away as he felt so drawn towards her.

If Jean-Paul was startled, the same could be said of Madame Perrie. She too, seemed mesmerised, and was greatly impressed with the Frenchman standing so close to her, his eyes boring into hers. Neither had spoken, and the whole atmosphere was charged with emotion.

The silence was suddenly broken as Jean-Paul – remembering his manners – stepped back, relinquishing her hand as he did so, and clicking his heels in salute, he bowed from the waist.

Recovering her composure Madame Perrie sat down, indicating to her new employee to do the same by pointing to a chair very near to her.

"Did you have a good journey Monsieur?" she inquired, speaking in dulcet tones. Her voice was soothing, rather than sharp or rasping. "It must have been somewhat tedious for you, so many days at sea," she added.

"In actual fact Madame, I quite enjoyed it," Jean-Paul explained. "There were incidents, naturally. Some were quite frightening, but on the whole the time went fairly quickly for me, as the Captain of the *Marie-Louise* spent much of his spare time narrating the ways of the Mississippi, and New Orleans."

"Well Monsieur! I am more than delighted that you have arrived safely." She told him, "I understand from my mother, Lady Pendavan, that you are interested, and available, of course, to help us in managing our affairs. You will work with me until you are used to your many duties, at which time I can then relinquish some of mine," she added.

"Madame! You can trust me implicitly to do any work you wish," Jean-Paul said, speaking with strong conviction, "I shall work long and laboriously, and shall not flinch at any task that you may put before me." He ceased speaking momentarily, and then, "I feel most honoured that Lady Pendavan and your good self have given me the opportunity to begin a new life," he continued. "It is what I have always dreamed of, and hoped for."

Just then Betsy appeared at the drawing room door – after first giving a light tap – to inform her maitresse that dinner was served.

"Monsieur! Let us proceed to the dining room before our meal becomes cold." So saying, Madame Perrie rose from her chair, beckoning Jean-Paul to do likewise.

* * * * *

The dining-room, long and sparsely furnished, was situated in an ideal position to receive as much air as was possible in the extreme heat. Double doors, and windows at either side all opened on to an unconfined space so that the owner would not feel penned in. Positioned directly below the ceiling, above the dining table, hung a fan that agitated the current of air, easing the heat considerably.

Whilst the meal was in progress silence prevailed. As Betsy had promised, the meal was something special, and met with the full approval of Jean-Paul, who had never partaken of a Southern dish. The last course was extremely satisfying too. There was a selection of sweet meats, consisting of jellies, preserved fruits; puddings, with lashings of thick cream and bonbons. Everything in fact to suit any one particular individual's taste.

With the meal completed, Madame Perrie, accompanied by Jean-Paul, returned to the drawing room to partake of refreshments. There were, as well as the usual pots of tea and coffee, varied liqueurs and spirituous liquors if so required, but the Frenchman much preferred the more refreshing drink of tea. He wasn't really a spirit person at all, having little penchant for the aromatic substances.

Eventually, when both were fully relaxed, the conversation reverted to the subject of the plantation, and Jean-Paul's forthcoming duties. There was much to discuss, in particular, the daily routine or the vast estate that carried a crop of fully grown plants, needing rapid harvesting. "This task is most urgent in case the weather pattern should change," Madame Perrie explained. "At the moment it is kind to us, and for certain ideal for the amount of work entailed," she went on. "But should the conditions alter, which they could so easily do, the full blown crops could be completely destroyed, in no time at all," she added.

Jean-Paul listened intently to his employer. He had no intention of interrupting her. For it was important to him to understand his duties, and accept them on her terms. All he wished for was to please, and allow her the opportunity to rely on him implicitly.

"I am most fortunate indeed to have such excellent workers on the plantation," Madame Perrie began again. "So as you would expect, they have little need to be driven, mainly I believe, because Zeb, my overseer – who incidentally is laid low at the present time – is so good with all the slaves. He is both firm and fair at the same time, and they respect him for his understanding. Hopefully, he should be well again, and back in harness within the week," she told Jean-Paul, trying, it would seem, to put him at his ease. "However, I must be honest with you," she continued. "There are sure to be some difficulties. That is a certainty, but I shall be near at hand to support you," she added, smiling in a friendly manner.

"On the morrow we shall go directly to the plantation, to supervise, and help with the cotton picking," Madame Perrie went on to explain further. "Naturally, this will necessitate a comparatively early start. Betsy will awaken you at six with your first meal of the day, and we shall need to leave here us soon as you conveniently can; firstly, I shall go to the stables for the horses," she continued, "they should be saddled, and ready for me to collect. "Our stables house a goodly number of excellent thoroughbreds, some highly spirited, but Leroy, our groom is sure to select the right one for you. We refrain from using the pure breeds on the plantation, as it wouldn't be fair to them," she added,

Rising from her seat, she suggested they both retire early, so as to be fresh for the busy day ahead. So, with the promise of more discussion on any subject of his asking, they wished each other good night, and walked away to their respective quarters.

* * * * *

Chapter Eight

Feelings Akin to Love

The dawn, with its grey shadows, fast disappeared as suddenly the sun struck, its brilliance glistening through the early morning haze, and lighting up the sky with a rich array of dazzling orange and gold colours, stretching as far as the eye could see. In the distance, distinguishable only by their outline, silhouetted against the light, the two riders rode their horses at a steady trot.

The early morning air, with a slight freshness that could last only until the excessive heat scorched everything in its path, brought forth and diffused an agreeable mixture of scents that intermingled with the earthy smell rising from the ground as the horses' hooves, over and over again, disturbed the soil.

Jean-Paul felt the excitement stir within him as his body moved in rhythm with the horse. He was very conscious of the animal's strength as it proceeded briskly along, showing its paces.

Lost in their own thoughts they rode in silence for the first part of the journey. For he himself, Jean-Paul had plenty to think about. That was for sure. He had to admit to a sudden exaggerated and quite unquestionable nervousness now that the day had really begun in earnest.

These feelings had first occurred during the night when his mind flitted from one thing to another, mostly, he had to agree, if he was completely honest with himself, his employer, and her extreme beauty, whose image - even at this early stage - was already imprinted on him for all time.

The morning call had come early enough, and to Jean-Paul it seemed his sleep had been somewhat fitful. It must have been two hours or even more before he closed his eyes and succumbed to the sheer comfort of the bed, until he was awakened by Betsy, with a warning from her that his first meal of the day would be brought in half an hour, allowing him just a short interval to be suitably attired for the days' duties. This he did manage to accomplish, with some difficulty, although he was seated at the table just as Betsy entered the room with all the eatables.

The meal, often chosen and partaken by most Orleanians - so Betsy informed him - was a choice of meats, highly flavoured and well-seasoned, and cooked as the usual *à la grillade*, served with a heap of *pain perdu* slices of bread dipped in beaten eggs and milk, and deeply fried. Steaming hot, these were laid more or less regularly upon one another in a shallow flat-bottomed vessel of earthenware, and the aroma coming from them, as well as from the meats, filtered across the room, making Jean-Paul realise how hungry he was.

Betsy fussed over him, and made sure everything was to his liking before she withdrew to the kitchen at the far end of the hall.

It was an enormous breakfast, and Jean-Paul partook of everything with relish. He found the meats appetising and distinctive, and made sure that he complimented Betsy on his way to the front entrance where the arrangement to meet his employer had been decided upon the night before.

She had already left the stables, and was in fact approaching on horseback leading a fine chestnut stallion - already saddled - with a magnificent flowing mane. His name was Henri she told Jean-Paul, who patted the horse. He placed his left foot in the stirrup, and swung into the saddle with great ease and skill, showing his horsemanship. A slight flick of the reins set the horse in motion, and they made for the plantation which, he understood, was quite some distance as they had to go to the section of the vast estate where the main work would be done. This area was the centre for gathering the cotton, and afterwards the dispersal and distribution of it.

* * * * *

Silence was forced upon them, mainly because the riders had to travel single file along the paths, which were not really wide enough to accommodate the two horses side by side. This made any conversation between them awkward. Had they talked, the morning chorus of whippoorwills, along with other sounds of wild life, and the dull thud of the horses' hooves as they hit the ground could possibly have gone quite unheeded, whereas the silence along the route was pleasantly acceptable to Jean-Paul, who was quite content to hold back and give Madame Perrie the lead. As well, it enabled him to glance at her as often as he wished without causing any embarrassment. He could not but help noticing that she sat her horse well, and looked good. Naturally, she was dressed to be comfortable.

She wore a soft brimmed hat that would provide good shade for her eyes. Her hair, twisted and interlaced into a long plait – tied at the ends with a ribbon – hung down her back on to a crisp white cotton blouse, opened at the neck, and tucked into breeches with strong boots pulled up over them. He was similarly attired.

Suddenly, the land opened out with plenty of space before them which enabled Jean-Paul to move ahead to join his employer who had already reined in her horse to wait for him.

Continuing the remainder of the journey, their conversation was quite varied. Madame Perrie, somewhat eager to seek information from this fascinating Frenchman, enquired of his life in France.

"Will you not miss the ways you are used to?" she asked of him. "And what of your close friends and acquaintances. Will you stay in touch with them?"

Jean-Paul's face clouded over momentarily as he recalled with sadness what had passed before. He still loved Semire deep down. His feeling for her could never change. But she had chosen another path far removed from his, forcing him to change his plans, albeit without an awareness of them, he had to admit in all fairness to her. Well, he told himself, she was in Paris, at her husband's side, and at his beck and call, and here he was in New Orleans, at the beginning of a new era, in the company of the very beautiful Madame Perrie, who was unattached, and fast becoming more dear to him by the minute. He was fully aware by this time that his strong feelings could eventually blossom into love. Naturally, he could never make the first move. She was his employer, and as such would expect the fullest respect from an employee.

He wasn't sure how much she knew of his reckless life in Paris, and wondered if Lady Pendavan had taken it upon herself to divulge his personal confidences to her daughter. He thought not, fully aware of that lady's integrity, and, as well, the fact that Madame Perrie was questioning him on certain matters, gave him to think that she knew little. He could explain one or two things to satisfy her curiosity, but he must deviate away from the actual truth. For a while, anyway.

"I should inform you Madame, that I have lived a very hazardous life in France, albeit an exciting one," be began. "With a flourishing wine trade, my adopted father gave me the reins – as the English say

– and I was fully expected to make important decisions for the benefit of the business. This entailed much travelling on my part," he went on to explain, "and, although I gained a certain amount of satisfaction from my effort, further demands were made on me, and things got completely out of hand to such an extent, that I decided that I had had enough, and was in the throes of making a change, when the tragedy occurred in Cornwall. The rest I believe you know," he added. "Your question as to whether I shall miss certain aspects of that part of my life, I can answer truthfully that I will, in particular my fencing classes, where I was esteemed and favourably accepted as 'Master Swordsman'. I am afraid the young blades of Paris will sorely miss my expert tuition," he remarked smiling broadly at his mock boastfulness, but clearly showing to his listener that he possessed a status he was most obviously proud of.

Eagerly attentive, and greatly impressed with what she had heard, Madame Perrie again addressed Jean-Paul.

"If you feel so inclined," she suggested, "I can arrange an introduction to a very skilled swordsman of a very high standard, who groups his many students together for their course of instruction at an auditorium in the French Quarter. He uses his sword scientifically, so I am certain that he will come up to your expectations," she added, with a smile, and a faint twinkle in her eye.

"This is most civil of you Madame," Jean-Paul said with feeling. "It would be most appreciated I can assure you. It would also give me the opportunity to contact my dearest friend, Dario de Laffiette, who resides in Paris, and is also an excellent swordsman. I will write to him almost at once, as he will be highly delighted to hear that I can continue with my fencing, as he is aware of my great love of the sport. He will also be anxious to hear of my safe arrival. We have grown up together," he went on to explain even further, "and have always been friends. So, as you may well guess, I sorely miss him, but I intend to keep in touch with a friend who means so much to me, as well, of course, as other acquaintances. That is sure," he added, remembering she had already asked if he intended doing so.

Madame Perrie glanced away from Jean-Paul to look at the scene before her. They had long since passed the outskirts of the plantation, and had now arrived at the centre section, where they would remain for the whole day.

Everywhere, the slaves had positioned themselves along the many rows, working laboriously, and at the same time, methodically. The slaves at the head of each row chanted in unison to keep them all going as one body.

Both riders reined in their horses and dismounted simultaneously, much to Jean-Paul's acute disappointment, as he had been very hopeful of assisting Madame Perrie from her high saddle to the ground. It would have been an ideal excuse to have made close contact without actually offending. As it was she alighted independently, and with efficiency, almost as though she was, at this stage, unwilling to be under any obligation to her new employee.

The horses were led away by two slaves to a stable, set well back at the fringe of the plantation. Here the men would tend the animals, after which they would be rested for the return journey.

Jean-Paul – who was quite fascinated by the speed and energy of the slaves – was able to quickly grasp the situation, and with spontaneous effort eventually joined in. His employer did likewise.

The plants, between four and five feet tall, were bursting with cotton, like white fluffy powder puffs. These were plucked from the hard shell, and packed into individual bales in considerable quantities in readiness for the journey to the 'Square' in the French Quarter. Once there, the desired quantity would be portioned out for transportation.

The exacting work, although back-breaking, was rewarding, and the day passed quickly enough, even so, it ended extremely late.

Jean-Paul couldn't remember when he had felt so exhausted. The constant heat had added to this feeling. At the end of the return journey he was ready to retire for the night. Although he was famished, he ate without being aware of what was put before him. He practically fell into bed after first being excused by Madame Perrie. After all, it was what that lady had anticipated, and prepared for his sheer physical exhaustion, was sympathetic in her feelings toward him.

* * * * *

Another four days were taken up with the same routine, until every piece of cotton had been collected. The crop had been extremely successful, so Madame Perrie had informed them all. She thanked everyone most profusely for their effort, and it only remained for the slaves to clear the mass of residue, which had accumulated all around the vast plantation, in readiness and preparation for the new growth.

Jean-Paul was informed that he was not required for this task. His employer had other plans.

* * * * *

Chapter Nine

Dominique

The day began like any other, but before it was to end there would come about some drastic changes where the present happy situation would be completely reversed.

No one could have foreseen what fate had in store, or the cruel blow she was about to deal the household. How could they when everything was running so smoothly?

* * * * *

Betsy had awakened Jean-Paul quite early as arranged with her mistress, served breakfast, and conveyed a message that Madame Perrie wished to see him in the drawing room as soon as it was conveniently possible.

Feeling much refreshed after a good night's rest, Jean-Paul looked forward with great zest to what lay before him, although he had no idea, as yet, what his employer had planned for the day, and wondered what she would suggest. He knew already that he wasn't required at the plantation, as he understood Zeb, the overseer, had now recovered sufficiently to return to his duties.

Jean-Paul felt somewhat relieved not to have to endure the tropical heat as he had done during the days just gone. He did suppose he would get used to it eventually. He would have to.

Glancing out of the window he was surprised to see, yet again, the weather still holding its high pressure pattern, giving promise of another fine day, once the overhanging mist had cleared. He was now well aware how suddenly the atmosphere could change in the area, from tranquillity to sudden violent storms, and he was curious as to how long an interval there would be before the change would occur.

He viewed the natural landscape, and noticed the leaves on the fine oaks dripping with moisture from the early morning dew, while the grass encircling the trees, so rich in colour, greatly embellished the whole picturesque scene extended before him.

Jean-Paul, overcome at the sheer splendour of the place, drew in a deep audible sigh of relief, and in his contented state, extended his arms above his head, and stretched to his full height. He had found his niche at long last, and was now in no doubt that he was destined for this occupation. Here was where his heart was, and nothing could alter that now.

He moved away, and walked over to the full-length mirror to take stock of his attire. Satisfied with his appearance, he made his way to the drawing room, where Madame Perrie waited to usher him in with a greeting that was full of warmth and friendliness, which Jean-Paul, with his quite impeccable manners and highly distinctive style, immediately reciprocated.

He was more than pleased to observe that her attitude visibly and most assuredly revealed a tendency towards contentment, and happiness. Emotions that were missing when first they met.

It did his heart good too, to think that in some way he could be partly responsible for this new phase, particularly as in the past few days they had noticeably drawn closer together, having spent so many hours in close proximity.

Now sitting opposite her in her own surroundings, Jean-Paul was full of admiration for everything his employer stood for. Her indefinable power of delighting was quite captivating. He couldn't fault her. If she beckoned, he would follow.

"I trust Monsieur that you had a comfortable night," Madame Perrie said. "I have planned a very full day for us both," she began. "It will be partly business, and partly pleasure, and I am sure Monsieur that you will be more than satisfied with the arrangements I have made."

She spoke excitedly, and her eagerness was clearly apparent to Jean-Paul.

"Ned will be here with the small phaeton in one hour from now, at nine o'clock," she went on to explain, "after which, he will drive us to the city, where at the square, in the French Quarter, slaves are to be auctioned. I shall expect to barter for a goodly number, providing, that is, that they have the characteristic qualities I am looking for," she added.

"It was at first my intention to send you on your own, to see how you would cope with the situation. But I changed my mind. After all, I couldn't throw you in at the deep end at this early stage, could I?" she said in a joking manner.

"You are as always most indulgent towards me Madame. But, with all due respect, do you not think – to relieve you of the task – that I could have the ability to barter quite successfully for slaves?" Jean-Paul asked of her. "After all," he went on, "I have been instructed well, not only by your good self, but by the Captain of the *Marie-Louise*, who was most informative about life on a plantation, and all that goes with it. Added to that," he continued, "I have also had the opportunity during the past days to make a study of your slaves, so I am sure I would be aware of what to look for."

"I am in definite agreement with everything that you say, and what you have suggested," Madame Perrie replied. "However, Monsieur, present circumstances necessitate my leaving the arrangements as they stand, even though I am really desperate for some relaxation. Unaccustomed as you are, and surely will be for some little while yet, to the wiles of the traders and, at times, even the auctioneers, I am quite certain that you will be very grateful for my presence, and my support, as slave auctions can be a very wearing experience. But the next time, whenever, I shall be only too pleased to pass over the sole responsibility to your good self."

She glanced at her fob watch attached to her close fitting bodice, and gasping with amazement as to how quickly the time had passed, hurriedly vacated her chair catching her shoe in the hem of her long gown as she did so, which threw her off balance. It was Jean-Paul's quick thinking that saved her from falling heavily to the floor, as with a sudden and rapid movement he darted forward and caught her in his arms. They stood locked together for a few moments, unable to move. He could so easily have succumbed to the heaven-sent opportunity to rain kisses upon her, and hold her closely in a passionate embrace, but just in time he remembered who she was, and who he was, so struggling with his conflicting emotions and firm principles, he released her, albeit reluctantly.

The next few minutes were full of confusion, but even so, both were waiting at the front entrance by the time that Ned arrived in the open carriage.

As the journey commenced, the sun, already high in the sky radiated so much heat that the temperature rose persistently, to such a degree as to necessitate Madame Perrie holding a parasol over her to shade the brightness of the rays from her eyes.

* * * * *

Neither employer nor employee had a lot to say during travelling time, speaking only when the occasion warranted. It became quite apparent to both passengers that constant conversation was decidedly not to be in the offing, due mainly to the slight feeling of embarrassment existing between them since the episode in the drawing room. But at least, the drive itself into New Orleans afforded them both much pleasure, with plenty to view on the way, for dominating the whole area were masses of exotic plants, quite magnificent in their striking foliage, and flowers perfect in their first flush ablaze with colour.

When eventually they arrived in the city, Ned drew the horses to a halt as near to the Square as was possible, to enable his passengers to alight from the carriage. They had to mingle with the crowd, for there were people everywhere, wandering aimlessly in all directions towards – it would seem – they knew not what.

As Madame Perrie led the way to the chosen position in the Square, for the sale of slaves, she found it necessary to assert all her strength in an effort to gain access through the multitude of people that had congregated to take part in the auction. Jean-Paul, following in her wake, worried only that she would do herself a mischief. Now and then a few amongst the crowd would stand aside to allow them both their gradual advance through to the section where the slaves were cordoned off for inspection. It was quite obvious to anyone familiar with the bartering of slaves that they were all graded in groups. The males were separated from the females, the old from the young and the weak from the strong.

Madame Perrie searched long and hard amongst those that she favoured, mainly to enable her to memorise their characteristics when the auctioneers would start the bidding. They were accustomed to the lady planter of Mon de Vue, and mostly all treated her, as always, in a specified manner. Her high bids for the strongest slaves, young or old, was a frequent practice. She would never quibble over a price already assigned to any particular slave, and those she would eventually acquire would be invaluable to her, and worth every dollar that she would part with.

Although most of the auctioneers were completely honest and quite trustworthy, Madame Perrie was well aware that one or two could be a little crafty in their dealings, tending to arrange transactions before the sale, mainly to compel a combination of speculative buyers to raise prices by securing the monopoly and so obstruct the course of fair bidding.

Madame Perrie explained all this to Jean-Paul, as they made their way back to the auction block, where the sale was about to proceed.

* * * * *

The throng of people pressing and crushing close against the raised platform in an effort to glimpse the first group of slaves that were brought into view, were surely plantation owners and overseers. It was Jean-Paul's candid opinion that they were, as he thought he could easily identify them because of their extreme interest, and eventually, their ridiculously low bidding at the commencement of the sale.

Even the auctioneer smirked openly at the absurdity of the starting prices, although at the same time he couldn't help but groan inwardly at the derisory treatment he received from the noisy crowd. He was well aware that many of the culprits were lookers-on, and as the instigators of trouble, would urge the crowd on. He should by now be used to the usual mockery and scoffing amongst them, but their bad behaviour still had the power to rile him.

He sighed despairingly as he mopped his brow that dripped with perspiration caused, not only by the intense beat, but by sheer frustration.

Suddenly, above the constant noise, someone at the rear of the crowd shouted in a loud and carrying voice, a much more sensible and higher bid.

The auctioneer brightened visibly with the thought, after all, that his earlier worries may be quite unfounded, and perhaps now both he and his colleague could expect a good and profitable return from the proceeds of the auction. After all, he told himself, mostly all the slaves were in an excellent condition, and as such should each fetch a relatively high figure, to make the whole bartering well worth while.

He glanced around at the sea of faces before him, indicating as he did so, that he wished to begin the bidding again in earnest. He did however, make it very clear to all involved, that the foolishness and playing around must cease.

Within minutes the offers rose considerably, as the auctioneer made ready to praise the first group of over two hundred male slaves.

"These young males are a fine example of their class," he went on. "Born in slavery of slave parents they are, as you all can see, very fit and ideally suited for working in the fields."

He spoke in a persuasive manner, almost wheedling, to try and induce quick sales.

"Look here sirs. And Madame," he added, looking directly at Madame Perrie, who stood at the forefront of the massive crowd, "you can see for yourselves that I speak the truth," so saying he pushed several slaves forward, while at the same time – handling them not unkindly – turned each one completely around.

"You have only to look them over to know they will be diligent and hard-working," he continued, speaking convincingly.

The auctioneer wiped his brow repeatedly with an enormous 'kerchief, as the bartering went on and on. The hours slipped by – one, two; maybe three, or even four, until eventually the numbers diminished at a rapid pace, and the slaves becoming the legal property of the many planters, were now bound to absolute obedience.

Madame Perrie had herself acquired thirty-five in number – not totally unexpected amongst the other planters, as it was generally known throughout the delta that Mon-de-Vue was by far the largest plantation, except perhaps one other just below the 'Vieux Carré' owned by the grandest of Creoles, the Marquis Bernard Marigny, who was thought to be one of the most wealthy of men in the Mississippi area.

Now that many satisfied traders were leaving the Square, the crowd began to thin out, sufficiently enough to enable Madame Perrie to observe her near neighbour, Earl Revington, pushing his way forward towards the platform in an effort to purchase the few remaining slaves at give-away prices. She shuddered with the feeling of repugnance that the man seemed always to invoke in her, as she too moved away from the Square, with Jean-Paul following close behind.

Together they walked slowly across Decatur Street, through to the French Market, where the people jostled one another in their eagerness to watch pralines boiled in black iron pots and dropped on marble slabs to cool. Quite a favourite sweetmeat amongst the folk of New Orleans, so Jean-Paul was informed by his employer as they both advanced towards a small restaurant where she made the suggestion that they tarry a while to savour *café au lait* and *beignets* – unique square doughnuts – the aroma of which wafted towards them as they crossed the threshold to step down into a smaller section of the restaurant for light refreshments. Taking their seats at a clean and brightly laid table, they had to wait no time at all before being served hot beverages, and delicious doughnuts, of which they partook with great relish.

After a short interval, enough to regain some of their diminished energy, they left and made their way in the direction of Bourbon Street, and thence on to Royal Street, where as promised, Madame Perrie introduced Jean-Paul to the Fencing Master, Monsieur Chapeau, who was indeed more than delighted to make the acquaintance of the Frenchman who he knew at a glance was a real sportsman, and a man after his own heart. Both men arranged a tentative meeting a week from the day.

Still progressing along Royal Street, the next port of call was with the tailor, Monsieur Edouard Duvalle.

"A more obliging gentleman than you would ever wish to meet," Madame Perrie told Jean-Paul, before they entered the tailor's establishment.

A definite appointment was made after this meeting so that Monsieur Duvalle could receive instructions as to what his potential customer would require.

He bowed them out most graciously, in quite a self important manner. 'After all,' he told himself, 'am I not the finest tailor in the whole of Louisiana? He was well aware that the Frenchman's order could be substantial, that each and every garment must be utterly distinctive, and of superior quality. His chest swelled with pride and his opinion of his own excellence, as he returned once more to his exacting and laborious occupation.

* * * * *

Walking almost to the extreme end of Royal Street, Madame Perrie and Jean-Paul came to St Peter, where many of the fine buildings – mainly of Spanish architecture – stood out in their magnitude, one even more splendid than the rest. It was here that she halted, saying as she did so.

"This is my 'town house' Monsieur, considered by many to be almost a mansion."

She spoke judiciously, choosing to limit her praise and let Jean-Paul judge for himself after he had seen over the whole place. She couldn't say why, but it was important to her that he should like the home of which she was so fond. She intended to permit him to use the mansion whenever he so wished, particularly if his many duties necessitated frequent visits to the French Quarter.

They stepped inside an enormous entrance, which in turn led to a sumptuous hall, and a staircase of considerable dimensions. The walls were graced by magnificent pictures of life-like portraits and country scenes, painted by such well known artists as Van Dyck, Gainsborough, Watteau, Herring and Reynolds. Fine china and silver delicately positioned on splendid pieces of period furniture, placed to display their extreme beauty, and enhanced by exquisite draperies, were heightened to perfection by the crystal chandeliers hanging from the ceilings, that glistened and sparkled with reflected light, and tinkled with bell-like sounds at the slightest movement from below them. The whole scene suggested lavish expenditure, amassed – Jean-Paul had no doubt – from the wealth of cotton.

After viewing the remaining parts of the great house, and openly admiring what he saw, Jean-Paul was then introduced to the lady *chatelaine*, who immediately offered refreshments should the visitors desire them, but having been duly replenished earlier, they kindly declined. In any case, it would not be too long before Ned would arrive to collect them for the return journey to Mon-de-Vue. Madame Perrie preferred to travel in the light of day while the surroundings would still be visible.

Travelling in the open carriage, the two passengers appeared to be somewhat more relaxed. Jean-Paul enthused over the day, and both agreed it had been most enjoyable, and perfect in every way.

Madame Perrie hadn't had such pleasurable company for a very long time, and permitted herself to relate her feelings to Jean-Paul. They were both very aware by now of the strong bond growing between them, and because of it their manner became much more intimately familiar. Each time the Frenchman turned to glance at her, and speak, her heart bounded at a startling speed, almost as though it would leap straight out of her breast. For himself, Jean-Paul had great difficulty in controlling his amorous urge to take her in his arms, and smother her with kisses. His situation prevented these quite normal feelings, even though he now sensed a complete change in her attitude towards him. But he was most insistent with himself not to make the first move. It could frighten her, and bring about a barrier between them. For the time, at least, he must absorb her sheer loveliness. After all, a few months ago he hadn't even been aware of her existence. Now he couldn't imagine life without her. This, he argued with himself, could so easily happen if he were to rush things.

Lost in his thoughts of her he hadn't realised how near they were to the end of the journey until Mon-de-Vue suddenly came into view, and Ned drew the horses to a halt at the front entrance.

Jean-Paul stepped down from the carriage and turned immediately to Madame Perrie, who waited for him to assist her to the ground which he did by catching her around the waist with both hands, and slowly easing her down beside him; they remained standing in the same position for perhaps a full minute, or maybe even longer. He was very reluctant to release her at all.

* * * * *

The figure standing motionless behind the drapes at the window could see, but not be seen. The scene at the front entrance was clearly visible to her, and she could sense almost at once how things were between her stepmother, and the new 'Maitre' as Betsy had earlier described him. The Southern 'Mammy' had enthused so ardently about him that Dominique could hardly contain her impatience to meet him.

She had arrived without word or warning a few hours earlier, giving Betsy such a shock as to cause that 'Second in command' considerable misgivings. She knew that Dominique's sudden appearance at Mon-de-Vue could only spell trouble for her beloved maitresse, who was now enjoying life to a much greater degree since the new 'Maitre' had arrived at the plantation. She had shared the same opinion with her that this difficult young girl whose troublesome nature had caused so much hurt, after departing three months earlier, would never again return to her stepmother's home, but it would seem they were both very much mistaken, and she dreaded to think what this would do to her maitresse.

Minding her manners Betsy did offer some refreshments to Dominique, although she performed the duty somewhat half-heartedly, and then left the girl to her own devices.

* * * * *

As Madame Perrie entered the hall, closely followed by Jean-Paul, Betsy ambled towards them as quickly as her generous weight would allow to convey the news of the visitor, when that young woman suddenly appeared on the scene, swaggering in a most defiant way. Silence pervaded momentarily as both the women took careful stock of each other. To say Madame Perrie was startled was an understatement. It was a sudden shock for her to observe her stepdaughter standing there with the usual arrogant look on her face. She had thought not to see her again, and felt somewhat angry, and deflated at the same time.

Madame Perrie suddenly froze as Dominique moved nearer as though to embrace her, saying as she did so.

"Hallo step-mamma dear! I trust it is your intention to grant me an introduction to your new-found friend. Lately arrived, I understand." She spoke in a coolish, as well as snobbish and somewhat nonchalant manner, her voice quite lacking cordiality, although inwardly, had anyone known, she seethed with excitement.

Determined to ignore the girl's distasteful mode of behaviour – albeit outwardly – Madame Perrie said as calmly as she could manage under the present circumstances.

"Dominique. This gentleman, not long since departed from France, is named Monsieur Jean-Paul de Leon, and as luck would have it, has agreed to assist me by taking over a number of my most exacting duties and," she added, with a slight, but quite noticeable edge to her voice, "although you may find it difficult to accept, he is indeed a very good friend." She looked directly at him as she added further in a distinctly softened tone, "Monsieur, my step-daughter, Dominique."

Apart from clicking his heels in salute, and bowing stiffly from the waist, Jean-Paul took little interest in the girl, but Dominique, on the other hand, found the Frenchman most fascinating, and looked him over to such an extent as to make that gentleman feel most uncomfortable. It was whilst she scrutinised him, that Dominique's thoughts darted quickly from one to another in quick succession. It occurred to her that she would have no compunction whatever, or scruples even in using her cunning wiles to entice the handsome Frenchman away from her stepmother, who even she herself had to admit, was most beautiful. This admittance on her part fed her extreme jealousy and dislike of the woman who had dared to fall deeply in love with her own beloved father who she herself had adored with ardent passion, not wanting to share him with any other but herself, not even her own mother. And for this alone she would never forgive her stepmother. Her father's death had made her very bitter, and quite clouded her judgement in her hatred of his widow. However, Dominique had, at this point in time, decided to try not to antagonise her stepmother, especially as she intended to use her while redeeming what should be due to her. She was with child, three months on to be exact, and could remember quite clearly the very hour it was conceived. The man that had made her pregnant, was none other than her stepmother's near neighbour, Earl Revington, although no one could be the least bit wiser of her condition, and as well, no one could remotely know of their relationship, as they had both taken great pains to hide their short liaison. The father was not as yet aware of her condition, but soon would be if her devious plan worked. She had every intention of extracting monies from him by fair means or foul, even resorting to blackmail or voodoo, or even both should the need arise. In the latter she had been a most willing participant where he as an excellent teacher in the art of evil was concerned, and the knowledge of this she could, and would put to good use, even as far as her stepmother was concerned, for Dominique would stop at nothing to achieve that which she considered was rightly hers. Of one thing she was certain, she had plenty of weapons with which to fight, and she could deal her blows accordingly.

"Dominique. Are you intending to inform me of your reasons for this unexpected visit?" Madame Perrie asked, her voice penetrating the girl's thoughts. "Only I am truly at a loss to understand your reappearance here, especially as you departed Mon-de-Vue three months now gone – if I may remind you – in a not so amicable manner, and gave me the surety that I would never have to see you again," she went on. "It is a shock I must admit, and I am most sorely tempted to ask you to leave now, at once, before either of us may say something we shall regret."

Without any hesitation, Dominique was ready with her answer, speaking persuasively.

"I thought step-mamma you would be over-laden with extra work now that dear Papa is dead." She bit her trembling lip at the mention of her father, finding great difficulty in speaking normally with so much hatred coursing through her veins, but composing herself to a certain degree, she carried on, lowering her glance as she spoke, for she couldn't bring herself to look directly at her stepmother, who would be sure to see the sheer venom in her eyes.

"I felt somewhat guilty at having left you in such a displeasing manner step-mamma, and as well, leaving you alone to bear the brunt of the exacting work to do with the plantation, so here I am to offer my help." The lies sprang easily from her lips as she added: "Please do not refuse my chance to make amends for my behaviour."

Madame Perrie hesitated momentarily before she replied, her thoughts in a turmoil. She felt quite agitated, thinking all the while how every thing would now be spoilt with her step-daughter's presence at Mon-de-Vue. It would seem that her newly found happiness was to come to an abrupt end. Dominique would see to that, she knew. She could never trust her, of that she was certain, but she would have to give the girl the opportunity to make up for her misconduct, although her inner self argued against her own decision.

"I had not anticipated this happening at all Dominique," Madame Perrie replied at last. "Still, under the circumstances I can hardly refuse you. However, I must insist, for all our sakes, that you curb your customary ways, and your continual disregard of convention. So doing, perhaps we can live together amicably. I can only hope," she added, her voice hardly discernible, even to herself.

"I have changed, you will see," Dominique enthused. "All I ask is that you trust me."

"Betsy," Madame Perrie turned towards her second in command. "Take my step-daughter to her old room, which fortunately is just as she left it. See also that she is comfortable, and has all that she may need. And afterwards, Betsy, would you kindly serve light beverages and sandwiches in the drawing room for Monsieur and myself. If Dominique would care to join us later, she can do so," she added as an afterthought.

* * * * *

Later on retiring for the night, Jean-Paul was unable to sleep. Try as he might he could not fight off the strong feeling of impending doom, however much he tried. Like his employer he felt somewhat dejected , and very disappointed at the turn of events which had taken away some of the happiness that both he and Madame Perrie had assuredly experienced throughout the day, that had started out so well for them both.

* * * * *

Chapter Ten

Lull Before The Storm

Utterly incapable of endurance, Dominique experienced great difficulty in trying to be nice to everyone at Mon-de-Vue, so much so, that at times the continuous pretence was more than she could bear. She was already positively weary of the so-called pleasantries passing between herself and her stepmother, neither sincere. In consequence, the whole facade made her wonder how much longer she could control herself before showing her true feelings. But time was gradually passing; days into weeks, and weeks into almost two months when she suddenly realised that only a short interlude would need to pass before her future would be decided upon.

Dominique had lately devised a plan which she had considered carefully, and could now reflect upon. It had been her sole intention at first to visit Chartenelle and force Earl Revington to see her so that she could break the unhappy news to him of her pregnancy. She had no qualms in doing so, and knew exactly what his reaction would be, as he wouldn't want this to be generally known in New Orleans. But as far as she was concerned his physical emotions didn't come into it. She was the one carrying the child, and he had to pay for his mistake. And she would see that he did. But contacting him just hadn't materialised as yet. It was not that she had abandoned the idea of extracting monies from her past lover, only that she had set her sights at the Frenchman, and used numerous excuses to accompany him, either to the plantation estate, where his duties took up a great deal of his time, or the occasional visit to the 'French Quarter' when she could sit in close proximity with him when they travelled together in the carriage.

His manner towards her was mostly unyielding, so as not to encourage the girl, but this mattered not to Dominique, as his aloofness only helped to fan the flames within her. At first, it was just a game to her, to woo him away from her stepmother so that she could watch her suffer, but everything changed when after a few short days she became wholly obsessed with him, and her mind was preoccupied with the fixed idea of winning him over. Surely she could accomplish this,' she told herself. 'After all, am I not attractive to men, to all outward appearances that is?' She herself thought she was far superior to her stepmother, and seemingly well educated. Her dress sense was exceptional, and with youth on her side she surely could endear herself to him.

As the weeks remaining before she intended to strike went by, Dominique felt that she had made some headway, as the good looking Frenchman appeared far more relaxed when they were together. He would listen to what she had to say, and they could now converse, which was of great importance to her for what she had in mind.

For himself, Jean-Paul was actually deceived into believing the girl was genuinely adhering to her promise. But had he known, it was simply the lull before the storm.

* * * * *

At last the day had arrived for Dominique to set her clever scheme into motion. She selected the time as two hours past midday, when Betsy would be occupied with the preparation for cooking the last meal of the day, and her stepmother, Dominique knew, was at her town house, where presumably she had been for the past few days.

In her usual deceptive manner, Dominique was able to waylay the Frenchman on some minor pretext or other. Then all she needed was his full attention, as well as a sympathetic ear, and with the knowledge that they were both alone, decided the time was ideal for the first part of her plan in relating her tale of woe. Naturally, what she conveyed was a fabrication of the truth. Dominique used disjointed, and sometimes incoherent utterances to express the emotion, and explain her condition, added to which her speech was often hesitant as she forced the ready tears to her eyes, and cried quite openly, fully aware by this time how realistic her story must sound, and how pathetic she must look. So much so, that Jean-Paul, who was completely taken aback, and at the same time quite taken in by her, and aghast that she was with child, offered his support, and in so doing, allowed the girl the given opportunity she had been waiting for, to throw herself whole-heartedly into his arms and keep the deception going.

"I swear you... to secrecy," she said between her sobs. "My stepmother must... not hear of this calamity... until I am ready to inform her, so promise... you... will... tell no one," she entreated with him, drawing her breath in compulsive gasps, obviously under much mental distress.

Jean-Paul held her closer to him in an effort to comfort the distraught girl, saying as he did so in a very subdued voice.

"I swear to you on my honour as a gentleman, that what you have conveyed to me shall go no further. My lips shall be sealed." And he meant it. Not that he had any great liking for this very young, and partly French mademoiselle, he just felt very sorry for her in the predicament that she now found herself. But an onlooker looking in on the romantic interlude as it seemed – would put a different aspect on the whole picture which could only give a total visual impression of two people very much in love. And this is exactly what Madame Perrie's power of thinking was when – having returned earlier than expected from the city – she witnessed the tremulous, and quite emotional scene, the like of which could only serve to bring further repercussions on an already much strained household.

This was another victory for Dominique, giving her an added weapon to use against her stepmother, although at the time the girl was totally unaware of her good luck.

* * * * *

It was quite late in the afternoon on the following day that Madame Perrie could be found reclining in the drawing room, alone with her thoughts which were in a complete turmoil. Ever since she had received the devastating shock she had made a special effort in trying to diminish the emotional tension that had gradually built up within herself, and, as well, tried hard to come to terms with what she had seen, and that which she didn't wish to accept. It was what she had thought could happen, but had hoped the Frenchman would not succumb to temptation where her stepdaughter was concerned, and now it was quite obvious that he could not resist Dominique's continual enticement. With the agonising proof staring her firmly in the face, her worst fears were realised. For days now, she had been constantly aware of her strong feelings for the Frenchman that were akin to love. At first, the conviction was not based solely on reason, but gradually it became apparent to her that her emotions went far deeper than she had visualised, and now through a bizarre twist of fate she had lost him.

Madame Perrie, staring out of the window, although unseeingly, recalled to her mind what she had heard only a few hours earlier, the horror of which was still with her.

Dominique had requested an audience with her stepmother "on a most delicate matter" she explained.

Madame Perrie could think no other than that the girl wished to gloat over what had taken place between the Frenchman, and she herself, but surprisingly enough she appeared to be quite the opposite, with little resemblance whatever to her usual irritating manner. In fact, Dominique was distinctly subdued. That is if her stepmother could really and truly believe it so.

"Step-mamma," she began, having the grace to look somewhat guilty, "there is something that I have to convey to you, but it must remain a secret between us, at least, for a while." She sat down directly opposite Madame Perrie, as that lady indicated her to do so.

"I cannot soften the blow, so I shall come straight to the point," Dominique continued. "You will not want to hear what I have to say, I am sure, but I am with child, and the father is your new employee, and as you say, your good friend," she added, hardly able to contain herself using a sarcastic tone. She could observe already that she had given this woman, who had dared to love her late father, a devastating shock. How could it be otherwise, when her feelings for the Frenchman were openly displayed on her face for anyone to see? For this, Dominique could afford a distinct feeling of elation.

Madame Perrie could scarcely believe, or take in what her stepdaughter had imparted. Her emotions, already running high, threatened to stifle her. This then was the end of her dreams. She couldn't bring herself to speak. In any case, what was there to say after hearing such a bombshell?

The occupants of the room looked away from each other, lost in their own thoughts whilst silence prevailed, which was broken suddenly by Dominique, anxious now after planting the seeds to make her story good, and obtain the secrecy which would be essential to her plan, otherwise everything could be ruined.

"As you must be aware step-mamma," the girl began again, "Monsieur is considerably embarrassed because of the position he now finds himself in, so I am asking your indulgence, and to prevail upon you to keep the knowledge to yourself, until such time as my body shall swell with the child, and I can no longer hide the fact of my misdemeanour," she suggested, her tone now becoming persuasive, and wheedling at the same time.

Madame Perrie thought hard. She could hardly refuse what her stepdaughter was asking under the circumstances. In any case, how could she bring herself to broach a subject of such a delicate nature to Jean-Paul, for she too would be most embarrassed, to say the least? No, her lips would be sealed. At that she had made up her mind.

"Have no fear Dominique, your secret will be quite safe with me," Madame Perrie informed the girl. "And now, if you have nothing else to say on the subject, I prefer to be alone."

Dominique, who had the grace not to speak, shrugged her shoulders as she walked from the room. As the door closed behind her Madame Perrie's eyes welled up with tears. She had been so afraid lest her extreme distress should be witnessed by her young adversary and rival, and that she could not face. On the other side of the door, Dominique walked seemingly on air towards her own room in high spirits. That everything had gone well and according to plan, she knew. Far better in fact than even she could ever have hoped for. She had struck the deadliest of blows towards her stepmother, and this was success indeed. But even so, she realised that her next conquest would not be so easy or straightforward when she would decide to make her move towards the true father of her child – Earl Revington. A meaner man there never was, and cruel with it, although there was much fascination for someone like her to be loved sexually by such a man. Having been used this way had been good for her ego, but she was well aware that he had hoped never to set eyes on her again, so he was in for a shock, and she would enjoy his discomfort when notifying him. She had no illusions as to how difficult her task would be, but at least, she would, in this case, have truth on her side.

* * * * *

Chapter Eleven

Gris-Gris, Spell of Death

During the ensuing days and weeks following the harrowing event that had inflicted so much pain and sorrow on Madame Perrie, the atmosphere at Mon-de-Vue deteriorated to such a degree that tension between everyone became strained to the very limit.

Madame Perrie, who was now most decidedly unapproachable, had set up a closed barrier between herself and Jean-Paul, who was completely shocked and mystified at his employer's change of heart. Because his thoughts were full of uneasiness through dwelling continuously on the problems, he could get little rest, or peace of mind. He had almost persuaded himself that the whole set of circumstances must be put down to the unwelcome presence of Dominique, who had most assuredly driven her stepmother into a state of depression, to such an extent that seemingly the lady was unable to pull herself together. Jean-Paul, finding he was unable to breach any subject, decided to keep out of the way, and did so, more often than not. In consequence, the situation was becoming absolutely intolerable.

As for Madame Perrie herself, the wounds went so deep that she had decided she could no longer remain at the plantation. The present difficulties at Mon-de-Vue could not be resolved so easily, not for several months anyway, not until such time that Dominique would give birth to the child. And, after that, well there would have to be some changes, serious ones at that. She had no illusions as to the outcome. And until this would come about, she had made up her mind to take up indefinite residence in her town house for a well earned rest. Her only wish was that it could have been under different circumstances, when she would have enjoyed the change of environment; whereas she would still be grieving, but, at least, her sorrow could not be witnessed.

As yet, no one was aware of her plans. Not even Betsy, who feeling the need to convey her innermost feelings, chose to speak to Leroy, when he entered the kitchen from the stables to partake of his meal.

"Ise dat worrit abowt de maitresse," Betsy began, pausing to place a steaming hot bowl of vegetable stew in front of her listener.

"Yez se Leroy," she carried on again, "de maitresse, she don laf animort cose oh dat gal, woo now brins bad truble fer err." She tutted as she moved away to the far end of the kitchen where she attended to her chores, mumbling to herself as she did so. Betsy too, was in a distressed state.

Dominique, on the other hand was a trifle more affable than was her usual wont, although even she appeared, at times, to be preoccupied, with her thoughts elsewhere. What she had on her mind was taking precedence over all else. She had made her plans, and to all intent and purposes, felt they would succeed.

Her final decision to approach Earl Revington was made one week after her stepmother departed for the French Quarter, where it was now known she would not return for some little while. Dominique, was more than delighted with the news, and gloated again over her victory in driving her out. This meant, of course, that she could have Jean-Paul to herself, most of the time anyway. But the gentleman himself, terribly distressed at Madame Perrie's decision to leave the plantation, had no intention of allowing the girl any liberties whatever.

* * * * *

Earl Revington stood rooted to the spot as he suddenly recognised the figure on horseback moving slowly in his direction. He couldn't mistake her stance or bodily posture, although she was some distance away. He had thought to have seen the last of young Mademoiselle Dominique, and her return - he knew - could only spell trouble for him. They were so alike, and each were only too aware how far the other would go to obtain his or her own ends. For a while, during their very brief liaison the girl had been an exciting, and quite voluntary sexual outlet from his undemonstrative wife. He had to have excitement, and plenty of it, which was how he came to be dedicated to and bewitched by voodoo. He had over a period of time, become extremely skilled in witchcraft, and to him it was a system of religious worship, in which he was deeply involved. It was through this interest that he had entered into the relationship with Dominique, because of her liking for the same cruelty that always came uppermost in voodoo, that he in turn craved for himself. But it was a mistake to have indulged in intimacy with such a calculating wench, and now he could not but deny his complete aversion to this young miss, attractive though she may be. She mirrored his own devious and heinously evil ways and he did not like what he could see. Her enticement of him had, for a while, driven him almost to distraction, but she became too demanding by far for his liking, thinking only of herself. And here she was now, entering Chartenelle in her most brazen manner yet, caring not who would see her. Fortunately, the plantation house was a fair distance away from where he was standing, safe from prying eyes.

With his thoughts darting from one to the other, Earl Revington hadn't realised that Dominique was almost upon him until she suddenly drew the horse to a halt just feet away. He moved quickly towards her to assist the girl with dismounting. Not that he wanted to, but it was what she would expect, and to cross her would only aggravate any situation that could arise. She would have no qualms – he knew – in denouncing him as a voodoo worshipper of the worst kind, and if that wasn't enough, she could, and would most certainly bring to light the regular slaying of new-born infants for the many ceremonies that had, for some time, become essential to the rites. Her knowledge was dangerous, to say the least. He should never have involved her in his absorbing obsession. He was assuredly aware of that now. For beneath his bravado he had a fear of her, which had abated somewhat since her departure from New Orleans. Now, here she was back again, and little did he guess the reason for her visit, or of the blow she was about to deal him. And she wasted little time in coming straight to the point.

"Hello Earl, *chéri*," she greeted him, flinging her arms around his neck, and kissing him fully on the lips. "I have such a surprise for you," she went on. "Would you believe, I carry your child?"

Earl Revington had the grace to pale significantly, but said not a word. He certainly could not accept offhand what he had heard, for how could he be sure she was telling the truth, with her flair for promiscuity and casual cohabitation. If it were true – heaven forbid he had no doubt whatever that she would fleece him for all she could get.

"Are you absolutely certain that I am the father Dominique?" he asked, speaking evenly, quite matter of fact, although inwardly he seethed with a consuming anger, realising how easily she had cornered him. He had to think! Here was a blackmailer, if ever there was one, and he was a fool to have put himself in the position of being the victim, as he had used himself always to being the victor. He, who could lay any slave of his choice on the plantation, and no one to query his actions. He could, and often did get away with murder amongst his human chattels. But the position he found himself in at this point of time with a white girl below the age of consent, was a different matter. This could have quite serious consequences, especially if the *affaire* reached his wife's ears. A wealthy woman in her own rights, she mostly held the pursestrings, and she would think nothing of cutting him off without a penny, if she so desired, and for this – as she would consider it – uncalled for misdemeanour on her husband's part, she would make him suffer in all ways. As things stood now he never wanted for anything, and as he managed Chartenelle monies were readily available for his needs, and for the asking. But being so greedy and mean, he could never have enough gold, likewise his excessive appetite for lust. This knew no bounds. So, if this became common knowledge, he would stand to lose everything, and it was quite incomprehensible to him that any change could come about to alter his way of life.

"There is no mistake Earl, I can assure you. I am able to remember the exact hour that I conceived," Dominique answered him. Her voice clearly penetrating his turmoiled thoughts. "I consider – because of this – that you should set me up in a town house at 'Vieux Carré'," she went on, expressing herself with emphasis, so sure of her rights. "Not, of course, with such vast dimensions as my stepmother's 'grand mansion'," she added, speaking in her usual sarcastic manner. "A small place would suffice, and you could visit me, and see the child whenever you so wished."

Even as she spoke the words Dominique was well aware that her only thoughts were for Jean-Paul, certain that he should be the most important man in her life. Her obsession for the Frenchman had increased tenfold. She could think of little else, but at this precise moment she had to be assured, and concentrate on getting what she most desired – a place of her own, with a *femme de chambre* to tend to her every whim. Earl would for certain, arrange things she knew, somehow. He would feel compelled to do so, under the circumstances.

As for Earl Revington, he himself was well aware that he had met his match. 'What Dominique demands for her silence is impossible' he told himself. It would take everything he had to acquire what she had asked of him. No! he argued with himself. Something would have to be done, and soon. But for the time he would have to appear to go along with her quite ridiculous, although quite frightening idea, if only to keep the girl from resorting to desperate measures, which she would have no compunction in doing. He felt cornered, like a wild animal at bay, waiting to meet its end.

"Have you spoken of this to anyone Dominique?" he questioned her, trying his hardest to control his tattered nerves, anxious only to be assured that it was their secret alone.

"I have conveyed these tidings only to my stepmother, and she will say nothing as I have sworn her to secrecy," Dominique told him. "But I did not reveal to her the identity of the father," she added as an afterthought. She couldn't tell him that another knew of her pregnancy. Lies would always fall easily from her lips.

This information did help somewhat to stay Earl Revington's anxieties, also it assisted him to contemplate further on a deadly plan that was now beginning to take shape within his warped mind. All he required was for the girl to attend the forthcoming voodoo ceremony, and take an active part in the witchcraft. He couldn't foresee any problem in getting her there, as he was well aware of her addiction to the mysteries of the unknown, and her sheer excitement of the religious rites.

"I will think on what you have asked of me with much deliberation Dominique," he told her, "but do not venture here again to see me. We must meet away from Chartenelle," he emphasised. "I suggest we rendezvous at our usual spot before the solemn ceremony takes place, one week from the morrow."

Earl Revington knew this would feed her voracious appetite for the imagined rituals that would govern the whole scene.

"I cannot help but divulge to you the severe shock I have suffered at the news," he began again. "But you may depend I shall look to my responsibilities without undue delay." He hesitated momentarily, quite sure in his mind that the girl believed that which he was promising.

"I know of just the right establishment, after all, your position is infinitely more vulnerable than mine," he went on. "I can also arrange for regular assistance to see you through to the birth," he added. If she but knew, he was only trying to humour her while explaining at the same time, the lies falling easily from his lips so convincingly, that the girl could not but doubt his good intentions.

"I shall provide adequately as a gentleman, and maintain you as my 'paramour', which is how you will be classed. Not uncommon though, not amongst the residents of the area where you will be housed," he added. He should know, already having placed a young Creole thereabouts.

Dominique, highly delighted, yet somehow surprised with how things had turned out, couldn't believe her good fortune that Earl Revington – the meanest man ever – had agreed to her demands, seemingly, without any objection. She had only to wait a week for evidence that his prolific promises were sincere, and her life could take a new turning point. It would, she knew, be difficult to wait. But she had little choice. In any case, all that mattered was the end product, the prospect of which induced in her the stimulus of great excitation.

There was little else to be discussed at this stage, so having said their goodbyes, both Dominique and Earl Revington mounted their horses simultaneously to ride in opposite directions. The girl set her horse into a gentle trot towards Mon-de-Vue. It would have been most unwise to ride the animal vigorously in her present condition, as she could so easily lose the child within her, and then have no call on this most devious of men.

Earl Revington, on the other hand, rode away from Chartenelle at a great speed after whipping the animal into a full gallop in his eagerness to put his diabolical scheme into action without delay. He had no thought or sensitivity towards his horses – likewise his slaves on the plantation. They were to him just a means to an end as far as he was concerned, and appropriately earned him the name of 'cruel taskmaster'. He had by now reached the dense undergrowth, so had to slow the horse's progress down to almost a gentle trot as he made his way towards the swampland which he could reach blindfolded, having made the journey – of much difficulty – so often.

Suddenly, he came into a small clearing where a family group squatted before an awning. The centre figure was a heavily built negress, by the name of Fotella, gifted and skilled in the art of casting spells with her extraordinary cunning in 'black magic' and advanced knack of using 'effigies', and she was the person he had to see. As he approached nearer, she eased her enormous weight off the ground and waddled slowly towards him as he, having already dismounted, made to tether his horse to a tree close by.

Earl Revington was well known, feared and hated by many for the type of man that he was, but not so the negress, who was liked more for herself, and only feared for her extreme expertise in witchcraft. All she ever needed was a description of the proposed victim so that she could make an effigy in that image using pins as a gris-gris spell of death, and place a malevolent curse upon it.

The deed done to bring about Dominique's untimely end - with a promised fee - Earl Revington accepted a beverage which was offered him before he would depart for Chartenelle. To refuse would be as good as a slur against Fotella's family. He swallowed the liquid in two gulps, none the wiser as to what it consisted of, except the taste was very bitter, and therefore quite unpalatable.

Earl Revington journeyed home in a much better frame of mind. He could not even bring himself to whip the horse, unusually content to let it amble along at its own pace. He was in no hurry to reach Chartenelle, as he had plenty to think about. There was one thing he could not fathom, and that was why Dominique had delayed informing him of her pregnancy. 'She must be all of five months carrying' he told himself, aware as she stood before him of a thickening of her lithe body. So why had she waited? Knowing her for what she was meant she must have had an ulterior motive. But what? He would never know now. Anyway, what did it matter, she would soon be gone from him for ever, and that could not come soon enough. All he had to do was to wait for the inevitable to happen. He would then be free of the problem that had suddenly presented itself, and his life could then revert back to normal.

* * * * *

The week dragged by, and Earl Revington could not but help admit to a certain anxiety until it would be over, and he could breathe freely once more. He had no doubt whatever that the gifted negress would be successful in what she had to do being thorough, as well as dedicated to her cause, so everything should go according to plan. But his confidence would have sadly waned, and he would have had great cause for concern had he been aware that Dominique had in her possession a diary with all the damning evidence set down for anyone to see, although for the moment it was housed in a safe place.

* * * * *

At last the day of the 'solemn' ceremony arrived. It was – with its usual routine – much the same as any other day, except that it was destined to end in a bizarre and horrific manner.

The week of waiting had been for Earl Revington one of the worst experiences he could ever remember. There was so much at stake, and if anything went wrong, he was not really sure how he could handle it. Only time would tell, and he was here now, in the area around the vast swamp where the many worshippers were gathering, in their excitement, in groups.

The place was very mysterious and sombre, and full of dark forces, which could be felt all around immediately on arrival. With relatively little light, except from the odd lantern placed here and there, the whole scene generated an eerie impression to all present of the many creeds – amongst them, several Creoles – that gathered together in their devotion to a specified purpose.

Many had painted their faces, whilst others had disguised their identity with fantastic interweaving of most intimate animal forms in comically distorted designs. The remainder resorted to masks – some so bizarre as to be quite ludicrous and absurd, and only a very few had chosen attractive concealment of the face in their masquerade. All in all, the assembly appeared most grotesque, and a complete source of morally evil corruption, that must only welcome some form of divine punishment.

Earl Revington became aware, almost at once, of Dominique's arrival. She was dressed in a thick woollen shawl of many colours which she had very conveniently draped over her head to cover her features. The garment also hid the signs of her already swollen body. Although he himself had quite naturally been looking for the girl, he felt sure within himself that no one else took the least notice of her which for him, was all to the good.

Looking around him the master of Chartenelle perceived the huge negress, Fotella squatting close by, and could hear rather than see what she was doing. He was well aware that she would be holding an effigy within her large and most capable hands as she chanted and rocked to and fro over the minute image. He could imagine also, the gris-gris spell with pins that she would already have become engrossed with. It was only left now to administer a special potion to the unsuspecting girl who – in less than an hour – would be completely devoid of her right senses, enough to cause severe hallucinations and trance-like behaviour, almost as though she would have been hypnotised. But, at first, she must be permitted to witness the beginning of the ritual to satisfy her lust for the infliction of severe pain, that always enhanced every ceremony.

A young cockerel that was considered pugnacious, and disposed to fight, had been selected for the first sacrifice after human bones, hair and fingernails – stolen from cemeteries – were strewn in disarray over the open ground.

The torturous slaughter of the male bird by slow blood letting was a most chilling spectacle, but for the voodoo worshippers, to witness any form of suffering, was to enjoy. When it became apparent to them that the second sacrifice was about to take place, they all partook of what was known as a magic potion to intensify their unbridled passion for such atrocious deeds.

The choice was a young pig, again slaughtered slowly, but in this case the poor animal took far longer to expire. Its squealing, and cries of pain and terror fell – it would seem – on deaf ears, for the watchers, working themselves into a form of frenzy had already reached a paroxysm of mania, brought on by sheer adulterated passion and lust for blood albeit only temporary – and in their animated suspension, had already trespassed into the darkness of the black art.

Meanwhile, Earl Revington, purposely sitting in close proximity with Dominique, so that he could be alerted to the expected development of her behaviour, noticed that her eyes had become visibly glassy and, realising the girl was fast approaching the final stages of the drug, decided he must put into action immediately the conclusive part of the plan, although, surprisingly, much sooner than he had at first anticipated, or hoped for.

Beckoning to a tall negro standing close by, whilst at the same time assisting Dominique to her feet, and turning her in the direction of the deepest and most dense part of the swamp, and pushing forward the girl, he told his slave to follow her at a safe distance but sufficiently close enough to be able to witness what was about to happen. This, then, would enable Earl Revington to report an accident, of which he would have tried his utmost to avert by sending assistance in the person of the negro. It must appear that Dominique took the wrong turning. No other at the ceremony would be in a fit state to contradict the story, should they be asked, which was very unlikely, under the circumstances.

Both men were fully aware that the girl would most assuredly meet her death with all the dangers that would surround her. But Earl Revington felt not even the tiniest twinge of remorse in his capacity to inflict pain. The girl meant nothing to him, and all he wanted was to be rid of her, and the problem she presented as soon as possible. The negro, on the other hand, was intent only on obeying his master's orders, even though he was fully aware of the man's cruel nature. He had much to be thankful for by becoming his property. He was known by all the slaves on Chartenelle as 'Boss Man's Shadow', as more times than not he would be seen at close quarters with him. There was nothing he wouldn't do for his master, and in return, Earl Revington treated the negro with a certain respect, as he knew his slave would give his life for him.

Without speech since childhood, the negro – appropriately nicknamed 'Jonie Mute' – unavoidably witnessed the violent murder of not only his parents at an African Mission, but the whole body of white missionaries who, in their divinely appointed work for conversion of the people, had been organised in the district. All had been cut down where they stood. On discovering the boy – the only child at the mission – the killers so deemed to spare his life, but in their barbaric style of savage cruelty had torn his tongue from its very roots, mainly, it would seem to be assured of his silence, but mostly from pleasure resulting in so gruesome a deed, inflicted on one that could not defend himself.

Sold in slavery at a low cost being considered worthless, of little account, and certainly no threat to anyone, he eventually became a slave on Chartenelle, where he had served his master with deep devotion for nigh on twenty years, and as a result had become invaluable to him.

Jonie Mute knew his life could be in great danger too, except he had his wits about him and knew just where to step, whereas the hapless girl was witless, and utterly at a loss as to what she was doing, or where she was going. The young negro was aware also of the malevolent curse upon her, and that her death was assured by the evil spell of gris-gris. He could only think that she must have committed a most grievous wrong against his master, for the man to deliberately resort to such monstrous extremities.

Only a foot or two at the most behind the girl as they moved slowly ahead, he could not fail but notice her unsteady gait which worsened by the minute – likewise her faltering steps. Streamers of 'Spanish Moss' hanging from the many tall trees brushed their faces as they passed beneath the undergrowth, and trailed back on to the water that, full of menacing shadows, and black as night brought home forcibly to the negro the dangers lurking beneath its sombre gloom. With tension building up Jonie shivered, and sought some comfort from the lamp that he carried close to his side.

Although Jonie Mute was prepared for the inevitable, when it actually happened the shock he suffered was intense. He stopped dead in his tracks as, with a sharp cry that rent the air when her foot slipped, the girl slid down into the swamp water to be pounced upon, and pulled beneath the surface by an enormous roaring alligator. In a matter of seconds all was over, and silence prevailed once more.

Almost always, Jonie Mute was able to hold in check his strong emotions, as well as the occasional attack of nerves – only to be expected working for so demanding a boss man as Earl Revington. But, in this case he was totally unable to control the severe shaking of his body as he hurriedly retraced his steps to reach the clearing where his master awaited him in anxious anticipation for the presumptive evidence.

Although the negro managed to convey the information in the customary way he had of expressing himself by conventional sign language which only the two men could decipher successfully, his manner was extremely agitated as the fear of the horrifying incident – still uppermost in his mind smote repeatedly at his heart, threatening almost to choke him.

On hearing of Dominique's untimely end, the expression on Earl Revington's face was one of immense relief, while at the same time he did – even if somewhat begrudgingly – spare a sympathetic thought for the state the negro was in. When he had sent Jonie into the dense undergrowth, he hadn't realised the slave's acute terror of the swamp, especially when, with others, he had witnessed such fatalities on many occasions. After all, the master of Chartenelle thought, it was nothing new, or unusual for some alligators to stalk the area in readiness to pounce on potential victims. Mind, he himself had to admit to an aversion to the man-eating predators of the swamps.

"I can quite understand your panic Jonie," he said, hoping to calm his terrified slave. "But she was a most wicked girl indeed and, as such, could only have brought me immeasurable trouble, therefore you must surely see that she received the retribution she so rightly deserved." He waited for this to sink in before adding, "I really thought you would be used to such attacks by now Jonie, so I am really and truly sorry to have put you through such trauma." In this case the evil man meant what he said.

"I suggest you try and put from your mind what you have seen this night, and return to Chartenelle where I shall join you later," Earl Revington told his slave. "After I have reported the proposed accident – as planned – in the right quarter, I shall, of course, need to break the news to the girl's family. So, off with you Jonie, and make for home," he finished, placing his arm across the negro's shoulder in apparent affection.

* * * * *

As Earl Revington halted the horse at the front entrance of Mon-de-Vue, the groom hurried over to take the reins and lead the animal to the stables where, after a good rubdown to remove the steaming sweat, the horse would have all the fodder it could eat.

Leroy did not like the look of the man who had – by this time – mounted the steps, and waited impatiently for an answer to his ring on the facing ornate bell.

Past the hour of nine in the evening, the house was ablaze with lights – both inside and out, the latter arrayed cunningly so that their imposing rays lit up the whole clearing.

Betsy came to the door, surprised to see such a visitor calling at so late an hour, but before she had any chance at all to enquire his business at the plantation, the man spoke out immediately, giving the Southern 'Mammy' no time at all to say anything.

"I am Earl Revington, your near neighbour. May I enter for I have news of a most disturbing nature to impart to your mistress?" So saying, the master of Chartenelle stepped forward in haste into the large vestibule eager, it would seem, to get a tiresome task – as he saw it – over and done with.

Earl Revington had left the ceremony immediately after the event to journey into the French Quarter, whereupon he wasted no time at all in reporting the girl's untimely death to the *gendarmerie* on duty at the *Corps-de-Garde*, who took the news of the fatality in a manner somewhat full of aggression.

"When ever will people learn their lesson not to wander in such obvious places of danger," he stated in a grumbling attitude, quite exhausted from the result of his daily duties that consisted of so many statements, as well as numerous enquiries. All he wanted was to return to his home as soon as his relief arrived. But now, because of a human death, it would take well over the hour to enter all the necessary data for immediate reference.

"De Maitresse, she no ere," Betsy began, her clear voice penetrating Earl Revington's recall. "She dan gon awey for de rest," the large 'Mammy' carried on explaining, "but the new Maitre, he iz ere, and I fitch hem fer you. Pleese to wate in ere," she added, ushering the man into the drawing room.

Jean-Paul could not make any sense to Betsy's garbled and very confused message as he made his way along the large hall to enter the room where the visitor waited.

"I am Monsieur Jean-Paul de Leon," he began, "and attend to any business whilst Madame Perrie is unfortunately away from the plantation. So how Sir, can I be of assistance to you?" he asked, bowing from the waist, and clicking his heels in salute.

"I am Earl Revington of Chartenelle, Madame Perrie's near neighbour," he said once again, realising that the 'Southern Mammy' had not been able to convey his message. "It is distressing news I am afraid," he went on, not relishing to inform this upright Frenchman what had transpired earlier, mainly because he felt that such a man would, for certain, see through him. Well, it had to be done, and the sooner the better.

"There has been a fatal tragedy this night involving Madame Perrie's stepdaughter, Dominique." He hesitated momentarily, wondering how best to say what he had to, knowing full well it was mostly lies. "She wandered off the Chartenelle paths into the swamp, and met her unfortunate death from an alligator that lay in wait for such a victim," he explained as best he could. "We tried to give assistance, but it was to no avail," he added, relieved now that the ordeal was over, for good or bad.

Jean-Paul was simply aghast and struck with amazement at the shocking news. For, however much he had disliked the girl, it was a most terrible end to her life, as well as to the child within her body. He didn't know what to say, under the circumstances, other than to bring the visit to an end, after first making sure of the obvious.

"I take it that the tragedy has been reported to the *Corps-de-Garde*, Monsieur Revington?" Jean-Paul enquired of the man. "Only, I shall have to contact Madame Perrie to convey the sad news, and she will need to know that you have done so. She can then make the necessary arrangements, without undue delay. Not without difficulty, I may add," he went on, "as the lady in question is, at present very low in spirit."

"I am indeed most regretful to learn of Madame Perrie's indisposition Monsieur, and can only hope that her health will improve quite soon."

The master of Chartenelle spoke convincingly, acting quite at variance with his usual conduct and selfish manner in an effort to put himself in a completely different light.

"I did report the tragedy, and have been informed that there will be no investigation as such to ascertain the cause of death, so the verdict can only be one of misadventure," Earl Revington said, as he made to take his leave. "This should cause Madame Perrie less distress than is usual when a fatality occurs," he added, descending the wide steps to the clearing.

* * * * *

Jean-Paul remained standing at the front entrance even after both horse and rider had long gone out of sight. He had watched with disgust as Earl Revington hurriedly leapt into the saddle to whip the animal into a full gallop, which caused it to rear dangerously and almost unseat the rider, and scare the groom, who had to move back a few paces out of the way of the flying hooves poised ready for attack. It took several minutes to calm the horse down and entice it to move forward. But eventually it galloped away from Mon-de-Vue at full speed.

The Frenchman abhorred ill treatment of any animal, particularly horses, and to see them whipped and treated cruelly distressed him greatly. In this case, what he had just witnessed only confirmed what he had already surmised since the man appeared – that he would be quite unscrupulous in all his dealings. There was a darker side to Monsieur Revington, of that Jean-Paul was certain. The lines of cruelty about the mouth were quite unmistakable. He felt something was very wrong, and his story not entirely true. This feeling had persisted all the while, even more so now since the man had left. He found the whole situation most disturbing, and upsetting for himself with having to relate the horrifying facts to his employer, who would – unless he made haste – be retiring for the night.

He turned on his heel and re-entered the house in search of both Betsy and Ned, to explain as best as he could what had happened, and to request the use of the small phaeton so that he could make the journey into New Orleans, and call on Madame Perrie at her town house as soon as possible. Ned, the good fellow that he was, insisted on driving the phaeton himself, and explained that he would be ready to leave within ten minutes – just long enough to harness the horses, and as well, allow Jean-Paul time to pack a few necessities for his stay overnight, which he had decided on.

* * * * *

It was almost an hour later that Jean-Paul entered La Demeure. The *chatelaine* ushered him into the imposing drawing-room, where his employer reclined on a low *canapé* in a somewhat lethargic manner until she realised who her late visitor was, then it was that her attitude changed from one of surprise to unmistakable pleasure, which was most definitely mirrored in her eyes for the Frenchman to see before she lowered them.

"Is there some problem that brings you so suddenly into my presence at so late an hour Monsieur?" she asked, in a slightly stilted manner, quite obviously holding her emotions in check, and not admitting, even to herself how delighted she was to see this handsome man once again that she knew she loved, whatever had come between them.

Jean-Paul, finding the greatest difficulty in controlling the most desperate urge to take her into his arms came straight to the point, after first taking her hand within his own to place a light kiss upon the long tapering fingers, which he declined to release.

"I am afraid Madame, the news that I have to impart to you is terrible. Your stepdaughter, Mademoiselle Dominique, has this very night met with her untimely death by a saurian predator of the swamp, where she strayed into its lair. There is no mistake," he went on, observing Madame Perrie's look of sheer incredulity, as well as – it would seem – her inability to make any comment trying, no doubt, to come to terms with what she was hearing.

"The fatality has been reported," Jean-Paul explained further, "and the *Corps-de-Garde* has made the decision that under the circumstances, there will not be the usual investigation. They are quite satisfied that death was caused by misadventure. Incidentally," he added, "the person who brought the news was, as it happens, your near neighbour, Monsieur Revington."

As Jean-Paul rightly conjectured, there had been little love lost between the girl and her stepmother, but even so, the shock must have been intense in the extreme for his employer, coming so unexpectedly as it did. She had noticeably paled and, as yet, still hadn't spoken.

She couldn't, had Jean-Paul known, for the mere mention of Earl Revington filled her with a chilling dread. If he had somehow been involved, and surely he must have been to visit Mon-de-Vue to convey the news, then there had to be more sinister overtones that must come to light. In this case there was no body available to contradict the frightening fatality, so she could not help but refuse credence to the story. Her feelings now were of regret. Regret that she hadn't shown more tolerance towards the girl, who had, after all, every right to fall in love with the Frenchman, as she herself had done, although he had chosen Dominique by making her pregnant, and as she saw it, falling in love with her. Had she not proof of such? Madame Perrie was fully aware that the girl's dislike of her stemmed from the love her father felt for another woman while her own mother lay bedridden. It was this which had no doubt fanned the hidden depths of jealousy and hatred that had considerably worsened with the death of her mother, and the subsequent marriage of her beloved father to the woman he professed to love so desperately. How could the girl forgive such blatant behaviour, as she saw it? It was no wonder the girl's eyes had filled with venom whenever she glanced directly at her stepmother. The more these thoughts flitted through her mind, the more Madame

Perrie became distressed, and quite contrite at heart. She also felt a complete numbness at the sheer extremity of the whole thing. And now there was Jean-Paul to consider. How must he be feeling with the loss, not only of the girl he appeared to love, but a forthcoming child as well. But here, Madame Perrie was somewhat mystified that she could observe no grief upon the Frenchman's open features as she would have expected. And, as well, she could have sworn he seemed a little more than pleased to see her once again, after the separation. This most certainly wasn't the behaviour of a grieving man, but she could not think clearly at all now, with her mind in such a terrible turmoil. The quite devastating shock she had received would seem to have taken far more out of her than she cared to admit to herself. Now, with only a few hours remaining of the night, she must take what little sleep she could. But even with the state she was in, she spared a thought for Jean-Paul, who she imagined, must surely be exhausted.

* * * * *

When the following morning dawned, it began in a predictably subdued manner inside the grandiose La Demeure, where the first meal of the day was partaken of in silence. Although there was still much to discuss, and many things to see to, neither had attempted to broach the subject that must have, for certain, been uppermost in their minds. And both must surely be aware that what lay ahead could not in anyway be thought of lightly.

Outside, things began to take on a different aspect. The mist was already up from the river and rolling across the swamp towards the centre of the city. In the trees the birds began their soft twittering, that would eventually turn into full throated song, as the early morning light slowly crept across the sky, with the promise of another beautiful day.

New Orleans itself was a world of mystic beauty, to stir even the coldest heart. At this hour though it was in a somewhat sombre mood, but soon the city would come to life in its vibrant way like a pendulum that regularly throbs with movement, as the inhabitants went about their everyday duties, in particular, the 'French Quarter' – or 'Vieux Carré', as it was more affectionately known. Here the streets were busy already with hawkers selecting individual places in which to haggle and peddle their small wares. In no time at all, their intermittent cries of promised bargains echoed around the wrought iron embellished balconies of the very attractive houses in the narrow streets – as they tried to out-do each other in their eagerness for hopeful sales, that would awaken anyone from the deepest slumber to investigate.

* * * * *

Jean-Paul, walking briskly along the busy thoroughfare, could not but help intermingle with the hawkers and pedlars, who were everywhere. He was on his way to register the death of Dominique, and, as well, make the necessary arrangements at St. Louis Cathedral, for a short service of respect for her.

Madame Perrie, who had felt she was unable to face further pressure, waited until breakfast was completed, and – accompanied by Jean-Paul – retired to the drawing room where she requested him to stay at La Demeure for the day at least, to assist with these distressing matters, and because she could not face the long hours alone, even though the *chatelaine* was there. The woman would be about her duties anyway, and unable to spare very much time away from them. Besides, should she not admit to the longing she had for the Frenchman to remain with her. She had missed him so desperately after spiting herself by leaving Mon-de-Vue, which she realised now, had been a sudden spate of jealousy that had made her make such a decision. She had flattered herself that Jean-Paul would want to see her, if only to know how she fared since moving into her mansion, and in spite of her determination to hold him at arms' length she hoped, deep down inside, that he would pursue their deep friendship further, even though supposedly his heart was with Dominique, but now that she had been removed from the scene – albeit so tragically – perhaps things could revert back to what they were. Madame Perrie had already decided that she could never imagine Mon-de-Vue without him. His interest was vast, and he possessed a strength of understanding and tolerance. He had proved himself right in his judgement of character; would listen to all complaints among the slaves, and was fair in his ability to attribute blame, if any, where it should lie. She knew all these things about him, not merely as an employee, but someone she could turn to at any time to confide in, besides her deeper feelings.

A sudden knock upon the door interrupted her musing, and she bade whoever it was to enter. It was Biddy, second in command to the lady *chatelaine*, who appeared in the doorway to convey a message that Madame's driver wished to have urgent words with her.

Ned, politely removing his cap, was duly ushered into the drawing room holding a roughly wrapped package which he handed to Madame Perrie, explaining at the same time what it was, and how he came by it.

From what she could understand Betsy – realising how distressed her Maitresse would be over the tragedy – had taken it upon herself to sift through, and sort out Mademoiselle Dominique's belongings, which is how she came across the book of messages – as she called it – hidden between garments in a deep drawer, whereupon she showed it to Ned, who thought it looked important, and decided to drive into the French Quarter, to place the book in his employer's hands for safe keeping.

Thanking Ned for his thoughtfulness, Madame Perrie settled down to read the object in question, as soon as he had departed for the plantation.

* * * * *

It was a well-written diary, dating back to when Dominique was at the tender age of ten years, and contained desperate secrets many of which were – it would seem – a fabrication of the truth, by a mentally disturbed girl.

To say Madame Perrie was shocked, and yes! surprised at some of the entries, was quite an understatement. That so young a girl could be so venomous, and steeped in seeking revenge on the offender – as she saw it – her stepmother, filled her with revulsion. The facts revealing the girl's utter vindictiveness, and the cleverly planned retribution to be exacted on her victims to cause infinite pain and sorrow, drove away all feelings and compassion that she had allowed herself towards her step daughter. Reading page after page she realised that the girl had been far more dangerous than she had at first envisaged. The daily entries were frightening as she read on to the end, noticing that the last entry was made on the day of her death, which was a complete revelation to her. On discovering the shattering truth she was now aware of the terrible injustice she had herself meted out to Jean-Paul. He had, after all, not been the father of Dominique's unborn child! The contents of the diary proved this beyond a shadow of doubt. Earl Revington was the true father, confirming Madame Perrie's fears that there was more to the girl's death than met the eye. Not that anything concrete could ever be proven against a man who, although capable of so much evil, could always go undetected. If the *Corps-de-Garde* had seemingly accepted the bizarre details put before them, then that must assuredly put an end to any further enquiry. She hoped sincerely that this would be the case, after coming across a particularly startling entry in the diary which Dominique had deliberately directed against her own father.

Madame Perrie could not but help leaf back the pages to the quite offending item to stare once more, somewhat unbelievingly, at the most blatant words, already seared into her brain, as she focused her eyes upon them.

"*Dearest Mamma died to-day,*" it began. "*Not a shock for me as such, for I have been expecting this to happen ever since discovering Papa's secret liaison with the English lady working with him at the hospital. I know that Papa, as a qualified doctor has easy access to certain poisonous substances, and I have good reason to suspect that he selected one of such to administer to Mama, in an effort to hasten her death. And, he has certainly accomplished what he desired, mainly for the love of this other woman. I hate Papa for what he has done. I shall never forgive him. Ever. Or her,*" she added.

* * * * *

Madame Perrie couldn't believe that her dear departed husband had contemplated committing such an atrocious deed. She always understood Andre's forte was to save lives, not destroy them. But his passionate love for another woman could have driven the warm-hearted person that he was to the ultimate crime. She had to admit to the possibility as no one can ever be sure of what another will do under extreme circumstances. So perhaps, in this case, Dominique could have spoken the truth. She may even have witnessed the supposed murder. Or had the girl written the entry moreorless as an indirect question as to how the crime might be done? No one would ever know now.

Madame Perrie made her decision to destroy the diary immediately, which she did, by tearing each page into shreds. Not a word of what she had read would ever pass her lips. This was a solemn promise to herself, for the disastrous innuendoes could not only implicate herself, and smirch Andre's character, but certain individuals would have a mind to interpret on the allegations, and therefore, imply the very worst. But she must convey the news of the rightful father of the unborn child to Jean-Paul.

A distressing situation all the way around, and one that she must carry with her always. Low in spirit she had been, and low in spirit she still would be, until she could apologise to Jean-Paul for her unforgivable behaviour towards him. Her feelings of guilt would prevail for sometime to come. And she pondered on how their relationship could revert back to what it had been. The lady certainly had a fit of the doldrums.

* * * * *

Into this web of entanglement stepped Lady Pendavan, lately arrived from England, with news of a most startling nature.

* * * * *

Chapter Twelve

Yellow Fever

Seeing dearest Mama appear before her so unexpectedly came as a desperate shock to Corrie who, with her emotions uppermost, was unable to speak, or stay the tears that welled up into her eyes and spilled over on to her cheeks as she rushed towards her mother, ready to fling herself into that lady's most welcome arms.

Lady Pendavan, not completely blind to the fact that her beloved daughter was in the depth of despair, waited with the utmost patience for Corrie to unburden her heart which she did eventually, on recovering her composure.

Corrie explained everything in great detail to her mother excepting, of course, the dreadful accusation that Dominique had made against her own father. As she had already decided, no one must know, not even must she divulge such tidings to understanding Mama.

Astounded, and at the same time greatly shocked by what her daughter had conveyed to her, Lady Pendavan was hesitant to impart her own devastating news, as she was well aware that what she had to say could only cause further distress to those she loved dearly. She hadn't foreseen the obvious possibility of Corrie and Jean-Paul becoming attracted to each other and – as she saw it – a deep feeling of love developing between them. This information had really shaken her, and made her realise how urgent the issue had become. So the sooner they were both told of their brother and sister relationship, the better for all concerned. But first, she must reveal to Corrie the facts of how her cousin – whom she absolutely adored – had met his tragic end.

Holding her daughter's hands firmly within her own, Lady Pendavan gently told Corrie the whole distressing story.

"You see my darling," she went on to explain. "Thorley lost the will to live without his beloved Elizabeth, so to him death was better than a burden, which is what he felt life had become, and he decided to end it all, by his own hand. I am sorry to be the bearer of such sad news, especially to you," she added.

Lady Pendavan knew Corrie would take this as badly as she herself had done. She still could not believe that Thorley was gone from her forever, never to be seen again. She had loved him as her very own son, for that is what he had been to both Antony and herself since the day they had adopted him after the deaths of his parents. She had herself known of the deterioration of Thorley's health, and his continual battle with himself for sometime now, and prepared though she had been, news of his premature demise came as a desperate shock. Now with anguish she recalled his last fleeting visit, when he had turned to her and said in a voice hardly discernible:

"I was born to sorrow and tears dearest Mama, and my heart has been broken many times, but never more than it is now. And it can never be mended. Not ever," he finished, as he clicked his heels in salute, bade her goodbye, and left.

Lady Pendavan came out of her reverie with a start, aware that Corrie sat as one in a trance, seemingly unable to grasp what she had just heard, the shock so great. Her face had paled considerably, and her hands twitched nervously, revealing to her mother what an emotional state her daughter was in.

"Understandable, of course," Lady Pendavan told herself with Corrie having suffered two very severe shocks in one day. And here she was about to administer a third, far and above more devastating – under the present circumstances – for both Corrie and Jean-Paul. It smote at Lady Pendavan's heart to have to worsen the situation, but she had no choice in the matter, for not only was Jean-Paul entitled to learn of his true heritage, but in no way could she keep quiet, and consequently add incest to the already troubled Pendavan family. So, she decided to speak at once, and get it over with.

"Corrie, are you listening to me dear?" she asked, hoping to get her daughter's full attention to what she was about to reveal. "Only it is important that you are aware of what I am going to say, for it is of a most serious nature."

Certain now that Corrie was listening intently, Lady Pendavan came straight to the point.

"Corrie," she began. "Now that Thorley has regretfully and sadly passed from this world, it is only correct and fitting that the rightful heir to Pendavan should be informed of his heritage. I could say nothing of this whilst your cousin was still alive," she went on to explain, quite dreading the impact she was about to make, "but now I must reveal his name. It is your employee – Jean-Paul, who is the new Master of Pendavan, and as well, my very own long lost son, Jason. He is, therefore, your dearest brother my darling," she added in a very subdued manner.

Corrie made to rise from her seat beside her mother, only to fall to the floor in a dead faint, her face ashen, thankfully oblivious albeit only momentarily – of the devastating repercussions that her mother's revelation would have on both herself and Jean-Paul. And as Lady Pendavan knelt down beside her prostrate daughter and chafed her hands, the scene was witnessed by Jean-Paul, who having received no reply to his tap on the door to gain entry, had just walked into the room. Startled, and quite nonplussed as to what could have happened to cause his employer to be stretched out on the floor and lying as one dead, he strode quickly across the room to kneel also beside the woman he loved, to offer some assistance, when he recognised Lady Pendavan. A pleasurable surprise to be sure, but at that moment his only concern was for the figure lying utterly insensible.

"*Qu'est-ce qu'il arrive*?" Jean-Paul asked anxiously, lapsing back into his supposed native tongue in his apparent agitation to know what had happened. An intense fear smote quickly at his heart as he gazed lovingly at the still figure, who made no movement whatsoever. While in the Cathedral, he had made up his mind to declare his deep love for her, and ask her to become his wife. That was until he had heard some whispers of the dreaded 'Yellow Fever' which had already struck in parts of the city. Even the Holy Father had warned him not to tarry too long. At first, Jean-Paul began to think it might be hearsay, but observing two quite separate incidents as he wended his way through the French Quarter, brought home to him how serious the situation could become. Two men, in different areas, dropped to the ground like stones, while people moved quickly away, clutching their throats, their faces stunned with fear.

Jean-Paul had hated to walk by on the other side, but he had no option. He couldn't risk taking any danger back to La Demure, as he thought, and here he was now, believing that Madame Perrie had already succumbed to the terrifying disease.

Jean-Paul, dragging his eyes away from the motionless figure and looking directly at Lady Pendavan, began to voice his fears when, just at that precise moment Corrie stirred slightly, and her eyes gradually opened to focus on those she loved. Struggling to rise to her feet, she glanced directly at her mother who, with the assistance of Jean-Paul, managed to settle her daughter on the low *canapé*.

"Have you divulged your startling news to Jean-Paul yet Mama?" she enquired shakily, daring not to glance in his direction to witness his reaction to the shock he was about to receive, if he hadn't already been told.

Shaking her head, Lady Pendavan wasted no time at all in coming straight to the point once again, as she had done to Corrie. Whilst Jean-Paul glanced enquiringly from one to the other, completely mystified.

"The information that I have to impart to you, Jean-Paul, will be most startling and to you, quite unexpected," she began, looking directly at her son. "And, although it can only be advantageous to you, unfortunately, under the present circumstances, the news is sure to cause you a certain amount of distress. I hope you will understand that I can do nothing to avert this happening, or even spare you the hurtful consequences that will come about," she added. "You see," she went on to explain further. "I discovered that you are my long lost son, Jason, and as such, you are now the new Lord Pendavan – Master of the estates, and therefore, Corrie is your sister."

Lady Pendavan waited for this to sink in, saying not another word. She could not help but observe the different expressions flit across her son's face, of complete disbelief, in refusing credence to the statement, excitement, of course, which was only natural, wonderment, and now, as reality took over, severe anguish, pain and perplexity, as he fastened his eyes on Corrie.

Reeling from the shock, and shaken visibly, Jean-Paul knelt down beside his sister completely lost for words with not knowing what to say at that precise moment.

Lady Pendavan, sensing that things must be said eventually between her children, quietly left the room to allow them time to come to terms with what she had imparted.

It was exceedingly much for them both to take in everything at once, as she admitted to herself, but felt sure that everything would right itself, once they unburdened their innermost feelings. She felt quite exhausted now that she had conveyed all the information, and could only wait to be approached when the time was right for them to do so. For now, it was taken out of her hands.

* * * * *

In the few days that followed the astounding news, Corrie's health deteriorated to such an extent that the doctor was summoned to attend her. She appeared to be sickening for something untoward, with alternate feverish turns and cold shivers, and her face would be pale and pinched, and then burning with a fire inside her. In the city the epidemic had reached alarming proportions, and caused numerous fatalities, with the promise of a lot worse to follow before the disease would subside. The Creoles mostly walked free of it, as they were wine drinkers, and sampled little water, which carried the Yellow Fever. In some cases, whole families would be laid low, with no one to turn to for help. More often than not the few worn out physicians would be too late to save them, which did nothing to boost their morale.

Lady Pendavan was duly contrite, aware that her devastating news had helped to lay Corrie low. It had taken both brother and sister some little while to come to terms with such tidings, coming so suddenly. But now, with Corrie's illness upon them, no one could even think on these things, only what the outcome of the attacks would lead to.

Unfortunately, the doctor, disquiet in his manner, identified of the dreaded disease by his patient's symptoms. There was no doubt in his mind whatever that Corrie had succumbed to the Yellow Fever. He explained there was little anyone could do for her, just let the disease run its course, and with God's will, perhaps she would survive. "A cool watered compress can be used often across her forehead to help relieve the severe body heat, and hopefully bring down her high temperature," the doctor suggested, seemingly trying to lessen the blow, and perhaps give a little hope to the worried listeners. "It is most imperative to break the ever mounting fever," he added. "But should this fail, we could bleed her, for sometimes the fever can be cooled by a diminution of the blood." He walked slowly from the sick room, his complete weariness showing plainly to Jean-Paul, who accompanied him to the front entrance, to see him off the premises. And, as the doctor stepped out on to the front path, he turned once more to face the French man, saying hurriedly: "If all seems hopeless, send for me again, and I will bleed her. God go with you all," he added.

* * * * *

Lady Pendavan devoted her full time to nursing Corrie, hardly ever leaving her side. The *chatelaine* brought food and beverages at regular intervals. But the ensuing days began to tell on her considerably.

Corrie, her lips swollen and covered with blisters, her body fiery red from the fever, twisted and thrashed from side to side on the bed in her delirium. Her mother repeatedly held a cold compress to her head, and bathed her every hour or so to try to bring the fever down. At times, she thought Corrie had departed this life, but she still hung on. Jean-Paul entered the sick room from time to time, anxious to help in anyway that he could. It grieved him to witness such suffering in his sister, and worried him intensely to observe the desperate change in his mother, who appeared to him just a mere shadow of her former self.

It was two weeks to the day when Lady Pendavan had begun nursing her daughter, that she felt great concern for Corrie's life. Her condition had seemed to worsen, and there seemed little hope for her. She had already discussed with Jean-Paul the possibility of another visit by the doctor for blood-letting. So the physician, having been summoned, arrived at the precise time that Corrie seemed to take a turn for the better. The fever had abated as suddenly as it had begun. She was wet from head to foot with her own perspiration and, as the doctor rested his hand against the patient's forehead, it felt cool to the touch.

"Thanks be to God," he muttered half to himself. "She will get well very soon now providing she has plenty of sleep." He glanced at Lady Pendavan, who was almost all in, but greatly relieved at his news.

"If I may be so bold and say Madame, you look a bit unwell yourself," the doctor stated emphatically. "Surely there is another soul in the house who can sit with the patient? I suggest," he went on, "that you retire to your own room Madame, now that the worst is over, and rest for in your present low state you could succumb to the disease." The doctor spoke deliberately to prove his point. So saying, he quickly went on his way having done all he could – a man greatly changed in the short time since he was last at La Demeure, but at least, in this case, a patient's life had been saved.

Biddy – the second in command to the *chatelaine* – took over the role of nursing to enable Lady Pendavan to rest. She hadn't realised how weary she had become. Removing her outer garments, she quickly climbed into bed between the cool sheets and was soon sleeping peacefully. When Jean-Paul looked in on her an hour later he was thankful, and stood momentarily marvelling at the thought that this wonderfully kind and most beautiful lady was his true mother. His heart swelled with pride and the deep love that he felt for her.

* * * * *

Corrie quickly recovered, and was almost her own self again when Lady Pendavan took to her bed, a victim of the disease. It attacked fast and furious, and her suffering was terrible to witness. The physician called and standing at the foot of the bed with a defeated look on his face, showing the weeks of strain and stress, as well as sorrow, he quietly shook his head. This patient was very close to death, he had no doubt in his mind. He had little heart for relaying his fears for his patient's life to the worried looking brother and sister. Time enough for them to know, and face their sorrow when the inevitable was to happen. He just had to give them false hope. After all, in the face of it, what else could he do?

* * * * *

It was three days later that Lady Pendavan passed from this world. She had been attended by Biddy, who was half Creole, and immune to the disease. She had made her patient as comfortable as possible before leaving the sickroom for some respite. Corrie had taken over from her to tend to her mother's needs, willing her to get well again, when she realised that the patient had ceased to breathe. Corrie's piercing scream echoed around the whole mansion, to reach Jean-Paul's ears, as he worked quietly on the accounts. Dropping everything, he raced up the stairs at break neck speed and hurried towards his mother's bedroom dreading what he would find. His worse fears were founded when he saw Corrie's face devoid of colour, kneeling beside the bed and holding the lifeless hand that hung limply over the side of the white coverlet. The shock was intense for them both, even though they had half expected the worst to happen.

Corrie moved away from the still figure, and immediately turned to her brother for consolation. Her sobs racked her slim body, as she gave vent to her emotions, whilst Jean-Paul, crying inwardly, could not accept that the mother he had just recently discovered had been spirited away from him. His heart cried out in anguish for his loss.

Arrangements were hurriedly made, and the funeral took place at St Louis Cathedral, amidst that of many other victims. The queue was long, and the priest spoke shakily over each service for the departed. He too, was very weary and saddened by so many deaths. He himself had lost one of his own priests, a beloved man of many good qualities. 'When will it end?' he asked himself as he quietly moved in the direction of the vestry for more meditation and religious contemplation, which he felt he needed after the funerals.

* * * * *

It was a month to the day before everything began to return to some form of normality. Nothing could ever be the same. The physician had advised both Jean-Paul and Corrie not to return to the plantation until the epidemic ended. He thought this advisable, in particular for Corrie, having been a victim, although quite recovered by this time. He realised that her brother must be immune to the disease, for which he was thankful, but even so, felt that no risk should be taken in transferring the epidemic further afield.

The love and affection was steadfast between brother and sister. They were a great comfort to each other in those dark days. They also knew now that they had been drawn to each other from the very first day they had met, not as they had at first thought as lovers, but deep down as kindred.

A few days before their return to Mon-de-Vue, Corrie informed her brother of the wonderful gift that Lady Pendavan had further bestowed upon him. She had already decided upon this before leaving England, that Jean-Paul should have her half-share in the plantation. It was her way of rewarding a beloved son for his worth. He was greatly overcome with emotion at his mother's considerable kindness and the trust she had put in him, and he vowed there and then that he would never let her down. For the time however, he had no intention of leaving Corrie to return to England. There were plenty of willing hands at Pendavan to keep the wheels turning. Corrie needed him now, more than ever, for it would take her sometime to adjust.

Once again fate was to intervene in the future of the Pendavan family, although they had no way of knowing, until a visitor arrived, this time from France.

* * * * *

Chapter Thirteen

Return to Pendavan, With a Bride

The heat was intense and the sun shone high in the cloudless sky of deepest blue, promising little change in the weather. It was almost tropical, and had been like this now for many weeks while the epidemic ravaged the city. "Thanks be to God," the survivors said as the disease subsided, then vanished as suddenly as it had commenced. No one ever had any warning when it would strike or when it would end. Now, all sent a heartfelt prayer to their maker for being spared.

Jean-Paul and Corrie had been back at Mon-de-Vue now for almost a month, and things began again where they had left off. It was just as though they had never been away, although the scars went deep. Betsy was thankful to have them both telling her what to do in the nicest of ways. Missing them tremendously, she had gone about her duties like a puppet, with someone continually pulling the strings.

It was during the end of the second week of their return to the plantation, that a letter from France arrived for Jean-Paul. He knew immediately it was from Dario, his dearest friend. How often he had thought of him, and wished they could be together as before. He had never doubted for one moment that Dario would eventually visit him in New Orleans, and now at long last it was to come to pass.

Apart from the information regarding the journey which, according to the stated date, had commenced three months past, with a passage booked on the *Franco-bor*, to take all of ninety days, the letter was totally devoid of news as such, excepting that Dario explained he had to depart Paris very suddenly and, he added, "not for the reasons that you will, of course, anticipate, my friend. But all shall be revealed on my arrival, for I have much to impart to you." The letter finished – as always – with Dario's usual flourish.

And, so it was, that Jean-Paul, having made the necessary enquiries as to when the ship would dock at the port of New Orleans, found himself waiting with great excitement at the wharf, in an open carriage driven by Ned. It seemed an age waiting to welcome Dario as he would step off the gangway on to *terra firma*, especially in this damnable heat. He still was not used to the tropical weather.

Suddenly, he recognised the well-known figure as he appeared to step down on to the gangway laid from the quarterdeck to the shore. His luggage was quite sparse, proving how sudden his departure from France must have been.

Jean-Paul leapt from the coach in a matter of seconds to be waiting at the base of the gangway. When Dario's gaze alighted on his friend, the pleasure on his features was plain to see. Both men embraced, their emotions coming uppermost, and then Jean-Paul guided Dario to the carriage and Ned urged the horses into a light trot, fully aware that in this heat the poor beasts would soon tire if he drove them too hard. This he would never do. Ned loved the horses, and treated them with the greatest respect.

The conversation in the carriage was varied. First of all, Jean-Paul wished to know how Dario had fared on the lengthy journey. It would seem by his reply, that he enjoyed every minute of it with little or no problems, just one or two skirmishes amongst the crew, and even this was quickly brought to an end. The weather had been kind in the sense that there had been no storms, although the heat had been stifling, and Dario was quick to notice that he had come from one heatwave to another. Both passengers mopped their perspiring brows from time to time between their conversation. Jean-Paul related all that had transpired over the past weeks, including the startling news of his quite unexpected heritage, and the wonderful discovery of his very own kindred. He spoke sadly of the terrible loss of his mother, so soon after their unusual reunion. His voice broke with the memory of the tragedy so fresh in his mind, but he quickly controlled himself.

"It is as well my friend that your journey commenced when it did," Jean-Paul began to explain to Dario. "If you had started out six or seven weeks earlier, the ship would have been refused entry and unable to dock because of the epidemic that killed so many. "Take Corrie for instance," he went on to explain further. "My mother gave her life to save my sister, who almost perished more than once, but dearest Mama fought so hard to keep her with us, and that makes me go cold all over, when I think how easily I could have lost them both."

Silence prevailed for a while as the journey progressed with both passengers lost in their own thoughts. Dario could hardly believe Jean-Paul's good fortune, and felt so happy for him. Just the ideal kind of man to be the 'Lord of the Manor', and Dario knew that his friend could fill the role quite competently, especially when his task would be made considerably easier with what he had to reveal to him, and because of it, his success in life would be assured.

Now Jean-Paul, eager though he was to hear what Daric had to impart to him, was more concerned as to whether his friend was here for just a visit, or had he made the decision to make a new life for himself in New Orleans? If the latter, Jean-Paul could not help but ponder on the idea that Dario might take over at Mon-de-Vue, and work with Corrie so as to enable him to return to England, and take over his inheritance. He could not foresee any problems at Pendavan, with the steadfast support of Ruan and Michael, and, as well, as he had been resident at the mansion for many months, he would not feel like a stranger, and that was a good beginning for his new life.

Whilst these thoughts flitted through his mind, Jean-Paul realised they had arrived at the beginning of the long drive, leading to the imposing entrance of Mon-de-Vue.

Dario remained speechless, in awe of the magnificent surroundings, as well as the vast lands of the plantation, and the great numbers of slaves. It had to be seen to be believed. Now he could understand better all the things that Jean-Paul had explained to him in his letters, for it had been difficult to visualise from so many miles away. He was also very smitten with the plantation house. It did to him surpass everything, and coming face to face with Corrie was for Dario a most stimulating, and wondrous experience, something he would never forget, as he was well aware that he had fallen in love at first sight with this most beautiful woman – sister to his dearest friend. If he had but known, his feelings were identical to those of Jean-Paul, who had felt exactly the same on his arrival.

As for Corrie herself, she took to Dario immediately. His manners were impeccable and his whole attitude likeable. In fact, he could not but help conduct himself with the utmost propriety, having been born a gentleman, so he would never lose that finesse.

Betsy, on instructions from her Maitresse, showed the visitor to the section of the house which had been allotted to him, where everything had been painstakingly arranged for his comfort. More than satisfied with the exceptionally warm welcome he had received, Dario made haste to freshen himself after the particularly dusty journey from the wharf, which had caused him to perspire most profusely. Then he set about selecting a complete change of clothing, fit enough to enable him to take his place in the dining room for a special meal, and afterwards to relax in the drawing room, where eventually he could relate fully all his news to his hosts who were eager to hear what their visitor had to say.

With everyone finally in the drawing room in a relaxed mood, then, and then only did Dario begin to recount his startling story.

* * * * *

His somewhat abrupt departure from France, he explained first.

"Having killed a man by my sword in an arranged duel, you will, of course, Jean-Paul, understand that it was essential I leave Paris immediately, for my own safety, especially as the victim was none other than Count Jean-Philippe Maille – husband to my beloved sister – as you, my friend are already aware, she suffered so badly at his hands. What else could I do under the circumstances?" he asked, adding: "he deserved to die," and then went on to explain further.

"I was so furious, and my rage increased tenfold as I was made aware of how he had besmirched her character, and continually belittled her with the bestial depravities and obscenities he put her through by forcing his lewd and drunken cronies upon her and, at the same time, extorting monies from them for having their lustful ways with her."

Here Dario paused momentarily, clearly distressed at remembering what had happened. But although there was a lull in the story, Jean-Paul made no comment, anxious only to hear all. Naturally, he was terribly shocked, and could hardly believe what he had heard, and could not fathom the outcome anyway. But even so, he could only describe his innermost feelings of sheer excitement and delight that Semire was, at last, free of the Count.

Dario's voice broke through his friend's thoughts as he began again.

"All this, and much more was divulged to me one week before I commenced my most unexpected journey to America. It came by way of a visitor from the Chateau Abbaye, and none other than Semire's very own *femme de chambre*, Michelle. She arrived quite late in the evening attired in a long cloak and hood to hide her identity. She was in quite a distressed state. Her face was pale. She was very agitated and shaken, and when she explained the reasons for her manner, and why she had to see me, I could understand it, and was soon full of sympathy for her, for what both she and Semire had been through was diabolical. We talked well into the early hours of the morning, and with what she had to reveal my worst fears were realised, as I felt right from the start that Semire had walked into a well laid trap, but even so, I little guessed how devastating her life at the Chateau had become. How often had I contemplated making an entry into the building to rescue her, but it never materialised without your assistance my friend."

Once again Dario took a short break from speaking, which gave Jean-Paul the opportunity to offer him a liquor, or something else that perhaps he would prefer. After having chosen his beverage, Dario reverted back to where he left off, having already emptied his glass. He hadn't realised how thirsty he had become, but speaking continually was dry work.

"Michelle described everything in such fine detail that I felt as though I was seeing everything for myself," Dario informed his listeners. "It was a bitter pill for me to swallow I can assure you," he added, anxious now to get the complete story off his chest. "I shall relate the whole series of events exactly as I heard them. So please bear with me my friends."

* * * * *

The wedding at the Chateau went well, without any known hitch. Michelle tended to her future mistress in every way that she could, and put Semire at her ease as much as was possible, under the circumstances. There were no outside guests permitted, as the Count had stipulated, only the staff of the Chateau. Even so, there was much pomp and circumstance in evidence because of the type of man that the Count was. It was well known amongst the higher circles that he was very clothes conscious, almost a dandy. But at least, he did look the part, and Semire made the most beautiful bride in the fascinating Maille wedding gown, added to which her own outstanding beauty surpassed everything. After the ceremony, drinks, and a variety of foods were available for the staff, as well as for the bride and groom. Eventually, Semire, exhausted with the preparations, and all that had been going on around her, retired to her room, where Michelle was already waiting to assist her. They took to each other right away, and from then on were never apart. The marriage was supposedly never consummated, for the simple reason that the Count in his view owned her and his only desired end was to use her for his own selfish reasons. He was a mercenary man, and made money his God. It was the only thing he ever really cared about. As a supposedly discreet blackmailer, his riches were assured. He was noted to be one of the most wealthiest noblemen in France, and therefore considered to be influential in all walks of life.

* * * * *

One week after the wedding, Semire's duties as hostess to the Count's cronies began in earnest. She had spent most of the seven days confined to her bed chamber, where Michelle spent many hours painstakingly brushing the Comtesse's hair with deft strokes to keep it shining, and to make it more beautiful – if that was possible – than it already was. During this time they conversed with each other, and Semire learnt a lot more about the Count, which didn't improve matters at all. She knew she was most fortunate to have a sincere friend in Michelle, and during the ensuing weeks ahead she had every good reason to be grateful for the supportive loyalty bestowed upon her by the young woman. In fact, Semire knew not what she would have done without her, especially as there was no other at the Chateau to whom she could have turned to in her hour of need, and certainly not the *chatelaine*. Semire had taken a great aversion to Gorte, after she discovered that she was a spy for the Count. She hated to hear her walking through the dark corridors in the vicinity of her bed-chamber, dragging her left foot in a sort of limp. It sounded quite eerie in the late evening, more so as she had a most disturbing habit of rattling the many keys she carried on her person, attached to a heavy chain where they hung suspended, and she would swing them to and fro as she walked. Semire could always sense when the gaunt looking half woman, half man, would stop to listen outside her door, where she would remain for several minutes – her breathing quite heavy – and then move away to go in search of the Count, to make her report that the Comtesse and Michelle were safely closeted in their abode. It would be soon after this ritual that any one crony of the Count's choice would be accompanied by Gorte, and safely deposited at the bed-chamber where Semire would be waiting – supposedly – in readiness for the man's paid favours. This was an enforced order by the Count, which in no way could be disobeyed by his wife. No one dared ever to go against him, that is, outwardly. It was Michelle's quick thinking, and deep concern for her mistress that brought about the continuous deception that took place the first night, and thereon after, every night, until eventually things came to a head.

* * * * *

Both Semire and Michelle hated the bed-chamber, but it was to prove a godsend to them both when they planned to outwit the Count, and play him at his own game, but they had to be careful.

The room had a high ceiling with small windows for seclusion. The whole area was dark, dismal and heavy with numerous drapes that concealed recesses and framed panelled walls, many of which were adorned with portraits of the Maille brides, their features brought most cleverly to life. In the centre, away from the wall, stood a huge king sized bed, also draped with curtains for privacy. Tucked away in one corner was a door that lead into a small side room where Michelle slept. Semire was to share this room with her for the many weeks to come whilst they tricked the Count.

Michelle obtained – with some difficulty – a small container of medicinal laudanum to be administered in drops into a small drink, not harmful, but which would put the strongest of men out, and strong enough to put an already drunken man into a deep sleep. He would know nothing until he would awaken in the morning and, believing he had had his way with the Comtesse, would leave, well satisfied with the world, and would pay the blackmailing Count his dues.

This routine continued for many weeks, and Semire was affected so much with the constant worry that the Count might discover what was taking place, although both women were very sure that they were not careless. But there was Gorte too, who had to be observed in case she became suspicious, and go to her master. Often she could be heard speaking to him in her native tongue, with the most irritating guttural sound to her voice. Feeling guilty, both Semire and Michelle often thought that Gorte had already realised something untoward was happening and seemingly appeared to be watching them, and listening in the hope that they would give themselves away. But one thing they were sure of, and that was the curtain draped bed which thwarted any prying eyes.

The turn of events began to take their toll on Semire's health. Her nerves were taut, and everything seemed to get on top of her. So much so, she thought the Count must observe her attitude and make some remark.

However, the morning of the day that would change everything dramatically, arrived with no warning of what was to transpire, until the first meal of the day was brought almost to a close.

The Count made to vacate the enormously long and magnificent table, in the centre of the huge room. He spoke to his wife as he replaced his chair beneath the table.

"I intend to visit you in your bed-chamber this night my dear," the Count said, speaking in a sneering manner, as he walked the full-length of the room towards Semire, still sitting to complete her meal. "After all," he went on, "I thought it about time that I should bed my own *femme*. What say you my dear?" Taking her slim fingers, and raising them to his cold lips he brushed them lightly in the form of a kiss, that had no feeling whatsoever. Affection was most definitely not one of his attributes.

As the door closed behind the Count, Semire sat as one turned to stone. What she had dreaded had now come to pass and was ready to explode about her ears. Now the truth would be out, and her husband would – during their intimacy – find that she was still a virgin, and therefore her deception must come to light. She pushed her table utensils away from her, unable now to stomach the remaining contents, and as she did so, rose from the table and walked quickly to the dining room door to return to her bed-chamber and see Michelle, to voice her rapidly gathering fears of her husband, and tell of the consequences that must come about after what he had suggested.

Michelle, somewhat shocked by what she had heard, and distressed at the state her mistress was in, hurriedly helped her down on to the *canapé*, where Semire rested back her head and closed her eyes to help ward off the rising nausea that threatened to engulf her.

'There is only one thing for it,' Michelle told herself, 'we will have to escape from the Chateau this very day.' So, discussing it with her mistress, they both came to the conclusion that it was the only thing they could do under the circumstances. Although the thought of making the attempt was frightening, it was the answer. Fortunately,

Pierre, Michelle's betrothed of long standing, who worked as a footman on the staff, was off duty for a few hours this very day, and it was, perhaps, possible to obtain some form of assistance from him. Michelle, already aware of a secret way out, would need to have a coach and horses waiting in readiness to take them to the Convent of 'Our Lady' where the Comtesse would remain in safe keeping from the clutches of the Count. There was a trap door cleverly disguised at the back of the Chateau, that Pierre had discovered a few years earlier, when Michelle took over her new duties to the first Comtesse. The very young girl that she was, at that time, sensed a secret from the very commencement of her service, and eventually when the young wife expired under mysterious circumstances, Michelle felt that a younger Gorte aided and abetted the Count, who must have needed some form of support. Nothing had ever come to light whatever it was that had transpired. And, to this day, more than ten years past, Michelle could not but help suspect that the evil Count, and his equally evil *chatelaine* shared some dark secret somewhere in the Chateau.

Michelle, eager to escort the Comtesse through the winding tunnels beneath the Chateau that would eventually lead out into the countryside, was extremely anxious to get word to Pierre as soon as was possible, for time was the essence, when there was so much danger to face. Then all it remained for her to do was to make sure her mistress was attired in suitable warm clothing, in particular, a cloak and hood to help hide her identity. She herself would need to dress likewise, so as to appear to others as though they were peasants. Neither would be able to take any luggage as such, which worried them not. All they could think of was to be free of the Count, and his cronies.

Whilst Michelle was away from her mistress to hopefully organise everything, the Count, aware through Gorte that the Comtesse was alone – but not guessing why – decided to visit his wife in her boudoir.

When Semire saw who her visitor was she felt inwardly nervous, and quite embarrassed at the same time, it being the only occasion since her marriage that her husband had ventured to this part of the Chateau to be in such close proximity with her. It took her by surprise also, believing he would be calling later at night, with the escape hopefully having already taken place. At first, she felt concerned that their plans could have been discovered already, and the Count here to gloat over his findings. 'What else could possibly bring him to my bed-chamber at this early hour?' she asked herself. Not many minutes passed before the truth dawned on Semire, and she realised his purpose, and what he intended to do when she saw plainly the licentious look displayed openly on his face as he lunged suddenly towards her, and almost ripped her day gown from her body as he forced her back on to the large bed, and made to straddle her. Semire, trying her hardest to ward him off, knew it was hopeless to try and fight off such a crazed man, whose only thought was to take his wife by fair means or foul. But at that moment when she felt all was lost, hurried footsteps could be heard in the corridor moving in the direction of the bed-chamber, which startled the Count who, not wanting to be caught in a compromising position, quickly straightened up and walked from the room without a backward glance, passing a surprised Michelle on the way.

Semire, visibly shaken, but very relieved to see Michelle, whose only concern at that moment was for her mistress as she observed her torn gown, and listened to what had taken place.

"I dread to think what could have happened had you not returned so promptly Michelle," Semire told the *femme de chambre*. "He tried to rape me, and there is no way that I could have warded him off," she added. Her thoughts running amok, when she realised how quickly her precious virginity could have been taken, and by someone she hated. She had fought to keep it all this time, with the help of Michelle, of course. She shivered with an uncontrollable fear by what could have come to pass.

Michelle, with complete forethought, quickly conveyed the good news that all arrangements had been made with Pierre, which helped considerably to avert the Comtesse's worried thoughts. But she omitted to impart what Pierre had pointed out to her, that the whole event could be extremely dangerous, especially if they were discovered to be missing, as both Pierre, and Michelle had no way of knowing if the escape route was known to anyone else, in which case, and if so, they could be followed, trapped, and once more ensconced in the Chateau. But as it transpired the escape went without any hitch, although the journey through the rough subterranean passages burrowed into the hills around the Chateau, and the surrounding area, was quite harrowing. At first, it was as though they were lost, and panic took hold of them, but eventually, with luck, they climbed out into the sunlight, where just a few yards away a coach was waiting for them. Once ensconced inside, the driver flicked the reins of the horses, and they set off at a fair trot. Sighs of relief were in evidence, and everything took on a different aspect for the three passengers. The nearer to their destination they came, the safer they felt, and relaxed more. Once the Comtesse was safely closeted at the Convent, both Pierre and Michelle made to return to Paris in the same coach, he to revert back to his duties at the Chateau, and she to ride on to the house of the De Laffiettes, where she would have urgent need to converse with the master of the house, and let him know what had transpired with regard to his sister, and the Count.

"And that is exactly how it happened," Dario explained, as he came to the end of Michelle's startling story.

"As you might guess my friend, Michelle can never return to work at the Chateau, so remains at my abode for as long as she needs, or may wish," Dario went on to say. "Pierre could not offer her any assistance, as he himself lives in at the Chateau. So there was nothing left but to house her. I feel very much indebted to the young woman anyway, for what she has done for Semire, and shall be for ever grateful," Dario went on to explain even further. "Likewise Semire herself. She too, feels the same way, and is happy to have Michelle living at our old house. I went to the Convent the very next day to see Semire you know," Dario went on to say, laying stress upon the fact. "I wanted to see her, to find out how she was faring. One could see only too clearly that she has been to hell and back. That she has suffered, my friend, is for sure. She was so relieved to be out of the Chateau and away from the clutches of the Count, and would have loved to be with Michelle, but I thought it too dangerous for her to leave the Convent, at that time," he added.

Dario went on then to complete his part of the story.

* * * * *

"The very next day," he began again, "I called at the Chateau to request an audience with the Count, whereupon I immediately challenged the evil man to a duel, and explained the reasons why. I had to get it over with, once and for all as my anger was at boiling point. And I needed satisfaction."

Dario broke off here to partake of refreshments, prepared with foresight by Betsy.

"I couldn't believe that I might actually lose my life, but it mattered not if I did, as long as I was given a chance to avenge my beloved sister. I did not like the vindictive feelings that kept coming uppermost within me, but it was important for me to exact retribution for the offence upon her. How otherwise could I live with myself?" he argued. "It would be better to die with honour, than live with constant shame," he added as an afterthought.

"The Count accepted my challenge there and then without any hesitation," Dario began again. "As the adversary he suggested the time, and the place, and I accepted in the face of it, after all, what else could I do?" Dario asked of his listeners, and then went on to repeat what the Count had said.

"'Shall we say De Laffiette, that we commence at eleven tomorrow, right here at the Chateau, in the Great Hall. I prefer to be on my own ground,' he said, a half smile playing around the corners of his cruel mouth. 'A doctor, a priest, and my second will be in evidence,' he added, in a matter of fact way, almost as though he knew already how things would turn out.

"With his known skill and considerable expertise with the sword, he must have been assured of his ability to be the victor. In all fairness to the Count though," Dario went on to explain, "he was not aware of my skill with the sword, and that I too hoped to be the victor. As I was about to leave, the Count passed a remark in a somewhat thoughtful manner.

"'I always said your sister was very clever as well as very beautiful De Laffiette. To outwit me needed some real pluck on her part, as well as much staying power,' he added, then changed to his usual sneering manner.

"'I warn you, Monsieur. As soon as I have killed you, I shall hunt your sister down until I find out where she is hiding, and bring her back here to the Chateau, where she belongs as my wife. This is no idle threat,' he added, his face taking on a sinister look.

"We shall see," Dario answered him, as he walked out into the open, glad to breathe the clear air, and be free for the moment of the evil that permeated the Chateau. He gave a slight shiver of apprehension as he stepped once again into the coach, his face bearing an expression of extreme seriousness, whilst his thoughts ran amok. He just had to slay the Count, and save Semire from a life worse than death. The man would have no compunction in hunting her down like a wild animal, and caught, she would return once more to the sheer hell that she had hopefully escaped from. The more he thought about it, the more determined he was.

Dario decided there and then, that he would use whatever time he had left to practice his cut and thrust style, much used by him with the young blades of Paris. Not having seen the Great Hall at the Chateau, he could only surmise what it entailed. The area must be large from its name, and presumably ideal for a duel to the death. He sent a heartfelt prayer to his maker, for guidance. He knew to kill was a sin in God's eyes, but it would be a fair fight and, if he was the victor, then France would be free, and well rid of the most evil of men, in particular, his beloved sister who otherwise would always live in fear, for once returned to the Chateau, she would never have the opportunity to escape again. The Count would see to that.

* * * * *

The day dawned grey and humid, suitable in a sense for death and its sombreness.

Dario selected one of the young blades who was very quick with the sword and who would be ideal for his second, especially to see a fair fight. He certainly didn't trust the Count.

At a quarter to eleven, the coach, once again, drew up outside the Chateau, where Dario and Marcel alighted.

Dario glanced up at the dullness in the sky, and wondered if he would see another dawn, but the hope that he would gave him courage, and the sheer anger he still experienced against the Count urged him on to be the victor.

Both duellists and their seconds were attired in similar garb, fitted black breeches, with white silk open neck shirts. The footwear worn was light half length black leather boots.

Dario and the Count spent the first few moments before the actual duel commenced by limbering up, as well as flexing their swords. Then it began in earnest, as the 'seconds' gave the go ahead.

The Count started his sword play in a somewhat teasing manner just to let his opponent see how clever he was, but as Dario matched the Count's cut and thrust with gusto, and versatile movements, the teasing ceased, as one expert matched the other. This went on for some time until suddenly the Count caught Dario a glancing cut across the top of his left arm with his sword edge, ripping sleeve and skin to bring forth a steady flow of blood. The Count, thinking this would discourage his opponent, fought like a fiend, and goaded Dario all the more by resuming the cut and thrust, saying as he did so, "Monsieur, now that I am about to finish you off I want you to know that you did not lose at the gaming tables. I cheated purposely to get you in my power to obtain that which I had required for a lengthy time – your sister!"

As the Count finished speaking, and whether Dario caught him off his guard he wasn't sure, but he dealt the fatal thrust straight through the man's heart, as with a look of sheer amazement, he fell dead to the floor. His second rushed to the Count's aid, but realised there was nothing he could do. It was all over. Evil had been avenged, once and for all.

Meanwhile, Dario was having his arm treated with a tourniquet to stop the bleeding. He couldn't believe it was over, and that he had actually killed the Count. He breathed a sigh of relief as he rested momentarily to recover his equilibrium. And as he became more controlled the doctor presumed to advise him to leave France without undue delay.

"It is always so in these cases Monsieur," he went on to explain. "Even though this was both an agreed and arranged duel, the Count's untimely death could necessitate your appearing before the Tribunal where awkward questions could be asked for which you may be loath to answer." The doctor hesitated momentarily, thinking how best to say what was on his mind. He liked this young man, and thought him extremely brave to have undertaken a duel with such an evil man, who could have so easily killed him.

"I should mention that the Count's blackmailing activities have been, for some time, known to the authorities, but they could not obtain any actual proof because many of his victims were too scared of the Count to divulge his secrets and, as well, the man had so many influential acquaintances in high places, that he could get away with almost anything, even murder," he added, pursing his lips as his trained eyes searched Dario's face. "The police could – because of the duel, and the fact that you are the victor – assume you to be one of the Count's many victims, and if you should be, or have been in the past, you could be put through quite a harrowing time. So once again Monsieur, take an old man's advice and leave France rapidly. After all," he went on, "you have rid our good country of a terrible scourge, and your deed will be quietly appreciated, I can assure you." He smiled at his own quip, whilst assisting Dario to his feet, and then shaking him firmly by the hand, wished him *adieu* and *bonne chance* for the future.

Dario, still somewhat confused, walked slowly to the waiting coach and asked the driver to take him directly to the Convent of Our Lady. He could now relate to Semire what had transpired, and let her decide for herself what she would wish to do for the future.

As Dario had already surmised, his sister made her choice immediately to take up residence at their home with Michelle. To be free of the Count was all that she had ever wanted, and because of her courageous brother she could now walk without fear. She realised also that she would never want for anything, as the widowed Comtesse. But thinking on this made her spare a thought for his other victims, of which there were a goodly number.

Dario explained also that he would now leave France altogether, having decided already to travel to America, to see Jean-Paul. It was his dearest wish to be with him once again to try and make up to him for how he had suffered through his compulsion to gambling.

Dario refrained from mentioning that Jean-Paul was still alive and well, for, uncertain of his friend's future plans, he decided not to tell her. He knew that Semire would be quite inconsolable with the shock, so if she was to be informed of the news, then would it not be best for Jean-Paul himself to break it gently to her?

Now all that remained for Dario to attend to before arranging a passage on the first available ship sailing to the New World, was to see Semire settled in her own home with Michelle, so that he too could have peace of mind.

* * * * *

"Well, my friends," Dario explained, "that is the end of my story as to how, and why I am here. If my presence is tiresome for you both, and you wish me to take my leave, then I shall quite understand and set about making alternative arrangements for my future."

But Corrie would have none of it. Her brother's friend was here, and here he was to stay. She quite understood that Jean-Paul would now wish to return to France as soon as possible, and thereafter to Cornwall, where he would take up residence at Pendavan. So she made her decision there and then with no hesitation.

"I would like you to remain here at Mon-de-Vue, and take over my brother's duties," Corrie suggested, brimming over with sheer excitement. "That is, of course, if you are agreeable Dario," she added, using his name quite naturally as though she had known him always. She had heard so much about him from Jean-Paul, that she felt she knew all there was to know, and because of it felt very much at ease in his company.

Dario accepted Corrie's kind and thoughtful offer, considering it an ideal situation for all three of them. What could be better after all, for it would leave Jean-Paul with no worries whatsoever, knowing that Corrie would be safe, and in good hands.

"I shall miss Jean-Paul," Corrie went on to say, "that is certain. But I understand it is now imperative that he returns to France, and then to Cornwall. After all, his duties lie there now, not here with me. It is what dearest Mama wanted. Therefore, she will be aware of what is happening, and rest in peace." Her eyes filled with tears at the thought of her mother. She had had so much to live for on discovering her dearly loved long lost son, and if he could be happy, that is all that mattered.

As for Jean-Paul himself, the next few days were extremely busy ones as he was very much occupied with making the necessary arrangements for his journey to France. He was quite ecstatic that both Corrie and Dario had taken to each other so well. He could leave New Orleans with good heart, and would be aware that his dearest friend would take great care of his sister, whilst he could now concentrate on seeing Semire, which would, he knew, be something of a desperate shock, however much his appearance would be what she most wanted. Fortunately, his journey could commence almost at once as the ship that Dario arrived by, the *Franco-bor* would be taking the return journey two days hence, which suited him perfectly, as he could not wait to see the woman that he had always loved deep down in his heart. That would never have changed whatever the circumstances. Jean-Paul realised that he would be quite intolerably impatient on the journey, but he felt that his love would give wings to the ship.

Meanwhile, all preparations were completed, and the hour of departure was at hand. Both Corrie and Dario accompanied Jean-Paul in the coach to the wharf where the ship would embark. Their goodbyes - as was only to be expected - were somewhat emotional, but even so they were all happy, each in their own way, when farewells could be a joyful occasion. As Jean-Paul alighted from the coach he reached inside his flared coat, and brought forth a small package from the deep pocket, and passing it to Dario, he spoke in quite an excited manner.

"This is for you Dario, my dearest friend. I want you to have my half share of the plantation as a parting gift. It will make both you and Corrie equal partners, so that you can work 'with' and not 'for' my dearest sister. What say you my friend," he went on, "are you not highly pleased?" Jean-Paul observed the pleasure on Corrie's face as he added, "dearest Mama would agree, would she not, my sister?"

Both Corrie and Dario were quite overcome with emotion and each in turn hugged Jean-Paul to them, their eyes speaking volumes. There was no need for words between them, especially with Dario, for he knew Jean-Paul of old and that if he wished to present someone with a gift, it was best to accept so as not to offend. And he did accept the most wonderful gift that his friend could ever present to him, with good grace.

* * * * *

Jean-Paul kept his eyes focused on the two figures standing at the wharf and waving until they were no more than two minute dots in the distance. The *Franco-bor* was now well out into the harbour of New Orleans, and gradually would leave the port behind, and here he was once again travelling towards a new life full of happiness.

* * * * *

The shining black coach drawn by four gracious greys, their full manes and tails flowing with their movements, pulled into the road where the house of the De Laffiettes was situated. The driver, already aware of the exact position of the imposing building halted the horses with ease to enable Jean-Paul to alight from the coach with his luggage, which he left on the boulevard while paying the driver. This done, he approached the main entrance and pulled on the ornate bell to gain entry, and receive assistance with his luggage. In a matter of minutes the heavy door was opened to reveal a man of considerable age, whom Jean-Paul recognised immediately as Chebec, the *maitre d'hôtel*, who quickly ushered the visitor into a large and impressive hall where seats were positioned here and there, and beckoned Jean-Paul to be seated upon one of them while he announced him to his mistress.

"What name shall I say Monsieur?" Chebec enquired, not recognising the man who had visited the house so many times in the past, while at the same time he pressed a bell push near to where Jean-Paul sat.

"I am Lord Pendavan, lately arrived from America, and would appreciate speaking to your lady of the house, if I may," he added.

It was at that moment that a much younger manservant crossed to the entrance and brought the luggage into the hall.

When the Comtesse received the message from Chebec, that a visitor by the name of Lord Pendavan was waiting to see her, she was quite nonplussed for she knew no one by that title, as far as she could remember.

"Please show the gentleman in Chebec," she said, concerned as to who he was, and what he could want with her. Since her traumatic experiences with the late Count, she mostly always felt nervous when anyone called.

Just then the drawing room door opened, and Chebec ushered the visitor into her presence, with Michelle bringing up the rear.

Semire could not at first place him at all, after all, he had changed somewhat since she had last seen him. But as he moved nearer to her, she clutched her breast to stay the fluttering within. The shock she suffered was quite intense as she realised who her visitor was, but at the same time was somewhat mystified at the name he had given. 'Was it Jean-Paul, or another in his image?'' she asked herself.

As for Jean-Paul himself, with his usual impeccable manners, he made to stoop over her hand in the customary manner of a Frenchman and, with dignity, brushed her fingers with his lips, whilst inwardly all he wanted to do was to crush her within his arms, and rain kisses upon her. But he quickly controlled himself with much difficulty, scared only that he might distress her if he moved too fast. After what she had suffered Jean-Paul knew he would have to tread gently. Firstly, he must relate everything as it happened since he left Paris to board the brigantine *Navire de Long Cours* for his fateful journey to Cornwall. The story would take some hours, so to begin with refreshments were quickly administered, which was greatly appreciated by Jean-Paul, who was absolutely famished.

Eventually, well satisfied with the excellent foods that were put before him, he began to recount the whole series of dramatic events since last he saw Semire.

* * * * *

It was the early hours of the morning before Jean-Paul concluded his recital.

All the way through Semire uttered not a word, too interested in listening most intently to everything that he revealed, and not wanting to miss anything, in particular, the episode with Corrie. Before she heard the true facts regarding their brother and sister relationship, she became acutely jealous of Jean-Paul's feelings of love. Semire argued with herself, of course, that she was at that time married to the Count, and far from Jean-Paul, but only because she believed he had perished in the storm. She would never have contemplated entering into the ridiculous marriage had she but known that he was still alive. Now the more she watched and listened to him, the more she realised how much he meant to her, and knew she would be prepared to marry him, if he decided to ask her. 'But would he?' she asked herself, for now that Jean-Paul had inherited an estate, and the title that went with it, he may have other plans which might not necessarily include her. Even so, she still argued, he had travelled directly to France to see her before visiting his mansion in Cornwall. That must mean something surely. One thing that did give her hope, was the fact that he had planned to marry her, and take her to America – with Dario also – whilst she herself was already married, and ensconced at the Chateau with her new husband. It was as well at that time, that she knew nothing of this. Now she could only wait and see what the morrow would bring forth. She would not have long to wait, with the time now past three, and everyone retiring for whatever was left of the night.

* * * * *

It would appear – from the conversation that took place whilst the first meal of the day was in progress – that no one in the house slept for those few remaining hours before dawn.

Jean-Paul, in a guest bedroom, had tossed and turned with his mind in a complete turmoil, pondering whether Semire still had the same deep feelings of love for him that she had before his presumed death which could now have changed her whole attitude. After all, hadn't he himself succumbed to his love for Corrie, when Semire was out of his reach? But now that this lovely woman was thankfully free of her deplorable bondage, his love for her came uppermost, and to him was well worth pursuing. So much so, that he intended to propose marriage to her that very day. 'But will she accept?' he had asked himself numerous times, especially on the journey back to France from America. In fact, the love of Semire, and how things could, perhaps, work out for the both of them, had kept him quite occupied throughout an otherwise anxious, and sometimes boring ninety days. The one thing that did give him some cause for concern was that if she did accept his marriagė proposal, would she therefore agree to uproot herself from France, to live at Pendavan in Cornwall? He could only hope that she would.

And so it was that later in the day Jean-Paul broached the subject of marriage with Semire. He had bided his time until just the right moment when, with butterflies in the pit of his stomach, he moved closer to the woman that he loved, lifted her hand to his lips in a gentle caress, and in almost a whisper, spoke the loving words that Semire had been waiting so desperately to hear. She loved this man – who had always been a gentleman, and was now an English Lord – with a consuming passion, of which she had no doubt whatever. He was the man of her choice. With her discerning taste, how could she have chosen otherwise? And now he had asked her to become his wife, an honour indeed. So she accepted without any hesitation, and agreed – as he asked – with exciting anticipation to begin a new future in Cornwall. She knew she would like nothing better than to live at Pendavan, and share Jean-Paul's heritage. After hearing his fine description of the imposing mansion, she made up her mind that she could live out her life there with him.

* * * * *

The approach to Pendavan was something that Semire would never forget. It was so grandiose. The large and imposing wrought iron gates swung back with ease to allow the coach to pass through and enter the long drive leading to the mansion, where in a matter of minutes the driver drew the horses pulling the coach to a halt. Jean-Paul then assisted Semire to the ground, and to the huge entrance, and into the magnificent hall, where all the staff waited in line to greet their new master and future mistress. Michelle, who walked quietly behind Semire, gave a quick curtsy of greeting in the usual habit of the French *femme de chambre*, whilst Jean-Paul, in his usual manner, clicked his heels in salute, naturally recognising most of whom he had met when he resided there during his lengthy indisposition, that now seemed such an age away.

The housekeeper – Mrs Rushton, or Rushie as he had called her while she had nursed him, moved forward in recognition, her face showing clearly the obvious pleasure she felt on seeing him again.

"I received your urgent message Sir," she told him, "brought directly by the courier, and everything is in readiness for you both, as you requested." She hesitated momentarily, and then in a very tearful voice carried on speaking.

"May I say how terribly sorry I am to be made aware of the death of your dear mother, which has truly shocked and distressed not only myself, but all at Pendavan. Particularly the boys," she added. "They are completely devastated."

Jean-Paul thanked her for her kind condolences, and taking her hand within his own, raised it to his lips in a show of affection.

"I know just how you must all feel Rushie, of course, and Ruan and Michael also. I am still deeply shocked myself. But I will explain everything to them," he added. "But in the meantime, may I introduce Semire, my future wife."

After the introductions were all over, everyone dispersed, each to go about their own individual duties, whilst the housekeeper escorted her new master, and as she understood, the woman who was to be, quite soon, her future mistress, both to their respective quarters. Jean-Paul in the East wing, and Semire in the West wing, where they could relax and take stock of their surroundings.

Semire realised at once that Jean-Paul had not exaggerated. Pendavan surpassed all that he had said, and that she could ever wish for her new abode. It would be most pleasurable residing in such a magnificent and picturesque mansion. And she could not wait to become Lady Pendavan.

* * * * *

The ensuing days and weeks that were to lead up to the wedding day were comparatively busy with all the preparations.

Both Jean-Paul and Semire made an especial journey to London, for the sole purpose of selecting an outstanding wedding trousseau, just as years before his beloved parents had so done. Arrangements were made at the same time for the garments to be delivered directly to Pendavan, by courier, and this was eventually carried out with only a day or so to spare before the big event would be upon them.

Everyone at the mansion was most attentive, and exceedingly kind to the bride to be, treating her already as one of the kindred.

Jean-Paul, as promised, spent many hours with Ruan and Michael, to try firstly to ease the pain of their tragic loss, and accompanied them on horseback throughout the large estate, to familiarise himself with the many duties that would face him in the future as Lord of the Manor. He met the tenants, and invited them all to the wedding. While he was thus occupied, Semire was more or less left to her own devices, but not in the least bored, as Rushie – she had been asked to call her that – spent as much time with her as she could spare. There was such a vast amount to tell Semire, which could only serve to improve her confidence when she became Lady Pendavan. Rushie knew of this lovely young woman's terrible traumatic experiences from Jean-Paul, who thought his housekeeper should be aware of the circumstances that had befallen his future wife. Whilst at the same time that certain confidences seemed about to be shared, Rushie herself decided it was the ideal opportunity for her to reveal to Jean-Paul the truth about the jewels that he had understood were lost in the devastating storm, in which he had almost perished. She recalled it to her mind now as though it had only happened yesterday.

"Your mother, Lady Pendavan – anxious for your safety because she believed you had come by the jewels dishonestly as a smuggler, out to make a handsome profit – decided to conceal the offending items which she discovered amongst your tattered clothing apparel. Only your mother and myself knew of the hiding place," Rushie explained further, "and it was most imperative to keep it so," she added.

"It would appear," she began again "that your ancestors used the place of concealment, because when your parents discovered it, they found evidence to prove its use over the ages, particularly one of them, who was a known highwayman who travelled the Cornish roads regularly. So your mother decided to use it also, only doing what she considered was best for your future welfare. I am sure," she went on, "that had she realised your promised commitment to help your friend, Dario de Laffiette, she would, most certainly, have made provision for his debt to that evil blackmailer to be settled once and for all. Your dear Mama was a very wealthy lady, and such a wonderful person. She would have willingly helped anyone, whatever the reasons. I do miss her so very much," she added, the ready tears welling up into her eyes. But quickly mastering her emotions, she suggested to Jean-Paul that he follow her to the library where the jewels were concealed.

After being shown the hiding place, and seeing the jewels safely nestled amongst the other enclosed items, Jean-Paul decided to leave them where they were until the wonderful news could be conveyed to Semire who, in turn, would send word to Dario, that the family heirlooms were intact, and safe after all, and in her possession. Both brother and sister could then decide what to do about them. As for Jean-Paul, he felt that a heavy burden had been lifted from his shoulders. For the presumed loss of the jewels had always depressed him, deep down, and somewhat blighted his new-found happiness.

When Semire received the good tidings from Rushie, with regard to the jewels, the joy of knowing their whereabouts could only be measured by the expression of profound relief on her face. It ended for her quite suddenly the guilty conscience she had continually suffered for parting with something that had been in her family for years, and passed down to each heir. But Dario's honour was all that had mattered to her at that time, and she had no option but to do what she did. Anyway, she argued, they were Dario's property now, to be passed on to his heir if he deemed to take a wife, and from what Jean-Paul had inferred, and reading between the lines of Dario's recent newsletter from New Orleans, it would seem a great romance was already budding between him and Jean-Paul's sister Corrie. She did sincerely hope that a marriage could be arranged, and come about very soon. She couldn't wait to meet the woman she knew her brother loved so very passionately. Thinking of these things did manage to momentarily bring back grave memories of her late despicable husband.

It was one year to the day since Dario had slain the Count, as Semire remembered only too well. She very rarely thought, or even spoke about those terrible times, and only then to Michelle, if the conversation were to unavoidably turn in that direction.

Before closing her mind to all that had transpired, Semire, having had to sift through the personal papers and important documents of the Count, as well as – with the assistance of his personal *avocat* – his finances, discovered an immaculate black leather bound book that held the names of numerous blackmail victims, including Dario's, although his had been neatly crossed through, supposedly at the time of her marriage to the Count. This distressed Semire so much that she sat down immediately at the *secretaire*, and with much deliberation, wrote a letter to each individual, asking them to contact the *avocat* of the late Count Jean-Philippe Maille, whence they would hear something to their advantage.

The Count, last in line, with no heir apparent, left Semire – as his lawful widow – to inherit everything – the whole estate, his masses of accrued monies and, as well, the enormous amount of monies he had extorted by intimidation, and such like, from the victims he had been blackmailing. In fact, the Count had most certainly had an *embarras de richesse* – with more wealth than he could have known how to deal with. So Semire thought it only right and proper to ease the present situation, and try to put right the terrible wrongs that her late husband had done. So it was arranged for a certain sum of money – quite generous, in fact – to be paid to each of his victims.

This done, Semire once again left the Chateau for the last time, not wanting ever to return. There was an unhealthy atmosphere surrounding much of the place with its scores of dark corridors and recesses. Semire had always felt that someone or something – she could not explain what, would pounce on her, and spirit her away to talked of hideaways, and secret passages. With a comparatively large staff, one could not but help overhear conversations amongst them. The whole Chateau would appear to be a secretive place. Semire was more than certain there was something that needed to be discovered, and brought into the open. Perhaps, in the future this would be so. But as she would not be there, it would not be her sole provocative to delve into. She was thankful to be free of the evil surroundings. Even so, she had no intention of depriving the people who were employed there of their respective positions. So the belated Count's lavish home continued to progress without the past owner. It was mentioned by the *avocat*, that certain wealthy guests could stay there as a paying proposition, mainly for the future upkeep of the enormous building and vast grounds.

Semire left the decision to the learned man. After all, she had put him in charge of everything, and would only be involved if the necessity arose.

* * * * *

The day of the wedding dawned warm, very still and somewhat hazy, with the promise of special weather, ideally suited for the most important event that can only happen once in any one person's life time.

It was understood by the whole community that this would be the most remarkable and outstanding wedding that had taken place for many a long year.

Everybody would be attending the marriage ceremony to be held in the Gothic Church in the vicinity, where Jean-Paul's beloved parents had years before plighted their troth and thereafter had lived at Pendavan, where their son and his bride would do likewise, and live out their lives also.

It had been decided to hold the reception – to receive the scores of guests which would be assembled for the sole purpose of wishing the bride and groom every happiness – within the grounds of the mansion, where everything had been arranged on a grand scale, with the most sumptuous and delicious foods delightfully set out on long trestle tables – covered by snowy white tablecloths – with delicate and most tasteful detail. Nothing had been neglected, even in small matters, enough to tempt even the most difficult to please.

* * * * *

The silence in the Church was broken suddenly by the sounds of surprise and gasps of sheer admiration, mixed with not unexpected feelings of envy for the beautiful bride who, having walked down the aisle, was now standing in her rightful place beside her future husband.

Ruan had accompanied her to give her away, whilst Michael took over the exacting role of best man to the groom. Both had accepted the tasks with honour.

Semire, adorned in the most exquisite gown of heavy white lace, appeared ethereal in her extreme beauty. The unique style which suited her to perfection had a fitted bodice that emphasised her figure the neckline having a stand up frill, lower at the front, with the whole framing her face. The sleeves, extremely full from the shoulders, and caught at the wrists, also with frills, topped a straight line skirt lifted slightly in the front, at the feet, enabling her lacy and dainty footwear to be seen. Whilst a train – fitted from the back waist – hung in folds, and reached along the floor at least three full-lengths of the gown itself. Her hair, swept upwards in a mass of curls, was adorned by a diamond tiara that caught the short veil high above so as not to cover her face.

The picture she made was magnificent, beautiful in all its entirety, and standing half a head shorter than the groom, they made a very handsome couple.

Jean-Paul had selected his clothing to compliment Semire's gown. He was attired in a black velvet cut away coat pleated from the waist, with fitted breeches to match, added to which he wore the finest silk white shirt with long lacy cuffs, hanging well below his coat sleeves, with a lace jabot to match, caught at the throat by a diamond pin. Black leather boots completed his array. And, with his long and very thick dark hair, greying at the temples, styled and caught back into a black velvet ribbon, also his beard trimmed and thinned extensively, he could only have the fine look of a typical English Lord of the Manor.

The marriage ceremony, which surpassed everyone's expectations, was quite unforgettable to all who were present. Likewise the reception that followed when the guests wandered around the spreading lawns and beautifully kept gardens. The ladies, attired in their quite magnificently styled bustle gowns, all in exquisite colours, with matching hats in all shapes and sizes, and shaded by their dainty parasols, were accompanied by their male companions who were smartly dressed in the usual fashionable cut away jackets, with fitted breeches, and buckle shoes.

When everyone had gradually partaken of the varied rich foods and the many beverages, available to suit all tastes, then the guests began to leave, fully satisfied with the day's exciting celebrations.

Lord and Lady Pendavan, with their impeccable manners, escorted all the guests off the premises, until at last they were alone in their part of the mansion.

Whilst Semire was assisted by Michelle to remove her wedding attire, and step into light fine gossamer night garments of sheer exquisiteness in readiness to join her husband, Jean-Paul was likewise preparing himself for his beautiful *femme*.

* * * * *

The bed-chamber was most magnificent. Splendid items of furniture enhanced the whole room that was tastefully decorated in the palest of green, with alternating rich wooden panels throughout the widely spaced walls, adorned with fine prints of countryside scenes. The high patterned ceiling of brilliant white lent extra height and width to the whole room. And centred on the main wall was the most attractive highly polished wooden bed, complemented by white lacy curtains, and frilled pelmets surrounding the overhead. Sparkling white bedding with frilled pillows gave a most inviting look to Semire, who entered from her boudoir adjacent to the bed-chamber, Michelle having already retired for the night.

Semire laid down upon the cool sheet, and pulling the top cover up over herself, closed her eyes, wallowing in the extreme comfort. In minutes she was fast asleep, and remained so even when Jean-Paul joined her a short while later. He had not the heart to awaken her, in any case, he was quite content to lie by her side and savour her extreme beauty. The man expressed the tenderness within himself, and the devotion he carried within his heart for so brave a woman who went through the gates of hell for the sake of her beloved brother. He would never cease to love her, that was sure.

He raised himself on his arms and glanced down at the lovely face of his very own wife lying close beside him. He delicately traced her clear brow with his finger tips, and wondered at the passion in his heart. He fondled her hair, silky and glowing, as the mass – brushed so lovingly by Michelle – lay spread out across the pillow, framing her face. He hesitated momentarily, then carried on across her eyes, down over her cheekbones and on to her soft full lips, pouting in sleep. He bent and lightly brushed them with his own, and then the love he felt for her came uppermost, and he pulled her into a close embrace as his kisses became more demanding. The passion in his caresses startled her, as she awakened from sleep, but soon she returned his kisses with fire and desire, her body trembling and responding to her husband's manhood, making their marriage complete.

* * * * *

Jean-Paul stood at the open window overlooking the sea that was very clearly ruffled. He could hear the waves awash over the rocks in the coves far below Pendavan. He had first approached the scene – not able to sleep as dawn crept slowly across the sky, pushing the night shadows away in the distance. Occupied with his thoughts he had no idea how long he had been standing there, until he became aware of the incipient gleam of the sun, now quite perceptible above the horizon. Glancing behind him he could see that Semire still slept peacefully, her beautiful face serene in repose. As he once more glanced out of the window to observe the vast expanse of water spread out for miles around, almost encircling Pendavan, his face saddened for the terrible hurt he felt for the deep loss of his mother, not only for the short time that he had been privileged to know her, but for all the long years without the knowledge that she had even existed. If only fate could have intervened earlier so as to have enabled him to show the deep love he held in his heart for her! But gone from this world she was, so it was now up to him to do everything he could that she would have wished for, and have been proud of. Nowhere in his life had the call been stronger than now to make a success of what had come to him through fate alone.

Romantic adventurer that he had always been, and in a way, would still continue to be, he was now poised to realise his ambitions that included his beloved 'femme', and the hoped for family they had already planned for. Pride of possession overwhelmed him as he thought excitedly of the son that could be born as his heir, to carry on the proud name of Pendavan. His cherished dream would then be complete.

* * * * *